MEET THE Earl AT MIDNIGHT

GINA CONKLE

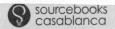

sourcebooks
casablanca

Published by Sourcebooks Casablanca, an imprint of Sourcebooks, Inc.
P.O. Box 4410, Naperville, Illinois 60567-4410
(630) 961-3900
Fax: (630) 961-2168
www.sourcebooks.com

Printed and bound in Canada.
WC 10 9 8 7 6 5 4 3 2 1

*This one's for you, Dad. You encouraged a quiet
teenager to take risks and try new things.
Guess what? She did!*

One

Edge of London
March 27, 1768

IF A WOMAN'S OLD ENOUGH TO WEAR A CORSET, SHE'S old enough to know midnight meetings spell trouble. Lydia's sleep-fogged brain weighed this undeniable fact against family duty. Of course, duty won. Why else would she be cocooned inside a shabby hack on a dark and blustery night? The quicker she extracted her stepbrother from his latest mess, the quicker she'd be cozy again in her warm bed. Bleary-eyed, Lydia peered at the Blue Cockerel. The inn's shingle, a blue rooster cracked up the middle, squeaked a lively rhythm. The establishment was hardly worth a map's mention. Worse yet, the driver stopped a long, puddle-filled distance from the entrance. Lydia glanced down at her best and only pair of buckle shoes; tonight, the limits of family loyalty would be tested.

Outside the hack, her stepfather, George Montgomery,

protested the driver's fare. His pockets always held dust better than coin. He groused and huffed but eventually dug deep for the requisite payment. That's when he caught her eye.

"Look lively, gel. Storm's kicking up...don't have all night," he snapped, wrestling down his hat against blasting winds.

"You asked for *my* help," she muttered and exited the hack.

Icy gusts nipped her ankles. Shivering, Lydia pulled her short red cloak tightly about. This time the blighter went beyond the pale. After all, wasn't he the one who pounded on her door, yelling she must come at once? Her trips to London were so rare, and she barely arrived two days ago. Why was her presence at this run-down spot so important? She hop-stepped from one cobble-stone to another, piecing together fragments of what George had said on the ride over.

"Tristan's in a mess...really done it this time...need your help...keep quiet and cooperate...be a good gel... best for the family and all that."

"Good girl, indeed," she scoffed, absorbing the information.

As a woman of four-and-twenty, she had shed that biddable nature long ago. Not that he would know. Sparse communication weakened already thin family ties. A heady dose of drowsiness kept her quiet; all the better to be done with this business. Her stepbrother stirred up trouble one way or another.

Then her shoe squished in some questionable muck.

"Lud, even the road isn't decently cobbled." She inspected the damage and foisted her skirts higher. "No need to ruin a hem on this fool's errand."

Right then, the heavens conspired against her. A shock of rain poured down on her head, thunder boomed, and Lydia rushed after George. He pressed a shoulder to the inn's ramshackle door, and they burst into the common room.

Empty, it was.

Oh, a dying fire and a whiff of an unnamed, unpleasant aroma welcomed them. Lydia shook damp skirts and spied a boot wipe. The Blue Cockerel raised a notch in her estimation for offering the amenity. In the act of scraping one shod foot, she paused, her foot hovering over the bristled wipe. Old George's eyes nearly bulged from his head. She followed his stare to shafts of light spilling from a poorly hung door abovestairs. Signs of life. Lydia righted herself and noticed his Adam's apple bobbling up and down in the way of a nervous lad.

"George?" She touched his sleeve. "Are you well?"

"Well? 'Course…feel fine, fine." He slid a finger inside his collar and craned his neck like some strange bird. "Let me do the talking, eh? All else fails, think of your mother."

"*Mother?*" Suspicion edged her voice. "What's she got to do with this? Aren't we here to get Tristan?"

"We are. We are." George doffed his hat to finger comb stray graying hairs, avoiding eye contact.

Footsteps, a steady cadence in blackness, drew her attention again to that cracked door. Lydia peered into the gloom, and uncomfortable cold penetrated her skin. A sylphlike figure paced back and forth, back and forth. The tiny hairs at her nape quivered from another kind of chill.

There it was.

A large shadow. That monstrous shape, a floating specter, flickered past gaps in warped wood. Light slivered away when the figure moved. An occupied room at a public house shouldn't cause concern, but she swallowed hard at the sound of those eerie steps. Someone abovestairs waited for them. This had to be a different kind of trouble.

"Let's get Tristan and go home," she said, her voice uneven.

"Right." George tugged at his waistcoat and kept a cautious eye on that door. "Remember, be on your best behavior."

Lydia grimaced at George's back but followed him up creaking stairs in silence, doing her best to stave off worrisome nerves. How odd, this place. Everywhere, tables heaped with dirty dishes and half-empty tankards of ale, as if someone cleared the inn on a moment's notice. A pair of beady-eyed rodents, bold in their watch, hunched over a crust of bread. Lydia hugged her cloak tight, unable to shake the haze of being off center and ill placed. Even more, she was poorly prepared. In her haste, she failed to comb her hair or don a corset. Though well covered, she squirmed at that brazen fact. As she took a bracing breath, the room's odor assailed her again.

"Ugh, sour rags." She pressed a hand under her nose. "That's the horrible smell."

Somehow, identifying that mundane lack of housekeeping helped her calm.

George's fist pounded the door. "Shh, gel."

"Why? Are we insulting the rats?" She rolled her eyes.

"Enter," a male voice called from within.

A push against warped wood, and metal hinges

whined their slow, high-pitched complaint. The door swung wide. Strangers—two men, tall and rather large—occupied the tight space. Tristan was nowhere in sight. A narrow, rumpled bed stretched vacant and forlorn. That alarm went off in her head again, yet George stepped into the room and waved her to follow. Lydia stepped past the threshold, and her inquisitive nature shushed those warnings for a better look at what she found inside.

A huge, sun-bronzed man leaned beside a tiny window, as nonchalant as you please. Her jaw dropped at the sight of him. Bald as an egg, he was, and sporting a full beard with three little braids to boot. A gold hoop gleamed from his ear. A pirate? Or a ruffler? He brought to mind those beefy men who roamed unsavory streets, smashing heads first, asking questions later, though he was nattily dressed in ruby-red velvet under his frock coat. Despite her best manners, she gaped.

Ah, but the other man was more mysterious, what with his collar flipped high and tricorn pulled low. A plain, oiled cloak covered him from his face down to his battered boots. A slit of eyes was the only sign of humanity. Any moment now, Lord Mysterious, a high-wayman for sure, would brandish a musket, and they'd be done for.

"Montgomery," the cloaked man greeted George and gave her a fleeting look.

"Milord." George, hat in hand like an errand boy, spoke to Lord Mysterious but jabbed a thumb at her. "I've done as we agreed and brought her, but I haven't yet broke the news to…to her mother, leastways. There'll be hell to pay, if you know my meaning. Women can be all weepy and such about these things."

"Your parley with Mrs. Montgomery is no concern of mine," said Lord Mysterious.

For a highwayman, he spoke rather well...and George did address him as *milord*.

What was this again about her mother? And where's Tristan? Lydia hugged herself for warmth and inched closer to the door's shadows. George failed to inspire confidence the way he wiped his forehead and squirmed. She couldn't be sure if that was sweat or rain on his face.

"If I may, milord, you're a reasonable man. I was wondering, really, that is, I was thinking there must be another way."

"Another way?" The cloaked man's voice held a soft, menacing note. "You came to me with this bargain."

Bargain? What bargain? Her head snapped to attention. Lud, but she should've pressed for details. The unsettling way her stepfather kept curling and uncurling his wide-brimmed hat didn't bode well.

"If you could find a mite of forgiveness...maybe give me some time to find another remedy?" George spread his arms in supplication. "Lord Greenwich, please...surely, in your youth, you've done some reckless deeds—"

"Don't." Lord Greenwich's voice cut short George's blather.

The elusive Edward Sanford, Earl of Greenwich.

Thunder cracked overhead. The window's wavy panes rattled.

The cloaked man was none other than one of England's highborn sons, and Tristan and George's employer. Her sigh of relief was loud enough that both strangers glanced her way.

Tristan's in a pickle if nobility's involved, but at least

they weren't in the company of common thugs. All things considered, a rare view of the eccentric Earl of Greenwich made the midnight rouse worthwhile. The men conversed in low tones, and Lydia indulged her curiosity, blatantly staring from the folds of her hood. Shameless behavior, of course, but why dither over that? Any woman in her shoes would do the same.

The Phantom of London. Enigma Earl. The Greenwich Recluse.

You had to be hiding in a cave to have not heard one of those infamous monikers. A scientist of note, he vanished a few years past from the public eye. Broadsheets claimed he never ventured out in the light of day. People whispered of a carriage bearing the Greenwich coat of arms, an ominous black conveyance tearing about Town, curtains drawn. Some said the earl suffered from madness. Some said he was stricken with a hideous, disfiguring disease. These silly stories came to mind because she read them to Great-Aunt Euphemia, who thrived on a steady diet of gossip pages.

Lydia pushed back her hood a fraction for a better look at London's favorite phantom. When he raised his head, she glimpsed dark eyebrows and strands of gold-brown hair framing what must be his face hidden behind the collar. Apparently, the *Enigma* was blond. She smiled, recalling the whimsies of Town chatter when it eventually made its way to humble Wickersham. Shrouded as he was, one could see why so many peculiar assumptions abounded. Truly, George conversed with a slit of eyes. At that picture, a yawning laugh escaped her.

"Something funny, gel?" George snipped.

"Did I laugh? Sorry about that." Lydia covered her mouth, not caring a whit. "I thought we were here to save Tristan, not have a midnight meeting with your employer. Not sure why I'm here."

"Like I told you in the hack. Silence, gel—"

Lord Greenwich stopped their exchange. "Be nice, Montgomery, or you'll find me less lenient. No more delays. She goes with me…as per the agreement."

Lydia snapped to attention. All vestiges of her hazy drowse vanished.

"What did you say?" Her head tipped toward the earl.

Lightning flashed. Pulsing brightness danced behind the nobleman's shrouded bulk.

"You heard me."

"Yes, I heard you, but I thought we were here to save Tristan. What's this about an agreement?"

His dark eyes narrowed on her. "You are here to save your stepbrother…in a manner of speaking."

"Then where is he?"

"His whereabouts are not my concern."

Now this was all very cryptic. Lydia planted a hand on her hip, and taking a deep breath, tried for clarity.

"But I thought he was in some kind of minor scrape."

"There's nothing *minor* about your family's troubles." The earl scoffed, and his cultured voice sharpened. "I wouldn't call your stepbrother borrowing money from some unsavory types *minor*. He came begging for help not long after he started his apprenticeship. My man of business"—he gestured to the well-dressed man near the window—"obliged him with a loan. When Tristan couldn't repay that debt, he stole from Sanford Shipping. Your stepfather made matters worse by trying to cover it up…from *me*." His lordship's tone lightened at this. "Even lifted some coin for himself. But we waste time. You know this already."

Lydia digested the news: Tristan and George were thieves; the earl found humor in the fact that they tried to pull the wool over his eyes; and he assumed she was fully apprised. Worse yet, Lydia was somehow embroiled in this mess, a mess that looked to be more than a paltry few coins lifted from a till. She glared at her stepfather, who shrunk under her withering stare, and then she faced Lord Greenwich.

"The apple doesn't fall far from the tree, my lord, and this sounds like a worse muddle than what's typical. But I fail to see what this has to do with me." Irritation building, she enunciated each word. "If you please, sir, the hour is late, and my skirt is soggy."

She shouldn't take a nursemaid's scolding tone with nobility, but thunder cracked overhead, a reminder of the nasty storm, and her patience ran dry. She had things to do come daybreak. The hearth's fire flickered orange light across his lordship's exposed slice of humanity, and his dark-eyed scrutiny softened.

"I understand this is all very abrupt, Miss Montgomery. We need to begin with proper introductions. I am Lord Greenwich." The earl gave a small bow and motioned to the bald man. "And this is Mr. Jonas Bacon, my man of business."

Her gaze snapped to Mr. Bacon's hulking form. He managed a thin veneer of respectability by the fine clothes he wore and the good grace of a noble's company. Man of business? What kind of business was one question banging around her head among the others crowding for space, but good manners prevailed. Lydia curtsied greetings before taking a deep breath and trying anew with sleep-deprived tolerance.

"Yes, I know who you are. I've gathered that much. But what do you mean by this agreement?"

The earl's dark eyes widened under his black brim. "Are you telling me you know nothing?"

Doubt threaded his words, but she wouldn't let that bother her.

"I'm very much uninformed, sir. I knew my stepfather was in your employ as clerk, and recently Tristan, but this is the first I've heard of any thievery. Terrible news…but I'm at a loss as to how my presence makes a difference."

That slash of topaz-dark eyes searched her face, and the fine hairs on her neck bristled again. Heavens, she had nothing to hide, unlike these men. His lordship exchanged a glance with his man of business. Five of Mr. Bacon's fingertips braced a washstand in relaxed repose, yet his indifference belied a pair of alert, assessing eyes. The earl sighed behind the collar as he faced her.

"My apologies, Miss Montgomery, I was led to believe you were an informed party"—he cast a sharp-eyed look at George—"on *all* aspects of this predicament."

George coughed, and his thin body hunched within his greatcoat.

"Allow me to explain," the earl continued. "More than a fortnight past, I confronted your stepfather with evidence of the theft. Of course there'd be a trial…certain conviction due to overwhelming evidence…incarceration at Newgate…unfortunately for your mother, the Compter—"

"*The Compter?*" she yelled. "Are you mad? My mother won't go *there*…least of all for something George did."

"—until the debts have been satisfied," Lord

Greenwich finished. "Of course, being past your majority, you are in no way under familial obligation."

Her stomach lurched at his casual discussion of her mother in that ancient Cheapside prison. Damp, moldy bricks reeked of death and excrement, casting its horrid pall long before the edifice came to view. Debtors and their families toiled in darkness, slogging for years before gaining freedom; others wasted to nothing, forgotten by the outside world. Scrawny children, released in daylight, begged and scrambled for ha'pennies while standing in filthy gutters, all in the name of repaying family debts. And the horrors of a woman alone...she shuddered. Lydia was of an age and free; her mother, shackled to George, was stuck. Forever.

"There must be another way." Her voice rose with each word. "How bad *is* this blasted debt?"

He raised a gloved hand to halt her onslaught of words. "No hysterics, please—"

"You talk of sending my mother to the Compter, and you're *bothered* by hysterics," she bit each word at him and took a step closer.

His lordship's eyes closed a moment, as if he dipped into a well of forbearance. "If you'll remain calm, I'll finish."

Lydia scowled at George, who was too busy wiping perspiration from his forehead; she'd get no help from that quarter. She wouldn't put it past him to implicate her mother in some way just to weasel his way out of any consequence.

"There is an amenable solution...a plan, if you will."

"Yes, I'm most interested to hear what plan was concocted *without my knowledge*," she said, glaring at the earl.

"Please understand, Miss Montgomery, I thought you

were in full agreement to the solution your stepfather presented." The cadence of his voice slowed. "Call it a creative remedy to satisfy an urgent requirement of mine."

"I don't care what you need. My mother will not go to that hellish place."

"Careful, Miss Montgomery," the earl cautioned. "You're in no position to make such pronouncements… such is the way of things with theft and debt, an imperfect justice system to be sure."

Lydia inhaled quickly, about to give his high and mightiness the sharp end of her tongue.

"Wait." He raised a gloved hand. "I'm not without compassion. Understand, the power to resolve this matter rests in your hands."

Lydia was sure she had the red-faced bearing of an angry fishwife. But he was nobility, and George and Tristan were clearly at fault.

"Go on, then." Her arms clamped over her chest, bunching damp garments. "You said something about a plan."

"Your stepfather overheard a conversation I had with my solicitor at Sanford Shipping. He knew of a particular and rather urgent need of mine. To get to the point—he offered you."

"Offered me? You want to employ me to pay off this debt?" Lydia canted her head sideways. "That's what this is about?"

Lord Greenwich had the nerve to be amused. At least she took the muffled sound behind the collar to be a laugh. Beside him, a heavy log rolled and split apart in the hearth. Firelight flared a bright dance of orange and yellow, exposing his splinter of skin.

"No, Miss Montgomery, I don't want to *employ* you." He paused, and topaz eyes scrutinized her. "I need you for a different purpose."

Though bare of corset or stays, Lydia couldn't shake the sensation of whalebone pinching her ribs. Breathing became difficult. Male stares bored into her, waiting. Her fingers dug at scratchy wool and muslin.

"Me? Why?"

His lordship sighed overlong and repeated in a monotone voice, "Because Tristan and your stepfather stole—"

"No," she huffed. "I'm *not* a half-wit. I mean, why this odd trade? Makes no sense. If not to employ me and repay the debt, then what for?"

The earl's shoulders squared. His dark-eyed look reached across the space and pinned her.

"More precisely, I need your body."

Two

Even a fish could stay out of trouble if it learned to keep its mouth shut.

—Proverb

"YOU *ARE* MAD AS A MARCH HARE." THE RUDE WORDS slipped off her tongue. "Why would you need my body?" Lydia's leather shoes scraped uneven planks as she inched backward.

"I assure you, I'm quite sane." The earl watched her, clear-eyed and focused. "I need an heir. I'll expect you to provide one for me, and possibly a second in due time."

He stated his requirements as if this were simply a matter of course. They could have been discussing a mundane transaction of flour or wool. The deafening rush in her ears competed with the steady drum in her chest, muddling her brain. As the midnight hour approached, her life opened an unwelcome door, and the cascade pouring down on her was not appealing by any stretch. She had plans of her own and was quite done with men.

"And if I refuse?" Lydia asked, her voice barely above a whisper.

"I will seek justice."

Her mother's gentle face clouded her mind, but under the folds of her cloak, Lydia's hands covered her abdomen. Her womb was a negotiation piece. Babies... children were meant to be the fruit of something close to perfection between a man and a woman...something close to that perfect, dreamlike memory of her mother and long-dead father. Children deserved to grow into their own dreams and desires, not live as pawns or game pieces for the fulfillment of others.

The pressure, so much to absorb, caused a nagging throb. Lydia's hand moved to her forehead. Her fingertips massaged her temple, wishing away George, Mr. Bacon, Lord Greenwich, this whole mess. She squeezed her eyes shut, only to picture her mother once again, and a different coldness that owed nothing to the weather crept over her. Lord Greenwich's smooth, hypnotic voice broke the silence.

"Come. Step into the light."

Lydia opened her eyes. Beside her, George licked his lips as his glittering, avaricious gaze bounced between her and Lord Greenwich. That calculating gleam of his...the irksome man saw an opening to bilk the situation.

George raised his index finger. "Perhaps, milord, we can renegotiate—"

She groaned.

"Jonas," Lord Greenwich called behind him.

Mr. Bacon nodded his shiny pate and grasped the unspoken request. The velvet-clad brute moved off the wall with surprising grace for one his size. Then, some shuffling of feet, a firm redirection or two, and his lordship's man of business gripped the back of George's cloak with one hand, removing him, like a broom sweeping out refuse. The big man finished the job by shutting the slanted door neatly behind him.

"Perhaps I spoke to the wrong Montgomery." The earl tipped his head in invitation. "Please. Come closer. This evening's been an unexpected trial."

No harm in that. The bewildering night might end well, if she could just have a sensible conversation with his lordship. After all, a peer of the realm ought not to marry a woman of little consequence, especially when one considered the dynasty in question. Matters could be negotiated, if only the earl would be reasonable.

But Lord Greenwich studied her with a different potency in his dark eyes. Lydia lowered her lashes, aware of how men's minds worked. She needed to regroup and gather her wits, but the earl must have sensed her wariness, or so she guessed when he extended a gloved hand.

"Please. This need not be unpleasant." His voice lulled her. "I promise I won't bite."

"Meaning sometimes you do," she snipped.

A muffle of low, masculine laughter floated from his collar. "Only on a full moon."

His quip surprised her much like a clue revealed. Still, this midnight meeting defied reason, best she use caution. When she didn't move, his hand dropped to his side. His lordship's presence grew bigger in the tiny room, though he stood a safe, respectable distance.

"Very well then. Why not take off your cloak?" he coaxed.

"How like a man," she said, eyeing him from the safety of her hood. "Get a woman naked, first. Solve a problem, second."

That earned her another low, masculine chuckle.

"Now, now," he chided. "I'm *not* asking you to undress, only that you remove your cloak. As you informed all, you are wet and soggy." Lord Greenwich motioned to the blazing hearth. "You could stand here and warm yourself…dry your damp skirts."

How did he manage to be commanding and reasonable at the same time? With a sigh, she pushed back her faded red hood and stepped closer. The welcome fire warmed her ankles nicely.

"I am, if anything, ever accommodating," she said, tart-tongued.

Her sharpness missed its mark. Instead, her target tipped his head with great interest, almost fascination, when her face came into view. Topaz-brown eyes inspected every exposed inch of her visage, searching her with blunt curiosity. A spark as hot and fast as flint striking stone shot through her. Flummoxed, Lydia squared her shoulders and tried for businesslike composure.

"I'm sure something can be done to rectify this debt."

"Your cloak."

"My cloak?" she repeated, running her palms over damp wool.

"Remove it."

Something in his firm tone brooked no disagreement. Her leaden hands obeyed, loosening the frogs and loops under her chin with graceless plucking. Her well-worn red half cloak, a sign of her modest station, parted and swayed, all while his gaze roamed over her, head to hem, waiting. A stag, tense and alert, scenting a doe came to mind. This was one way a woman could find herself flat on her back, as well she knew from times past.

Wind and rain squalled outside as the last closure

came undone. Damp wool slipped from her shoulders. Though fully clothed, she couldn't shake the sense of being stripped bare under his lordship's keen scrutiny. Lydia clutched her cloak in both hands and made a rumpled shield. There really ought to be more space between them.

Lightning slashed the room. Quick flashes split darkness behind Lord Greenwich. His acute study drifted up her skirts to pause just below her neckline—he stared at her bosom, and her traitorous, corsetless bosom pointed back. Was it the cold air? Or him? Lydia inched her cloak higher, and his lordship, undaunted in his perusal, returned to his intense study of her face. Was he pleased? That she entertained such a question shocked her.

The earl clasped his hands behind his back. "Turn around."

She gave an indignant huff and glared, not budging an inch. "I will not."

"If you please, Miss Montgomery." He made the request sound courtly. "I'm only asking you to take a turn."

The cloak, rough scratchy wool, bunched tighter in her hands. "Next, you'll want to check my teeth."

His lordship twirled his finger. "A single rotation will suffice."

Being at the mercy of his good grace reminded her to get this done and over with…all the better to move on to a more reasonable solution. Her mother's welfare beat a constant drum in her head; thus, she obliged him. The water-stained ceiling became the safest place to look as she crossed one foot over the other, beginning a slow circle.

"You know, my lord, I have a small amount of my own funds. Well, not much, really, but if we could discuss this tomorrow. At luncheon perhaps? I might have a solution of my own."

"No. We do this my way."

Fire crackled and floorboards creaked from her slow circling movement. A tickling sensation flowed over her, touching everywhere. Her lack of corset set her cheeks aflame. Yet, his scrutiny was fascinating. She bemoaned her wrinkled, outdated dress. Did he notice? Or did he notice her smooth skin and glossy waves of sleep-mussed sable hair, of which her great-aunt raved? The earl's impertinent gaze ranged everywhere.

"If you're quite through, my lord," she said with some starch.

Lydia pressed the cloak closer. Lud, but he needed a set down. She'd dealt with overzealous farmers and country squires in the past and knew how to put men in their place. Men were all the same, no matter their status. The quality of their clothes differed, but all were flesh and blood underneath. A biting remark formed on her lips.

He reached for her.

She froze.

Lord Greenwich's gloved hand hovered near her face in the gentlest fashion, as if he wanted to touch her but held himself in check. They stood that way for a few, eternal seconds. Only his warmth touched her cheek. So close, she smelled oiled leather and saw the stitching on his glove. Why the hesitation?

Long moments stretched, measured by the sound of rainfall. His brown eyes studied her lips, her hair, even the outline of her ear, as odd as the notion was. His lordship examined her as if he would memorize shape and texture without contact. He angled his head, the black tricorne casting shadows, and something passed between them: something elusive and slight when his gaze met hers...a current of curiosity that must have beckoned him to test her.

A lone, leather-clad finger trailed over her cheek, so light. Lord Greenwich's subtle connection caused tantalizing shivers, shivers that followed his whisper-soft caress on Lydia's skin. His exploring finger slipped under her chin and angled her face toward firelight.

"You're a thorough one," she said breathy and low. "No doctor's ever examined me thus."

His dark gaze flicked to hers. "Even phantoms have their standards."

The tip of his glove grazed her neck, a mere hint of touch. His eyes fixated on that fraction of her exposed flesh, following the line his finger traced. Unexpected warmth swirled across her body, yet her feet were stuck. His hand dropped to his side, and the earl stepped back, breaking the current.

"You realize I offer marriage?" He clasped his hands behind his back and spoke matter-of-factly.

They were back to the evening's transaction. But her breathing, heavier from the singular invasion of his gloved hand, hadn't recovered.

"A legitimate heir requires as much," she managed, trying to sound like a woman with some wits about her.

"You would lack for nothing. As my wife, you will have every luxury, I daresay more than—"

"My mother," she blurted. Was she giving in to this bargain?

Lydia needed to gauge the man who held all the cards, and this discomfiting sense that all was out of her control. Even more, she needed him to remove that infernal greatcoat, or at least have him drop his collar. Hadn't she done as much for him?

He cocked an eyebrow. "Yes. What about your mother?"

"Leave my mother alone. No harm befalls her." Lydia twisted and bunched her cloak, rationalizing what was important and what was not. "Tristan and my stepfather can rot for all I care, but I don't want my mother to suffer for anything they've done."

"Of course. You have my word. She will live as free as she pleases."

Free. She smirked at the notion. That was a relative word where her mother was concerned. Still, he agreed so quickly. Hands clasped behind his back, his lordship was all business. Yes, she had to protect her mother, but her whole reason for coming to London also hung in the balance.

Her plan could not be pushed aside any more than she could stop breathing.

And one ought to consider how the Sanford name could help with *that*.

Her mental scale tipped in favor of this preposterous agreement. She was in no hurry for marriage fetters with any man, if ever at all, thank you very much. However, a peer of the realm could open doors, doors previously closed to her. Lydia's mental scale slanted more toward the earl's scheme.

Her chin tipped high. "And I want a measure of freedom."

Lord Greenwich crossed his arms. The action caused

his collar to slip lower, revealing the top of a blade-straight nose.

"You're in no position to make demands, Miss Montgomery." His cultured voice firmed. "Especially, oddly phrased ones."

Lydia licked her lips. She should have asked for funds. He probably expected as much, but she lacked the cunning for that sort of thing. She wanted what she wanted, however out of the ordinary that may be. Her cloak knotted into a tighter ball in her hands. Like a juggler at a country fair, her mind tossed each notion and problem up high and worked to keep track; then a new one joined the whirl.

"On the contrary, my lord, no respectable family of rank will marry their daughters to you because..." Her voice trailed off as she searched his collar, unable to meet his eyes.

Lydia recalled the scandal pages, each with their own lurid story of a failed liaison with another noble family. The common theme in all the gossip rags claimed the engagement fell apart last summer when his betrothed slashed her wrists and nearly bled to death. Nasty business it was that drove the family into seclusion. The earl's notoriety as *The Phantom of London* grew. Was he horrid to that young woman?

Reading about the disgrace made little more than passing news for her and her great-aunt. This close to the earl, discomfort poked Lydia's conscience like a stick. Gossip charged a hefty price: she saw it in his eyes. Shame must have stung him, and all of England played voyeur, entertained by his private pain. Nevertheless, her empathy had its limits. Lord Greenwich tilted his head back and looked at her as an unexpected chess rival.

"Apparently, I underestimated you." His voice softened. "It's true. Certain circumstances have made the possibility of marriage…difficult." He paused, and his tone turned weary. "You asked for freedom. What kind of freedom?"

She hesitated. How to word this? After all, what she wanted was out of the ordinary.

"To…to…pursue the same quiet interests I enjoyed in the country, with the occasional stay in London, where I'll—"

"I don't participate in Society." He nearly growled the words at her.

"Yes, I understand this." She searched the exposed part of him. "I…I only wish to maintain my…interests, such as they are—" Lydia squared her shoulders and looked him in the eye with a different approach. "Give me free rein, my lord, and I'm confident that I can be of assistance to your needs. As often as you like."

His head snapped to soldierly attention. That last distracting bit was a tad bold, but men were rather simple. Wasn't food or sex what most men clamored for? Keep those appetites sated, and a woman could do what she wanted. Lord Greenwich stepped forward, invading her space. His dark eyes narrowed as he searched her face.

With the hot fire at her back and cloaked man leaning close, there was no place to go. Silence stretched between them, save the rain easing to a light patter outside. A ceiling stain turned into a steady drip; its subtle ping of water droplets hit a porcelain bowl on the floor with hypnotic rhythm.

The bottom of his cloak brushed her skirt. She couldn't be sure if the earl was trying to read her or intimidate. Lydia's neck tensed, ready to snap, but she

met Lord Greenwich's stare, despite his invasive closeness. Stiff-armed, stiff-necked, she pressed her cloak to
her ribs.

His eyes crinkled in the corners. "Very well, Miss
Montgomery, we have a deal."

Her jaw dropped. She stared at him as wide-eyed as
her great-aunt's cow. Lord Greenwich took a step back,
pointing at the cloak she clutched to her chest.

"You'll want to put that on, won't you? There's a storm
outside." The lines at the corners of his eyes deepened.

"Yes, yes, of course." Stunned, she fumbled with her
cloak and managed a wobbly smile.

The cloth had rotated into a tight ball. A mass of jumbled nerves, she whisked her hand from the mess, and the
garment dropped. Lydia and Lord Greenwich knelt to
the floor at the same time. They crouched low and close;
her head almost touched his hat. As she reached for her
cloak, her bare hand bumped his gloved fingers.

Her quick inhale was slight. "Oh."

The touch was trivial, yet Lydia couldn't help but
check for visible signs of normal flesh and bone. What
woman wouldn't? Her study of his gloved appendage
must have gone on too long. When she glanced up, she
met the earl's hard-eyed gaze.

"Checking for a hideous claw?"

She flinched, locked by his dark stare and whiplike
sarcasm. There was a rustle of movement, the slip of
leather against leather, but she dare not look down. One
of his eyebrows rose in challenge.

"Aren't you going to look?"

She winced, but her gaze took a cautious path to his
high collar, then dropped in a rapid fall of curiosity to

the second sign of humanity from this arcane man. Veins roped the skin of a very normal, rather large, but nicely shaped masculine hand. Gold hairs sprung from bronzed flesh. Scraped knuckles were darker brown, leading to long, tanned fingers. Odd, a recluse wasn't supposed to be so tan.

How would those fingers feel on her skin?

The unbidden question sent a jolt through her body. He flipped the appendage over for her to see his palm dotted with calluses at the base of each finger. A plain white linen cuff obscured his wrist, but Lord Greenwich had a different reaction to her study.

"You see, Miss Montgomery, I'm human. Every. Inch. A human."

Each razor-sharp word hit the mark. Lydia's face tingled with unwelcome heat. In spite of her blunder, she looked him square in the eye.

"I don't doubt your humanity, my lord. I simply wonder about the complete stranger who bartered for my body. This situation, after all, was heaped on me with only a moment's notice, late at night when most souls are abed. And *you* stay hidden in your cloak."

"That's the deal I offer. I like my privacy. I'm sure you've read the gossip columns," he mocked. "They've mentioned as much."

"Begetting an heir, my lord, involves more exposed flesh than your hand," she said.

Oh, that was brilliant.

"I'm familiar with the process."

Lydia squeezed her eyes shut at his dry tone; he must think her rather dim. She smarted as much from his gibe about gossip pages as her impulsive tongue. More unwelcome warmth spilled over her face and neck. If only the floor would swallow her now.

Lydia stood up and smoothed damp palms down her muslin skirt. Perhaps she'd try for reason at a later time. Lud, but she needed her bed. A body couldn't keep a clear head without decent sleep.

Lord Greenwich rose to full height and, in gentlemanly fashion, held open the cloak for her. She stepped back into the cloak but studied his ungloved hand folding the garment's edges over her shoulders. His mannered voice vibrated close to her ear.

"In due time, Miss Montgomery, you'll see much more than my hand." His warmth and nearness sent a shiver skittering across her neck. "But first, we have the business of finding our way home."

"Home?" She whipped around to face him.

"Yes. Greenwich Park. My home."

The fire made his brown eyes sparkle. That's when she saw a white cleft on his skin, a minute scar, next to his right eye. She breathed a sigh of relief and made an effort to smile.

"Of course. You'll return to your home, and I'll return to my mine."

"No, you're coming with me."

He was irritatingly calm and in command. Certainly he didn't expect her to go home with him this very night. Despite her bravado moments ago, all was moving much too fast. That unwelcome whirling sensation came back with a vengeance. This truly was going to happen.

Now?

Lydia swiped at a bothersome strand of hair that fell across her face.

"Milord, the hour is late. I'm tired. You must be tired. Of course, you realize…" Her voice faltered, and she took a shallow breath. "I…I expected to return home. To *my* home." She swallowed hard. "Surely, you don't expect…"

"Expect what?"

Hands clasped behind him, Lord Greenwich exuded pragmatic patience. Or was he playing with her? Something in the slight arch of his eyebrows made her wonder. If only he'd lower his collar, then she could see his face, all the better to read him. But her patience thinned to near snapping, and her vision narrowed on him.

"What I mean is, no *true* gentleman would even think…" Her voice trailed off again. Lydia stomped her foot and groaned her frustration. "Blast it! You're impossible. This whole situation's impossible. I'm tired. And you know very well what I'm trying to say."

"A moment ago, you were concerned about the business of our begetting an heir. You even expressed the need to see more of my flesh. Now you're turning missish over a simple carriage ride to my home. What's it to be?" he asked.

"I…" Words failed her.

She was sure there was a teasing smile behind that collar. His lordship baited her, and she was simply too tired and flustered to set him straight about that missish business. He must have grasped her rattled state. With precise care, he slid the leather glove back on his hand.

"Let me put your mind at ease, Miss Montgomery. I grant you this evening has been unusually difficult. If you're concerned about Society's strictures, don't be. I do what I want, when I want." Fingers splayed, he methodically tugged on the glove for a tight fit. Lord

Greenwich studied the gauntlet a moment, then pinned her with his dark stare. "I am not a rutting monster. We sojourn to my home tonight. For sleep. Nothing else. In the morning after you're rested, we'll talk. Does that put your mind at ease?" He didn't wait for a response but walked to the door and pulled it open. "Shall we?"

Shadows cast darkness over him. An air of arrogance and expectation and, she guessed, fatigue enveloped him. The evening's drama wore thin for him as well. Drained of keen thought, Lydia followed him as if he were a lodestone. The earl offered his arm for escort, and her ungloved hand slid over his thick leather sleeve. Lord Greenwich was not a man of small stature, this much she could tell. Maybe it was the sureness of his step as they descended, but he walked with confidence, and that went a long way in soothing her.

Belowstairs, George and Mr. Bacon waited for them by the hearth. At least the smaller rats had been chased away.

"All's well, then? You'll not seek the magistrate, milord?" George called out to them as he wiped his forehead. "I'm free to go?"

"Free?" Lord Greenwich scoffed. "Go home, Montgomery. I'll be in contact."

George didn't even consider her. His lack of concern didn't sting—more the notion that she had no say in the matter rankled. That these men bartered her like common goods grated deeply. Lord Greenwich must have felt her stiffen, because he placed a hand atop hers resting on his arm. The gesture reassured but did nothing to abate her ire.

"Feel good about selling me to save your skin?" she jeered.

"I made sure you, your mam, and your sister were fed all those years, didn't I?" George jammed on his hat.

So that's how it was? Lydia inhaled sharply, about to say something ill-mannered, when the earl squeezed her hand. A firm warning grip it was.

"Go home, Montgomery, before this turns into a family brawl."

George's wide mouth clamped shut, giving him the maw of a toad. His eyes beaded as he glanced from the earl to her and back to the earl, but he took his leave, mumbling under his breath. He banged a table in quick departure and left the inn door wide open. His heels clicked, fading in the night from his hasty retreat. Mr. Bacon closed the distance to the open portal, tipping his head in the direction George had run. The hissing storm swirled his frock coat around legs as big as tree trunks.

"I'll keep a careful eye," he said, setting a Dutch cap on his bald head. He nodded at her, and his gold earring glinted. "Miss."

Lord Greenwich moved his hand to the small of her back and led her to the door. The familiar connection told Lydia the balance of power was his: she belonged to him. Unfazed by the storm, the earl strode to the center of the drive, and arm raised high, called for his carriage. His actions were ordinary, and one could daresay, considerate.

He stood, a steadfast form, impervious to howling weather. Lydia recalled tidbits about the infamous Earl of Greenwich. The whole Greenwich dynasty, in fact, fell on one disaster after another, as if cursed. Such curse business sounded like foolish nonsense, helped sell scandal pages, but she admitted it was very strange how calamity camped at their door. Once they were golden:

successful shipping concerns; father and youngest son renowned for their scientific prowess; the eldest son cut a dashing figure in Society; each family member beautiful like Renaissance art, or so people said.

Now, one of England's greatest sons was reduced to a midnight meeting at a backwater inn.

In the darkness, hooves clattered. The black lacquer coach approached. The earl directed the large conveyance toward the inn door. At least she wouldn't squish through mud and muck. Nobility had its benefits. Lord Greenwich spoke over raging winds as he came to the door.

"You're not turning missish on me again. I could have a footman chase after Mr. Bacon, but he's a sorry substitute for a chaperone." Rain beat down on him, but he set a hand to his chest in dramatic chivalry. "I assure you, your virtue's safe with me."

"Quite," was her tight reply.

Over the storm, she detected a note of tolerant reassurance. Lydia opened her mouth, ready to say something tart, but the tired, shuttered expression in his eyes stopped her. The middle of a downpour was not the time to trade quips about virtue. Better save that delicate subject for later.

A footman, his periwig sodden, attended the carriage steps and raised a candle lantern to light the way. With all formality, his lordship swept his hand toward the open door.

"Miss Montgomery, after you."

Lightning split black skies, revealing the carriage's fine forest-green leather and brass-studded interior. A dream-like quality of stepping off a cliff into a chasm enveloped her. Lydia braced herself and dashed into the vehicle, and Lord Greenwich followed close behind.

"To Greenwich Park."

The door snapped shut. The light was gone.

Lydia fidgeted against the squab, letting her eyes adjust to blackness. Without a word, the earl settled his head into the corner and crossed his arms. He tugged down his hat and stretched one booted leg across the seat, bracing the other on the floor. She waited for him to say something. Anything. Lydia cleared her throat, hoping for some acknowledgment of her presence.

Nothing.

Black carriage curtains swished back and forth as the vehicle rumbled down the road, allowing occasional light to splash the interior. Her vision traced his lounging frame swathed in bulky leather, where a rounded paunch might hide beneath for all she knew. Lord Greenwich's collar covered his face. The man refused to unmask himself even in pitch dark. His head lolled, keeping time with the carriage's bumps and sways.

"He sleeps," she whispered.

With her eyes adjusted to the dark, Lydia spied a heavy blanket folded next to her. She draped herself in wool and hunkered down. Cloth tickled her chin, and her mind fairly buzzed in the steady vehicle. She wasn't fully reconciled that this would truly happen.

How could she delicately extract herself without reprisals to her mother?

Her mind turned to another matter—a matter she could hide from his lordship for the time being. She'd have to. Her fingertips grazed her abdomen. Would *that* be her way out of this mess?

Men could be particular about these things. She shook her head and smiled at the mysterious man stretched out before her. If she truly found herself stuck, what wife doesn't have a secret or two she keeps from her husband?

Three

If you must live in the river, befriend the crocodile.
                                            —Indian Proverb

"MISS MONTGOMERY...MISS MONTGOMERY..." A PER-sistent male voice intruded. "We've arrived."

Lydia rubbed sleep-grained eyes. The earl. His slit of eyes and hat pulled low appeared less ominous: gold-brown hair came loose from his queue and spilled over his collar, quite the ordinary, mussed traveler. She yawned and stretched, not genteel but satisfying, until cold air nipped at her face and hands.

In the drive, wind drove heavy mist sideways at a footman who stood a respectful distance, his candle lantern swaying. Beyond him, a wide sweep of curved gray steps led to a large open doorway—a dark, ominous cavity. Lurid visions of dust and cobwebs and bats camped in her brain. Such notions were probably foolish, yet a body could only wonder.

"What time is it?" She groaned.

The earl, oblivious to the driving mist, pulled a silver fob from his cloak.

"Precisely half past midnight, but the hour's irrelevant." He returned the glinting timepiece to his pocket and extended a gloved hand. "Come. You'll find the house more inviting."

She frowned at the imposing edifice. The footman standing in the drive shivered. He needed to be abed as much as she. Stalling, and thereby keeping the servant from the comfort of his bed, equaled the height of inconsideration. The warm wool blanket dropped to the floor, and Lydia set her hand in the earl's firm grip. She stuck her foot outside, but awareness wasn't with her. That cavernous black doorway claimed her attention, and therein was her problem.

Trouble came in mere seconds, as it usually did for her.

The step was slick. She slipped. The sole of her leather shoe slid off the step's edge.

"Oww!" she yelped as her foot banged the graveled drive hard.

Legs buckling, down she went, like a graceless sack of flour. What's worse, she slammed into the earl, her shoulder punching his midsection.

"Ooomph!" Lord Greenwich grunted but moved quickly to save her from falling all the way to the ground.

Her face mashed against leather and linen. Strong hands held her arms. At least she didn't knock the earl down. Grabbing for purchase, her fingers touched warm wool…buttons…skin.

Her face pressed into fabric, she murmured, "I'm so very sorry."

Lydia tried to right herself, but relief turned to horror: she was a mortified eye level with the pewter buttons of

Lord Greenwich's breeches. Stalwart English mist snapped sense into her. That and seeing his placket bunched low in her fist. Her fingers grazed smooth flesh. Another, more interesting sliver of Lord Greenwich's skin was exposed: pale, intimate skin just below his navel. Lydia yanked back her hand, and a pewter button went flying.

"Oh no!" she cried as humiliating heat flared across her face and neck.

"Miss Montgomery? Are you injured?" Lord Greenwich asked above the wind, slowly lifting her up.

He sounded unperturbed at having a woman's hands on the front of his breeches. Their bodies pressed together, and in the upset, Lydia's hood slipped from her head. Drizzle wet her skin and hair. Oh, how she wished the cloak would swallow her up and blow her to another district.

"I'm sorry. So clumsy of me."

"Not to worry," he said above increasing wind. "Did you twist your ankle?"

Lord Greenwich held her close. Concern reflected in his eyes. Considering the circumstances, plenty of leather and wool made a proper barrier between them, enough to satisfy the stodgiest matron, but the alarming proximity was too much. Lydia jerked free and, without thinking, stepped back. The earl stood bolt upright, strands of his gold-blond hair whipping in the wind. Even in darkness, she caught the narrowing of his eyes.

"Forgive me for intruding on your maidenly sensibilities. I thought only to stop you from falling to the ground." His harsh words bit like frost to bare flesh.

He must think me repulsed.

She clapped a hand over her eyes and groaned. This

was not the first time her hand was on the front placket of a man's breeches, but now was not the time to clarify that point. More to the matter, she needed to clear up this debacle, but that would not be. Lord Greenwich's bootheels pounded the gravel drive in his hasty exit. When she lowered her hand, he took the stairs two at a time, his leather cape sweeping wide like a huge bird of prey.

"My lord, please…" Her voice was lost in the night wind.

Either he didn't hear her entreaty, or he ignored her.

"Oh, blast it!" Lydia clutched her skirts high—showing too much leg—for a dash to the door.

The footman's slack-jawed gape stopped her short.

"As if you've never seen the like," she retorted. "Just go warm yourself."

Teeth chattering, he bobbed his head. "Yes, miss. Good night, miss."

Lydia bounded up the stone stairs, excess cloth from her skirts bunched high. She needed to set things right. She burst into a dim interior and stopped to shake her wet garments. Her noisy entrance didn't distract the earl. He snubbed her—she saw as much when his back stiffened—and went right on speaking to two women holding guttering candles, the sole light for the cavernous entry.

She near burst to explain, but the need to say something to Lord Greenwich was overruled by impertinent curiosity. A plump, older woman and another woman, whose face was hidden from view, listened to the earl. Both, apparently servants roused in the middle of the night, wore thick robes.

Amidst his lordship's muffled instructions, the hidden

woman turned sharply in a flutter of pale blond hair, as if to get a better look at the miscreant hovering at the door. Lydia cringed; he must have relayed the minor misunderstanding by the carriage or some other unflattering news about her.

Lydia's fingers started flicking at a frayed thread inside her cloak, and then she looked overhead. Not a cobweb in sight. Her shoe tapped the marble floor: the black-and-white expanse stretched underfoot, making intricate geometric designs where not covered with carpets. His lordship ignored that toe tapping and kept his shrouded profile to the older woman. Her graying braid bobbed up and down her back as she nodded. Finally, he turned to Lydia.

"Miss Montgomery, this is Edith Lumley. She will see to your comfort. If you need anything, let her know." He raised a hand toward the other woman, who stepped forward. "And this is my housekeeper, Miss Mayhew." With a curt nod, he finished, "I bid you good night."

That last pleasantry was quite a proper set-down.

What's more, the housekeeper was shockingly beautiful.

He said *Miss* Mayhew, not the generally preferred *Mrs.*, which nobility hired or women of that class manufactured for appearances sake. Lydia gaped at the housekeeper and murmured greetings before turning to the earl. Lud, the man moved fast, going without a candle to light his way. Did he have a beast's night vision? The black hall swallowed him whole, with his boots echoing retreat.

"Your lordship, please…" she cried after him.

There was a momentary hitch in the earl's step and then a quickened pace. Somewhere in the deep shadows,

a door opened and clicked firmly shut. Lydia wanted to
crumble from the indignity witnessed by these virtual
strangers. Miss Mayhew, a vision of flaxen blond perfection, frowned toward the dark hall and then at Lydia.

"Let us see to your comfort," the housekeeper said,
smoothly turning to the older woman. "Edith, please
take Miss Montgomery to her room. Unfortunately, I
must attend to something else."

Miss Mayhew, cupping a lone candle, floated down
another dark hall, but not before turning her mouth in a
small, disapproving moue at Lydia. Owl-eyed, Miss Lumley
nodded and placed a comforting arm around Lydia.

"Don't mind his lordship, miss. He's usually an affable
sort. Sometimes he needs to be alone with his thoughts."

"Please take me to him, Miss Lumley. I must apologize—"

"Apologize? Now, now, miss. Not to worry. And
please call me Edith," she said, patting Lydia's back as she
led her to some stairs. "Sometimes a woman has to let a man
stew before *he* needs to apologize to *her*." The older woman
winked. "I'm sure 'twill all be right as rain come morn. And,
Lord knows, we've plenty of that these days, haven't we?"

Gentle pressure guided Lydia. Miss Lumley stopped,
and concern crossed her features.

"If your ankle's well enough, that is? His lordship mentioned you might've hurt it getting out of the carriage."

"Yes, it's fine." Lydia twisted around, trying to figure
out which door hid Lord Greenwich. A slender white
line lit one part of the hall, but the maid pushed her along
to the stairs.

"Good enough, miss. Though not 'miss' for long,
right?" The maid chuckled. "Ah, it'll be good to have a
lady take charge of the house. Of course, Miss Mayhew's

done a fine job, but a wife gives a home the personal touch…and children soon, we can only hope."

Now that was doubtful. His lordship couldn't be bothered to hear an apology, much less look at her. At the mention of the stunning housekeeper, a niggling question pressed its point: *Why did the earl seek a stranger to provide an heir when a beautiful, unmarried woman already lived under his roof?*

After the door snapped shut, Edward peeled off his hat and cloak, tossing aside his armor to the outside world. He needed his study's comfort and solitude. Even the air smelled better in here; his lungs expanded, testing that notion. Leather-bound volumes brushed with oil, the flat scent of beeswax polish on wood, and…

Tick, tick, tick. His mind, however, moved like a constant clock, keeping rest at bay. Categorical thinking divided the evening into neat columns. Column one: he coerced a woman to his home—a woman with vivid green eyes and smooth skin, though he couldn't fully vouch for the latter, since he'd touched her glove to skin, but appearances were promising.

He'd used all the weapons in his arsenal to achieve Miss Montgomery's acquiescence: persuasion, reason, family wealth and name, a little humor…and yes, threats.

Column two: he needed her—a simple detail encased in messy reality. The flesh-and-blood part of him admitted he wanted her. What was meant to be a simple transaction at a tumbledown inn turned into the unexpected. That surprising business of caressing her neck, albeit with his gloves on, set him back a notch.

Prowling his study, Edward contemplated that verity. His father's silver fob pressed inside his hip pocket, a reminder of familial duty. Time ticked by with the persistence of an astronomical clock. The universe moved forward, and so must he.

Nothing else would be accomplished tonight. He chuckled, recalling the astonishment on Miss Montgomery's face when he stated she'd go home with him. Tonight. Considering the evening's proposition, her assumption that he would demand conjugal rights this very evening made logical sense.

But he was not a rutting monster.

Drawn to the shelves, Edward moved along rows of favored tomes. His hands skimmed one gold-embossed spine after another. Flamsteed's *Celestial Atlas* caught his eye. Someone incorrectly shelved the folio in the history section. Probably Rogers, the new footman charged with the study's care. Edward grinned, recalling the lad's delight when given leave to borrow books at will.

A favorite, *Greek, Roman, and Persian Governments in Antiquity: A Comparative History Complete with Variorum* stopped him. He breathed clean leather and reached for the preferred text. Right as his fingers touched the spine, an intrusive knock at the door begged entry.

Go away.

The evening's transaction weighed on him: a burden to properly care for the unknown woman abovestairs. Edward pulled the book and let it fall open, flipping idly through its pages. He needed this respite.

"Go to bed, Rogers," he shouted at the paneled door. "I'm fine."

Tap. Tap.

Whoever was on the other side wanted an audience; sanctuary and solitude would be short-lived.

"Enter."

An angelic blond head peered around the door. Of course. Claire.

"I'm not bothering, am I?" She slipped in, not waiting for a response.

"Never." He glanced at her and leaned his shoulder against the shelf.

"I know better than that." She smiled, walking toward him with one hand behind her back. "You kindly tolerate me."

Edward focused on the page. "Hmmmm…tolerate you…to the contrary, the household knows *you* tolerate me." His fingers skimmed the text. "Whatever it is, leave it on my desk."

Silence.

He read the last paragraph, and just as his index finger began to turn the page, the upper space of his vision caught Claire, statue-still with a half smile on her face. This would not be a cursory deliver-the-post-and-leave kind of visit.

She wanted details.

Women always did.

Besides, females were rarely satisfied until they had a man's complete and undivided attention. That fact etched itself in his brain years ago: he preferred to ignore it. But a long history with Claire demanded he give his full attention; solitude and study would have to wait. Edward didn't lift his head, but his gaze rose over the massive tome to Claire's cool presence.

"I take it this conversation requires all my powers of concentration."

"Edward," she cajoled.

The book snapped shut, and he slid the tome back on the shelf. Edward crossed his arms loosely.

"I'm at your command."

"What happened tonight?" One elegant brow rose in question. "You gave such spare details in the hall. I guessed Edith's presence prevented you from saying more, but do tell. Something horrible must've happened to make you so angry. Was it that business of her pulling away from you by the carriage?"

He frowned, annoyed at the rapid spread of news in his household. He had informed her of Miss Montgomery falling from the carriage step, nothing more, but one feminine shoulder lifted with nonchalance.

"The coachman gave me his version in the kitchen." Her face softened. "You know we mean well. Everyone in this household cares a great deal about you." Her voice gentled. "Or did something untoward happen at the inn?"

He snorted. "I threatened to throw the woman's mother in the Compter. Some would call that untoward."

"You'd no more toss her mother into that place than me or Edith," she scoffed sweetly.

"Miss Montgomery doesn't know that. Besides, her stepfather failed to inform her of the night's business."

Claire inhaled sharply. "Oh dear. She didn't know *why* she was meeting you tonight?"

Edward shook his head, and tension bunched his shoulders and neck. He wanted this interview done. Why did women want a man to bleed everything? Especially in the murky arena of emotions. He didn't have the heart to ask her to leave. Yet.

"Then the whole thing must have been a terrible shock." Claire's fingertips fretted at her neckline, no doubt in solidarity for the set-upon Miss Montgomery.

"She took it surprisingly well. As well as one could expect when confronted with"—he made his fingers spread like claws, and his tone shifted to melodrama—"an infamous, reclusive beast who sweeps her away to his dark lair."

"Edward, don't. You're nothing of the sort." Claire stepped closer, reaching out to him, though not touching.

"Most of the realm has a different point of view."

The hand hidden behind her back slid forward. "Perhaps these will provide worthwhile diversion. They arrived late this afternoon." Claire's slim fingers held a large, official-looking post and another smaller missive.

The elegant, embossed calligraphy in the upper corner of the official post piqued his interest: *The Royal Society of London for Improving Natural Knowledge.* He accepted the letters and turned the large one over: Lord Blevins's red wax imprint. Edward broke the seal and scanned the brief letter.

"Now this makes for an interesting turn," he said, studying the parchment.

By rote, his footsteps took him to the wide leather chair dominating his desk. Without looking, he folded his body into the chair as he read and reread the note.

"Hmmm…amusing," he murmured and sent the post skidding across polished wood.

He put his booted feet on the desk, crossing them at the ankles, and opened the smaller letter. He scanned the note and dropped it on his desk. Across the mahogany, Claire seated herself.

"Do tell." She linked her fingers and waited, posture perfect.

"Mr. Cyrus Ryland needs a consult about a patent he's considering. We've maintained lively correspondence. Now he wants to meet in person."

"And, you plan to receive him?"

"Yes." He chuckled at her shocked expression. "What door in England doesn't open to one of its wealthiest citizens? Besides, I'm sure he's not coming to gawk. He means business."

"I've read about him. Owns half of England. Stodgy, fat, and boorish, I'm sure." She smiled, and her gaze fell on the larger parchment. "And that?"

Edward steepled his fingers. "An invitation from none other than Lord Blevins, the Royal Society's newly minted president. Wants me to present my latest discoveries at a symposium in June…and *respectfully* requests I submit an abstract a fortnight prior to the presentation."

"That's wonderful. You must go."

"No." Edward's steepled fingers tapped his chin. Plans for tomorrow's dissections took root. But this development…could it be a long-awaited victory?

"Why?" Claire leaned forward and touched the desk's edge. "He obviously wants to make peace with you."

"More like he wants me to apologize for the leaflet before God and man."

"Don't be so quick to think the worst." She grinned like a schoolgirl trying to hold back forbidden giggles. "But that caricature of him…" She shrugged a slender shoulder. "I see why you think he wants an apology. You accused him of stealing your work, Edward, and in a very public, humiliating way."

"What other options did I have? I was barely out of university. Blevins had position and reputation in the scientific community." He looked pointedly at her. "And he *did* steal my work."

"Exactly. What's it been? Three years since the pamphlet?" Her index finger tapped the offending sheaf. "This is his olive branch."

"It's been four years. And unequivocally *no*."

Claire shifted in her seat, a prim smile on her face.

"All right then. Think of your father. He'd be thrilled." She mimicked a lofty tone and leaned closer. "Family reputation lives on and all that."

Edward found himself opening to her infectious humor. She softened his sometimes hard edges, but the die was cast.

"My father's cronies no doubt prodded Blevins to extend the invitation out of pity...or curiosity...find out once and for all what happened to me." He shook his head and rubbed his jaw. "No, I'm content with staying here and publishing my findings. They can read about my work. Besides, there are more pressing matters, in particular one residing abovestairs."

Claire's delicate brows pressed together.

"There is that," she agreed quietly. "Does Miss Montgomery understand the full...*urgency* of things?"

Edward tipped his head back. "Very delicately put. And no, she learned the genesis of the bargain only this evening." He scrubbed both hands across his face. "I prefer to approach this one issue at a time."

"Well, you have—what is it?—ninety days to work this all out, right?"

"Less than eighty days...seventy-nine to be exact, since midnight came and went."

He tugged off the black velvet tie wrapped around his queue and rubbed the back of his head and neck. Pressure and weariness washed over him. Claire was gracious enough to take note and rose from her chair, and when she did, returned to her role of Greenwich Park's solicitous housekeeper.

"I bid you good night, then."

"Good night, Claire."

Edward didn't follow her exit from the room; the astonishing missive drew his attention to his desk. He stared at the invitation as if he could conjure motive and meaning, but freedom to think was cut short again. A pale blond specter at the doorway faced him, speaking quietly across the room.

"She really is quite lovely."

"What?" He glanced up, half listening.

"Miss Montgomery. She's very pretty."

Claire's fragile smile spoke volumes. Edward leaned back, unwilling to divulge more about the evening or Miss Montgomery. A polite dismissal was about to be given. No need. Like a wisp of smoke, Claire slipped from the room.

Four

All our knowledge has its origins in our perceptions.
—Leonardo da Vinci

THE LUSH VERMILLION PATH BROUGHT TO MIND A ROAD paved with hidden promises. What or who lurked behind each closed door she passed?

Lydia rolled her eyes at her overzealous mind, but soaked up every visual detail.

Setting aside fanciful notions, she trod the plush pathway, really a fine Oriental carpet of rich red that streamed a long, regal hallway. A chambermaid, or team of them, must spend hours buffing and polishing the walnut paneling to its present perfect sheen. Exotic hothouse flowers flared explosions of color from porcelain vases atop delicate-legged tables; definite symmetry balanced table placement and flower arrangements.

Greenwich Park looked nothing like a madman's dark lair.

The maid motioned to a door on the right. "Here we are."

The brass doorknob shined. Impeccable. Miss Lumley

swung wide the door and bustled about, lighting matched candelabra. She banked the fire, and light flooded a coliseum of femininity. Lydia stood in the doorway aghast: the entire room vomited shades of pink.

Disquiet at being in a strange man's palatial home turned to blatant assessment.

Before her wasn't a matter of low-class design. White furniture, French and expensive, conveyed delicacy. Each item reflected the past decade of continental decor, which made her smirk. The pieces likely found their way from France during the Seven Years War, something only well-connected nobility could manage, while the rest of the populace made do with sturdy English goods.

Lydia stood aware of another boundary, a line between stately elegance and a space that screamed excess. The room, awash in blaring shades of pink and yellow silk, cried insipid womanhood.

She winced. Wealth and nobility never guaranteed good taste.

A writing table sat near a window, but the room's owner wasn't much of a writer, for ink would surely splatter and stain somewhere on all that white.

Miss Lumley beckoned her into the room. "Come, come. Oh, here, miss, I've gone and forgotten all about taking your cloak. Poor dear. Tired and damp. We'll get you into something dry. You'll need nightclothes, won't you?"

The older woman opened an armoire with doors featuring blank-faced, poorly painted cupids, their pink posteriors comically oversized, on chubby, cloud-floating bodies. Such gaudy, immature art was an offense to muralists everywhere. The maid pulled a frothy white nightgown and white velvet robe from the cabinet and shut the door with a snap. Miss Lumley laid the effusive garments on the bed and helped Lydia with her buttons.

"Those should do 'til we get your things." She chuckled, nodding at the robe and sleepwear. "Men and their haste."

Lydia's dress slackened as each button came undone. Comfort and drowse made Lydia stretch her neck, and her gaze collided with an attractive blond swathed in gold silk. The regal woman stared at her with an imperious air from a painting above the mantel. Two small white dogs flanked her skirts, prepared to yip at the interloper.

"Whose room is this?" Lydia stared back warily, though the painting was excellent.

"Why it's yours, of course." Edith tugged off Lydia's sleeves. "Step out of the dress, if you please."

"But who's that?" With an eye to the portrait, Lydia held the bedpost as Edith peeled away her dress and patched underskirt.

"Lady E., er, Lady Elizabeth, his lordship's mum." Miss Lumley tossed the garments over her shoulder. "This is, or was, her room, which now, of course, will be yours. Let's get this on, shall we?"

The maid bunched up the frothy nightgown. Copious pink and yellow ribbons, shiny strips of silk, dangled in the air. The garment must belong to the woman in the portrait. Lydia shook her head and raised her hands in protest.

"Oh, no, no thank you. I'm fine with what I have." She glanced from the painting to the maid, not willing to wear countess garb, even for sleep. "I'll stick with my chemise."

Edith frowned at her thin, short-sleeved chemise, eyeing a threadbare spot.

"At least take the robe. You'll catch your death of cold without proper garments."

Lydia grimaced. No corset and only one underskirt. She stood in her chemise and drawers with nothing else but a pair of stockings. Even when her dress and underskirt dried, she couldn't very well walk around the earl's home corsetless. Wearing the cloak indoors would be silly, all in the name of modesty.

"I suppose his lordship shouldn't see bobbing breasts about his house, should he?" Lydia announced.

"Oh, my." She chortled. "You're a cheeky one, miss. Just what his lordship needs, I think. Now, be a good girl and put this on. I see the gooseflesh on your arms. Best be sensible, I always say."

Lydia hesitated but slipped into the luxurious robe, belting the pliant velvet. The lush fabric caressed her arms, tempting her with shimmering softness.

Her brain couldn't help but latch onto the question: What exactly did his lordship expect of her? Other than an heir and a second, which seemed like overly functional thinking. The earl spoke of children, babies, after all. She contemplated probing the older woman for information, but the energetic maid had lost herself in what must have been a mental "to do" list.

The maid poked the fire, and above her head, Lady E. stared, full of hauteur and sophistication. Lydia, never one for fashion, leaned on the bedpost.

"Does the countess live here?"

Miss Lumley replaced the poker and moved to the

bed. She slipped her hand under a pink bed ruffle. Out came the rim of a chamber pot.

"Just so you know, miss." She tapped the porcelain rim and stood upright. "The countess? Live here? Oh no, her ladyship has apartments in Bath and her own estate, Ashton Manor, nearer to Lady Jane, the earl's sister she is, and her little ones." Edith winked and lowered her voice. "Don't worry. Lady E.'s at least a good two or three days' journey from here. She's not big on visits to Greenwich Park anymore."

Lydia absorbed this news and slipped her hands into the robe's deep pockets, while Edith retrieved her candle from the dressing table.

"All's well prepared, I think." The maid cupped the flame and smiled. "At least I hope so, since we got word of your coming. Of course, tomorrow will be much better when your things arrive."

"You had word of my coming?" Lydia fisted her hands encased in velvet.

Lord Greenwich was confident of his plan.

"Why, of course. We were informed of your arrival two days ago. Such a bustle to get the room ready. But if you're quite comfortable, I'll be off to get a mite of sleep." Miss Lumley pointed at the long pink cord near the dressing table. "Give that a tug if you need anything."

Lydia's only decent clothing departed the room on the woman's shoulder. She grinned: a melodramatic escape from the phantom's lair would not be an option tonight.

Once the door closed, her toes wiggled on the fine pastel carpet. She leaned a hip against the bed and slipped off her stockings, all the better to feel the expensive pile under her feet. The old stockings floated to the floor.

That's when the porcelain winked at her. She leaned over and pulled out the chamber pot all the way.

"Pink. Of course."

Her heel nudged the ceramic bowl back, and Lydia flopped onto the voluminous comforter. Her splayed fingers rubbed and swirled over the pink silk bedcover, and that's when she remembered: her fingers had touched Lord Greenwich's abdomen, firm male skin, pleasant to the touch.

The earl sported well-exercised, hard flatness…an interesting state for a recluse. This was not her first exposure to a man; nor was she one for fits of hysteria at the sight—or feel—of male flesh. But then Lord Greenwich wouldn't know that. Her gaze wandered to the elegant portraiture.

"How do you feel about your son marrying a woman like me?" She crossed her arms. "But therein lies my trouble. To save my own mother, I must do this. Wouldn't you want your son to do everything he could to save you?"

Lydia slid off the bed and picked up the brass snuffer to extinguish the candles. She paused, hand in midair, glancing at the dominating portrait.

"I don't relish marriage to any man. No more than you probably relish me marrying your son."

And there was that slight misunderstanding that needed to be rectified. She rubbed her tired eyes and set the snuffer down. A shaft of light beamed from under an adjoining door. Of course, the door to the earl's room. Lydia tucked a thick lock of hair behind her ear.

"At the very least, clear the air," she decided aloud.

The soles of her feet sped over the luxuriant pile,

and her fist poised to knock on the adjoining door. She stopped short and cocked her head. Voices, a man's and a woman's, carried faintly. Lydia stared at the narrow beam under the door. Was that Miss Mayhew's voice? What game did his lordship play? A valet perhaps would attend at this hour, but not a woman. Her apology and confession fell by the wayside. Lydia grabbed the doorknob, ready to give Lord Greenwich a few choice words.

Five

SHE SCANNED THE ROOM, HEART POUNDING, AND braced herself for...silence. Not a soul was present. There had been voices, in particular his lordship's voice, somewhere in all this...mess.

The whole room cried disaster. Mismatched furniture competed with an abundance of books. Three bookstands acted as stems for massive tomes. Near those bookstands, a large, poorly crafted table held sizable sheaves of paper. Maps from the look. Everywhere, volumes stacked in such a scrabbled mess.

Not at all what one expected of nobility, then again, neither was the adjoining pink monstrosity. Large pillar candles blazed brilliantly, leaving excess wax pooled on tabletops. A man's clothes piled in haphazard array across a rough sea chest. A pile of breeches taunted her, reminding her of where her hand had been less than an hour past, and the humbling fact that she owed Lord Greenwich an explanation...no, scratch that, *explanations* in the plural. Moments ago, she'd made base assumptions about him and his housekeeper.

Worse yet, she'd marched uninvited into a man's bedchamber well past midnight. Her record of decision making this eve left much to be desired.

And then she spied him.

A dark blond head showed above the back of a large leather chair. Lord Greenwich, oblivious to her presence, faced a roaring fire, his stocking feet propped on a leather stool. Lydia slowly, carefully let the air from her lungs. She could turn back. Wait for morning. Her hands clenched into fists. When she opened them, Lydia willed control.

"My lord. A moment of your time, if you please."

Her words shot like a musket blast through the quiet room. Masculine feet jerked off the stool, and a male hand set a crystal glass on a side table with care. Firelight played inside the jostled amber liquid.

"Miss Montgomery. I thought you were asleep."

He didn't stand up to face her, but his tanned fingers gripped the crystal glass.

Emboldened, Lydia strode a few paces forward. "I'm surprisingly awake." She rubbed her chilled hands. "When I saw the light under your door, I thought I heard voices…"

"That was Miss Lumley taking the laundry."

"I see." She fidgeted, feeling a little silly about her suspicions. "I'm glad you're up, because I want to speak with you. With the evening's excitement and all—"

"Go to bed." The terse command came from the chair's expanse, cutting her short.

"What?"

"Do as you're told and go to bed." His voice carried across the space, sharp on each syllable.

"Wha…" Lydia choked down an indignant snort.

Lord Greenwich's earlier considerate, gentleman's veneer had worn off and been replaced by the type of nobleman she'd run into far too much: young, privileged, and full of themselves to excess. She was in his home, after all. Something snapped within her adaptable nature, and she closed the distance, her bare feet making quick swipes on the rug.

"So that's how it is. Get what you want, and those polished manners of yours disappear. You may be the high and mighty Earl of Green—" Lydia stopped in her tracks when he stood up.

Her spine chilled. The back of him looked menacing. His linen shirt hung loose, and firelight limned broad shoulders through wrinkled fabric. Lord Greenwich stood tall and imposing, his mane of blond-brown hair hung free just past his shoulders, more highwayman stirred from repose than aristocrat at ease.

"Don't come any farther," he commanded and gripped the mantel with both hands. "Return to your chamber, *if you please*."

"I do not *please*, sir," Lydia said, but she finished the space to his chair with caution. "I will not be ordered about like a child."

He inhaled sharply when she moved closer, and his back expanded like some kind of cornered beast about to spring. The part of her brain crying for restraint could not douse her ire.

"What's wrong with you? You orchestrate my removal from my home in the dead of night. Then, you threaten my mother if I don't go along with your ridiculous plan." Her volume increased with each condemning phrase. "And, talk about the height of bad manners… you, you *rudely* show me your back—"

"I'm trying to spare us both any discomfort," he snapped. "Stay where you are."

"I came only to clear up some misunderstandings." Lydia moved beside the great chair and hooked bothersome hair behind her ear.

"Don't come any closer." His long fingers rubbed the back of his neck. "Whatever it is, consider the matter cleared. Now, *please*, return to your room."

He said the words as if he were the very soul of patience, with a touch of pleading as he finished. Lydia made an inelegant sound and moved closer just to spite him. She wanted to shake that lordly shoulder and make him face her.

"I realize I'm not a lady of nobility, but at the very least, acknowledge my presence, sir." She clamped her arms under her breasts.

"I deplore histrionics," he said. "And status of birth matters little to me." The earl chuckled, a dry, humorless sound, as he kept his face to the wall. "You'll find I'm equally rude to those of my class, if not more so."

His bald statement threw her. Lydia shifted on her feet, not knowing how to respond, and the way his shoulders bunched and tensed under his shirt, she had poked and prodded the cornered beast, testing his limits.

"I'd hoped discussions could hold for morning, when we're both rested and in a better frame of mind"—his head dropped, chin to chest—"but apparently you can't wait."

Before her eyes, the beast uncoiled, and Lord Greenwich turned to confront her.

Her hands shot up to her cheeks as shock splashed her cold.

"Your face…"

"Yes. My face." His scornful smile told her she wasn't the first distressed maiden to see him.

Half of his face, shadowed by gold and brown whiskers, showed male perfection, but the other half, a bizarre pattern of scar lines and puckered flesh. Truly, staring at his face was akin to seeing a painting of two men, split down the middle. Lydia recoiled as much from the hot anger flashing in his eyes as from astonishment. The chair hit the back of her knees. Down she sat. Hands on hips, he loomed over her.

"I can't be sure if you're irritating or obtuse," he said, growling the words.

She swallowed hard. "Most people find me very agreeable."

One doubting brow rose. Untidy hair spread across his shoulders; more dark brown sprung from his nape, some of it curling. She had it all wrong at the Blue Cockerel; the *Phantom of London* was more menacing than mysterious.

"Very agreeable, actually," she whispered, wide-eyed.

She took in every detail of his face: the blade-straight nose, the small white cleft, that tiny scar she noticed by his right eye, long brown lashes, gold-tipped in the light, and wide, frowning mouth.

"You're staring," he said. "Didn't anyone ever tell you that's the height of bad manners?"

Lydia's eyelids shuttered at having her own words

dumped back on her. She forced herself to concentrate on the front of her robe. The earl's harsh bark of laughter made her squirm.

"On second thought, why not get your fill?" Lord Greenwich leaned in close.

His hands braced the chair arms; she shrunk from the sharp, glinting eyes a mere hand's breadth from her face. The aroma of scotch and lye soap came with every overbearing inch. Her curious questions, the need to know and see what had been hidden from her at the inn, turned fuzzy in the face of peril.

But heaven help her, she looked.

Tawny hair fell forward, framing handsome features and taut skin browned from the sun. The grain of his unscarred skin stretched over twitching jaw muscles. And the other half...lines moved in maplike array across his left cheek. What must be small burns dotted his skin into pale discoloration, going down his neck.

"Get a good look at the Greenwich Recluse, Enigma Earl, or whatever drivel London's busybodies call me these days." Well-formed lips pulled tight in a grimace. "Of course, you must have the complete picture."

Lord Greenwich stood up and yanked his shirt to expose part of his chest: more lines, more small dotted burns, and puckering flesh on one section of his upper torso. Lydia flinched deeper into the cracked leather chair. His lordship took a step back and released his shirt. His hard brown eyes turned weary and hooded.

"Had enough?"

Numbness dissolved into an altogether different feeling. Pity? Confusion? Lydia dropped her head into her hands. Thankfully, her hair curtained her, giving respite for the moment. If he'd wanted her to feel small, he'd succeeded.

"If only I'd known, this could've gone much better," she groaned.

"Nothing could make this better."

Her head snapped up.

"I'm sorry for this, so sorry…for what happened this evening, truly…for everything…George's and Tristan's theft, what happened out front tonight…everything. But what did you expect? That I'd stay in my room to await your bidding?"

"Sounds reasonable," he said, glaring at her and crossing his arms tightly across his chest.

"Oh, please," she snipped. "A total stranger whisks me away after some secret, late-night meeting, expecting me to wait like a biddable mouse for who knows how long?" She folded her arms across her chest. "What would you do if you were in my place?"

His jaw muscles ticked under the scars, as though he weighed her argument and found solid reasoning.

"I said we'd talk in the morning. And the middle-of-the-night meeting was your stepfather's idea. Remember, I thought you were fully informed. And as you so *aptly* pointed out at the inn, my previous matrimonial arrangements haven't gone well. Circumstances turned critical. I was prepared to move quickly."

"What do you mean?"

The earl leaned a shoulder on the mantel. "Not relevant at this time."

She wanted to probe that cryptic comment, but his topaz eyes glittered in a way that issued warning bells in her head.

"What is relevant, Miss Montgomery, is the fact that

you came to my room, requesting a moment of my time—" He spoke softly as the corners of his mouth turned up in an unfriendly smile. "Unless exhaustion has finally claimed you."

With him standing there angry, in stocking feet and open-necked shirt, Lydia's equilibrium went askew. Dark-eyed and unkempt, he looked primitive. No, he *was* primitive and bore no resemblance at all to a refined earl. Her right hand gripped the neckline of the robe, closing it high under her chin.

"I know nothing about you."

"Edward Christopher James Sanford, ninth Earl of Greenwich." He said each syllable with the enthusiasm one gives a list for a trip to the market. Yet his eyes... they blazed, sharp and assessing, like he could read her every thought.

But what happened to you?

She couldn't help that. He knew that question hung between them; she guessed as much in the hard glint of his eyes and the tightness about his mouth. Was he daring her to ask the impertinent question out loud? No instructive social manual existed to tell a woman how to engage reclusive noblemen in cordial conversation well past midnight. What was she supposed to do?

Behind the earl, a log split in two, both pieces rolled apart inside the massive hearth, and pulsing orange embers spilled near his feet. She flinched, but the sudden noise didn't bother Lord Greenwich.

"A-And?" she asked, pulling her robe tighter under her chin.

"And what?" He sighed, starting to sound more annoyed than fierce.

Her lips parted, but no words came, couldn't because the sensation of wool filling her mouth made talking difficult. Under the weight of his harsh glare, Lydia squirmed inside the chair: her velvet-clad bottom rubbed the leather, making the only sound amidst awkward silence. Asking the obvious question would wait for another time. Then one of his eyebrows rose slowly, imperious and lordly in effect.

"Perhaps you can begin by telling me why you barged into my room at this late hour."

She didn't immediately respond. He'd deftly moved the conversation away from questions about his face and saved her from blundering anew.

"You mentioned something about misunderstandings," he prompted, drumming his fingers on the mantel.

"There are some things you should know," she said, glancing toward his door. "Earlier this evening, when you saved me from my clumsy fall, I wasn't bothered by your catching me or your closeness. I was embarrassed."

He gave no response. Not even a shift in position or batting an eye. So, he'd give no quarter. His hard-eyed, stark silence was condemning enough, as if he'd judged her and found her statement lacking. She made herself sit up straight.

"Lud, you're making this difficult. I was embarrassed at having my hand on the front of your breeches. Is that plain enough?" Lydia folded her hands in her lap and exhaled her relief, freed by unvarnished directness.

Lord Greenwich placed an open hand at his hip and studied her.

"Your reaction had nothing to do with my presumed madness?"

"No."

"My supposed diseased state?"

"No."

"Or that I'm some kind of malformed, rutting beast?"

"Of course not."

He'd fired each question at her, she'd answered truthfully. Lydia swiped at hair that fell across her eyes. She stared up at him, almost daring his perusal. Then, the barest hint of a smile showed on the earl's face.

Her whole body eased back into the chair, and rigidness melted from her spine. Glad for the respite from the tense atmosphere, she decided to face that *other* issue another time. There was only so much bravado a woman could muster in a single night. Lydia smiled brightly and put her hands on the sides of the chair, ready to rise.

"Well, then I shall take myself off to bed, and we can both get some sleep."

"Wait." He held up a hand. "You said that you had some *misunderstandings* you felt I should know." His eyebrows snapped together. "You spoke in the plural. What else did you plan to tell me?"

Her jaw dropped. His lordship had paid enough attention to detail to catch every nuance of what she'd said, very unlike most men of her experience. Relief over their simpatico, however brief, drained, as did her courage on the other point. She wanted to slink off to the safety of sleep, hide under thick covers, and not emerge for days.

"That can wait for morning, my lord."

She tried a smile, but by the way his eyes narrowed, a muddled, caught-in-the-thick-of-trouble look must have been written all over her face.

Lord Greenwich shook his head. "Now is as good a time as any. After all, *you* came to me."

"Oh, but…" Whatever argument died from her lips under his scrutiny.

She contemplated a lie, if only for a second, to relieve the pressure of his penetrating stare. Lydia noticed the rich amber liquid in his lordship's glass, very nice scotch whiskey, she was sure. A bracing swig would be welcome right about now. She swallowed hard and took a deep breath.

"I'm not a virgin."

Lydia's hands clasped neatly over her abdomen. Lord Greenwich's gaze dropped to the protective gesture.

"Not a virgin," he said softly.

"No." Her thumb brushed the robe's velvet belt. "I'm not sure what George told you about me, or if that was a requirement in this unusual transaction, but with your need of an heir…ah, perhaps that might be an issue." She glanced up at Lord Greenwich and tried to gauge his reaction, but the man stayed stiff and unreadable.

"He inferred you were pure as the driven snow…but go on."

She winced. "In the carriage, I pieced facts together. I was sure you didn't know, and of course, that detail would be important to you. Usually is to family lines, isn't it?"

Lydia stared into the fire behind him. The late hour and warm, hypnotic fire lulled her. With the worst of what she had to say over and done, easiness with the earl loosened her tongue.

"My stepfather has a talent for trickery." She peered up at him. "Once I understood the whole situation, I realized you likely didn't know why I live in Wickersham. I was a bit of a hoyden in the past, caught in a compromising situation and packed off to my great-aunt's house some four years ago. Ironically, I left to spare my mother eviction from the old steward's cottage, which happened later from something George did. We lived there by the benevolence of the Duke of Somerset after my father died." Lydia kept playing with the velvet tie. "But the duchess thought me a bad influence. She, along with some houseguests and one of her daughters, stumbled upon me in the barn"—she looked down at her clasped hands and chose her words with care—"with, ah, a man of close acquaintance."

"Then having your hands on men's breeches isn't a stretch for you, is it?"

Her head shot up. "That's a touch rude."

"Not as rude as the trap you and your stepfather have set for me, is it?"

"I've done no such thing," she said, her voice sharpening.

"You're as quick with deception as old George, aren't you, Miss Montgomery? I played nicely into your hands. The cash-strapped family of no rank marries nobility. Oh, you'd all be set up well." His dark eyes sparked. "I should've known at the inn. What you said to me…bold as brass."

Lydia sat up taller. "I came here to spare you any false assumptions. I'd like nothing more than to be free of this absurd arrangement, which as you may recall, I had no hand in making."

"What?" he scoffed. "No convenient marriage for the unmarriageable hoyden? You're pretty but not that pretty."

She blinked, unsure how to respond to such insult

and accusation. He'd twisted her best intentions into something horrible. Lord Greenwich's face contorted from one dark emotion to the next, but that stare down was brief. He lunged at her and yanked her within an inch of his chest.

"Or does this have something to do with my scars? Now that you've seen me, having second thoughts about your scheme?"

Lydia's hands fluttered in defense. Her palms pushed against the warm, hard wall of his chest.

"No," she said, her voice a hoarse whisper through rapid breaths. "Your scars don't bother me, took me by surprise, yes, but I'm not a schemer, least of all with George."

Gone was the calm, arrogant noble, replaced by a wild-eyed beast caught in a snare. His hands gripped her upper arms, manacles that clamped hard. Eyes narrowed and nostrils flared, he searched her face. Surely she'd struck a nerve with something in the mess that was this evening. She'd spoken the truth.

"You're hurting me," she whispered. "Please."

He released her. She slumped into the chair, but her heart kept a wild thump against her ribs. The earl's chest rose and fell with rapid, deep breaths. He looked away from her and rubbed his scarred cheek.

"I'm not sure what to make of you, Miss Montgomery. I realize this has been a most unusual night." Lord Greenwich's gaze slid sideways back to her, as if adding up the sum of the evening's parts. "On the one hand, you appear lovely and sometimes well spoken. On the other, you tend toward the com—" He stopped himself.

"Common." She supplied the unfinished word, holding her head high.

"Yes." He shrugged quick agreement.

"You don't insult me with the truth. I am exactly what you see, my lord: an honest, barely educated, commoner of some past disrepute." She dared a cheeky introduction of her own and tipped her head to him. "Miss Lydia Anne Montgomery of nowhere important."

The scarred corner of his lordship's mouth curved up, giving him a dangerous, if humored, brigand's smile. That miniscule change shifted awareness; they were an arm's length apart, and all of her sensed him, as if they touched. Both had been deceived this evening and were sorting through the confusion, but excitement ebbed, and a crashing wave of weariness claimed Lydia as she rose from the chair.

"You understand, then, I must leave in the morning. We can put this unusual arrangement behind us, and you're free to search for a more suitable wife."

She gave the quiet pronouncement and moved to go. Lord Greenwich's hand stopped her. His long fingers slid over her velvet-clad arm, stopping at her elbow.

"Wait. Please. I've developed a bad habit of underestimating you. You are something of a riddle."

Complexity, then, was not an unwelcome attribute for the Earl of Greenwich. They stood rather close, and in his room, the informality of their attire was not lost on her. Another flush prickled her skin, and one hand clutched the robe's collar high under her chin.

"I've come to think the same about you, my lord, in our short acquaintance." Her head canted to the side. She was unsure of what to make of this new turn.

He motioned to his chair. "Please."

Lydia, her eyes hazed with sleepiness, expected Lord

Greenwich to be glad to wash his hands of this mess—of her—but she took the proffered seat. She couldn't refuse him. His lordship straddled the footstool facing her, bracing both hands on his knees.

He took a deep breath, and his chest expanded under the linen weave of his shirt. "I state the obvious when I point out we're both tired and not in the best frame of mind. Nor were matters helped that we were caught off guard this evening."

"A few surprises, to say the least."

Sitting this close, she noticed his shirt stretched across his shoulders. Edges of deep scars showed through pale linen.

"But there is the matter of your family's dubious circumstances, and I still need a wife. Soon, as a matter of fact." He paused, as if he chose his words with care. "A woman of experience isn't necessarily a bad thing in these circumstances, is it?"

Her back stiffened.

"We've already established what you think about—"

"Hear me out. Please."

His last word, less commanding, put her on equal footing. The dangerous brigand turned into a reasonable barrister laying out his middle-of-the-night case with persuasive gentility.

"Go on."

"At the inn, you asked for freedom to pursue what you will. Why not here? With the full weight of the Greenwich name to support you? And there is the matter of your mother's best interests…how you can best aid her." His hands opened in appeal. "I'm happy to offer her my protection, if that helps. Besides, our arrangement ought to work well. Almost all my time's devoted to my work. You'd be left to your own pursuits." He finished with a rueful smile. "Most marital unions follow a similar formula with great success."

Fire haloed his shoulders and tawny hair from behind, casting a golden glow around Lord Greenwich. The dangerous brigand turned reasonable barrister was now an archangel with frightening appeal. Her head drooped as all of her fell prey to the lure he set.

When was the last time a man proposed something beneficial to her?

The offer was no longer a mad scheme, but began to sound logical, even congenial. With the Greenwich name, she'd be more likely to help her mother, too. Exhaustion pressed her from all sides, and Lydia nodded.

"I'll stay."

"Good. I'm glad we were able to have our discussion now." He smiled, and faint lines creased the corners of his eyes.

Somewhere in her chest, warmth swelled into a faint connection with him. Under that pleasantness, her eyelids drooped. Lydia wanted to ask for a blanket and curl up in his large chair, such was her tiredness and ease at that moment. An ember snapped and crackled behind the earl, and the fire sent a spray of sparks. Lord Greenwich got up and took the poker from its iron stand, jabbing the cozy blaze.

"There is one thing," he said, turning around to face her.

"What's that?"

"We'll wait one month, a necessary precaution, if you will. It will stress my timeline"—his full lips pressed into a flat line, looking like all the world pressed down on him—"but it must be."

His shoulders bunched under his shirt as he leaned both hands on the iron poker.

"A month?" She shook her head, confused, until hot truth hit her.

He said nothing, but his pointed gaze spoke volumes. That warm swell toward the earl, a tiny but growing thing, dissolved into lukewarm puddles of hard wax.

"Of course. You mean to wait for some assurance that I'm not already pregnant." The words came flat and lifeless.

The way his eyebrows furrowed into a straight line, Lord Greenwich's face reflected a grim barrister bearing judgment on the convicted. Was he waiting for her to burst into dreaded histrionics? The earl acted as judge and jury: to him, she equaled some kind of blowsy wench. Hadn't he already said as much? Neck-stretching pride stopped her from saying anything further. She wouldn't stoop to defend herself. None was needed.

The province of a woman's life was never truly her own. Men could drop their drawers as often as they pleased, but women always paid the price. Lydia's smile stretched into a tight line.

"Of course. One month."

She rose stiffly from the chair, chin tipped high to his stare that she was sure followed her. At the door, she mustered every last ounce of good manners for the final courtesy.

"Good night, milord."

His lordship surprised her and set a hand on his chest and gave her a chivalrous bow.

"Good night, Miss Montgomery."

Was there a flicker of regret in his eyes?

Lydia slipped into the other room and shut the door between them. Molded panels pressed her back. She stared at nothing in particular, disappointed that his lordship was no different than other men after all. Nor did he think well of her. The very notion stung deeply.

Six

Women are a necessary evil.

—Proverb

EXCRUCIATING NEED FOR A FORBIDDEN WOMAN NEVER made a good start to a man's day. Edward climbed out of bed, and every inch of his body roused to the knowledge of Miss Montgomery's proximity beyond the adjoining door. Some parts stirred more than others, but the worst of it? The lady in question was prohibited and by his own proclamation—a classic paradox.

All the more reason to lose himself in the blessed focus of work: science gave her siren's call, and she tolerated no competition.

Scraping blade to skin in smooth strokes, Edward acknowledged harsh facts in tepid morning light; a woman invaded his well-ordered world last night, and he raised the gates, letting her in under the interest of familial duty. Yet his gaze wandered to that adjoining door through which she charged unwelcomed last eve. Was he too hasty with that month-long demand?

A nasty nick to his chin brought him back. A spot of

blood swelled, and a thin line of red streaked the iron blade with sanguine warning: *proceed with caution*.

Edward moved through the quiet house and found his way to the center of his world, his greenhouse. With the rough wood of his workbench under his palms, rich soil perfumed the air, anchoring vast arrays of plants begging to be studied. Yet Miss Lydia Montgomery, wrapped in virginal white velvet, kept dancing before him.

Edward squeezed his eyes shut then spread them wide. He blinked and tried again to examine the white blossom under the magnification glass. Fimbriate petals morphed into a chocolate-haired woman with a proud walk and delectable form wrapped in white velvet.

A chocolate-haired woman?

He rolled his eyes. "Next I'll compose sonnets in her honor."

Edward was certain his one-month requirement insulted her, but the rationale of simple biology won the day.

He tried once more to reassemble his thoughts. The open journal filled with tables of facts and measurements, his deplorable chicken-scratch notes, and messy diagrams failed to bring typical clarity. Palms flattened on the workbench, Edward's chin hit his chest, and the placket of his breeches brushed the table's edge. Yes, mindless, baser parts of him sung their own tune, praising the dark-haired invader.

"Hux, do we have any coffee?" His bellow bounced off the high glass ceiling.

"Coffee, is it yer're needin'?" an ancient voice wheezed somewhere behind a mass of green fronds and exotic, unfurling buds.

"Yes. Black. Strong. Hot." Edward opened his eyes.

Huxtable, a bantam-sized man of advanced years, ambled over and set a watering can amidst rows of loam-filled tins.

"I can check," he said and disappeared into a smaller room in the corner of the greenhouse.

Edward hitched a hip on the worktable and rubbed his eyes. A curious thing, this fascination with a woman he hardly knew and of no particular significance to his life prior to last night. She went along with minimum dramatics, threats to her mother notwithstanding. However, he was sure he'd made an accurate assessment of her stepfather: a pettifogger to be sure.

He rubbed his scarred cheek. The month-long waiting period stressed his already tight timeline, but would resolve any doubts regarding Miss Montgomery's condition and tease out possible deception. This morning's torment proved an unexpected thorn in his flesh: the reality of a man long deprived of a woman's charms. Huxtable's approaching shuffle and the aroma of coffee gave him blessed relief.

"Aye, here ye go." Huxtable passed a cracked mug to Edward and settled on the opposite table with a steaming cup. "Don't mind me sayin', but ye look a bit worse for wear." He tapped a finger to his own whiskers. "Nicked the chin, too, I see."

Edward put the welcome black liquid under his nose and breathed in the dark roast's heady aroma.

Huxtable grinned, revealing chipped, tobacco-stained teeth. "Bad night, was it?"

He sipped the scalding brew. "I returned from London late."

"And I hear with a certain pretty, dark-haired miss stowed away in yer carriage." Huxtable waggled wiry brows over his mug. A few gray hairs corkscrewed longer in his bushy brows.

"Yes, she's pretty and dark haired." Edward nodded and took another sip as he stared past the glass wall. "News travels fast in the kitchens."

"It does indeed," Huxtable ruminated, sipping from his mug. "And I'd say she's a rather determined one, too."

"How'd you conjure up that information?"

"Easy. I can see it in her walk. She's a comin' this way." The servant raised his cup toward the door, rasping self-satisfied laughter.

Edward twisted around to see a woman charging toward the greenhouse, her long hair whipping about in brisk morning wind. Arms swinging and long strides eating up the lawn, Miss Montgomery ignored the winding gravel path for a more direct line through damp grass toward the greenhouse. He groaned. His inner sanctum was about to be breached.

"First my room and now my laboratory. The only two places I crave solitude, and she violates them both."

"A woman after me own heart." Huxtable's curt nod emphasized his long-voiced opinion that Greenwich's lord and master needed to get out more.

Edward shrugged off that stale argument to see Miss Montgomery stop outside the door. She pressed her face against the smudged glass. Likely, she couldn't see him through the dirty pane or past overflowing greenery inside, but that didn't stop her. She pushed her way in with a whoosh of air and stood, leaving the door open wide. She cupped both sides of her mouth and called out to him.

"Lord Greenwich? Lord Greenwich, are you here?"

"Shut the door. You're letting warm air escape." He barked his irritation and added, "A greenhouse thrives on keeping heat in, cold out."

When she spied him, Miss Montgomery smiled and waved.

"Sorry," she yelled across the vast room before pushing the door closed. "Miss Lumley told me I'd find you here."

"A logical conclusion, since this is where I do my work. Undisturbed. Usually," he grumbled under his breath.

"Not this morning, I wager." Huxtable wheezed and chuckled as he sipped his coffee.

Edward kept his casual seat on the high workbench, but his other boot pressed harder into the gravel. He tried to relax. This was his space after all, barred to most. Miss Montgomery would learn her place. The sooner she grasped this, the better. His mouth opened to issue that edict, but the lady in question strode toward them bright-eyed and looking remarkably well rested. In fact, she glowed: sparkling bottle-green eyes, pink cheeks, dazzling smile, wind-mussed hair, and all.

"Good morning, my lord," she said in good cheer and clasped her hands at her waist.

"Good morning." He took another sip from his cup.

She faced Huxtable, and the jaunty old man pulled his short frame upright, eyes twinkling.

"Huxtable at yer service. Part gardening genius, part servant and friend to hisself." He snapped his heels and tipped forward in his version of a bow. "Welcome to Greenwich Park, miss. Can I get ye a coffee?"

She bobbed a curtsy and smiled. "Miss Lydia Montgomery. And yes, I'd love a cup."

"That won't be necessary, Hux. Miss Montgomery won't stay." Edward gave her a pointed look and added, "I'm sure she must be exhausted after such a late night, and have need of more rest."

"No need. Once I put head to pillow, I slept quite well, thank you." One thick, feminine eyebrow rose. "And as I recall, you mentioned last night a *morning* discussion regarding various details about our…the arrangement. It is morning, however late, and I'd rather not delay."

"Not even to complete your morning toilet?" he said behind his cup, giving her unbound hair the once-over.

Huxtable sucked in a loud breath. Edward didn't mean to be unkind; what was meant to be an observation came out sounding bad, but Miss Montgomery stood undaunted. Intriguing.

"Oh." She laughed softly and checked her dim reflection in the glass. She brushed back stray wisps of hair and faced him again. "Don't have my own things, remember?" She pointed at a small stain on his shirt. "What's your excuse? You've certainly overlooked a few articles of gentlemanly attire this morning, milord."

Huxtable coughed into his shoulder. "Gives as good as she gets, milord. I like her already."

Edward checked his garb: an older linen shirt minus neckwear, no waistcoat, buff-colored breeches, and the same well-worn leather knee boots. He'd shaved and clubbed his hair at least, not that he really cared. A glimmer of admiration for Miss Montgomery sparked. He wasn't the easiest person to be around by any stretch, but Huxtable saved the moment.

"At least his shirt's tucked in proper like. Doesn't

always manage that. He's not usually testy in the morning. Not much sleep last night, but you look lovely, miss. Why we watched you come across the lawn, what with your hair flyin' about and all."

Edward cringed. Miss Montgomery must think they ogled her like a pair of overzealous lads. And she knew very well why he'd had so little sleep…at least part of the reason. The odd thing was she looked at ease despite his prickly demeanor, and the smile she gave Huxtable would probably send his ancient heart into arrest.

"Thank you, Mr. Huxtable. Now about that coffee you offered? A bit of cream, if you've any."

This didn't bode well. A cup of coffee meant conversing. Here.

"O' course, miss." Huxtable fairly skipped off to the supply room to do her bidding.

Edward wanted to issue his edict that the greenhouse was closed to visitors, when Miss Montgomery clasped her hands behind her back and stretched her lovely neck to examine the high ceiling. The whole place flooded with natural light, even on overcast days. That light played over her, making her eyes shine like polished sea glass.

"I've never seen a greenhouse quite like this. Bigger than some homes. You even have large trees growing inside. Incredible."

"It is both a greenhouse and a laboratory." Pride found its way into his voice. "It may not be the cleanest greenhouse, but it is the most prolific, with the rarest, most sought-after specimens in England."

Her head tipped farther back as she visually explored the magnitude of the place. Two stories high, half-brick, half-glass, the place was impressive. Sometimes he got lost in the minutiae of what he found under the magnification glass, that the scale of his surroundings disappeared. Her awe made a pleasant reminder of how far he'd come.

"And warm, too," she said, unclasping her red cloak, letting it slip from her shoulders.

Dark hair spilled in a shiny cloud down her back. The full circles of her breasts pressed against her dress. She was neither small nor large, not quite the full size of his hand. The center of his palm tingled at the image of placing his hand there. Ample cleavage spilling over plunging square necklines was the mode of the day, yet Miss Montgomery's rounded neckline stopped modestly at her collarbones. He stared at the light green fabric that swathed the skin high on her chest. Would the flesh be the same smooth, fair shade of her cheeks? Or whiter?

Her shoes crunched gravel as she circled about, taking in the expanse overhead. "I see why your skin lacks the paleness one might expect of a recluse."

He tensed, poised for the worst. Instead, she set her cloak on a nearby table and touched the leaves of a juvenile potted tree; her fingers caressed dangling, yellow-gold fruit. The tip of her nose touched the luscious orb, and she inhaled, long and slow. Wasn't she going to explain her comment?

"Ahh." Her eyes closed a second, and she smelled the fruit's perfume. "What's this?"

"Chinese pear."

A lone feminine finger traced the skin, following the subtle indent that bisected the round pear. But what was this about his skin and being a recluse?

Would she make disparaging remarks about his scars, as did his last betrothed?

Edward cleared his throat and braced himself. "How did you come to this conclusion about my skin?"

His question pulled her from the lure of the unusual golden fruit, and she faced him, blinking.

"Your skin? Oh, yes." Miss Montgomery tipped her head back as her hands waved at the surrounding glass. "Wide-open glass everywhere, constant sun exposure. Your skin's bound to darken if you spend all your time here." She gave him a triumphant smile. "Mystery solved."

He took another sip of his coffee, tensed for the worst. The fact that she likely had more questions about him settled in, as did the lack of commentary about his scarred visage. But his morning guest acted more struck, like a child in some kind of wonderland. She stepped closer to a wide window to trace a line on the foggy pane.

"A bit damp in here."

"You could say so, miss." Huxtable's footsteps crunched the gravel as he approached with her mug of coffee. "Here you go. With cream." Huxtable pointed at light condensation frosting the window. "Tells me I'm doing my job right, keepin' the tile stoves going... invention of some Swede scientist of his lordship's acquaintance. Special kind of stove keeps the whole place warm. Best for the plants. Makes 'em think they're still in the West Africa jungle."

"West Africa? How exotic," she said, eyes rounding. She sipped her coffee, and her fingers plucked at her neckline, lightly fanning her collarbone. "A bit balmy."

"O' course. That's why we don't stand on ceremony

with waistcoats and such. Too warm." Huxtable chuckled. "As a boy, his lordship was always hiding them fancy wigs his mother made him wear, and stuffin' coats and such into nooks and crannies in the house."

"A little slapdash about his dress as a boy, then?" She smiled behind the steam wafting upward from her mug.

"And the same he is full grown." Huxtable grinned.

This walk down the annals of boyhood verged on being too personal.

"Hux, perhaps you could check the compost for me and see if the morning post has arrived."

"And I've been dismissed," the old man said with a flourish. "But let me say, pleased I am that yer here, miss." With a wink and a tug on his forelock, Huxtable jammed his pipe between his teeth and ambled away.

Miss Montgomery pulled up a tall stool and sat facing him. She wasn't fastidious about her skirts on the rough, splintered stool. One shoe heel hooked on a rung, and the other braced the floor, an exact mirror of how he sat. Both hands cupped her mug, and her gaze wandered around the vast greenery.

"Your greenhouse is impressive. All of Greenwich Park that I've seen so far is impressive. I couldn't imagine the job of cleaning the place. Must take an army."

He took another sip and made a humming sound of agreement. Details about cleaning never crossed his mind, best left for Claire. Then again, Edward scanned the broadsheets once in a while; since he shut his door to Society, people postulated ridiculous ideas about him and the state of his home. Would Miss Montgomery be any different? His thigh tensed again, and the sole of his boot wedged into the gravel.

"Your home's nothing like I expected," she said before taking another sip.

"What did you expect? A beast living amongst cobwebs and bats?" he asked in a droll tone.

"I wondered about the state of things." Her fingernails drummed the cup, clinking porcelain. "You were much nicer last night, you know."

"You mean when I ordered you out of my room?"

"No," she said, drawing out the *O*. "I am referring to when you were discussing our mutual predicament at the inn. I came here with the intention of having a pleasant conversation with you, my lord. Not to wage battle."

That got him square in the chest. He was being a horse's arse. His sister, Jane, would have said as much and given his arm a feisty slap if she were here.

"My manners aren't in top form this morning." He made an effort to smile. "I'd like to say circumstances have made me the man I am today, but that wouldn't be true. I've always been private, preferring science to society. I take people in small doses."

"Private's what you call it," she said, not budging from the stool. "I see."

He sighed. "This is as good a time as any, Miss Montgomery, for me to politely lay a few ground rules. Visitors are barred from my laboratory, and I prefer not to be disturbed when I'm in my room. I like my solitude."

Her eyes rounded. "Are you asking me to leave, my lord? *Right now?*"

"I am." He held up his hand when her eyes flashed with the beginnings of feminine ire. "Please, wait. I realize this is a most unusual situation. I thought last night's discussion would suffice in lieu of this morning, but the inner workings of Greenwich Park are new to you, so I'm prepared to give you some leeway."

"Only *some* leeway, my lord? How good of you." She huffed. "I think I begin to understand. You have an irritating propensity for lordly arrogance."

Edward smirked at that set down. He deserved it, but his accuser was only warming up. Her face flushed becomingly as he sipped his coffee.

"Is that because you're the mighty Earl of Greenwich? Or do I alone bring that out in you...*my lord*?" Her mug clunked on the worktable, and she muttered, "Self-serving nobles."

His jaw tightened. Best to lay down logical parameters now.

"You also need to know that I can't abide hysterical women."

"Good heavens, no hysterical women allowed? Then last night must've been quite a trial for you." She tapped her fingers with rapid counting. "Let me see if I've got this right: one, no coming in your greenhouse; two, no going in your room, and three, no hysterical women."

This was deteriorating quickly.

He took a deep, calming breath and cradled his mug in both hands. "You're getting perilously close to histrionics, and no, last night was enlightening. You are enlightening."

Her eyes narrowed on him as if to gauge his sincerity. She snorted in a most unfeminine manner, but his sincere compliment must've taken. His pretty, dark-haired interloper fidgeted and gave her attention to the Chinese pear tree while speaking to him in a world-weary voice.

"Discourse between a man and woman will, from time to time, become heated"—she crossed her arms tightly over her bosom and looked him in the eye—"even passionate. To expect otherwise is foolish."

At least she didn't shriek and kept something of a level tone with him. They stared, wary and watching like opponents saving energy stores for later, but the heat of their exchange dissipated. Last night, Miss Montgomery was pretty in demure white velvet; in the high color of the moment, she nettled and fascinated him all at once. She tilted her head, and daylight diffused by clouds made her eyes glimmer.

"This is not the best of circumstances." The corners of her mouth curled up. "We must be able to bear each other's company for a short time, at least…if you plan for an heir."

He raised his cup in salute and matched her triumphant grin with one of his own.

"Touché."

That simple acknowledgment on his part sufficed as a truce, though so far, she'd said nothing of leaving. A pair of birds flew overhead, chirping joyful songs to each other. He and Miss Montgomery followed the line of flight.

"It's a slice of paradise in here…a garden of Eden." Her soft voice mixed awe and woefulness.

When Edward's gaze returned to Lydia, he noted the slump of her shoulders and the edges of her teeth chewing her lower lip.

"My lord, I came fully prepared to continue last night's discussion, and you bit my head off about holding a door open and about my attire, which I'm happy to point out is due entirely to your own haste. You'll remember: I wanted to go to my own home last night."

She clasped her hands in her lap and waited. The volley was his. She looked at ease, and he admitted a growing ease with her and some admiration. Miss Montgomery posited herself in his lair with nary a note of nervous chatter or ridiculous tittering like other aggravating females of his unscarred past. Edward set his cup on the table and tipped his head, conceding the point.

"You have the right of it. Despite what I know is ahead, I wasn't ready to face the obvious change your presence here means. My solicitor, Mr. Aaron, dealt with marital details in the past. This is new ground for me."

"You courted a woman by a solicitor?" Her jaw dropped inelegantly.

He grinned. "Sounds bad, but, no, I didn't court by my solicitor. Negotiations, however, are a reality of my station. But I am of the opinion life would be easier if all relations were transacted thus."

"And all these years I thought it was about a man and a woman." She sighed, giving him a teasing smile before slipping off the stool to reexamine the Chinese Pear.

Miss Lydia Montgomery had a way of making things elemental; the awareness of this facet and her quiet intent slipped under his skin. Edward shuffled some of his books and picked up a lead writing stick. He needed to return to his work, could feel the push-pull drawing him.

Her fingers cupped the golden, apple-shaped fruit. "I should very much like to paint this."

"Is that a passion of yours? Painting?" he called over his shoulder.

"Yes, and I don't mean dabbling with watercolor."

The way she spoke with purpose, even slight disdain for watercolor, caught his ear. Edward turned around, idly rolling his lead stick in his palm. Her soft lips pressed in a line, as if she braced for the worst, then they opened with a bold request.

"I'd like to find a room with plenty of sunlight and make that my studio, one with all this wonderful natural light." Then she grinned cheekily. "Like your greenhouse."

"Oh, no, you'll not work in my space."

She winked. "Don't worry, too balmy in here."

But he had the distinct impression she was testing the waters of proximity and invasion of his domain.

"That would certainly help me to abide by your ground rules for places off-limits." Some of her hair slipped past her shoulder, and she finished quietly, "This was the nature of my request last evening. At the inn. I'd like to paint."

"That's your request? To paint?" He leaned a hand on the table, stunned.

"That's why I came to see you this morning." She clasped her hands together. "I need supplies."

"Such as?"

"Canvas and wood…I can make my own frames, mind you." Her hands slipped from the self-imposed vise grip and became animated as she listed her needs. "Oils, pigments, brushes, a small, sharp knife or two, some tripod stands, since what I have at my aunt's…"

He stared at her, tuning out the rest of what she said. Miss Montgomery looked away, apparently recalling mental pictures of certain items, tapping one finger after the other while listing out loud her artistic needs. Of all the requests she could have made—*painting*?

That she didn't say jewels, new wardrobe each year with all the fripperies, or her own carriage with matching four shocked him. Edward made a conscious decision to close his mouth.

"Painting supplies. Nothing else?" He crossed his arms and stared a second longer, looking for deception, but her eyes were open green orbs.

"Yes, that's it," she said, folding her hands at her waist. "If I may, milord, you seem surprised."

A disbelieving burst of air escaped him. "Previous negotiations with another woman were extensive, to say the least. Like establishing a small kingdom."

Her fingers plucked at a wrinkle in her skirt, and though Miss Montgomery faced him, her head tipped down a bit. She eyed him cautiously. "Then, my *painting* shouldn't be a problem for you to support."

"Greenwich Park has a hundred rooms thereabouts," he said, glancing at the grand edifice that made the back of his home. "You're sure to find something that works."

She rewarded him with a broad, glowing smile. A niggling voice in his head prodded him to ask more about her painting. There had to be more there, but at face value, this turned out to be so easy. Making her happy pleased him.

She picked up her coffee mug and cupped her hands around the old crockery. Wearied of so much talk, Edward longed for the gratifying solitude of work. Their morning exchange was more than he gave most people in a week. Plants, thankfully, never demanded conversation.

"At some point, I would be happy to give you a tour of Greenwich Park."

Now where did that come from? He had a treatise on

plant placenta theory to finish. Even working after dinner was not uncommon for him. When did he expect to find time to escort her about the place? Her beaming smile warmed him, but work beckoned.

"I need to get back to work. Give Claire"—he caught himself and tipped his head toward the house—"I mean my housekeeper, Miss Mayhew, the list of art supplies, and she'll take care of it."

A curious blankness filled her face at the mention of Claire. "Of course, Miss Mayhew the housekeeper."

She raised the mug and studied him over the rim. He took a step to escort her to the door, but she didn't budge from the stool.

"Miss Mayhew's quite a stunning woman for a housekeeper," she said and took a careful sip. "Very beautiful, in fact."

"Many have commented as much." He went tight-lipped, almost certain of the vein Miss Montgomery wanted to open.

Her green eyes searched his for an answer to the breadth of questions about Claire. Questions, he was sure, lurked in her mind. Something inside Edward sank with disappointment.

Women never ceased their inquisitions as to the nature of Miss Mayhew's relationship to the Greenwich family. In the years prior to his scars, when female houseguests came and went, women gave their comments on Claire, running the gamut from snide slurs to the outright catty: the natural response to fighting for and gaining territory with available wealthy, titled men. Some sought status, the desire to be the pinnacle beauty in the room. None of that mattered. Claire deserved his protection.

That Miss Montgomery would slip into the banalities of feminine competition proved a grave disappointment. Edward frowned as he turned his focus on a stack of pamphlets. He pulled one from the pile and flipped it open to the desired page. He tapped the lead stick on the workbench and glanced over his shoulder at Miss Montgomery.

"I'm sure you'll want to arrange your painting supplies and find that room. Ask Miss Mayhew, or if you prefer, Miss Lumley, for assistance." Then he finished with cold dismissal. "If you'll excuse me."

"Turned out so soon?" She cocked her head.

"I'll not discuss loyalties, household staff, anything, or anyone else." He spoke with—What had Miss Montgomery called it?—*lordly arrogance*. So be it.

"You are a puzzle, my lord." She enunciated each word. "A very private sort that has nothing to do with your injury."

His gut clenched: she spoke the truth, but this meeting was at an end. He tapped the lead stick on his journal.

"I've much work to do."

"I thought we were making progress toward some kind of understanding." She set the mug on the table and slipped off the stool with decidedly less spark. "I'd hoped to spend a little time with you, but I can see you'd like me gone."

She looked small and vulnerable, and he was sorely tempted to let this pass and allow her to stay.

"Perhaps another time," he said, turning to his workbench.

"Very well, then, my lord. I'll see you at dinner?"

"Of course."

Edward flipped the journal's pages. Behind him, Miss Montgomery's shoes beat a slow retreat. Out of the corner of his eye, he followed her as she slipped into her cloak and quit the place without looking back. He should have escorted her to the door, at least; that would've been the gentlemanly thing to do. Edward tossed the lead stick on the table and turned around to stare out the window where a light mist fell.

His sister often said he was his own worst enemy. He rubbed his scarred cheek, catching his faint reflection in the glass. The dim likeness echoed the way he used to look—a smooth-skinned visage that appealed to the fairer sex. Long ago he took that appeal for granted, never valuing that currency with females. What he valued little then mattered not at all now.

Or did it?

Glancing at the greenhouse door, Edward duly noted that Miss Montgomery didn't act repulsed on seeing him in full morning light. His gaze followed the—What was it Huxtable said?—*determined* woman. The red-cloaked form moving over the verdant lawn was certainly that and much more.

He would even go as far to say his lively new housemate was a little flirtatious in the most interesting way. The coming seventy-eight days might prove interesting indeed.

Seven

Every path has its puddle.

—Proverb

"COULD HE BE ANY LESS INTERESTED?" SHE SAID, stomping into the wretched pink palace and tossing her cloak over a chair. "Perhaps if I were a plant, I'd warrant a bit of his time and attention."

Lydia flopped on the pink-and-yellow-striped settee near the hearth, slumping ungracefully. She wanted to learn more about the arcane man, but that door had shut firmly on her moments ago. Oh, and forget trying to ascertain Miss Mayhew's role at Greenwich Park, other than housekeeper, of course. Housekeeper, indeed, she huffed in the silence and rested her chin on her palm. Lord Greenwich got prickly when Miss Mayhew's name came up in conversation. That didn't bode well.

What an off morning this turned out to be; nothing went as planned. Lydia stretched her legs across the seat and dangled shod feet over the cushion's edge. She ought to be in search of that solicitor's office on Lower Ormond Street, pursuing her own plans, not waiting on someone else's plans; instead, trapped she was, her wet hem smearing grass on the furniture.

No stranger to the inner workings of household cleaning, she swiped the green blades into her cupped hand and slid off the settee to drop them over the fire.

"Just as well I didn't find Lower Ormond Street," she said, consoling herself. "The blighter I was supposed to meet is probably one of those solicitors who can't keep his hands to himself."

Miss Lumley poked her head around the corner and spied Lydia's shoes. "Want your shoes cleaned, miss?"

Lydia lifted her hem for a better look at the offending items. "I've tracked in grass and greenery." She made a face. "Sorry."

"Not to worry on that score."

The maid entered and bent to the task of removing the shoes. The odd sight of someone removing her footwear made her feel childish.

"Please don't, Miss Lumley," she said. "The last time anyone tended my shoes, I was just out of leading strings. I can clean them myself. Sorry to have troubled you."

"Pish posh, miss, and call me Edith." The maid tapped a tarnished buckle and chuckled. "You're no trouble at all. This is my job. Best get used to having others take care of you, if you don't mind me saying so."

When was the last time anyone made an effort to take care of her? So often it was the other way around.

"Thank you, Edith." Lydia perched on the settee again.

"Speaking of greenery, you visited his lordship in the greenhouse?" Edith said, cleaning a shoe with rapid swipes.

Lydia smiled at the busy maid. The whole household

probably wanted to know what was going on between the earl and the unlikely woman he brought home. All and sundry must've recognized Lydia wasn't countess material. Of course they'd be curious belowstairs about what happened in their place of employment.

"Yes," she ventured cautiously. "Very impressive. The whole place."

"Certainly is from the outside, I mean." The gray-haired maid took her time rubbing the cheap buckle. "I've not had the occasion to be in there much."

Miss Lumley could be a potential ally in times of need. Or did the staff charge her with scouting duty on the dark-haired interloper occupying the pink palace? Lydia smiled wider on that score. Give a little, get a little. But how much to divulge? Her ears near twitched from the kitchen gossip she assumed they bantered. In the interest of budding friendship, she tossed out a crumb.

"The magnification glass was quite interesting, as were some of the plants." She shrugged and slumped against the settee's back cushion, curling stocking feet underneath her. "I wasn't there long enough to learn much."

…about his lordship, that is…

"You were in his lordship's laboratory longer than Miss Blackwood ever was." Edith's voice grumbled, and her rag shimmied across the shoe.

"Miss Blackwood?" Lydia hugged an ice-pink pillow to her stomach, hoping Miss Lumley would rise to the bait. Her fingers flip-flopped a corner tassel. "She would be…"

The dancing rag paused. "The lady formerly betrothed to his lordship." She gave Lydia a pointed look, pursed lips and all.

"Isn't she the one the papers say slit her wrists?" Her tassel flipping slowed.

"Humph! Don't be fooled. Conniving bit of baggage, she was. More drama in that one than all of Drury Lane, if you ask me." Edith's rosy cheeks darkened with a scowl, and her rag picked up speed. "Only wanted parties, she did, *and* jewels, *and* Greenwich gold. To think, growing up she chased after Lord Eddie and cried her undying love. That is until…" Edith's voice faded as she put a hand to her heaving bosom. "I forget myself, miss."

Lord Eddie, is it?

Edith set the shoes on the stone hearth and missed the way Lydia gaped at the familiarity. The maid was so caught up in calming down from her angry flare. Lydia couldn't imagine the mysterious brigand she met last night as a *Lord Eddie*. Edith stuffed her rag in an apron pocket and banked the fire before taking her leave.

"Oh, there is one thing, Miss Lumley."

She scooted off the settee and retrieved a list of art supplies sitting on the pristine desk. She'd already made this wish list earlier that morning, anticipating the earl's support.

"I discussed this with his lordship, and he bade me give it to you or Miss Mayhew. These are a few things I'll need." She folded the paper and passed it to Edith. "Some painting supplies."

The maid slipped the paper into her other pocket. "I'll give this to Miss Mayhew. She'll take care of it."

At the mention of the lovely housekeeper, Lydia opened her mouth to probe. A warning voice inside her head bade her not to dive into that muddle. Not yet.

"Thank you for taking care of my shoes."

"Of course, miss," Edith said with a wink. "And you hold fast with his lordship. He's really a good sort, he is."

A few tidbits had been dropped at her feet about Lord Eddie, but nothing of true substance. His childhood moniker made her smile at the elegant but austere lady staring down at her. She drummed her fingers on the striped upholstery. Things got very prickly when she asked about the housekeeper.

Tread carefully there.

Still, Lydia couldn't help but be a touch irked. Was he planning to marry her and dally with the housekeeper? Such an arrangement wasn't unheard of amongst nobility. Did his lordship have a thing for women of the lower classes?

"Miss Blackwood, a young lady of quality, besmirched. Miss Mayhew, a housekeeper, respected," she mused. "Just how does one win over the reclusive Lord Eddie?"

She tipped her head back and smiled at the absurdity. Lydia studied the adjoining door. Win over Lord Edward? *Was she mad?* That closed door, like the closed man, taunted her, a challenge. Most people liked her, really.

She chewed her thumbnail. Didn't he say he'd see her at dinner? Plenty of time to poke around his room, learn a bit more about the infamous recluse…a little information hunt. Nothing harmful in that.

Lydia glanced again at the portrait over the mantel.

A woman ought to know something about the man she's agreed to marry.

She had every right…to look at his things. At least whatever he liked to read. How else would she get to know his preferences? Her stocking feet found their way to the adjoining door, and she pressed her ear against the cold wood.

Nothing.

Really, there are worse crimes than going through a man's personal effects. It's looking only.

In the middle of pondering that sticky point, the doorknob turned under her hand. Just like that, the door opened. Her heart thumped as if she'd raced uphill. What was it he said in the greenhouse?

My room and my laboratory are barred to visitors.

Surveying his hodgepodge room, this was poor form; she'd just give things a quick peek, enough to quell this maddening need to know. Lydia schooled her breathing. She wouldn't get caught—the maids had already swept through the place. The bed was made, wood was stacked high by the hearth, and a few fresh candles replaced last night's melted stubs.

Embers glowed in the fireplace. That's when she noticed the open cabinet holding the amber-filled decanter and glass. As she walked closer to the open door, the smudged glass looked to be the same as what the earl drank from last night. The maids must've missed changing the glass, which gave her a naughty idea.

"Why not sneak a dram? None would be the wiser," she said to herself.

Lydia reached for the decanter. The heavy cut-glass carafe alone felt like a year's worth of spending money in her hands. She lifted the stopper and sniffed the single malt's smoky aroma.

"Mmmm." She closed her eyes and hummed her satisfaction.

Golden liquid poured smooth and viscous into glass.

Her first sip tasted of pure heaven: flavors of smoke and peat slid over her tongue, down her throat, all the way through her chest, warming her.

"Must be from the north of Scotland. And very expensive, of course." One sip followed by another brought renewed boldness.

Daylight, however gray outside, illuminated his lordship's reading area through bare windows. She hadn't noticed the faldstool chair last night. The Romanesque chair sat throne-like among the books and bookstands. Journals were flipped open. Messy sketches depicted flowers and plant diagrams. Lydia settled herself in the wide-styled chair and rested the glass on her lap.

"Something of a senatorial blue blood, eh, Lord Eddie?" She smiled and took an ample swallow. Scooting to the chair's edge, Lydia craned her neck to read the title on a book stand. "*A Discourse on the Six Planets of Our Solar System* by Lord George Sanford, Earl of Greenwich."

Her fingers traced the imprinted words drawing her in with a sense of history. "Like father, like son," she whispered, standing in awe to examine the tome, large like an atlas.

All of England revered the late earl for his work in astronomy and his generous nature to the less fortunate. The book engrossed her with its maps of the heavens and fanciful depictions of the solar system's six planets. Lydia pored over one page after another, setting the book on the wide table littered with maps. What was this fascination with maps?

She planted her elbows on the rough plank table, so out of place in an earl's room, and sipped more scotch.

Numerous pamphlets from the Royal Society of London for Improving Natural Knowledge, their edges curling and split, stacked this way and that in a corner. Lydia scooted the book across the table, bumping a forlorn-looking map holding court in the middle of the untidiness. Lines bisected crumpled paper over what must be an island, but the array struck a chord with her, teasing her mind. From where?

"A treasure map?"

Her fingers traced faintly familiar patterns on yellowed foolscap, leading to an *X*. On one corner, fingerprints left red-brown paint, smears more like it, unlike any pigment she'd ever seen. The table's edge bit into her midsection as she hugged the drink to her chest in one hand and leaned over for a better look. With her other hand, she brushed the red-brown tincture. Tiny flecks clung to three fingers.

"What is this?" She brought her hand closer for examination, rubbing her thumb over the color. "Dried blood!" she cried, jerking back as if the map had turned into a hissing snake, almost spilling her drink.

Lydia scrubbed her fingers up and down her skirt, but like all things exotic, the slashed *X* and scribbled notes bewitched her. Numbers, longitude and latitude most likely, made neat rows on one corner. Where was this mysterious place? And the faintly familiar design bothered her, hanging on the periphery of recall. She sipped her drink and hugged the glass to her chest.

"'Herein lies the...the'"—she squinted and leaned closer, angling the paper for the best advantage—"heavens, the poor soul who scrawled this needs to learn the King's English. The clero...clerodendrum... clerodendrum thom—"

"*Clerodendrum thomsoniae.* A bleeding heart vine." Lord Greenwich's voice shot into the room. "And that's Latin you're reading, the language of science and intellectuals."

Lydia whipped around, facing the direction of the cultured voice. As she whirled, a golden arc of scotch sprayed from the glass, raining wetness. To stop the spray, she jerked abruptly, overcorrecting, and the glass tilted, sloshing liquid on her dress.

The earl filled the doorway, leaning against the door-jamb, arms folded loosely, as if finding a woman snooping in his room was a common occurrence. A cringing chill scraped her skin, the same as when she was a child caught in the thick of wrongdoing. Fire sparked in his lordship's eyes and the way his scarred jaw ticked. *What would he do?* That molten stare of his raked her bodice.

"Your dress."

"My dress?" She shook her head, befuddled, until she followed the cant of his glare. "Oh dear."

A wet spot blossomed, the strong, smoky peat of scotch marking her with its stain like some kind of immoral woman. Grim-faced, his lordship moved across the room with long, quick strides. He reached for the glass she clutched to her chest in a death grip.

"I'll take that."

His chill tones sent goose bumps down her spine. Long masculine fingers slid over hers.

"I know this looks bad," she said, swallowing the lump in her throat, not letting go of the glass.

"Yes." Hard brown eyes stared back, giving no quarter. "Very bad."

"Awful...for many reasons," she whispered, dry-mouthed.

He pulled on the near-empty glass. She held fast. Her fingers pinched fine crystal as if the glass were some kind of talisman. Lord Greenwich's jaw muscles flexed.

"Give. Me. The. Glass."

Some strands of dark blond hair had gone awry of his queue, flanking his jaw. Lydia stared wide-eyed at the masculine hand covering her own, then met his hard stare.

"You won't hit me, will you?"

His eyes flared wide, as if the idea were ridiculous. "I don't hit women. But you will give me the glass."

"Yes, of course." Numbly, she followed the exchange of her hand curving in his, and stinging embarrassment made her study the carpet. That's when she saw the puddle at her feet.

"Lud! Look what I've done." She dropped to the floor, using the hem of her underskirt to alternately rub and dab the spot.

"The rug is the least of my concerns," he said, extending a hand. "Up with you."

Lydia knelt at his feet. She followed the line of scuffed boots, past traces of dirt smeared on his breeches, to the calloused hand offered to her. This thoughtful gentleman's gesture was in stark contrast to his anger. She swallowed hard as excruciating embarrassment at demonstrating the worst kind of invasive voyeurism crumbled under a weightier issue: her mother's fate.

Why hadn't she thought of her mother before snooping in his room?

"Come, now." The earl's proffered hand flicked at her. "While I'm sure my legs make for an interesting view, I'd rather we converse face-to-face."

Sarcasm aside, his words held a certain promise. Or

could it be the beginning of her getting the boot? Another chill skittered down her neck. This loomed like the worst kind of trouble but with ominous consequences. Unable to meet his eyes, Lydia set her hand in his. She moved upright, swallowing hard.

"I can explain."

Lord Greenwich placed the glass on the table and settled in the faldstool chair, sprawling his booted legs before him. He could be the very picture of Caesar giving audience to a humble citizen. The stern line of his mouth, however, promised dire judgment.

"Yes, I'd very much like to hear why you were in my room, *uninvited*, and rifling through my things," he said, propping an elbow on the chair's arm.

The earl leaned his unscarred cheek into his index finger and waited, acting as judge and jury on her person. Hadn't he done the same last night? The floor seemed flimsy under the soles of her stocking feet. No corset. No shoes. A woman could never gain the advantage poorly dressed. Lies, a fleeting temptation, failed to appeal: nothing from that avenue would be plausible anyway. Truth gave the simplest and best path. She clasped her hands together, hating the sunken pit that was her stomach, and hoped for mercy, yet her shoulders drooped as one already condemned.

"I…I wanted to learn more about you. That's all," she said, licking her lips. "I apologize for the intrusion. This was…I was terribly wrong."

His eyebrows shot up at her last pronouncement. The index finger pressing his unscarred cheek began a slow circle over his temple as silence ticked between them, but the light in his lordship's eyes hinted at his mind working those simple statements of hers, measuring them.

"And drinking my single malt gives you intimate knowledge of me?" His lips twitched with something between a cold smile and doubt.

"No," she groaned.

Her face and neck went warm; Lydia was sure all her exposed skin turned beet red. And the most pressing point wasn't her defense, rather what bothered him more? The invasion? Or the drink? Her brain couldn't form a coherent explanation for pilfering his scotch. Did one even exist?

"Are you given to heavy drinking, Miss Montgomery?" His question cut the awkward silence.

Her body jerked as if he'd hit her. "*Of course not.*"

"A drunkard, perhaps? It happens with some women." He leaned forward and pinned her with his intensity. "No need to act the outraged miss with me. Young women do not usually go skulking around men's rooms uninvited, going through their things. Nor do they drink strong liquor. Only those of the loosest morals would entertain such audacity."

She gasped at the implication. He assumed the worst of her. *Again.* And she had her answer: snooping in his room was the greater of the two evils committed this day. Her damp palms pressed her chest in pledge.

"I assure you, my lord, going through someone's personal effects is *highly* unusual for me." Her heart pounded under her hands.

"Is that so?" His eyebrows shot up once more.

How could a man's eyebrows be so irritating?

Lydia wanted to slap that imperious expression right off his face. A calming breath was needed. After all, his lordship did have the moral high ground here. She had some work ahead of her to put things right; best to dive headlong with the truth. Taking a deep, calming breath, she proceeded.

"On occasion, I enjoy a small dram with my aunt. A bottle we open a few times a year is all. It's a gift from a longtime admirer of hers, who visits from the borderlands now and then. I know it's unseemly for women, but..." Lydia let her words trail off and decided on a new approach. She held up thumb and forefinger, keeping a judicious inch of space. "I have only about this much every once in a while...very little, but, yes, I enjoy it. Is that a crime? And I came into your room with the intention of looking at your books. The drink was an afterthought. Nothing more."

"My books." He said that as both statement and question, part and parcel of whatever judgment swirled behind his brown eyes.

His lordship stared at her, weighing her words, while his other hand tapped his thigh. Agonizing silence stretched, mere seconds really, and Lydia placed a steadying hand on the table. She needed something to prop her up under that dark-eyed scrutiny, but damp spots touched her skin. She checked her palm, noticed a small spray of wetness, and her gaze flitted from hand to table.

"The map! Blast it!"

She hiked up her skirt and dabbed wetness off the crumpled, curling foolscap. Lord Greenwich sprung from the chair and snatched the map from her. He held the yellowing sheet high toward the window, examining every detail. Sunlight touched the planes of his smooth, tanned cheek. From this angle, he was every bit the handsome nobleman. He squinted at the map as his left hand skimmed the scrawled words.

"The map is intact…a few drops on the corner," he said, breathing a sigh of relief. "No harm done. I can still read the directions."

"You can read that scrawl?" She grimaced at the map.

"Hope so. It's my writing." His lips turned in a half smile as he set the map on the table.

His sleeve brushed her arm. She smelled the plain soap he must've used to shave with that morning. Clean scents of English mist and greenery clung to him. Lydia shifted away from the earl and swallowed hard.

"Is it a treasure map?" She gave all her attention to the map and clasped her hands on the table.

"Yes." His hand flattened the square paper reverently. "The best kind."

He took one book and used it as a paperweight on one curling edge, and smoothed his palm down the other. Glad to have the attention diverted from her blunder, Lydia stood a silent witness as his free hand grazed the page as one might stroke a beloved instrument.

"What you see here is my first effort as cartographer and botanist. The map represents my first and only scientific expedition to an uncharted island off Africa's west coast. And this"—he tapped the *X* twice—"was my unusual find." His bemused smile and faraway look morphed into something stony. "A treasure hard won by flesh and blood."

Midday sunlight broke through the clouds. His skin made a dark contrast to his white shirt and the sudden brightness flooding the room. He eased the map from under the anchoring book.

"You say you want to learn more about me?" His lips twisted in a bitter, tight-lipped smile as he raised the parchment next to his scarred cheek. "Notice any similarities?"

She gasped, unable to drag her attention from his face. Lydia's gaze levered from face to map, map to face, comparing the near-identical markings as stomach sickening horror set in. The map's myriad lines and Lord Greenwich's cheek shared the same awful pattern.

"Who would do such a thing?" she asked, though not expecting an answer. The question slipped out from shock.

What could one say to offer comfort? Words were trite and small compared to what he must have endured. Newfound admiration sprung as well. While all of England gossiped and guessed about his painful trials these past three years, Lord Edward soldiered on with tenacity. Lydia swallowed, searching his face, unable to voice even the plainest mumblings of comfort. He had half the visage and full vigor of a man in his prime years, but those glinting, topaz-brown eyes of his bored into her, reflecting a lifetime of—courage and depth? More of the unexpected revealed from this privileged nobleman.

Lord Greenwich sighed under her scrutiny and returned the map to the table, settling it with care.

"Barbary pirates attacked our ship. We were on a scientific expedition, and they thought to torture information out of me." He tapped the yellowed paper with efficiency, but his voice was slow and rough. "They got hold of my map. So certain were they that it led to gold and silver…that I withheld information to protect my treasure. It didn't help matters when they discovered I'd funded the expedition, and the treasure in question was plants." His sardonic smile covered a flare of raw emotion. "Drunken, angry pirates make a bad combination."

His brief explanation gave cursory facts, the telling

was not denied her, but when Lydia searched his face for more, a wall slammed down around Lord Greenwich. A strange pressure moved up her chest and into her throat as the whole vast room fell away, disappearing. She would not lose that fragile connection with him. Lydia reached out to touch his arm, needful contact for a reassuring bond. But with his lordship's rolled-up sleeve, her palm grazed his bare forearm.

Crisp, curling masculine hairs tickled her palm as her hand hovered over warm skin to finally settle, flesh to flesh. Tactile communication, a forward touch out of step with propriety, stilled him as much as it stirred her.

And she was alone with this man in his room. Again.

The earl's dark gaze dropped to her slim hand resting on his arm.

A rush of schoolgirl awkwardness flooded her. She pulled her hand away. Cool air brushed her empty palm, but his clean smell became a welcome, heady scent. Lydia's breathing notched up its effort to move air in and out, and thankfully, his lordship was equally affected. He crossed his arms, but his heavy-lidded gaze dropped to her mouth and lingered.

"I need to be clear: my room and my laboratory are forbidden territory. Keep out. I thought you understood this." His commanding words held no bite, swimming as they both were in a sea of awareness.

Lydia tipped her head sideways, exposing a length of neck. The move was flirtatious, but worked. Her quarry gave his full attention to the column of her throat, half-hidden by unbound hair.

"Wouldn't that make your plans for procreation a

bit…*difficult?*" she asked, letting quiet, saucy challenge have its way. "If I'm not welcome in your room, that is."

She was completely in the wrong here. The earl had every right to be incensed with her for this intrusive foray. She should take a more conciliatory tone, but something unsettled within her wouldn't let things rest. Perhaps because she was a woman who knew very well the lustful underbelly that inhabited every man.

She clasped her hands behind her, giving in to the perverse wish to tempt the reclusive Lord Greenwich. Truth be told, she still chafed at his absurd one-month waiting period, but Lydia held her tongue from going further on that score. She wasn't in very good standing, what with her history with men, her snooping in his room, and that dreadful error with his scotch.

Lord Greenwich looked her up and down, as if taking measure of an unusual creature.

His lips quirked. "A bold statement from a woman in a precarious situation. Pushing the limits of my benefaction?"

She couldn't answer why she wished to needle him about the privacy of his room and laboratory. In that short stare down of nobleman versus hoyden, the tanned V of his shirt and the earl's noticeable breathing rhythm mesmerized Lydia. He was just as affected by the riot of attraction that bounced between them. For that was most definitely what was going on, however unexpected.

Lydia shook her head. "I think not, my lord. You need me as much I need you." With a triumphant tilt of her chin, she finished quiet-voiced, "And I've just realized we're on equal footing."

"A dangerous assumption." His eyes narrowed, but his tone met hers, equal in velvet softness. "I'm not letting you off that easily. We must deal with your intrusion here."

"What? Are you going to bend me over your knee?" She laughed at the absurdity.

His mouth pulled in a harsh line, and Lydia's vulnerability hit her. She blinked at him, and her jaw dropped.

"You aren't sending me packing, are you?"

Eight

Deal with the faults of others as gently as with your own.
                                                    —Chinese Proverb

HOW COULD HE?

They stood close enough that her neck craned in her effort to maintain eye contact. But it was his lips, well formed and attractive, that snared her. A sculptor could have taken his chisel and smoothed the slight plane on his lordship's lower lip, leaving the rest of that brooding mouth alone. Pure fanciful thinking.

The earl was unreadable, but this much was clear: the tables had turned in her favor for a short space of time. The whole interchange turned informative, exciting even. Oh, yes, more revealing clues about this enigmatic man unfurled like large petals on a blossom.

But control was a fleeting thing. Lord Greenwich neatly turned the tables back to the error of her ways, and Lydia faced another startling fact: *she wanted to stay… at least for a while*.

The corners of his mouth played at a smile that failed to light his eyes.

"Logic dictates that I can't send you packing when your things haven't arrived yet, now can I?" his lordship said, picking up the near-empty glass.

He walked to the liquor cabinet across the room. Much of his hair had worked free of his black velvet queue. Daylight hit a few guinea-gold strands in the dark blond, yet, the hair at the nape of his neck was dark velvet brown. What would his hair feel like? As Lord Greenwich set the glass inside the cabinet, he spoke over his shoulder.

"I came looking for you because I was less than gallant in the greenhouse. I wanted to make amends. And then I found you violating the sanctity of my room." He shut the cabinet doors with a click and turned to face her with both hands at his hips. "An appalling lack of good manners, wouldn't you agree? In fact, twice now, you've entered my room uninvited. Do you have a habitual disregard for others? Or is my charm growing on you and you find me irresistible?"

He had the audacity to give her that brigand's grin. Was he toying with her?

"I can assure you, no to the former, and I'm not knowledgeable enough on the latter to say." She cleared her throat, trying for seriousness. "Today's behavior, my lord, is most unusual for me. I am *not* a snoop." She emphasized the *not* with all the starch of a proper nursemaid.

"Words, Miss Montgomery, mere words. You've been full of assurances and light on action since I met you last night." He crossed his arms over his chest. Pale sunlight filtered through clouds and touched him everywhere.

Not toying…flirting? At least his version of flirtation.

"I'm in your home, aren't I? Awaiting your pleasure."

The prim fold of her hands knocked any salaciousness from her words.

"True." He nodded. "But there is an axiom in science, a law of nature, if you will, that every action has an equal and opposite reaction. I think that applies here…call it a consequence to one's behavior." Then his gaze flicked over her head to toe. His eyebrows pressed together as if something bothersome came to mind.

"Is something wrong, milord?"

"Come here." He spoke with his lordly, commanding tone.

Warning bells went off in her head.

Lydia rooted to the spot. "I…what do you want?"

"For you to come here." One side of his mouth slid up. "In fact, I'd find it refreshing if you did whatever I asked the first time I issued a command."

"What?"

"Please," he added, tipping his head in gentlemanly fashion.

His high and mighty lordliness had the upper hand, but he'd softened the advantage with that "please."

"What are you going to do?"

"Why not come here and find out?" Eyes sparkling, he challenged her.

She gave in to the invisible pull, very much like a moth fluttering helplessly, perilously into a flame. Mesmerized, she held eye contact with him. Warm, swirling sensations built inside her body as she closed the distance to him. Lydia stopped a safe, respectable arm's length from the earl, but the dangerous glint in his eye hypnotized.

What he did next astounded.

Lord Greenwich bent on one knee before her. He

tipped his head and almost bumped her abdomen. His hands hovered close to her thighs. He put both hands on her skirt, grabbed the fabric—and gently pulled.

She looked down at her dress, horrified to see the faint outline of her thighs through her underskirt. The brief exposure was fleeting as Lord Greenwich lowered her dress skirt, a falling curtain to what was on display.

She moaned. Her skirt must have caught on her underskirt when she dried the map.

The earl knelt before her like a chivalrous knight of old and settled the hem around her ankles. His fingers skimmed the tops of her unshod feet as if testing the feel and shape of her. Heat grazed her, her lower body, her thighs and knees precisely where his hands had hovered, leaving a mark of warmth as he set her skirt to rights, shooting awareness everywhere.

"Your skirt was stuck above your knees," he said, explaining the obvious with a mischievous glint. "I couldn't let you go on with an unseemly display of undergarments."

Oh, he was not bothered by her unseemly display of anything.

Parts of Lydia flushed hotly again as it dawned on her: they'd conversed with the cloth bunched and riding an indecent height, all while she was rather bold with him. Her underskirts hung the proper length, thank goodness, and covered her legs, though their silhouette was clearly visible.

Lydia shut her eyes and groaned again at the indignity. Lud, she could be a piece of work.

His lordship had pushed the edge of propriety, and well he knew it. What's worse, her body had reacted—from his brigand's smile or his hands on her skirt, she wasn't sure. Lydia pressed a protective hand to her midsection.

"Thank you." She stepped back, needing some distance.

Lord Greenwich stood up and towered over her, and on purpose, she was sure.

His thumb and forefinger tweaked her chin. "Don't think you're off the hook for this uninvited foray into my room. You need to atone for this grievous behavior, Miss Montgomery, and flashing your underskirts won't suffice." His eyes sparked with a dangerous, playful light. "Everything has its price."

Her eyebrows shot up at his daring tone, and Lydia planted a hand at her hip. "Is this all some kind of game for you?"

"Game?" One side of his mouth, the scarred side, curved up. "If this is sport, then you're the most diverting woman I've had the pleasure of sparring with in a very long time."

Every nerve in her body shot to life again, sensitized, just when she'd calmed the riot inside her. Her quick inhale gave her away, telling him, she was sure, that he threw her off balance with his unusual compliment. Again. Lord Greenwich likely wasn't the type to wax poetically about the gentler sex. A woman would have to make do with his brand of verbal surprise. His slow smile spread to the smooth, unscarred cheek with what she guessed was satisfaction at silencing her.

"I'll give you 'til dinner to come up with three ways to make amends for coming in here uninvited."

"What?" she asked, her eyes rounding. "You want some kind of atonement for my looking around your room?"

"Yes, three. That way I can choose whichever is most advantageous to me. This will give you a *sporting* chance to please me." His brigand's smile widened. "Perhaps I'll choose all three. I never said I was a nice man, especially with women who don't follow the rules."

This situation had sped out of control like a horse galloping too fast. And what happened all too often with a rider who let a racehorse have his head? Disaster. She needed to rein in this maddening nobleman and this maddening situation. Lydia's gaze dropped to his exposed neck and the exposed fraction of his chest. His pulse ticked a rapid cadence against the skin at the base of his neck. His lordship was not immune to the excitement either. She was about to give him a starch set down, when someone coughed from the doorway.

Lydia jumped from the noise.

Miss Mayhew, rigid and proper in housekeeper gray, stood in the hallway just outside the door.

"My lord," she said and gave a proper curtsy. "Mr. Ryland waits for you in the study." Miss Mayhew looked at Lydia with cool features. "Miss Montgomery, your things have arrived. I thought you'd want to change, possibly have a bath."

"Yes, thank you."

Curiously, if the beautiful housekeeper had any designs on Lord Greenwich, she hid them well. The housekeeper likely detected some of the charged inter-play, yet Miss Mayhew's face remained a mask of demure, unemotional decorum.

Lydia needed to extract herself from the earl's surprising effect on her—like a strong drink one was unsure of but kept consuming. She needed badly to set this man on his ear and stop his assumptions about her. But first things first.

A good clean up and the right dress made all the dif-ference for a woman.

"A bath would be perfect," she said, trying for control.

Miss Mayhew disappeared in a rustle of brisk steps and stiff skirts. The stunning housekeeper's dress would never catch on anything; surely those starched skirts didn't bend or wrinkle. Lord Greenwich started to exit, but he paused at the doorway.

"We shall continue this later."

"And I'll use the time wisely to consider my ways." Lydia folded her hands at her waist, smirking at him.

"And come up with three, as you put it, *atonements*." He gave her a cheeky grin. "You'll make my trip up here worthwhile."

Lydia's eyebrows scrunched together as she remembered that something had taken Lord Greenwich from his work. "Why did you come here in the first place? You said something about making amends to me."

His hand rested on the doorjamb. "I was going to take you on a tour of the estate's art gallery, but we'll postpone that for after dinner. I need to meet with Mr. Ryland, and I saw the way your eyes lit up at the mention of a bath. Enjoy your respite, and you have your things to settle." He glanced at her bodice. One side of his mouth hitched up. "And you won't have to roam about corsetless."

Her arms covered her chest in a loose X. "And I was beginning to believe you're a true gentleman."

"Dangerous notion," he teased, and his dark eyes smoldered above his dangerous smile. "Remember, I expect no less than three choices from you."

With a slight bow, he quit the room. Lydia's arms slid down to her sides. Beyond the open adjoining door, she heard the maids chattering and pouring water into a tub.

No one came to shoo her from the earl's room. Studying the restrained disarray that was his room, Lydia tapped her mouth, deep in thought.

In some ways she was more informed yet more mystified by the man she'd come to investigate. Her gaze landed on the large messy table where maps and books sat. Ideas for his required atonements sprang to mind with ease. She circled his domain, smiling to herself: he'd left her alone in the very place he'd forbidden her presence.

Her smile spread. That mental image of a racehorse, near out of control, played in her head again. The earl had better hold on tight. With what she had in mind, his chaotically ordered world was about to change.

Nine

Conversation has a kind of charm about it,
an insinuating and insidious something
that elicits secrets from us just like love or liquor.

—Seneca

EDWARD RUBBED HIS FOREHEAD AND TRIED AGAIN TO read the intricate diagram. Focus eluded him; instead, his mind wandered abovestairs to a dark-haired woman in a bath. Schematics and chemistry turned fuzzy when pitted against the naked woman in his head.

"Is there a problem?" Cyrus Ryland's firm voice doused cold water on that inviting image.

"Problem?" Edward repeated, rifling through the sheaves. "Not at first glance."

"You've been *glancing* at the documents over half an hour."

Edward gave his guest a rueful smile. "Apologies. My mind is otherwise occupied." He stacked two thick documents on the side table. "I'll give them a read first thing tomorrow and send my response in the post."

As he sipped tea, Ryland sat with the ramrod discipline

of a general. One expected a master of commerce to drink something hard and bracing, but Britain's leading citizen claimed he rarely imbibed. Rumors abounded on how he'd gained his wealth. One didn't rise from son of a humble midland pig farmer to own half of England without a cloud of questions. Edward grasped the murky nature of rumors. Ryland's correspondence came direct and to the point. In person, Edward could say no different.

Solid as granite, Cyrus Ryland commanded respect upon entering a room. And the way Claire's cheeks flushed when Ryland glanced her way? One could speculate she found Greenwich Park's guest a far cry from fat, stodgy, or boorish.

She refreshed the king of commerce's tea and ignored Edward, not that it mattered. He wasn't thirsty. Ryland's slate-gray stare followed the housekeeper's every move until she exited the room. Apparently, Edward wasn't the only one sidetracked by a woman.

Edward cleared his throat. "Let me make sure I understand: Arkwright, inventor of the waterproof periwig dye, wants to partner with you in the manufacture of this new mechanism."

He didn't withhold his skepticism about the vast leap one made from simple chemistry for vanity's sake to complex machinery for practicality's purpose.

Ryland nodded, and threads of silver glinted in his brown hair. "A carding machine. Turns raw cotton into thread. Arkwright wants to relocate to Cromford in Nottingham. He needs capital to build the necessary warehouses." He tipped his head at the documents. "But I'm intrigued about the possibilities there as well."

"You're interested in the textile business?"

"I'm interested in growing my wealth." Ryland settled against the chair and sipped his tea, impassive gray eyes giving nothing away.

"Of which you hold an impressive amount, by all reports."

Ryland's brain worked like a clearinghouse of decision making, and Edward respected that, could see as much in months of correspondence. And when they'd met face-to-face for the first time that day? Ryland had assessed Edward's appearance in a split-second glance, and then moved to the business at hand. No probing questions. No bald commentary. Ryland was a walking beehive of pure strategy, all to increase his wealth and expand his business empire.

He respected Ryland for knowing his limitations: scientific intricacy wasn't a strong point, but he acknowledged that and sought advice. Now, Edward surmised, his guest had something to say that had nothing to do with the documents on the table. Edward's fingertips tapped a rhythm on the chair's arm, waiting. Ryland set down his dish of tea and brushed at an invisible speck on his breeches.

"I'm not one to pry—"

Edward stiffened, as much disappointed as anticipating the drollery to follow.

"—but financial records can be very revealing. Your finances speak well of you, Greenwich. Your priorities, your level head...often missing from men of your class and age."

Edward couldn't help his smile at the unexpected compliment. "Thank you."

"You've been one candidate I've considered for my

sister, Lucinda." Ryland's gaze flicked to Edward's scars. "But that's not plausible."

Edward tipped his head, acknowledging the edict. "Understood."

He wasn't bothered by plain speech. Lucinda Ryland had been one name bandied by his solicitor as a possible marriage candidate. There may have even been inquiries, but something stirred at the notion of any other woman occupying the countess suite.

Ryland gave a relaxed smile, the first crack of emotion since his arrival.

"I sit on the board of Lloyd and Taylor Bank. Facts and figures, how a man spends his money tells me a lot about his character." Cyrus Ryland paused, so like a sovereign considering what next to say. "Sanford Shipping needs new blood. With the success of canal building in the North, your schooners may soon become relics of the past."

With that blunt pronouncement, Greenwich Park's esteemed guest rose.

"Thank you for the insight," Edward said then motioned to the footman in attendance. "Rogers, please see Mr. Ryland to the door."

Etiquette demanded Ryland genuflect first, but Edward bowed. Somehow he couldn't help but sense he'd spent his afternoon with a great man, and the closed, convoluted nature of English Society had crowned the wrong man king. Even more, the visit laid new burdens and pressure on his already taxed shoulders.

Edward went to his desk, a hub in his universe of thought, and retrieved fresh parchment.

Deadlines dictated he put his—what had Ryland said?—level head into the next phase of his plans.

❦

Never in all his five-and-twenty years did Edward think the words "woman" and "scintillating" would intersect in his mind.

Such a notion defied logic.

He paced the dining room's massive hearth, his hands clasped behind his back. Oh, he'd met a witty female or two in the past, but this was maddening. No, Miss Montgomery was maddening; she had worked her way under his skin.

As he passed the hearth yet again, a stray ember skipped from the fire, landing close to his shoe. Vibrant orange light flared in small waves across the charcoaled piece. Fire fascinated the eye, drawing the viewer in close, but one needed to proceed with caution or else get burned. Wasn't that what had happened with the beautiful, vacuous Eugenia Blackwood? At that, the tip of his shoe kicked the offending ember back from whence it came. He set his hands on the cold marble mantel and let the inferno warm his legs.

The cavernous room was chilly, and the pretense of warming himself at the fire would force him *not* to pace and *not* to watch the door. Around him, footmen moved with efficient steps, lighting candelabra on the sideboard and setting the table.

Staring into dancing orange and yellow flames, he tried to recall the last time he'd anticipated his evening meal, or the company of a woman, with such thin restraint. To add insult to injury, he dithered over his choice of coat, deciding on a newer brown velvet embellished with gold trim at the wrists. Of course, he stopped short of digging out a waistcoat.

Where is she?

He pulled his silver timepiece from his breeches's pocket. Miss Montgomery would have to understand promptness was a virtue of considerable impor—

"Good evening, Lord Greenwich." Her soft feminine voice floated across the room.

Edward's head snapped to like a hound on a vixen's scent as his fingers slipped the fob back into its home.

"Good evening, Miss Montgomery."

She stood in the doorway, hands folded low, all scrubbed clean, and her glossy hair fashioned nicely—minus powder, that was all the rage, probably because there was none in the house. Miss Montgomery had taken some time at her toilet and availed herself to a maid with pleasing results. He couldn't claim to know the exact color of her dress, but it had a modest bodice and a pleasing dark hue that flowed over her form, nipping at her slender waist. The dark color shaded the graceful arc of feminine cheekbones, casting shadows and light just so. A woman of simple elegance had replaced the cheerful hoyden of this morning.

He motioned to the round table set very near the hearth. "Dinner awaits."

One of the footmen standing at attention helped seat her, and disappeared into the kitchen. His dinner companion's head tilted this way and that as she scanned the bare, windowless room.

"Except for the room's size, and the footmen in attendance, I could be in a Wickersham dining room," she said, smiling. Her gaze traveled once more around the room and table. "You have a rather unusual arrangement, my lord."

"How's that?" He flicked his coattails behind as he took his seat.

Her fingers skimmed the unvarnished table and singular knife and fork beside her plate. "I thought nobility preferred long, rectangular dining arrangements with formal settings. This"—she unfolded her napkin and glanced across the round table—"feels very intimate."

A door swung open, and two footmen marched forward bearing silver trays of food and drink from the kitchen. Edward cocked his head at the sound of their heels striking bare marble in the high-ceilinged room.

"Sounds like a mausoleum, doesn't it?"

"I wouldn't know." She grinned. "Never been in one."

He unfolded his napkin, digesting that difference in life experience. "Well, I prefer comfort first, decorum last."

The footmen set wide salvers, polished to a mirror's shine, on the side buffet. Dinner was simple fare: a generous slice of meat pie, and a tankard of the best local ale, but for Miss Montgomery, red wine from the cellar. Her thick brows arched as she took in the rustic, one-course meal.

"Do you dine like this every night?" She spiked her fork at the flaky pastry, removing layers of golden crust, on a hunt for what lay underneath.

When she found the simple meat-and-gravy center, steam curled up like a genie released from its bottle. Her nose twitched as she sniffed the food and speared a carrot slice.

"I assure you it's not poisoned." Edward chuckled as he split his pastry in two. "And yes, I dine this way because I grew up with formality in excess. As soon as it was prudent, I made things more to my liking." He pointed his knife and fork at the table and made a quick circle. "Are you uncomfortable with this arrangement?"

"No. Simply surprised." She lowered her eyes and sipped her wine. "When you say 'prudent' to change things, you mean after the period of mourning for your father?"

"No, I mean after my mother resigned herself that I was head of the Greenwich seat and leading as I saw fit." He waited on his explanation while a footman refilled his tankard with golden ale, and then raised his tankard in silent toast to his dinner companion. "Which took about a month. That's when I made changes in here."

"You haven't told me much about your mother, or your family for that matter." Her cautious knife strokes kept a careful slicing tempo on the porcelain plate.

They'd waded into new territory here, and some places, too many, made shaky ground at best and volatile terrain at worst. Edward popped a chunk of meat into his mouth to delay, a stall tactic he was sure Miss Montgomery duly noted. True, the balance of knowledge stood in his favor, but he owed her some information. Why, though, must matters go right to the touchiest spots, like probing a tender bruise?

"What's there to know? Most of England read about the Greenwich family the past few years in the broadsheets." He stopped for another draught of ale. "You'll see some of the family portraits tonight. Your artist's eye should ascertain plenty."

Edward motioned to one of the footmen for more ale, but not before catching an all too discerning light in Miss Montgomery's eye. Instead of pursuing that topic, she speared another bite, and her green eyes sparkled in firelight. Ale warmed him, playing with his equilibrium. Or was it his dinner companion?

He liked that what he tried to brush aside spoke volumes to her…could see it in her eyes; she'd no doubt navigated family disasters better than he. Edward dismissed the footmen and made a mental note of appreciation that Miss Montgomery was an atypical female. How satisfying to be in the company of a woman who didn't dig for more information when a door clearly shut.

"This meat pie is delicious," she said, her face writ with astonishment.

The hearth's warm blaze lit her features, casting soft shadows. Miss Montgomery sat up straighter, giving him a pleasant smile now and then. Good. She'd found her sea legs and was getting used to him. Her head tilted toward her plate, and she ate with genuine enthusiasm. Nor did she ply his ear with incessant chatter; thus, Edward surprised himself when he speared a hunk of beef and decided it was time to delve into personal matters.

"Why have you never married?"

Miss Montgomery's fork froze midair. "I could ask the same of you, my lord."

He chewed, angling his scarred cheek at her, and swallowed.

"You know one very substantial reason. I was barely out of Cambridge when this happened, though half of London's made sport out of their speculation about my marital concerns." He leaned his forearms on the table. "And you're avoiding my question."

"Perhaps it's as you put it last night: I'm pretty, but not that pretty." She set the wine goblet to her lips, but mischief played about her face.

"Ah, I see the writing on the wall." He raised his tankard. "Any rash comment I make will be used against me and require recompense." He swallowed more ale. "Of course, I have it on best authority that discourse between a man and a woman can get heated from time to time."

His cheeky reminder of her own words earned him throaty, joyful laughter. He liked the way her head tipped back, exposing her neck, a slim column of smooth, pale flesh.

"You are an apt pupil of women." Miss Montgomery dabbed the napkin to her lips. "I'm curious. What did your solicitor's report say about me?"

Right then Edward took notice, really saw Miss Montgomery in a new, fascinating light, another facet of a carefully cut gem. They ate for a time in pleasant silence. She was much more than a simple country miss thrown into an advantageous situation; her adroit sidesteps would make her a worthy ally and make for an interesting chase. A man would have to be on alert with her.

"Mr. Aaron had little time, I'm afraid, to delve deeply. His report was bare bones." Edward leaned back, and his fingers stroked the handle of his tankard. "You're the oldest daughter of the late Mr. Alistair Wright, steward to the Duke of Somerset, and Mrs. Abigail Montgomery, who remarried one George Montgomery, a clerk recently in my employ at Sanford Shipping. Your entire upbringing took place at the ducal seat in Somerset, where you occasionally were tutored with the duke's children, acting as companion to their older daughter when the family was in the country. After your father's demise, the duke allowed your family to stay in the steward's cottage because of his high regard for the late Mr. Wright. Your sister married and moved away. An unsavory incident occurred four years ago, at which time you removed yourself to Wickersham to live with a distant family relation." His fingers drummed his tankard. "How am I doing so far?"

"Magnificently." She tipped her head in acknowledgment.

"There was no mention of you enjoying the occasional dram of scotch, or your *experience* as a woman." He leaned forward, resting his forearm on the table, every muscle tensing. "Here's where things are less clear. Little is known about you in the four years in Wickersham."

As soon as he said that, her green eyes flickered with wariness. "And what do you know?"

"Everyone spoke highly of the young woman living with her great-aunt with rare trips to visit family in London. Neighbors waxed on about your helpfulness in times of need and your cheerful nature at the annual spring rout." He cocked his head at the mystery. "Strangely, the report listed no close friends, save for regular correspondence with your sister, and only two short-lived male suitors. More intriguing, no one could answer the question as to why a fairly attractive woman was on the shelf at four-and-twenty."

Lydia sat like a marble statue, a wan smile pasted to her face. "You've been quite thorough, or I should say your solicitor has been."

"I needed to be. Would I invite a shrew into my ancestral home?" His fingertips stroked the tankard's rim. "To my bed?"

Her chin raised a notch. Firelight flickered, playing

over her dark glossy hair. Dense, sable lashes outlined her eyes, and curling wisps dropped from her simple coiffure, contouring high cheekbones.

"You get ahead of yourself, my lord." Wine-red lips curved prettily. "Don't forget your edict to wait a month."

Every muscle in his torso tensed alert and aware to the tempting quarry across his table.

"But what about all the years beyond?"

As he said those quiet words, her lashes shuttered low, shielding her eyes from his intent stare. She brushed at the sleeve of her dress, and another wall was erected. Interesting. Miss Montgomery was the one hiding.

But what else could she possibly withhold from him? Women teetering on the verge of spinsterhood, who lived with ancient family members, did not live fast, exciting lives. What possible secret could she hold in check from him?

Edward sighed, and the chair creaked as he pressed into the back rest. "Very well, Miss Montgomery. Rome wasn't built in a day, nor will the accord between us come quickly. Everything in its time."

Her eyelashes fluttered upward. "You wish for accord between us? And here I thought you wished only for an heir."

Her coy words neatly parried to his thrust. Miss Montgomery opened her mouth a fraction from that mild, teasing sarcasm she gave him. The dark, wet space in the middle of those soft lips would drive him mad, if he let this go too far. Then, as if she knew, the temptress dabbed her napkin to her lips, hiding what tempted him most. Ale and the scintillating feminine company across the table warmed his blood. He stood on the brink of something.

"I wish to know many things, Miss Montgomery." Edward's fingers skimmed the edge of his plate. "At present, I'll settle for your list of atonements. You owe me a choice of three."

Though her mouth hid behind a napkin, her whole face lit with a smile. Miss Montgomery set the napkin on the table, her fingers kneading the linen.

"I'm happy to oblige." She stood up, and her chair scraped the floor before one of the footmen could pull it out for her.

His dinner companion missed the footman's approach: a future lesson for the future countess to allow people to wait on her. She turned and took note of the hovering footman.

"I messed that up, didn't I?" She grinned at Edward. "Should've waited for help with my chair."

He was too taken by the mischief in her eyes to comment.

"My lord, why don't we take that tour of your family's art? Then I shall present my three…ideas."

At least her first dinner with a noble wasn't a complete disaster. How was she to know one waited on a servant for chair movement?

All in all, the dinner went splendidly, save that minor misstep. Her mind focused on the vexing man across the table. She mentally cataloged *yes* and *no* topics: the reason for his scars and reclusive ways, however painful to recount, rolled off his tongue today, yet one question about his family and Lord Greenwich slammed shut. And forget trying to ascertain Miss Mayhew's status from his lordship or the servants; the housekeeper was the *most forbidden* topic. Yet, everything about his demeanor this eve struck her as a clever predator dallying with its prey, and he enjoyed every minute of the game—for that is surely what kept his interest attuned. This clue to his character was the most intriguing yet.

Lord Greenwich took the candelabrum from the sideboard and offered his arm with an infectious rogue's grin.

"I can't remember the last time I had such enthusiasm for art."

"Art? And here I thought you were eager to hear my offerings," she said, slipping her hand under his elbow.

"Hmmm, there is that," he said.

Her fingers splayed over the plush velvet covering his forearm. Oh, she had an inkling as to what his lordship anticipated her ideas to be: ideas that played to a sensual nature.

He was in for a surprise.

As they moved through the hallways, she sneaked quick side views of Lord Greenwich. His classic profile and smooth, unscarred cheek would cause hearts to flutter if he bothered with social niceties and went to Town in the light of day. The irreverent noble still wore no waistcoat or neckcloth. The exposed skin of his neck and top of his chest intrigued her. The edge of a scar showed at the open neckline, driving her mad with an itch to explore. Did Society dictate the need for neckwear solely to hide that forbidden flesh? The notion made her laugh.

"Something amusing?" Lord Greenwich questioned as he navigated Greenwich Park's hallways. Lydia opened her mouth to answer, but right then his lordship pushed against two very grand, gilt-trimmed doors, opening the way to a long, rectangular room.

He could have been Moses parting the Red Sea, so awe inspiring the effect.

"Oh, my."

Polished silver candelabra glowed from small tables every ten feet or so along the walls. The earl had had the servants prepare the room for them. No, for her.

Large and small paintings lined the walls, well-placed geometric puzzle pieces covering white space. Narrow windows stood between some paintings on one wall, and whenever the clouds parted, pearled moonbeams mixed with mellow candlelight. The whole place took her breath away…a sumptuous spread of fine art. Beauty, the rare and real kind, could overwhelm the senses; such was the visual feast that rooted her to the floor, until one particular gilt-framed piece beckoned.

"Is that a van Oosterwyck?" Lydia cried. Her arm slipped from his. She grabbed handfuls of her skirts for freedom of movement, taking a rapid pace toward an oil painting of flowers and a globe.

Lydia craned her neck, checking the signature. Lord Greenwich's footsteps echoed on the parquet from behind until his silent presence warmed her. He raised the candelabrum, all the better for her to read the signature, but she already knew.

"You *own* the *Vanitas*." She breathed the painting's name in reverence and shook her head. "You actually own Maria van Oosterwyck's *Vanitas*."

Edward leaned in for a look at the artist's signature. "Apparently so."

"I thought all her pieces went to royalty," Lydia sighed. "I've long admired her talent, her ability to support herself. As a woman, she was never allowed into her countrys' painters' guild. That's for men only." She pursed her lips on that pronouncement and sighed. "But the worse crime is such beauty's hidden away in a room where only a choice few can appreciate it."

Her voice, edged with brusque coolness at both injustices, relaxed when she leaned in to capture the details of a flower petal.

"Pity…such magnificence locked away. I had to see a copy of it in a book, a very rough block print." She straightened and faced him. "Someday, someone will have to explain to me why one's birth in Society dictates access and appreciation of art."

Lydia didn't bother to see how his lordship reacted to that. Another portrait dominated most of one wall. The giant piece lured her, as much the quality of work as the subject matter. She pulled away from Lord Greenwich, her heels rapidly clicking the polished wood floor.

Lydia clasped her hands behind her and craned her neck to absorb every detail. She pointed at the younger boy.

"That's you," she said with glee.

"It is I." Lord Greenwich raised the candelabrum to give her more light. His cheerful composure was that of a man who knew he'd struck a bull's-eye in pleasing a woman.

She squinted at the brushstrokes. Better to study this in the light of day. Lydia stepped back a few paces for perspective. A triangle of children, two boys and one girl with a golden spaniel resting at their feet, filled the portrait that was easily twenty feet tall. A large, older, dark-haired boy stood at the epicenter; no, he was the epicenter. One hand fisted at his waist, the strapping lad, barely in his teenage years, held a brass telescope against his thigh, complete with a commanding air.

The girl shared the same tawny-haired mane as the boyish Edward and was the youngest of the three. With each brushstroke, the artist had captured her spoiled nature in the pout of her mouth and willful, brown eyes, the same as both her brothers.

And then there was Lord Eddie, as Huxtable and Miss Lumley called him. Lydia wanted to hug the lad with plump childish cheeks. The handsome, pensive child gave onlookers an unrepentant glare, while one hand clutched a green book and the other curled in a fist at his side.

"You look like you want to run away. Or hit someone," she said, laughing out loud. The sound echoed pleasantly in the room. "You were probably done with the sitting before it began."

Lord Greenwich's rueful smile said she made the correct assessment.

"I was ready to punch someone, anyone, for that sitting…a colossal waste of time to my young mind. I had better things to do." He shrugged. "My father promised to take me worm hunting after that first tedious sitting, so I was appeased."

"Worm hunting? Incredible." She laughed again. "The very idea, your father, the great and revered Earl of Greenwich worm hunting…I can't imagine it."

"Oh, yes," he said, warming to the topic. "My father knew all the best places for worming and toad hunting, too, for that matter."

The open joy in his face as he perused the portrait took her breath away. She stared at him, couldn't move. The topic of his family was not a closed issue after all.

Lord Greenwich as an intense, arrogant man was threateningly handsome, but this peeled-back layer of happiness showed an altogether different kind of entrancing.

Smiling at the portrait, he lowered the candelabrum. "You know, I'm Greenwich Park's foremost expert on worming—" He turned to her and stilled.

His visage morphed from cheerful childhood recollection to saturnine intensity. The moment's levity slipped away, and they were a man and woman alone in a quiet place. Skin-tingling awareness melted her senses, as much as his smoldering stare that could burn holes through her dress. Her lashes shuttered, and she blinked. She had to look away.

"But that's for another time," he said. "Perhaps now you can share your three ideas."

His voice, liquid male and smooth, invited intimacy. The earl set the candelabrum on the floor, and when he stood up, Lydia slid her arm through his and pulled him close, as drawn to his warmth as she suspected he was to hers.

"Let's take a turn about the room, shall we?"

He said nothing but glanced down at her hand touching the same forearm she'd touched earlier in the day. They strolled along in silence with only the steady resonance of their footsteps sounding.

She loved surprising him. Serve the man right to keep him off-kilter. The balance of knowledge swayed too much on his side, and no woman ever served herself well by letting a man always have the upper hand. She savored his clean smell as their quiet footsteps meandered over the parquet.

The Earl of Greenwich was quite unlike any other

nobleman with whom she'd ever crossed paths: intelligent, handsome in appearance—the scars aside—and
not given to the ridiculous notion that his birth gave him
superiority over others or every right to live an idle life
of useless debauchery and dissolution. Beside her was a
man of purpose.

Lydia recognized a hazardous wish growing within,
the wish to make this man want her in every way. This
could be a slippery slope, if she weren't careful. She laid
her other hand atop the earl's arm in a comfortable grasp
and closed the gap between them, the gesture cozy and
familiar as their hips touched and their legs sometimes
brushed against each other.

"You gave me much to consider this afternoon with
your mandate, my lord. But truly, all I needed was that
warm bath, and the ideas came quickly."

"Go on." Lord Greenwich's pace matched hers.

"My first offering: I act as your valet. Your clothes are
piled everywhere in your room, so I asked Miss Lumley
about that. She confirmed my worst fears: you care for
yourself without aid of a valet. I shouldn't be surprised,
since you're very private, but"—her index finger traced
a loosening edge of gold trim at the wrist of his jacket
sleeve—"your wardrobe's badly in need of attention. I'm
good with a needle and the blade." At this last word, her
gaze slid to the small cut on his chin.

His fingers skimmed the scabbed-over nick from his
morning shave, but Lord Greenwich shook his head.
"Not good enough. If I wanted a valet, I'd hire one."
He angled his head at her, a teasing glint in his eyes.
"However, I could use some assistance with bathing.
Someone to scrub my back, perhaps?"

Lydia playfully slapped his shoulder. She loved the humorous brigand.

"You care not even a whiff for fashion, my lord?"

"Not a bit. Growing up, my brother eventually accepted—with resignation—our mother's mandates on attire. Later he came to embrace them with relish. As for me, I despise anything I'm *supposed* to do. Hence, you see a bare minimum of lace on the lad in the portrait back there." His head tipped at the massive painting dominating the wall. "Lace scratches my chin, bothers my neck, and gets in the way of my hands. When I was a boy, the seams and lace at my wrists were muddied and torn before the day was done. No amount of my mother's threats could make me place boyish curiosity on the shelf in favor of decorum. My father finally intervened and banished lace from my wardrobe." He favored her with a mischievous smirk. "And then there was peace."

"A bit recalcitrant," she said in good cheer, but her smile faded.

If their conversation were a stream, the waters turned turbulent as Lord Greenwich frowned.

"At odds with my mother more times than I care to admit…and my father, tolerant and understanding until his authority was needed to render an edict."

"Then he was not only a man to be admired in public, but privately as well."

"Yes, I loved my father. His loss was"—Lord Greenwich trailed off, and he stared ahead—"more than I can explain."

Lydia chewed her lip. More questions wanted to spring off her tongue, but wisdom held back that tide.

"Don't get me wrong. I…*love*…my mother," he said,

but his hesitation over that singular declaration was more like one trying to ascertain the missing ingredient in a dish of middling appeal. "But she's…"

He let his words disperse, finishing with a bland shrug. Lydia let the silent gap stay between them, and then his lordship narrowed his eyes at some vague point in the room.

"More the point, she pressed for whatever gave the best appearance of things, what *she* thought was best for you, instead of letting one act as one saw fit. My mother tried to force malleable young girls down my throat"—he touched his scar and finished dryly—"in previous days. She decided their biddable nature worked as counterbalance to mine. You know, opposites attract."

"And?"

"That works best with magnetic force fields, not always with human nature. The girls were duller than dishwater." His eyes rolled with mock agony.

"How terrible for you as a young man." She gave him a coy smile and patted his arm in playful sympathy. "To have Society's loveliest young women vying for your attentions."

He snorted at that. "More like get in my way. But we digress. I don't need a valet, Miss Montgomery. What's my second choice?"

They strolled quietly, passing portraits of blank-faced family members from other eras, each defined by modes of fashion and hairstyles of other times. Her shoulder grazed his arm, a bare rustle of wool against velvet. Candlelight bounced off gilt frames and mirrors. For the first time in distant memory, contentment flooded her.

The evening, however unique from others, counted as excellent. She didn't want this to end.

Lord Greenwich tipped his head. "Woolgathering?"

"No, my lord, simply afraid I may disappoint you. You have such high expectations." She turned her mouth in a playful moue. "My second offering: I will assist you in your greenhouse. In Wickersham I was rather handy in the garden. I grew lemongrass to make my own soap. I could make some for you as well."

Lord Greenwich stared ahead as he appeared to consider the notion, but shook his head in the negative.

"Your talents are legendary, I'm sure, but I must refuse the offer." His voice slowed, dropping an octave. "I'm very selective about who touches my varietals."

Lydia licked her lips, her mouth quirking over that playful innuendo. His eyebrows snapped together from that simple movement with her mouth. The dangerous brigand was back, and his gaze traced her face, eyes to mouth, catching a moment on her lips and back again to her eyes.

"I'm sorry to hear that."

The refusal was deflating. He must've known that, because he offered his brand of reassurance.

"To be fair, the flora in my greenhouse requires very explicit and unique attention. They're like demanding, high-strung ladies from foreign courts, except they're blessedly quiet."

Her head tipped back with laughter. "I shall remember not to talk too much, my lord," she said, squeezing his forearm. "But I've failed to appease on two of my three atonements. I'm close to a perilous end."

He shook his head, and his face pulled in a melodramatic frown. "I expected better from you."

"No, you expected something of a sensual nature."

Lydia said the coy words, hoping to throw him off guard with directness. The simple fact: her confidence melted under the heat of appealing male fixation. Lord Greenwich, when not focused on his work, turned into something of a dangerous flirt with his subtle humor and dark eyes—not the jovial type of man a woman could easily maneuver with a smile. His body tensed beside her when she dared name what lurked between them; yet his lordship's steps were steady.

"I could be tempted."

"About that...an idea to be sure, but there *is* your waiting period, my lord." Her fingers tapped the lapel of his coat. They stopped, and her hand slid from his arm, a whisper of skin to velvet the only noise in the room. "We can't tempt fate, now can we?"

"Thank you for the reminder." He looked away, sounding as grouchy as a baited bear.

They stood close. The air crackled between them. Lord Greenwich's nostrils flared as if scenting her, and the candelabra behind him gave a golden glow to his neatly combed queue. A faint shadow of dark facial hair, the day's growth, covered one side of his face, while the other was shiny scars and marred skin.

"Your first two atonements are child's play, Miss Montgomery. You have your final chance to impress me."

Or?

She wouldn't bother to ask what would happen if she failed to impress. Diverting tension thrummed between them, awareness so taut they could be touching. Lydia inhaled deeply, and his black-brown gaze dropped to the thrust of her breasts properly trussed in stays.

"I will sketch for you, plant diagrams and such." She exhaled once the words were out and squared her shoulders.

She would be taken seriously, not simply as a diversion for a man particular about the female company he keeps, but as a woman with talent and a soul hungering for more than the tiny morsels life doled out to her in piecemeal fashion.

Lord Greenwich's eyes widened. Idea number three stunned him silent. With her third offer, Lydia stood on the rim of a new precipice, headed to something big, bigger than anything she'd ever done. She clasped her hands at waist height, squeezing them tight to abate her fingers' faint tremors, and in what she hoped was persuasive solicitation.

"I noticed your journal drawings, both in the greenhouse and in the reading area of your room."

One imperious eyebrow rose at the mention of her earlier intrusion on his lordly space.

Her head dipped a fraction. "I know...I was *completely* in the wrong to go in your room and rifle through your personal effects." She licked her lips and raised her head, "But I'm sorry, my lord. Your sketches are deplorable. Your handwriting's even worse."

She must have struck a chord: gone was the flirtatious brigand. Lord Greenwich appeared to embrace the truth of his artistic shortcomings rather than be offended by her noting them. He stayed stone silent, with the slightest cant of his head, though not as one vexed by her critical comments, more like she'd shed light on a new and interesting theorem. Lydia's clenched hands touched her chin.

"Oh, I know you can hire a secretary to transcribe your work, but you'll have a harder time conveying

your ideas without excellent images and diagrams."
Lydia splayed her fingers high on her chest. "I'd wager
that I sketch, paint, and draw better than most people of
your acquaintance."

His brows rose at the boast. "Quite confident in
your abilities."

"Aren't you confident in yours?" Her hands slid to
her sides as she gave him a level stare. "Truly, I offer
this without excessive pride when I say that I'm a good
artist, *a very good artist*, and can help with that part of your
scientific papers. An excellent picture conveys a wealth of
information; a poor one only confuses."

"Intriguing." Lord Greenwich rubbed his chin. "I
must say, you've managed the impossible. Your third
offer not only astounds me but has some merit."

"Consider it the most basic partnership, easily ended
by either of us when no longer convenient. I might add
that I work quickly…quite fast at my sketches. You'll not
have to worry about me slowing down your progress."

Lydia held her breath under his scrutiny. Did she hold
her head higher? For she was sure he was assessing her as
a colleague, an equal. The revelation gratified her to no
end. Gone was the man who'd made the unusual bargain
at a ramshackle inn—Was that only last night?—and in
his place was a scientist, a peer in the realm of talent.
His lordship tolerated nothing less than the best from
himself and would demand the same of her. That alone
exhilarated her.

"I'm intrigued. Definitely. I won't present my papers
to the Royal Society in person, but have been contemplating sending a folio of my latest findings for distribu-
tion. Excellent pictures, clear diagrams are a must." His

eyes glittered in an unusual way, as if he was trying to read deeper into her person. "I admit some of my past sketches have caused confusion, as you put it."

"Then you accept my offer?" Her voice was on the perilous line of faltering.

She held her breath, waiting. His scarred face, calculating, severe, and uniquely handsome, was something to behold as the mental measurement of his decision came.

"Yes." Lord Greenwich's sharp inhale punctuated the decision. "Be in the greenhouse by eight o'clock, Miss Montgomery. I'll brook no tardiness."

Her whole body relaxed as she breathed out slowly. There was one more obstacle, her secret wish, to clear with him, but now was the time to outline that singular stipulation.

"Wait." She held up a hand to stall him. "I make my offer with one exception."

"What's that?"

"I work for you a few hours a day and then am allowed to pursue my painting as originally promised."

"Done."

She sighed in relief, a giddy happiness filling her. Lord Greenwich clasped his hands behind his back and peered down at her. She appreciated his decisiveness in the matter, yet he gave the impression of an exacting headmaster the way he stared at her, albeit a young, brooding headmaster. Then the earl put his hand at her elbow and steered her quickly toward the door.

"Your happiness may be short-lived."

"Why's that?" She glanced up at him, their heels clattering echoes against the high ceiling. "And why are we leaving the portrait gallery?"

"If you displease me, I'll exact payment in the form of my choosing." His hand on her elbow tightened. "And we're leaving so you can get a good night's sleep. I need you refreshed and ready to work hard. For that matter, I need sleep. I had so little last night."

As Lord Greenwich led her down another hallway, she was sure he muttered, "You've been enough of a distraction."

They took the familiar vermillion path past a blur of exotic blooms she recognized from his greenhouse, and Lord Greenwich halted outside her door. She faced him, about to protest. With her back to the portal, he leaned close, his velvet-clad arm brushing hers as he touched the brass doorknob. More blond hair tugged loose from his queue, framing his face.

"I'm not an easy man by any stretch. I'll have my due one way or another."

Ten

What is madness?
To have erroneous perceptions and reason correctly from them.
— Voltaire

THE SILVER TRAY HOVERING AT NOSE LEVEL COULD NOT be the harbinger of good news. Lydia sat up amongst a soft crush of pillows and hooked a tangle of hair behind one ear. From her upright angle, she recognized the familiar script, and lurking dread chased away the morning's heavy drowse.

"Good morning, miss." Tilly, the young, practical maid who'd helped her dress the night before, stood beside the bed, polished salver in hand. "This came yesterday with your things. Got lost in the mix with his lordship's correspondence. Sorry for the delay."

Lydia lifted the heavy brown paper from the tray—a message from her mother. She hoped all was well in the wake of her hasty departure, without even the chance to say good-bye. The maid held the tray, extending a slender mother-of-pearl penknife to open the missive. Another welcome side effect of nobility, someone waiting with a helpful convenience.

The letter crackled in her hands, written on unused brown butcher paper, the commoner's stationary to sidestep the paper tax. Lydia grinned at her mother's thriftiness and replaced the penknife with a quiet clank.

She sat bolt upright.

In between messy splotches of ink, her mother's alarming words jumped off the page.

> *Dearest Lydia,*
>
> *Don't do it! Do not marry in haste, or you'll invite unhappiness on your head and live with regret as I have. Too many women, in search of false security, make terrible mistakes with men, and they pay for it in misery the rest of their lives.*
>
> *But I'm afraid my letter bears only dismal tidings.*
>
> *George and Tristan disappeared. Gone to the Colonies for good, I hear. To George, I say good riddance! But I will miss Tristan so very much. The path he's taken these past few years breaks my heart. I had such hopes for him.*
>
> *I'm leaving to stay with Sarah, at least as long as she and Virgil will have me. Creditors have come knocking more and more of late. I'm not sure what I'll do, but it's high time I figure out what I should've done long ago— learn how to live as an independent woman forging her own happiness instead of believing it comes from a man.*
>
> *In your case, sacrificing yourself for Tristan's and your stepfather's errors goes far beyond family duty. Don't worry about me.*
>
> *Save yourself. Return to Wickersham immediately!*
> > *With all my love,*
> > *Mother*

Hands and sheaf slumped to her lap. She flopped into the bank of pillows and set a hand over her mouth, digesting the news. The weight of her mother's worries pressed her shoulders like a palpable burden. That George ran away was not so much of a surprise. But to leave her mother to answer what were likely *his* creditors? Just how much debt did he leave behind?

How like the blighter to leave her mother holding an empty purse, with creditors calling.

And what about Lord Greenwich? Her hand slid to the top of her chemise, clutching the fragile fabric. When he discovered this turn of events, the disappearance of George and Tristan, would this change matters? Certainly the earl wouldn't exact so-called justice on an innocent woman old enough to be his mother, when the true perpetrators had vanished. In the priority of things, his lordship struck her as wanting his heir much more than any repayment of thievery or debts. But did she truly know the lay of his mind on that score?

Lydia refolded the letter and placed it on the nightstand. She looked across the room where Tilly had already set up a tray of breakfast foods and was in the act of opening the gaudy wardrobe.

"Is his lordship up and about?"

The energetic maid stepped back, a plain leaf-green dress with underskirts and brown shawl in one hand, shoes in the other. She snapped the door shut with her hip.

"He was up with the sun, as usual, miss. In his study, he is, going over some business." She laid out the dress and tipped her head at the tray. "He instructed me to bring your breakfast up now, and said something about both of you needing to work in the greenhouse."

Lydia hopped out of bed, prepared to take advantage of a ready breakfast. Her mind reeled as she tried to digest her mother's letter. She picked up a slice of toast and dabbed a corner in the cup of jelly. She closed her eyes and savored her first bite—delectable rose-petal jelly—a luxury she could get used to enjoying. If her mother was at Sarah and Virgil's, she'd be safe for now. Lydia chewed the toast, ideas of how to approach Lord Greenwich rolling around her head as she crunched.

The carrot-haired maid stood by the dressing table, her hands folded demurely in front of her. "Will you be wanting me to fix your hair this morning, miss? Or do you want to take care of things, like yesterday morning?"

Her mind raced. She couldn't wait for eight o'clock. Surely his lordship wouldn't mind an interruption? She had to talk to him about her mother. Did he know this latest turn of events?

What if Lord Greenwich went back on his word about her mother now that George and Tristan had left England? This morning's missive was most unusual for her cautious mum. She'd put a lot of weight and trust on a single day and night with the earl; more of that indelicate pressure strained against her.

"I just need you to help me dress."

Genteel poverty made her self-sufficient about getting dressed, but the help of a maid would get her downstairs twice as fast. She dropped the half-eaten toast on the plate and swigged some hot, black coffee, then availed herself to Tilly for a quick dressing. The maid went about making the bed while Lydia splashed her face with bracing cold water and cleaned her teeth. A few rapid brush strokes to her hair, and she swept the mane into a hasty knot on the back of her head. Pins scraped her scalp; long wisps dangled for an imperfect mess.

She pinched her cheeks while speaking to her reflection. "This will have to do." Tucking her mother's note into her pocket, Lydia grabbed her favorite winter shawl and charged out the door.

She sped down the carpeted corridor and flew downstairs, seeking the earl's study. The door was wide open, jutting out into the walkway. As she approached, voices emanated from within. Lord Greenwich was with an obviously upset woman.

The housekeeper, Miss Mayhew.

Lydia jerked to a stop just short of the portal. Her hand lightly pressed the wooden door as she stayed out of view.

Lord Greenwich spoke in soothing tones. "I can't believe you'd ask such a thing, Claire."

Her voice rose with emotion. "*Why not?*"

"Shhhh, calm yourself."

He could be steadying a restless filly with the tenderness she heard.

"A lot of good this does for me now. Please. Take it. I can't bear to look at it anymore. It serves only as a reminder to painful memories...of love..." Miss Mayhew's voice choked, and she broke down.

"Claire...Claire..." he soothed.

Lydia's whole body froze from the shock of what she heard.

Memories of love?

She clutched her stomach, a strange sick feeling settling there. Worse yet, unwelcome possessiveness crept in hotly. Her most dire fears proved right about the earl and his housekeeper. She squeezed shut her eyes. What to do? Turn around and go back upstairs, pretend she never heard? Her shoulder pressed the cold wall. There had to be some kind of explanation.

Lydia peeked around the doorjamb to see Miss Mayhew's head on the earl's shoulder. One of his arms draped high across her shoulders, and the other rested on her upper arm, where a dazzling necklace, an array of bright blue baubles, hung from his hand. One of the precious stones was robin's-egg big. The necklace could feed half of Wickersham for a year and a day.

She turned from the scene and rested the back of her head on the wall as her mind tried to register what she'd seen and heard. Her eyes stared straight ahead, unseeing. These nobles played with lives the way neglectful children played with pets, showering treats and affection one moment, then moving on to another interest. From within, Miss Mayhew's voice near sobbed.

"Oh, Eddie, you know I must leave. Everything's different now. You're to be married and—"

"Don't worry about Miss Montgomery," he said in that soothing voice again. "I'm sure she'll understand."

Don't worry about Miss Montgomery?

A hot bolt of anger stiffened Lydia's spine. And just what exactly was she supposed to understand? She wanted to storm into the study that moment. But what was he all about last night, with his lordly innuendo and flirtation? Why bother to bring her here to act as broodmare, when a gorgeous woman stood at the ready, throwing herself into his arms, no less? The notion that he was one of those men who liked to play multiple women falsely, rang hollow and untrue. But what was this all about? A horrible pang churned in her stomach, the pain so sharp her hand fluttered over that spot.

The housekeeper gave in to sniffles and a woeful tone. "No, it's time. You're to be married, start a family"—at this, Miss Mayhew's voice broke, but she collected herself—"very soon. I must go."

"Don't go. Greenwich Park is your home." He paused, and the cadence of his voice changed. "Besides, these jewels belong to you. Do with them as you see fit."

"I'll…reconsider." She sniffed again. "I'm not even sure what I'd do or where I'd go."

"One more reason to stay, don't you think?"

Lydia had to peek through the sliver of space between the door and the doorjamb. Lord Greenwich grasped the housekeeper's hand and tenderly placed the necklace in it. Twinkling blue stones spilled from her palm, and he closed her fingers over the jewels. Lydia's forehead touched cold wood; her heart sank to a new low.

"Thank you, Eddie." Miss Mayhew reached up to kiss the earl's unscarred cheek. She jammed the outrageous jewelry into her pocket and dabbed at her wet cheeks. "I'm a mess, aren't I? Everyone will know I've been crying."

Lydia couldn't stand to hear any more of the audience that she was never supposed to hear in the first place. Painful disappointment pressed in on all sides like a jostling mob out of control. The Earl of Greenwich had just painted himself with the same self-serving, womanizing stripes as other males of his class. A scene from her painful past flashed across her mind. No, the same was true for men of all ranks and societal stature. She'd bolt from Greenwich Park this second, if it weren't for her mother. Lydia wrapped her shawl tightly about her shoulders, swallowing hard.

How could she ask him for help with her mother's creditors now? That'd put her even more at the mercy of his good graces, which was as appealing as chewing spikes.

Numb in body and soul, Lydia stared at the floor and put one foot in front of the other. Somehow her feet moved away from the study door, and for whatever reason, she sought the greenhouse.

Edward heard footsteps tread the hallway. A servant, perhaps, retreating with discretion to Claire's upset. Claire dabbed her eyes and smoothed her snowy-white apron. After she collected herself, she gave him a bleak smile and exited the room, back into the safety of proper stiffness and decorum as Greenwich Park's housekeeper. He scrubbed his face with both hands...so little he could do. Painful history could not be undone.

He pulled his silver timepiece from the pocket of his breeches. The cracked watch ticked vivid reminders of the last Earl of Greenwich. His father was the steady hand in life's storms. Would the late earl be sorely disappointed with his son's job at the helm of all that was Greenwich substance? Edward returned to his desk and worked on his correspondence.

One letter in particular to his solicitor demanded his immediate attention and could not be delayed. The quill moved across the page with firm, cursory instructions. He finished the last of that morning's work, and rang for Rogers as he sealed each missive.

Edward checked the timepiece again; half-past eight. Claire's interruption, though a needful thing, threw him off schedule. He was late for the appointed meeting in

the greenhouse with a certain woman of interest. He left
the letters on the salver in the middle of his desk, trusting Rogers would know what to do. His feet took him
through the house on a familiar path as dancing green
eyes invaded his mind. Miss Montgomery was a tad saucy
last night in the Gallery Room, a spark of fun, flirtatious
in a way that appealed to him. He never understood the
draw some men had to pouty, moody, demanding chits,
but Miss Montgomery's quiet, if sometimes bold, allure
drew him like no other of her sex.

His grin widened as he pushed open the double
drawing-room doors to let himself out onto the balustrade and down the steps through the small ornamental
garden deep in winter's sleep. His plain black broadcloth coat chased away some of the cold, damp air. The
skies, heavy with clouds, filtered sunbeams here and
there, turning morning dew into tiny crystals. Going
around a large urn, he moved down the slope's curving
graveled path and gained a clear view of the greenhouse's east side. Two hazy figures, Miss Montgomery
and Huxtable, conversed at a workbench pushed up
against the wall. As he pushed open the greenhouse
door, he hoped she was every bit as good as her boast
of last evening; he wouldn't mince words if her work
wasn't up to snuff.

Gravel crunched underfoot, announcing his arrival.
Huxtable pulled his ivory pipe from his mouth and held
it close to his chest.

"Mornin', I was just showin' Miss Montgomery here
yer journals and what not…things ye've been doin' of
late." Huxtable beamed like a proud father. "Her drawin'
is a good idea. A mite better 'an anything ye've done, I'd

say." Huxtable leaned into the table and motioned him over with the pipe. "Take a look."

Sheaves splayed the table; Miss Montgomery's lead stick, honed to a fine point, scraped quick, efficient lines across foolscap. A few of his sketches sat alongside two new sketches of the same flower but far superior to his work. Many children of nobility suffered through tutoring sessions to develop the basics of sketching; he failed them miserably. Edward held up a drawing of petals, pistil, and stamen, and Huxtable crowded in beside him.

"Did that while I watched this past hour." Huxtable's chest puffed out as if he did the diagram himself.

"Uncanny." He raised the sheaf to the light. "One might think he's actually looking at botanical anatomy rather than a facsimile. The leaf looks like it lifts off the page."

"Kind words, my lord." Cool words came from behind a curtain of tendrils falling across her cheeks.

Miss Montgomery faced the work before her, not bothering to look at him face-to-face. Was he getting the brush-off? Her fingertips, already darkened from the lead stick, moved with rapid efficiency, forming lines and shades and miniscule shapes on a third, more complex illustration. Edward didn't miss the quick daggers shot from the corner of her eye, though. Neither did Huxtable. The old man's eyes rounded before beetling back and forth from Lydia to him. Edward's jaw flexed and twitched. Warning signs flashed in his head: female histrionics ahead.

Huxtable coughed and muttered, "There's seedlings that need tending."

"Thank you, Hux."

Huxtable worked the pipe at the corner of his mouth and patted Edward's arm. Under his breath, Edward was sure Huxtable was warning, "Batten down the hatches, me boy."

A thick brown shawl that had seen better days draped her rigid back. He studied the movements of her slim hand over the page, deciding to try again.

"Good morning, Miss Montgomery."

She made a dismissive hum in return, not even looking his way. He'd try another approach.

"Your skill is amazing."

"Thank you, my lord." Her voice could freeze the windows, and this time she didn't deign to give him a side glance.

Heaven help me understand the moods of women. He leaned a hip against the workbench and crossed his arms casually.

"I can't help but wonder at your demeanor this morning. Is something amiss?"

Lydia faced him, starch stiff and green eyes flashing. Yes, something was definitely wrong. He hadn't lost all his powers to read the impossible female species, not that this green-eyed fury before him took deep intellectual capability to comprehend.

"Of course not, *my lord*. Whatever makes you think that, *my lord*?" She inhaled and pressed soft lips into a hard, unforgiving line.

"Quit 'my lording' me." He braced a hand on the table. "What's wrong with you?"

"Nothing. Nothing at all."

Her frosty tone could drip icicles. He stepped back, bemused, shaking his head. "Incredible."

The sensual, playful creature of last night was gone, replaced by an ice-cold miss. He took a breath of forbearance and tried again.

"Miss Montgomery, are you one of those females who expects a man to read your mind?"

"You ask that based on your *vast* experience with women?"

"What?" His head snapped back as if she'd slapped him.

Her fingers rubbed the lead stick, sending smudges higher across her thumb and index finger.

"Perhaps I should ask: What do you want, *Lord Eddie*?"

He flinched from her acid tongue. "Is reason and logic in a dress too much to ask for?"

Last night the familiar moniker of his childhood would have been music to his ears. This morning, between her sarcasm and mercurial shifts, the childhood pet name on her lips irritated. He shook his head, baffled. No, he wanted to shake her.

"You're such an arse." The words came low and wavering as she turned back to the table and sketched.

"Brilliant. We've reached a new low—juvenile namecalling." Edward set his hands low on his hips. "I've work to do."

He turned and walked away with thoughts to check the tile stove, anything to keep his distance. Confusion and disappointment clouded his thinking. At least her work was excellent thus far. She could stay. He'd give her some time to stew and try again in an hour—

Thunk!

A small object pinged off the back of his head and dropped to the ground. His hand rubbed the offended spot, a minor tap to his pate, as he turned around and discovered a small lead chunk at his feet. When he looked up, Miss Montgomery sat very tall and indignant on her stool.

"What's Miss Mayhew to you?" she blurted. "Is she your mistress?"

The words reverberated through the greenhouse.

Edward picked up the lead writing piece that surprisingly had remained intact, shaking his head. "You threw this at my head."

Bemused, he walked to the workbench. He rolled the piece over his palm and held it out, as if to provide evidence. The way she braced the wood, he was certain she'd toss that bench at him if she could. Miss Montgomery was like an exotic, foreign specimen with this unexpected flare of hers.

"Miss Montgomery, are you given to fits of hysteria?" he asked, more amazed than angry with the wish to get to the bottom of this puzzle.

Her gaze, shuttered and withdrawn, dropped to the gray shard and back to him.

"No." Miss Montgomery took a deep breath and settled her hands in her lap. "No, I'm rather a calm sort with most people." Her firm chin wobbled right then, and she near burst like fireworks again when she said, "But, I won't tolerate living with your mistress under the same roof. Miss Mayhew must go. Or I will."

He barked a disbelieving laugh. "You're in no position to make ultimatums in my home. And Miss Mayhew has never been nor will she ever be my mistress."

She charged ahead, apparently not registering what he'd said. "Oh, I know some nobility keep odd, secretive arrangements, but this goes beyond the pale." If possible, Miss Montgomery sat up even taller.

"Did you hear me?" He fisted both hands to his waist, pushing back his coat. "Miss Mayhew is *not* my mistress."

"Don't you mean *Claire*?" she snapped.

His eyes narrowed. "I repeat, she's not my mistress. I've never had one. Never saw the point."

Miss Mayhew studied his face as if she could read more behind his words. Her mouth pressed to a firm line, and Edward spoke to her with open hands.

"I'm not complex when it comes to people." He spread his arms wide, and his astonishment at the unusual morning grew. "If I already had a woman under my roof, as you put it, why would I seek out a stranger at the Blue Cockerel?"

Miss Montgomery looked away, and her eyebrows pressed together. He guessed her mind digested that fact. Edward's hands dropped to his sides, and the beginnings of triumph over this ridiculous morning grew, but he cautioned himself not to gloat. Logic alone could clear the air.

"Makes sense," she said under her breath, then faced him, licking her lips. "But this morning, I thought…"

"This morning?" His eyes narrowed with keen intensity.

The footsteps outside his study. He closed the distance between them and tossed the lead stick onto the bench. He admonished himself to act with caution as he stared back at the green-eyed termagant accusing him…*him*! But threads of control snapped, one after the other.

"That was you I heard in the hallway. Now we can add eavesdropping to your talents."

"It's hardly eavesdropping with the door wide open. The two of you made no attempt to curb your voices." Her eyes shot daggers at him again. "And what was that necklace all about? I saw it."

"Did you?" he said in a soft voice.

In that split second, thought and reason gave way to action, as patience, his last fragile thread, broke. He grabbed her wrist and yanked her from the stool. "You're coming with me. There's something you need to see."

Eleven

Love ceases to be a pleasure, when it ceases to be a secret.
—Aphra Behn

OF ALL THE TYPES OF MEN, BROODING RECLUSES PROVED to be the most difficult to understand, and she decided, the most difficult to manage.

Had she come to that conclusion when her skirts billowed like a flag behind her as they raced across the lawn, up cold stone steps to move swiftly across the balustrade? Or did that come to her when they charged past a flirtatious footman and downstairs maid caught amidst a hallway dawdle? Of course, his lordship didn't care that their mouths froze midsentence at the spectacle of a man and woman speeding down the hallway.

"Carry on as you were," he barked at the stunned pair, while Lydia's arm was stretched behind him from dragging her along.

Trotting to stay in tempo with Lord Greenwich's angry strides over the marble floors, Lydia resolved that he would understand one thing: she'd never tolerate a dalliance. Her chest heaved from exertion and rising indignation, and her heels clacked, barely keeping pace with him. Something else nettled her, a rampant, foreign idea building inside her—the right to demand fidelity.

Why?

She couldn't answer that. Everything blurred quite literally. But as she followed the broad, determined shoulders that headed who knew where, his lordship needed to know one thing: Miss Mayhew *must* go. Forget that minor reasoning he did in the greenhouse. Not all of life was based on logic and fact.

Then, of all places, the earl stopped just short of the art-gallery doors and let her go. He faced Lydia, and his scarred jaw twitched and flexed when he spoke.

"I will *never* force Miss Mayhew to leave Greenwich Park." He shoved the doors in a grand flourish. "This is her home."

"Then you don't need me," she huffed.

His lordship's eyebrows lowered in a heavy line over topaz-brown eyes, eyes that sparked with a strange light that she couldn't fathom. "In some odd way, I find I do. Though I question my sanity in coming to that conclusion."

Bewilderment mingled with rapid huffs of breath from their sprint. How could he say something like that? That he needed her? Or was it simply her womb? Lydia tried to collect herself after their mad dash from the greenhouse. She glanced around the gallery.

"You drag me from the greenhouse to look at art *again*?"

"This way."

He clamped a vise grip at her elbow, and they marched through the room with the earl intent on some distant point. Greenwich ancestors stared down at her, some forbidding and some comical in their antiquated attire. Lord Greenwich's scowl was as severe as the black coat he wore. Lydia's skirts fluttered, and her shoes clattered loudly, echoing off the ornate plastered ceiling as she tried to keep up with him. His long stride ate up the distance. What was he trying to do here?

"I assure you, my lord, this matter will not go away with the appeasement of—"

The earl glared at her, and that severe look won him a moment of silence. He moved ahead, his fingers digging five fierce points into her arm, when he abruptly stopped. She collided with him, her face brushing his sleeve.

"My lord," she said, sputtering.

He stemmed her oncoming tide of feminine indignation with a commanding move, taking her by the shoulders and pulling her flush to him. With her back to his chest, his hands kept her in place. They faced a smaller portrait, about the size of a tea tray, near the corner of the room. She'd missed this one last night: an assertive, handsome young man with a brass sextant fisted against his thigh.

"Your brother," she said, stating the obvious.

"Yes, my brother, the one born to wear the mantle as Earl of Greenwich. Perfect and unscarred." He gave the facts, but tender pain, like a fresh wound, limned his voice. "On his way to Sweden, his ship was attacked by a Rus ship. He died in his bed of wounds from the assault. Miss Mayhew nursed him and witnessed his last breath."

Lord Edward's hands warmed her shoulders, gripping with the kind of firmness that brooked no movement. She peeked over her shoulder at his stony features.

"I don't understand." She shook her head and stared at the strong, handsome features before her, a darker, bolder mirror of the man behind her.

"Miss Mayhew is a friend, like a sister to me, which is how things were growing up together. Thick as thieves, we were, but you won't find her portrait on Greenwich walls." His smooth, cultured voice vibrated above her head. "Do you understand? *I* was never more than a brother to her, and she was always a sister to me. Her affections developed elsewhere."

Dawning recognition seeped into her mind. The man at her back, intense and intellectual, and the man in the portrait before her, commanding and entitled—both cut from the same familial cloth, but so very different in their appeal. Lydia viewed the late heir, and then craned her neck to see the man behind her.

His mouth hovered near her ear as he whispered, "Tell me what you see."

Heat radiated from his chest to her back. She glanced at Lord Edward once more. So many emotions played across his face as he stared at the flat replica of his brother...love, awe, sadness. Her head swiveled back and forth between the two men: one dead and the other very much alive.

"*Not you.* Miss Mayhew and...and..." She pointed at the portrait, her jaw dropping.

Questions, the pressing need to know, waited at the tip of her tongue. What of the necklace? The morning's tearful outburst? What exactly happened? Lydia stretched her neck as she tried to read his face, deciding to temper herself. Lord Greenwich gave her a telling, rueful smile and nodded at the portrait.

"Miss Mayhew loved your brother," she gushed the admission.

"With all her heart."

The dashing, dark-haired Lord Jonathan could easily claim the heart of any woman who crossed his path; stunningly beautiful women would not be immune. Strength and masculine vitality radiated from him. Couple that with wealth and position, and troves of women were bound to lay their hearts at his feet. And from the stories told, they did.

Lord Greenwich's body pressed closer, his hands eased their grip, and he moved to stand beside her with his arm brushing hers. "Now you see. I give Claire the same protection and care that I'd give my sister, Jane."

With understanding came silent connection. Lydia waited. The rhythm of his breathing slowed, matching hers. Or did her body strive to match his? If he harbored any anger toward her for the unfounded accusations, she couldn't feel them. Acute awareness of the earl, a man very much alive, flushed her back, her bottom, her limbs.

"She loved my brother, and for a time, I believe he loved her." He inhaled deeply, and his tone went flat. "And then he hurt her. Badly. Like some coldhearted cad."

"What happened?" she asked, her voice a wisp of sound in the cavernous room.

His gaze, a kaleidoscope of love, disappointment, and awe locked on the portrait. "We grew up."

She watched traces of anger dissipate, replaced by fascination. There was no guile or arrogance in him.

He stared at the painting, a faint smile playing at his lips. "As children, we played together, whiling away our summers, fishing, making mischief."

His dark blond queue hung loosely at the top of his back. His unscarred profile bore the Greenwich hallmarks: straight nose and classical features, like beautiful

Greek statuary, above wide shoulders. Yet he was not the same kind of handsome as his brother.

Better than his visage, Lord Edward exuded depth and intelligence—too much for some, intriguing for her. He would never need people and social conventions as others did; privacy and solitude meant too much to him. And those he allowed close enough to matter would be held to very high standards. Lydia stored away that tidbit, a treasure piece of knowledge about this man, to savor and examine later. His face was a vision of jumbled memories behind stormy eyes. Loyalty was his gift to Claire. Would he shower that gift elsewhere? She wanted to draw him out of his reverie and draw him closer to her.

"What made things go badly?"

"Childhood affections turned into something more. I was more and more with my tutors," he said, rolling his shoulder loosely. "My brother and Claire became very close—too close according to my mother. She confronted Jonathan and told him under no circumstances would a steward's daughter be the next Countess of Greenwich."

Lydia inhaled sharply. "But I am a steward's daughter."

"Ironic, isn't it?" Lord Edward's eyes slanted at her. He faced the portrait again. "My mother paraded anything in skirts, young widows to girls fresh from the schoolroom, all in an effort to sway him."

"And?"

"Some he ignored, and with some, he dallied. He kept Claire hanging. She was always conveniently tucked away here at Greenwich Park." He frowned at the portrait. "In his selfish, youthful way, he still loved her"—Lord Greenwich shook his head, his eyes narrowing as if he could divine something from the silent painting—"then came the proverbial carrot, something Jonathan always wanted but could never have."

Lydia leaned forward for a better look at the present earl's face; truthfully, she wanted his full attention and touched his arm. His eyes hooded, Lord Greenwich stayed oblivious, lost in family history. He tipped his head at a small frame high up on the wall. That portrait of his mother showed an older woman in the same vein as the beautiful, commanding presence over the mantel in the pink palace.

"She gave Jonathan his own ship."

"Ahhh…I begin to see how things unfolded."

He clamped his arms across his chest, stretching black broadcloth tight over his shoulders. "How often do you hear of an heir taking to the high seas? My mother was so desperate to get him away from Claire that she'd risk losing him to the seas rather than to an inferior woman, as she put it." His mouth pressed into a hard line, anger etched the corners. "She feared they might run off to Gretna Green."

"What about your father?"

"My father was not…unopposed…to Claire, but he didn't rally to her side either. I think he saw two young people and decided to let things be." One corner of his mouth curved up as he set a hand over his heart like a quixotic. "He was, deep down, a romantic."

"But your brother, a ship's captain? To go as far as providing him a ship?"

"True. He had misgivings, but he allowed it in part to keep the peace, and in part, I think…" He squinted at a smaller portrait, a younger version of his father. "I think he understood what a trap the title could be, and allowed

Jon's passion. The pleasant surprise was how lucrative that
venture proved to be. Thus, Sanford Shipping was born."

Another clue to the enigmatic earl and his family fell
into place. Lydia scanned the wall. Each portrait became
a puzzle piece setting neatly into another. Gone were
blank stares, blank faces of the past; real men and women
whispered their faint stories. Her gaze flitted from picture
to picture, fathoming details, and unfolding secrets: Lord
George Sanford, father of the current earl, moderately
handsome, with a gentle soul's face, and beside him a
beauteous, haughty-eyed Lady E., as the servants called
her. What did she hide behind those imperious eyes?
What of the children caught beneath the weight of family
duty, dreams, and desires?

"Because your father was never able to fully follow his
passion, the same one you share. Your scientific work."
Lydia's fingertips touched her lips to stem the tide of
revelatory words. Then her hand dropped to her chest.
Sudden knowledge tumbled from mind to mouth. "And
you admire him greatly but refuse to let the same fate
befall you. You'll take your scientific work over all things
Greenwich, thank you very much."

The corners of his mouth quirked upward, but astonishment lit his eyes.

"Very good. I knew I'd chosen well." He winked,
and his shoulder bumped hers playfully. "We're
making progress."

She returned his smile. "But this whole arrangement
between us must put a crimp in your plans."

"Hmmm...all will work, I'm sure, before time runs
out." He glanced once more at the portraits, appearing
lost in thought.

Before time runs out? He'd spoken of time constraints before. What did he mean by that?

A twinge of a question wanted to follow that cryptic announcement, but Lord Greenwich didn't make eye contact. She was about to probe, when he smiled, as one confidante to another, and offered his arm.

"Shall we?"

Lydia leaned close to him as they strolled across the gallery, the warmth of camaraderie and a shared confidence forging a new bond, an intimacy of trust. Her cheek grazed his sleeve, and she breathed his clean scent: plain soap and warmth, if one could capture the scent of warmth. She would never have thought an academic could be so masculine and arousing, but the Earl of Greenwich was pleasant, intriguing depth in a man.

As they exited the gallery, he broke from her to shut the doors and turned again to face her. Grand gilt-edged doors framed him, but his lips twitched with that brigand's smile. His severe black jacket framed an open-necked shirt, buff breeches, and well-worn boots: Lord Greenwich was more country squire than high noble. His queue, a touch messy, contained as much hair as what came loose. He needed…fixing. What she did next seemed so natural.

"Your tie." Lydia faced him and rose on tiptoe. Reaching past his shoulder, her fingers breezed his neck as she pulled slowly on the black velvet strip until it came loose in her hand. "I've untied you, but we'll fix that."

Her gaze went from the gallery doors back to him.

His lashes hooded dark penetrating eyes. They stood so close, barely touching, but the charged current stopped her breath. Lydia saw each minute stitch on his coat collar. She glanced down, and mere inches of air separated her body from his. The earl's frame visibly stiffened, like a stringed instrument taut and ready. She searched his face, the scars, white and dark lines, some puckering and some straight, against tan skin, and then a barely discernible lift of his eyebrow.

An invitation.

She swallowed and let headiness overtake her. Lydia followed his lure, drawn to him, closing one intoxicating inch after another until they touched. Waves of awareness swept her body: his warmth to hers, hard planes to soft curves, and they fit. Lord Greenwich's hands slipped around her waist to the small of her back.

Her heart pounded, making breathing hard. Was there room for her lungs the way her heart was expanding? The sensory overload was too much. She shut her eyes, all the better to lose herself in his scent. Her forehead tipped into the exposed V of his shirt, and her face grazed the warm landscape of his chest. She breathed him in, the heat and scent of his skin, and let her lips skim fabric and flesh. Close as they were, the earl was an elixir, and she was drowning in him. Her fingers curled into fists, gripping his jacket for dear life.

His hands swept slow circles up and down her back, leaving a trail of warmth and comfort swirling across her back. He touched her the way a sculptor smoothed contours, patient strokes that brought a form to life. Her body tingled in response to the palpable pleasure. Calluses on his palms made snicking sounds on wool from a slow upward sweep to her shoulders, as if he would tactilely memorize her shape. His lips skimmed the crown of her head, and his voice came rough and thick.

"Lydia, I—"

"My lord, Mr. Bacon—Oh!" a female voice said from the hallway.

Lydia jerked from the embrace, scalded by another feminine voice dousing the moment's closeness. A very surprised Miss Mayhew halted in the act of coming around the corner, her mouth agape but quickly shut. Lord Greenwich kept one hand splayed across the small of Lydia's back.

"Jonas is here?"

The housekeeper's features morphed to bland coolness, and she clasped her fingers loosely at her waist.

"Yes, he just came from London and waits for you in the study with two large crates." She glanced at Lydia with blank eyes and at the velvet tie dangling from her fingers. "And, Miss Montgomery, your art supplies arrived as well. Where would you like them?"

Lydia, a riot of sensitized nerves, hid the incriminating velvet scrap in the folds of her skirt. Her mind raced, recalling the few rooms she'd explored on her way to dinner last night.

"The, the ballroom, if you please."

"Of course." And then she was gone, her starched skirts rustling from her exit.

Mortified, Lydia clamped her eyes shut and spoke under her breath. "Of all the people…"

Lord Greenwich removed his hand from her back, and the absence of it was noticeable.

"Tell me you're not still holding that misconception about her."

Lydia opened her eyes to find Lord Edward, arms crossed and mildly peeved.

"No." She exhaled the breath she must've been holding. But of all the people to intrude and witness that intimate moment.

Her brain had just begun to change the picture of Miss Mayhew from beautiful, mysterious housekeeper to a woman wronged and due some empathy. But this was not new information for Lord Greenwich to assimilate. He turned around and pointed to his untied hair.

"Would you?"

Of course, he expected her to take everything in stride in the same manner he did. Everything was old history for him, but for her there was so much to digest. And there was the matter of that embrace and near kiss.

"Oh, yes." Lead-like fingers went mechanically about gathering his hair: one part the drugging effect of their embrace and another a vague, unnamed emotion.

"I have one redeeming quality—loyalty—to those I count as friend, few and far as they are. I could never turn my back on them. Now you understand why I'd never send Claire packing."

Lydia stared straight ahead and gave him a noncommittal, "Mmmm."

The velvet moved through her fingers and began to form the required knot. That vague emotion took shape as she slowly completed her tender task. She noticed lighter skin rimming his hairline at his nape. Lydia stroked the black velvet, and her knuckles skimmed his flesh. Layers had been peeled back between them, uncovering raw vulnerability. Loyalty was not something the earl gave to many, but to those he did, it was unshakable.

She should *never* do anything to harm that loyalty once given to her—if he ever would.

Lydia brushed his shoulders of miniscule dust, like a shopkeeper's wife sending her husband off to his labors, and his lordship stood for the commonplace gesture. Her mother's letter, however brief, was a noticeable weight in her pocket. And she'd let her brain fall into a muddle with this man. But now was not the time to plead her mother's case. Soon.

Void of words, she let her hands drop to her sides, curling and uncurling them. Very much, she needed her hands on paintbrushes and canvas and paint, to mix pigments and oils, creating something new. How many days since she last painted? She needed linseed oil on her hands, a bland aroma to many but perfume to her. Her senses buzzed with the need to express herself in her favorite form: painting.

Lord Greenwich defied her brand of logic and understanding, turning her neat, ordered world on end.

And as surely as she breathed, Lydia wanted Miss Mayhew gone.

Twelve

Because a thing seems difficult for you,
do not think it impossible for anyone to accomplish.
— Marcus Aurelius

ROUGH, WATER-STAINED CRATES PROMISED GOOD news, or so he hoped. The pair of them, lined up end to end before his desk, was as out of place in the well-appointed study as rabble-rousers gathering for teatime. So was Jonas, for that matter, his shaved pate showing black stubble. His friend and man of business, garbed in coarse attire today, often bore the brunt of quick judgment from those assuming the worst, but common veneers often veiled treasures within.

Edward ambled quietly across the carpet with another question hanging: What would the artistic eye of Miss Montgomery think of the contents? That such a question sprang to mind made him smirk with self-deprecating humor. Her morning sketches pleased him. Her skills, so far, went beyond the typical "I-can-sketch" boast of many females listing their qualifications. What's more, he wanted her to be equally enthusiastic about what nestled in the straw. That he valued the opinion of an uneducated woman was at once humbling and enlightening.

Neither could he ignore truth's pressure: much rode on the success or failure of what they pulled from the crates today.

Jonas wielded a crowbar, and wood and nails whined at the Colonial's intrusion, but the crate's lid opened wide its maw to reveal an abundance of yellow straw. Jonas, his sleeves already rolled up, dug into the straw 'til he found a prize. Out came a bright blue and white dish, painted in facsimile to the high-priced Chinese style that was all the rage in homes, from merchants of some means to England's finest estates.

"Has Cookworthy done it?" Edward asked when he drew near.

Jonas glanced up from his labors and nodded. "Think so. Feels light to me." One meaty hand clamped a plate that he held up for scrutiny. "Looks the same as the goods from China."

Edward reached for the plate. "Let me see." He examined the dish, lifting it high to overcast daylight spilling through sheer white curtains. Light limned the thin, round rim of the plate.

Victory. The sublime marriage of art and science finally achieved.

"He's perfected the hard-paste process," Edward said with awe. "This one feels light as air." He tapped the dish on the desk gently, then banged harder. "Doesn't shatter."

They pulled out the porcelain piece after piece, lining up dishes on his mahogany desk, the bright white and brilliant blue dishware so out of place with the somber greens and browns of his study. They made a point of raising each one to the window's light, checking for telltale markers, translucent rims, followed by tapping the dishware for durability. They worked in silence, occasionally murmuring a comment or two. Then Jonas raised an oval serving tray to the light, shifting the platter this way and that.

"How goes it with your guest from the Blue Cockerel?" He passed the tray for Edward's inspection.

Neither man gave eye contact while keeping up the business of their tactile and visual inspection of the goods.

"She's surprising, stimulating, and..." Edward let his words drift as he traced the rough, imperfect border of cobalt blue paint on a small creamer.

"And?"

"Fascinating. Defies words." He put the creamer on its miniature plate setting. "David's report failed to convey her true essence."

"Is that possible?" Jonas stood up, dusting off his hands. "Hire a solicitor to investigate the *essence* of a woman? Especially one you'll be shackled to 'til your eternal reward."

His friend grinned from ear to ear as he rolled one of his thin beard braids between his thumb and forefinger. Edward shrugged away the jibe and went to pull the servant's bellpull near the window.

"What else could I do?"

"The normal things. Dance attendance on her, talk with her. You don't *read* about a woman to understand her."

"I'm not a complete imbecile with the fairer sex. You know very well the genesis of my bargain with her, as

well as my...time constraints and singular situation."
Edward set one hand at his hip and searched the space
beyond Jonas, seeking the right word to describe what he
wanted. "I seek...to enjoy congenial relations with her.
That's all. This is not meant to be a love match."

Jonas's eyes rounded a fraction. "Then there's the
possibility? Of love?"

Edward snorted at that. "Don't go maudlin on me. I
want a peaceful household. Period." With good humor,
he finished with a friendly verbal jab: "And what makes you
the expert on women? When's the last time you had successful parley with a woman that lasted longer than a minute?"

Jonas scratched his hairy cheeks, grinning. "Call me a
cautious combatant. Sharing what little I've learned with
a fellow foot soldier as I come and go."

"Precisely. You can afford your freedom, while I
cannot." Distracted, Edward checked the window where
dust billowed in the distance. An oncoming carriage?

"Have you sampled her charms?"

That snapped his attention back to Jonas. His friend's
direct question was not a surprise; they shared deep trust
earned by trying times, but the query struck a tender
nerve. He didn't want to sully Miss Montgomery's
already tarnished reputation, and more important, he
didn't want his friend to think less of her.

Edward leaned his hip against the windowsill and
chose his words with care. "Let's say we're observing
certain proprieties."

Jonas stopped twirling his beard braid and studied him
a second in that flat, assessing way of his. That thread
of conversation ended when Rogers appeared in the
doorway, adjusting his livery.

"You rang, my lord?"

"Yes, please ask Miss Montgomery to join us for tea and—" Edward pivoted toward the window, every sense alert.

He groaned at the sight of the ominous carriage tearing through the distant Greenwich gate. He squinted to be sure, and like any stalwart warrior facing a difficult skirmish, he swore softly under his breath.

"What is it?" Jonas asked.

"Make that tea for four," Edward called to the footman.

He gripped a handful of curtains, making certain he'd correctly identified the oncoming carriage, but there'd be no denying the owner of the black conveyance trimmed with lots of flashy red and yellow.

"Very good, milord." Rogers bowed and was in the act of shutting the door.

"And, Rogers."

"Yes, milord?"

"Gird your loins, man."

The footman blinked, holding the door half-open. "Beg pardon, sir?"

"Alert the staff, especially Miss Mayhew, my mother's come to call, and by the muster of trunks strapped atop her carriage, she'll be with us a few days." Edward nodded at the oncoming carriage and four, not relishing the next hour, much less the next few days.

Rogers's eyes bulged like two marbles. "I will, sir."

Jonas began to replace the dishes in the crate. "Shall I make myself scarce?"

"No. Stay. And leave the dishes. I'd like Miss Montgomery to see them." Edward crossed his arms as the coach, pulled by immaculate grays, heaved to a halt. "It'd be good for the countess to see them as well."

Jonas reached behind his back and pulled a pair of pistols tucked into his breech's waistband. Then he grabbed another hidden in his boot.

"What shall I do with these?" His large hands gripped the barrels, muzzle down, but his eye sparked with mischief. "Or do you need to arm yourself?"

"Tea is still a peaceful pursuit. Or will be in my home." Edward yanked open a drawer in his desk, but his attention focused on the minor uproar beyond the window. "Put them here."

Jonas settled his small armory and shut the drawer to brace five fingertips on an open space atop the desk while watching the production outside with a bemused smile. Edward was thankful his friend abided the countess's sharp, disapproving tongue with good humor and patience. He grasped a handful of curtains for a better view of the unfolding drama on his front drive. Cold emanated from the clear, tall panes. His mother never comprehended how her good life came to fruition, nor did she understand the sacrifices he made to keep the deathbed promise given to his father, a promise of deep personal cost.

His rubbing shoulders with commoners kept her in the manner she dearly enjoyed, such as paying for the pair of footmen who scurried from the back of her ostentatious carriage. In mere seconds, those strapping lads had adjusted their wigs, tugged on bright red livery, while brushing travel dust from their sleeves. One set red lacquer steps at the carriage door, while the other unrolled a narrow red carpet stretching the distance to the front stone steps. The brawny lads exchanged a speaking glance, nodded once, and taking a deep breath, one opened the door with a flourish while the other raised his arm as a banister for the elegantly clad virago stepping from the carriage. First came a well-shod foot, a high-heeled golden silk shoe tied with an oversized red bow, followed by another well-shod foot, and volumes of gold and white silk.

Jonas picked up some loose straw from the floor and stuffed it back into the crate. "Not a planned visit, I take it?"

Edward waved from the window when his mother caught sight of him, and a delicate frown marred her perfect face. She would not condescend to wave; instead, her gloved hand patted the high sweep of powdered blond hair off her forehead while her maid fussed and fluffed her ladyship's ensemble. Public displays of affection, even on Greenwich Park's front drive, never made for good appearances.

"Planned? No, but inevitable." He sighed, letting the curtains fall. "Before the meeting at the Blue Cockerel, I sent word to her about my plan to marry Miss Montgomery. Should've waited on that."

"And now she comes to meet your intended." Jonas unrolled his wrinkled sleeves as they moved to the seating area by the hearth.

"More likely to voice her disapproval of my decision."

"Does that matter?" Jonas put on his plain, black-skirted coat and settled himself in the leather great chair, facing him.

Edward removed his jacket and slung it over the back of his chair by the roaring hearth. That small rebellion of his youth would remain. He took his seat with an eye to the door.

"Approve or disapprove," he mused aloud, tapping steepled fingers together. "I don't care, but I want her to like Miss Montgomery…at least be affable to her."

"Like her? Doubtful. Your mother'd find fault with Queen Charlotte's daughters, if any were old enough to wed."

"What about you?" he asked, watching his friend for subtle reactions to the sudden question. "Do you like Miss Montgomery? What little you know of her, I mean."

Jonas's black brows shot up at that. "Does it matter?"

Edward was spared having to answer that nettlesome question when the countess entered the study, and all fell within cannon range of her sharp opinions. His mother swept through the partially open doorway unannounced, patting three blond coils perfectly arrayed over her collarbone. She gave the half-open door a slight frown. In his mother's opinion, doors in an organized household were opened all the way or shut completely: anything else signaled a home on the brink of shoddy management.

She moved past that minor household catastrophe, her wide silk skirts swishing a fierce sound as terrifying as any cavalry charge. She stopped short of her forward march and waited in the middle of the study like a captious general pulling rank.

"Well?" She clasped lily-white hands together high on her waist. Her arms formed parts of two perfect triangles, with lace-encrusted elbows jutting from her sides.

The countess had come to do battle.

Edward slipped from his chair, stiff armed and stiff necked, as he moved across thick forest-green carpeting.

"Welcome, Mother." He lightly touched her shoulder and bent his unscarred cheek toward hers.

Of course, he honored the rules on how to greet her: maintain an inch of space so as not to disturb the light dusting of pale powder on her cheek. Her rouged lips kissed the air beside his ear, but one soft hand gripped his arm with iron will, not letting him pull away.

"I hope you had a good journey," he said. "What brings you to Greenwich Park?"

"I did not, thank you very much. How could I, after I received your dreadful missive? And you know quite well why I'm here." Her sharp glance shot toward the fireplace, where Jonas rose from his seat. "Where is she?"

Edward ignored the question and escorted her to the settee facing the fire, and propriety first, motioned to Jonas. "You remember Mr. Bacon."

"Good to see you, ma'am." Jonas bent low from the waist.

"I see you still prefer spending time with rough Colonials." She sniffed, causing her nose to tip a notch higher, but at least she gave Jonas a tight smile.

"Jonas is a friend and does excellent work for Sanford Shipping. And he's from the East Midlands, remember?"

The countess perched herself on the settee's edge, her back plumb-line straight, but her manicured fingers dug into his arm as he leaned near, only a step away from the safe haven of his great chair. Today, she could not be bothered to give further commentary on Jonas; his mother had bigger battles to wage.

"I ask again, where is this *commoner* you claim you'll wed?" Her voice shook with unrestrained ire.

"Right here, my lady," Lydia called from the doorway, her voice breezy and light.

She clutched her brown shawl around her shoulders as her skirts swung from long, purposeful strides. Miss Montgomery walked over to the hearth to face the half circle of people, but lowered herself in a deep curtsy to his mother first, even before Edward began the introduction. Good. She innately understood that appeasement protocol.

"Pleased to meet you, my lady. My lord." She nodded at Edward and gave Jonas a shallow dip, finishing with measured caution. "Mr. Bacon. How nice to see you again."

Miss Montgomery planted herself on the brown-and-green-striped settee, wiggling her back into the corner, adjusting loose pillows for comfort. The furniture shook a little from her movements, and her hem was wet with bits of grass clinging to some threads unraveling there.

His mother's stern stare grazed Miss Montgomery's simple, outdated attire, faded from years of wash and wear. She lingered on the brown shawl peppered with holes. The countess gave the woolen wrap the distaste one saves for an awful, hideous insect. His mother hummed a disapproving sound in her throat, and crossed elegantly shod feet at the ankles, allowing artful red ribbons to show under her pristine silk hem.

"*This* is to be the next Countess of Greenwich? Tell me you jest. You cannot marry her." She shook her head, and cylindrical gold curls bounced from the emphatic quake. "She's terribly inappropriate for the position. Just look at her."

"You don't have a say in that," Edward said, leaning into the chair's wide back, but all of his body tensed for the inevitable attack. He braced himself over a more pressing question: What would be Miss Montgomery's response? "And Miss Montgomery's not filling a post. She's becoming my wife. Big difference."

The countess snorted, really a slight huff, since women in her position made no such indelicate sounds. His mother harbored a differing opinion on the role of countess.

"Have you no regard for the lineage?" she sniped.

From the doorway, Claire entered, followed by Rogers and another footman. Both men were wide-armed with trays laden with tea and finger foods, but at least the distraction spared him a moment of battle. Good.

"And here's Miss Mayhew with some tea," he said, smiling at his ally-in-arms.

A flicker of malevolence crossed Claire's face before she pasted on her serene housekeeper's mask.

"And yes, Mother, I'm familiar with family history. The desirable and undesirable parts."

His mother failed to acknowledge Claire, as the housekeeper whispered instructions to the servants. The countess's tourmaline-blue gaze slid from the silent Jonas and Miss Montgomery back to him.

"Edward, I would rather we take tea *en prive*." One golden eyebrow arced with suggestive command as to how emphatic her preference.

"No. Miss Montgomery is very much a part of this, and Jonas, like you, has just journeyed here and is no doubt hungry and thirsty." He tipped his head toward the dish-covered desktop. "And he comes bearing gifts, for which I'd very much like to hear your thoughts, as well as Miss Montgomery's."

That he sought her judgment on something appeased the countess, at least he assumed so by the flash of surprise in her eyes. Alas, the peace was short-lived.

"I'm glad you seek my opinion in some matters, but this plan of yours…" His mother's rouged lips pursed so hard, tiny lines sketched the outline of her mouth.

The footmen set the trays on the wide oval table before the settee. And Miss Montgomery leaned too far forward to retrieve the delicate rose-painted teapot, but her hands stopped short of touching the porcelain.

"Shall I serve, my lady?"

"Oh, please do," his mother said with an unkind gleam in her eye. She turned to Edward, and her accusing glare spoke volumes: *Watch her inept skills at tea.*

Edward couldn't be bothered with Society's ridiculous requirement that women present themselves well at tea. The notion that tea service ranked high in marital requirements struck him as absurd, an idea he voiced a time or two in the past. To drive home her point on this salient issue, the countess wore the closest thing to a sneer as Miss Montgomery clinked and banged her way around fine china, demonstrating finesse on par with Jonas's ham-handed talents in serving refreshments.

But the winning salvo belonged to Miss Montgomery.

"I, for one, would like to express my enthusiasm for his lordship's plans of procreation," she said, her perceptive green gaze sweeping from him to the countess. "Consider me an eager and willing partner to carry on the family lineage."

Jonas coughed behind his balled fist.

The retreating footmen banged into each other behind Jonas's chair as they stared bug-eyed at Miss Montgomery.

And the countess inhaled sharply. His mother failed to anticipate her adversary sharing the settee. Edward could almost read his mother's mind as she tried to weigh Miss Montgomery: Is the young woman soft in the head? Or a complete brazen? He pressed his lips together, holding back his grin at the unexpected conversation twist.

His Miss Montgomery, one hand gripping the embellished handle of the teapot, turned a careful eye on the stream of tea pouring into another rose-petal cup. The pitcher went horizontal for a moment, and she smiled with an insouciant light in her eyes.

"You know, my lady, his lordship interviewed me extensively, and in a manner of speaking, I'm quite appropriate for the...*position*—"

Jonas doubled over with another loud cough but managed to say, "You sound very congenial to me."

"Oh, dear, Mr. Bacon. Please, drink some tea for that cough," she said with some concern, passing a cup and saucer.

"Thank you, miss." His hulking friend accepted the proffered tea with a jovial smile.

Edward shot Jonas a stern glance. He didn't need another voice fanning flames of conflict by dumping earlier, privately stated words into the arena. Jonas was never a big talker, so that quip of his came as a surprise. But the best way to shut the man's mouth was with food and drink. Miss Montgomery became an accidental ally by quickly delivering tea to Jonas, but then she turned her focus back on the countess.

"His lordship found I'm more than adequate for the task." One corner of her hoyden's mouth curved up as she verbally caressed that final word. She tipped the pot, and finished splashing tea into the last cup with only a dribble hitting the tray. "Of course, you would have concerns about this, it's only natural."

Edward watched her play hostess, holding back the odd mixture of mirth and reproof that played in his head. He wasn't sure if he should kiss or scold the minx the first moment they found themselves *en prive*. The idea of his lips touching hers brought a new spark to this uncomfortable venue. But her brazen innuendo set the countess back. Good, Miss Montgomery could hold her own doing battle with his mother, and her quick reconnaissance of the situation, along with her choice to adroitly stand her ground, impressed him.

Both footmen, however, lingered in the background too long as they gawked. Claire's polite cough came from the doorway, and they quit the room in haste.

Claire frowned at the lads, who were sure to get a set down once out of sight. Miss Montgomery needed just such a scolding, if he could deliver it straight-faced, but he'd give her the lead for now and see how far this went. That his mother was momentarily speechless, near gulping hot tea, was a battle coup, and judging from the paleness of her features under her powder, she raised a tentative white flag of surrender.

"I can see my son finds you most entertaining. He has a penchant for surrounding himself with"—his mother paused and gave a pointed look at Jonas with his braided beard—"unique and colorful people not of his station. I do not deceive myself. You are simply another one of the oddities with which he surrounds himself." The countess held her cup elegantly and finished, "But what, pray tell, will happen when you go out into Society?"

His mother replaced her cup with a triumphant clink. The regrouping had already begun.

Miss Montgomery fidgeted on the settee, and drops of tea splashed her fingers and skirt. "Lud, but I hadn't anticipated that." She kept her eyes glued to the offending liquid, setting her cup down with a rattle and clank, to snatch a napkin. "Perhaps you can give me some guidance? Daughters of the nobility are taught proper decorum. Why not me?"

His mother's blue eyes glittered as she watched the napkin unravel from its careful fold. The cloth flopped about like a helpless fish on land as Miss Montgomery wiped her fingers and rubbed the napkin across two coin-sized spots on her skirt.

"We speak of young ladies of noble birth." She huffed again as the corners of her mouth drooped. "Their training takes *years*, and begins early in their upbringing. And you, my dear, are not fresh from the schoolroom." His mother's small nostrils flared as she delivered that thinly veiled set down.

"Then my maturity works in our favor, doesn't it? Because I'm a fast learner." Miss Montgomery winked at the countess and reached for a petit-four with her fingers. A crumb fell into her lap as she popped the tiny delicacy into her mouth, then she brushed the crumb onto the floor.

The countess's perfectly plucked eyebrows pressed together at the ill-mannered display, but Jonas kept a stoic face in his corner of the arena.

Lydia chewed the tiny confection quickly and swallowed. "I'm putty in your hands, my lady. I ask only that I have an hour or two to sketch for his lordship and a few hours to paint for my own pleasure, and then I'm yours for countess training."

Miss Montgomery reached for a larger pastry, balancing the flaky crust on her jumbled napkin. His mother's eyes narrowed on the continued evidence of rustic manners.

"Painting?" The countess lifted a small plate and pinched silver tongs on a miniature biscuit. "You do watercolor? I've enjoyed a bit of painting from time to time."

"Watercolor? No, I work strictly in oils." She took a healthy bite, and apple filling squished out the side onto the napkin. She chewed, swallowed, and swiped a corner of her mouth. "Such a blasted mess I'm making. Tea was much simpler with my great-aunt, what with the smaller tray and simpler food."

Jonas chuckled softly from his corner and nodded his agreement before taking a healthy swallow of tea. The Countess's stiff spine went straighter, though he didn't think that possible. She sipped slowly from her cup and watched the fire in silence, her face a mask of decorum and stillness.

The unfolding play turned from skirmish to truce, but Edward, setting his teacup back in its saucer, didn't trust his mother's slight, amicable shift in conversation; this was a change in tactics. She didn't come all this way to give up in one meeting. No, she'd come at Miss Montgomery or him or both with new armaments. He'd never known his mother to quit easily, but then, Miss Montgomery deserved praise for courage under fire. The fact that she was not a simpering country miss probably set the countess into another momentary retreat.

"Oils." Jonas spoke into the arena, reaching for a plate

and heaping it high with the table's offerings. "I thought only portraitists and professional painters used oils."

And then Miss Montgomery dropped an altogether different salvo into the theater of battle.

"After we're married, I plan to sell my artwork. In London. The sooner the better." Miss Montgomery set her becrumbed napkin on the closest tray and licked her lips. "It's what I've been working for these past three years."

"What have you been working for? Selling your art? Or marriage?" Jonas asked, selecting a biscuit from the mound of food on his too small plate.

"My art, of course."

Another facet revealed itself from the diamond in the rough known as Miss Montgomery. Edward glanced at Jonas, whom he expected to be full of mirth at the pronouncement, but instead, a different light shone in his friend's eyes. His man of business tipped his head in something of an admiring salute. Miss Montgomery may not have garnered Jonas's friendship, but she'd surely won his respect. Work was not a dirty word to his friend. His mother, however, let decorum slip when her jaw near unhinged. Of course, that moment was short-lived, for she needed full use of her mouth to heap words of malcontent.

"Edward! She can't be serious. Did you know about this crude merchant's behavior?" His mother asked the question but charged ahead, not waiting for his reply. "That will besmirch our good name. People of our class purchase goods. We *don't* hawk them on roadways like street urchins."

"Of course, I'll not *hawk them* as you say on street

corners, my lady." Miss Montgomery made that statement as if she were the voice of reason. "I'll be discreet and sell them through a solicitor in your London town house when I host an art salon."

"What?" The countess gasped, and her head swiveled from Miss Montgomery to Edward. "You cannot allow your future wife to engage in anything so, so vulgar as… *commerce*." She spoke that last word as if it were vile on her tongue. "This plan of yours to marry a commoner is folly." Her chin pointed as high as her neck would allow. "I'll not stand for it."

Edward's elbows pressed into the chair's plush leather arms. He didn't answer right away. His mind ticked, mulling over this new side of Miss Montgomery. Fundamentally, he had nothing against commerce; business simply failed to hold his interest compared to science. Mercantile endeavors provided minimal appeal but had become a financial necessity. That a *woman* could engage in such a practice bore careful consideration.

Weren't there plenty of English wives of the craftsman and artisan class who partnered with their husbands, thus adding to family coffers? Logic supported this notion. But none of those women were the Countess of Greenwich, a factor that carried some weight.

"Edward. This is unconscionable." His mother's voice was close to shrill when he failed to respond. "Did you know about this?"

The cup and saucer rattled in her hands, threatening to upend on shimmering skirts.

He raised his hand, halting the feminine stream of words from the settee. "You know how I feel about hysterics."

Miss Montgomery spoke into the fray, tugging her

shawl tighter about her shoulders. "There are plenty of female artists. Why Clara Peeters of Flanders does wonderful still lifes and supports herself admirably—"

"Ahhh," the countess groaned, shocked speechless. She touched her hairline where Edward was sure a *mal-a-tête*, real or fake, formed.

"And there's Lavinia Fontana, an Italian artist. People pay a pretty penny for her work," Miss Montgomery said with firmness, defending her position like a stalwart soldier.

His mother winced and groaned anew at the mention of something so crass as a pretty penny. Jonas finished off his biscuit in silence, his alert stare darting from one woman to the other, and Miss Montgomery battled on with her defense.

"And there's Maria van Oosterwyck. Why you have one of her paintings here in your own gallery."

Edward pushed off the chair, deciding to interject objectivity into the heated arena of female emotions. No, with his mother, simple reality would do. He wasn't decided yet on what exactly to do about Miss Montgomery's ambition, but he'd dissemble that topic later. There wasn't time, however, to negotiate for another future countess. His deadline loomed, and he rather liked the current candidate sitting in his study, truth be told.

But he needed to deal with one issue at a time, and Edward grudgingly admitted his mother had some parts right. Miss Montgomery needed lessons in comportment, if only to ease her navigation of Society as mother to the Greenwich heir would require. Women could be such cats, making life miserable for another of their sex, if they so decided. Miss Montgomery deserved a fair start, and his mother was the perfect teacher for that realm. But first things first. He needed calm in his household.

Edward strode to his desk, where tangible materials for his point waited. Some bits of straw remained scattered on the floor, crunching under his boots. He heard the loud rustle of silk behind him as the countess must have swiveled around on the settee to follow his path to the open crates. When he looked over, he saw a great deal of the whites of her eyes.

"Edward, are you listening?" His mother gripped the back of the settee as one might grab the rail of a small boat—while watching her larger ship sink.

"They're all fine artists, my lady. Their work's well received here in England." Miss Montgomery's voice raised a notch in volume and firmness as she defended what was clearly a passion of hers.

His mother groaned. "Yes, *Continentals*, all of them." She pivoted on the settee, and when facing Miss Montgomery, her voice rose to quavering heights. "It's simply *not* done in England."

Edward picked up the small creamer pitcher he'd examined earlier, remembering his joy and awe at the triumph of science and invention. He glanced at the tableau before him: his mother outraged, her earbobs swinging from the furious movement of her head jerking from Miss Montgomery to him; Miss Montgomery's glass-green eyes were as set as her stubborn chin; and Jonas, sitting a safe distance behind the battle line of upset women, hiding his amusement in what now must be lukewarm tea. Edward cradled the creamer in both hands and planted his hip on the side of his desk.

"Ladies, would you join me?" One boot braced the

floor, while he hooked his knee over the desk corner. "I've some things to show you."

His mother touched her temple and spoke sharply. "This is not the time to discuss Greenwich dishware."

"I say it is." The firmness of his tone brooked no disagreement as he faced the women. "Both of you. Over here." Then he tipped his head and softened the command. "If you please."

Miss Montgomery's mouth pursed like a recalcitrant schoolgirl, but she slid off the settee. She sauntered over, jamming her arms across her chest, and the holes in her shawl stretched even more across her shoulders. His mother followed, sighing and pinching her skirts. She moved to the other side of Edward, keeping a mutinous distance.

He waved an arm over the display. "Please, examine the dishes and tell me what you see."

His mother huffed but picked up a soup bowl, and Miss Montgomery held out her hand for the creamer cradled in his.

"May I?" She gave him a level gaze.

Her eyes burned dark green, but the way her gaze flicked from the small dishware and back to his eyes told him she would bear him out on this. Good. He liked that quality; that bespoke the ability to give and take reason. More women needed this, in his opinion.

"What you hold in your hands, ladies, is the perfect joining of art and science: the work of a chemist friend of mine, William Cookworthy." He took a slow breath and said quietly, "A commoner whose genius may save us with the manufacture of light, pretty porcelain dishes affordable for the masses."

Miss Montgomery's gaze snapped wide as he spoke. Did she comprehend his subtle clue? She stepped closer, and that simple movement into his sphere stirred his senses. Her lemongrass scent, a slight whiff, reached him. Her head tipped in that subtle way when she listened intently, and a new, smoldering current radiated between them.

But beside him, his mother bristled as she turned the soup dish around for cursory inspection.

"That's all well and good. But I fail to see how dish-ware saves anyone," his mother said with stinging sharpness. "Your preoccupation with science, your scientific friends…it dwarfs even your father's past preoccupation. And this"—his mother clutched the bowl with both hands, as if she would use it as a battering ram—"this *dish* is a paltry thing compared to the matter of the Greenwich family line. Why are we wasting time here?"

Eyes locked with Miss Montgomery, Edward rubbed his scarred jaw, and his gaze traced her green eyes and dropped to her full mouth. He hadn't tested those lips yet. Why not? He was so close outside the gallery. The way one of her thick brows shot up, she knew the lay of thoughts. Was he that transparent? The brown shawl was adjusted across his quarry's shoulders, a subtle statement that that avenue was shut for the moment, and he'd better finish his point.

"Because, I expect these dishes, and many more like them, to keep you living in the manner to which you are accustomed." He broke eye contact with Miss Montgomery, and facing the countess, he picked up a plate. "The sale of this plate and many others like it will pay for lots of fancy carriages, maintain both your luxurious households, and keep you in those shoes you insist on buying at prices that boggle the mind."

His mother's red lips clamped in a tight line, but she replaced the bowl carefully to its spot on the desk.

"Edward. What are you saying?"

"I'm saying that if you want to continue to receive your exorbitant annual allowance, we need commoners, and we need commerce. This hard-paste porcelain"—he tipped the flat of the plate toward his mother then returned it to the desk—"sturdy and inexpensive, will enable us to continue living well."

Miss Montgomery studied the creamer, turning it over in her hands.

"What you see here," Edward said while waving his arm over the desk, "will lead to the fruits of commerce, however vulgar that may be to your delicate ears. Truth is, after Jon's death, Sanford Shipping fell into disarray. Between that and Father's illness, the family coffers dwindled. The Greenwich entailment yields middling rents, and Father's investments of years ago went dry long before he died."

"Then make up for it with an advantageous marriage," the countess said, tipping her nose high.

"And repeat that debacle with the Blackwoods?" His mouth stretched into a wide, unfriendly smile. "No thank you."

"There are others," his mother huffed.

"I'd rather handle fiscal matters the only way I know how: science." He crossed his arms over his chest. "Cookworthy approached me about a partnership last year. His chemistry was sound, and Sanford Shipping, thanks to Jonas, had a good year. So, I invested. Now he's perfected what the Chinese have mastered for years, a hard-paste porcelain. As we speak, our solicitor attends the patent of our joint partnership with Cookworthy Dish Manufacturer. The success of which I am confident will buy as many ostentatious carriages as you could ever imagine owning."

"Oh, Edward." Lines bracketed his mother's mouth, but this startling knowledge stymied her for the moment.

"You tolerated Jon's foray into shipping because it provided a distraction—"

The countess's head snapped to attention, and his words that flowed so easily froze. A mosaic of emotions etched fine lines around his mother's eyes. Edward softened his voice, treading with care in that most painful of places.

"But Sanford Shipping proved to be a boon. Needful commerce, if you will."

Dull aches, like an awful healing bruise, pressed him everywhere as he recalled the agonies of the past. Despite their distance, he was still his mother's son; he needed to tread with care. For no matter what barbs they exchanged, from testy words to harsh rancor, when the countess hurt, so did he. Edward never forgot the day Jon died. His mother cried bitter tears, wailing eviscerating self-recriminations for supporting the first ship that turned into a sizable venture, the venture that swallowed the life of her firstborn son.

After Jon's death, she was so fragile. To bring that history to the fore hurt them both.

She hated all things to do with ships, which made what loomed on his horizon all the more thorny. His mother lightly brushed a dish and turned shrewd eyes on him: she didn't rise from daughter of a borderland baronet to elevated noblewoman without the skill to hone in on the unsaid.

"Very well, I understand the dishes, but why the rush to marry a woman so far beneath your station?" His mother reached out to touch his sleeve, the first true show of tenderness since she arrived. "You're a young man in your prime, still rather handsome, despite your scars and…" Her voice trailed softly as she searched the smooth and scarred planes of his face. "In time, we'll find the right woman for you."

"That's just it. We're running out of time." He gritted his teeth at what was coming.

"So you've mentioned a time or two before," Miss Montgomery said as she set the creamer back in its spot. Her direct green-eyed gaze demanded unvarnished truth. "What do you mean by that? And don't dare brush me aside."

"One of our ships, *The Fiona*, leaves in precisely seventy-eight days." Edward sucked in a deep breath, the same as he did before diving in for a cold swim. "I'll be on it. Gone for two, maybe three years…on a scientific expedition sailing the world. I accept that there's the possibility I may not return…and wish you both would do the same."

Thirteen

If you want to know the mind of a man,
listen to his words.

—Chinese Proverb

LOATHSOME QUIET HUNG OVER THE CAVERNOUS STUDY, a pall as oppressive as a sudden death notice. Emotions jumbled through Lydia, but one of truth's bitter pills surprised her: the earl was like every other man of her life's acquaintance, who in the end, would leave. She harbored the heart of a realist. Men were driven to sate their lusts, be they of the flesh or selfish ambition.

And women of all types and relations were left scattered in their wake.

The earl, like other men she'd known, inveigled matters solely to meet his needs, drawing a woman close with a promising beginning, then left, or would leave, at his convenience. Well, Lord Greenwich hadn't left yet, but his eyes, distant and shuttered, told her in some ways he was as good as gone.

Why did men have such difficulty staying?

"But you could die." The countess wheezed as one hand braced the desk's edge. "You cannot leave me."

Lydia clutched the ends of her shawl low across her abdomen. A protective gesture? But the countess, the way she blanched under white powder, sharp, blinding pain writ years on her fine-boned features. Lydia couldn't say she cared for the noblewoman, but the gut-wrenching news her son delivered just then would level any woman hanging onto her progeny by a thread. She had to act.

"My lady." Lydia wrapped a comforting arm about the countess's shoulders. "Come take a seat near the fire."

The countess accepted her assistance as Lydia shot Lord Greenwich an incriminating glare, but his eyes stayed woefully blank. He rubbed his scarred cheek and watched Lydia coddle his mother, withdrawn from the displays of emotion. What? Did he think his mother wouldn't be affected by this latest news? Men and their irritating bluntness. She settled the countess on the settee, and like a mother hen, sat near the older woman, fussing over her, pouring tepid tea that was refused.

The earl moved to the hearth and rolled a new log onto the waning blaze. He poked and prodded the fire to new life before he turned around to address the consequences of his words. Mr. Bacon, Lydia noticed, sat straight-faced and silent. The blighter probably knew all along what his lordship planned and was in on it. Thick as thieves, those two, and Lydia's harsh stare swept accusingly from one to the other. Lord Greenwich was man enough to speak up first.

"Now you know why I need a wife and that she is...*enceinte* before I leave. I'm making every effort to protect the line, as well as the family coffers, if I fail to return. That was the nature of the promise I made to Father before he died, though he was especially concerned about financial arrangements." His lordship tapped ash from the poker before replacing it on the stand. He clasped his hands behind his back and gave Lydia an apologetic grimace. "Forgive me. This is indelicate but necessary."

"But you could die." The countess, with her tear-glossed, red-rimmed eyes, repeated the words like an accusation. "I need you to stay."

"It's possible with storms, disease, and"—he touched his scarred cheek—"the occasional seafarers bent on murder and mayhem. But I could very well return safe and sound." Then he nodded at his desk. "At least with this new business venture, you will both be financially set."

"But you hardly have time to…to achieve an heir," the countess said, verbally dancing around so delicate a topic. "And there's no guarantee of a male child."

"I realize this, but plans were set in motion last summer when I thought all was resolved with the Blackwoods." He squared his shoulders, but flatness in his eyes and the line of his mouth made him impassive. "Then Miss Blackwood came for a visit."

Uncomfortable silence hummed in the sitting area. No one, save Edward, could truly fathom how painful that visit was. Oh, Lydia wanted to hunt down that silly girl and slap her good. Then she scanned the faces of Mr. Bacon and the countess. Both held very different but very powerful connections to his lordship. Something ran deep between the Colonial and the earl. The Greenwich household's man of business nodded at the earl as if he understood; however, the countess ran counter to all agreement, with her head swiveling side to side as she dabbed watery eyes. Lydia sat in solidarity with the countess, straight-backed and angry.

"Why?" she asked.

"You mean why do I go?" A vertical line marked the space between his brows, and he looked again like the menacing brigand she met a few nights ago.

The earl stood by the hearth, and with his booted legs spread wide, and open-necked, dirt-smudged shirt, he appeared a man of land and sea. He bore the stance of one already on a ship, commanding others to his will. There was nothing dangerously flirtatious about this man. He stood with a purpose that would not be thwarted.

"I will not be moved by feminine tears or pleas to stop this venture. After the first expedition was cut short due to the attack on our ship, I thought I'd recover and turn around for another." His cultured voice took on a note of iron. "But for too long I set aside those plans in favor of family responsibilities: trying to see Jane settled, then searching for her after she ran away in a fit of juvenile rebellion, taking exhaustive care of my mother, and attending the business of all things Greenwich, all while trying to recover from my wounds and neglecting my research. Not anymore."

"But, Edward, you are the *last* of this line." His mother clutched a frilly handkerchief, dabbing watery eyes. "You cannot take any more risks."

His chin dropped to his chest. For a moment, he was the Earl of Greenwich shouldering multiple burdens, but when he raised his head, that man was gone. His thick blond hair was barely restrained by his queue, and those scars, lines and shiny burn spots, stretched over twitching jaw muscles. The man before her bore the intense look of someone with a deep-seated need that must be met, and science was the siren that lured him.

"Father set aside his dreams of astronomy to pursue what was best for the Greenwich name. That work diminished to almost nothing when he spent more time in the House of Lords, even though that wasn't his passion, and well you know. But he filled the role admirably." He paused, and his chest expanded when he took a deep breath. "And even you'll agree Jon wasted his youth in idle, debauched pleasures until he was given purpose. That purpose connected with his passion, his talent in shipping and business. He was good at it. And we prospered."

"And it *killed* him," the countess cried, her body shaking.

Lord Greenwich's brown eyes burned with anger. He opened his mouth as if he were about to speak, but the earl clamped his lips into a narrow line, and he turned away. His lordship leaned an elbow on the dark mantel ledge and stared out the window. Lydia guessed he was going to say something about his brother and Miss Mayhew, and she admired his restraint. But that gain was minimal in life's costs and rewards: he still chose to leave, and that rankled.

"I am stunned, my lord, that you'd bring me here to turn around and leave." She leaned forward on the settee to emphasize her point. "Even I can admit how out of my depth I am with the nobility's silly rules, rules for everything from an able-bodied woman waiting for a footman to help her with a chair to tea service. And there is the matter of selling my artwork. Something you agreed to help me with."

"No. I agreed not to take legal action where it was

justly warranted. And I recall we agreed you would have freedom to paint—" He held up a hand when Lydia opened her mouth to blast him with a few choice words. "I never said anything about helping you in Society or aiding you in selling your art."

"But I'd just as soon stop breathing than not pursue my art!"

"Then we understand each other very well." His dark topaz gaze shot across the space.

Lydia's half-opened mouth froze as that honesty sank into her soul. What had life been like for her these past three years? Had she not quietly sought solicitors in London's cut-rate back alleys for artistic representation when her finances allowed the occasional venture into Town? Slimy, unscrupulous fellows, they were. Yet, even the few she'd met, men more interested in carnal payment that she refused to give, failed to deter her.

Truth really was so simple: painting fed her person the same way that science fed his. Lord Greenwich had charted his course in secret as much as she had done with hers.

Compromise would be impossible.

His shoulders squared under what must be the sense of a tremendous weight, but he pushed on.

"My father and brother finessed their way through life…politics, shipping…both were skilled with people, where I lack all patience," he said quietly, speaking only to her. "My passion, my purpose is science. I've buried this too long."

His firm, cultured voice cloaked a plea that she understand him, and that plea wrapped around her more seductively than the cleverest touch. Her legs tensed, as if she would spring from the furniture at any moment to…

what? Touch him? Lydia gripped the ends of her shawl in both hands, and locked her gaze to his. They could be the only two in the study for all the intensity that flowed between them.

Somewhere in the periphery, Jonas coughed, and the countess sniffed while making use of her handkerchief.

"Time I went to my room and got settled." Jonas rose from his chair and moved around to the settee. "Countess, may I escort you to your room? I'm sure you're in need of rest."

In the nature of a true gentleman, the Colonial offered his arm to the countess, who gripped the beefy forearm like a lifeline.

"Yes, I, I need to lie down." Her voice sounded frail.

Lydia glanced down in her lap, twirling the shawl's fringe, and waited for their exit. Once the door clicked shut, she looked up to see his lordship watching her with smoldering heat in his eyes. Odd how mutual understanding could be an elixir between a man and woman. Lord Greenwich's chest rose and fell under his linen shirt, a steady, hypnotizing rhythm that she couldn't help but follow. Her gaze rose to his lips, the scars crisscrossing his cheek, and she wanted to touch him. Badly.

"I find I want to kiss you, my lord, but I'm baffled by that, since I'm also angry with you at the same time."

"Why?" His lips quirked in a half smile at hearing her quandary.

She slumped back in her seat, sitting in a way no future countess would ever be caught doing. "Because you're turning out like every other man of my existence. Here today. Gone tomorrow. Not that I wanted all of them to stay. There were some I was glad to say good riddance to."

"Such as that farmer you took a tumble with? Or the likes of George Montgomery?"

"Yes, both…though for different reasons." Her eyes spread wide, and her mother's letter came to the fore. "He's gone, you know, as is Tristan."

"I know." His handsome mouth pulled in a line of sympathy. "Jonas watched them board a ship at dawn after our meeting at the Blue Cockerel. They're bound for the Colonies."

Lydia's palm rubbed the square paper still in her pocket.

"Leaving my mother to face…" Her words trailed off from quavering bitterness, and she stared at the floor. She gripped her stomach. A stone could've settled there for all the heaviness. "All those debts. Apparently more than what you mentioned at the Blue Cockerel."

She looked at Lord Greenwich, ready to plead on behalf of her mother, but the tenderness in his brown eyes took her by surprise.

"Wait. Did you know about the other debts?"

"I learned of them, yes." He gave her a warm, genuine smile. "My solicitor is a busy man these days. He gathers the notes as we speak."

Did the light around him grow a little brighter? Was the *Greenwich Recluse* a knight in shining armor?

"Thank you, my lord," she gushed, her shoulders slumping as that burden lifted.

"And I'll pay every last one, even grant your mother an annual stipend after our wedding."

Then his actions weren't all generosity of spirit, but a calculated maneuver to keep her firmly in place.

"Of course, my lord," she said, brittleness lacing her voice.

He couldn't simply perform a kind act; there was a logical means to his ends. Had to be. And keeping her body available for the blasted Greenwich line was something he needed to cross off his list of things to complete before sailing off to who knows where.

His dark eyebrows raised a notch. "One would think that news would please you. Rescuing your mother, providing for her all the rest of her days, not exactly what we originally agreed to, but I understand the need to care for one's mother."

Lydia winced at that truth. She wished he would've offered to save her mum simply for the goodness of it, but he did go above and beyond, looking to the care and concern of others. And their bargain fundamentally stayed the same, benefitting her by removing her mother's debt and by providing a secure future, thus, removing that worry. Save the sticky issue of selling her art, Lydia was very well situated.

"I thank you for your generosity." She fiddled with her shawl, pulling it tighter.

"You're welcome," he said, but a thread of caution entered his voice.

Under his watchful eyes, Lydia could be a young woman just out of the schoolroom, talking with her first suitor, but that was ridiculous. She was older and wiser when it came to men. And what the earl said next brought that into glaring reality.

"You could thank me with a kiss." The corner of his mouth kicked up, bunching the scarred cheek. "If I'm not mistaken, you were very ready to kiss me before."

"No." She folded her arms, a want to dig in her heels taking over. Why did she have the off wish to cry right then?

"But it's only a kiss. No harm in that." He set both hands at his waist. The smile that spread over his face was pure brigand's mischief. "You all but threw yourself at me outside the gallery today."

She laughed at his outrageous comment.

"I did no such thing, my lord." But she could tell by the darkening of his eyes, her laugh, a low, husky sound, did things to him. "But by your own mandated schedule, we'll have barely enough time for any of *that*. You won't reconsider and stay? At least postpone your voyage?"

"No." His brigand's smile faded.

The ease of the moment dispersed. They were at an impasse. His lordship stood more like a statue at the hearth, with his fingers drumming the mantel, while Lydia adjusted her shawl. But neither rushed to exit the room. She wouldn't lose their growing closeness in the face of his determination to leave England. At that, her eyebrows scrunched together.

"Why seventy-eight days?" she asked softly.

"Because my competitor, Joseph Banks, leaves on a similar expedition with Captain Cook sometime in August. If I leave in June, I'll have a two-month head start." He leaned a relaxed shoulder on the mantel.

"But I read once that you both were friends."

"Hmmm, yes, since university." He nodded. "Friends and the greatest competitors in science."

"But he makes the rounds in Society."

"Regularly, and I'd say at the expense of his work. He hasn't published in the past year, but yes, he's well liked by many. Certainly the ladies are drawn to him."

"If there's one thing your mother and I share, its firm agreement that there are other women who'd jump at the chance to marry you." She tilted her head as honest words spilled from her. "You are rather handsome, the scars notwithstanding. You also have an interesting mix of intelligence and distance, which appeals to many women."

"Trying to escape the phantom's lair?" he asked, the corners of his mouth twitching.

Lydia linked her fingers together in her lap. Interesting that her compliment about his appearance, however inelegant in delivery, left him unaffected. "Being realistic."

His low chuckle came smooth and mellow, like the fine scotch he drank.

"Miss Montgomery, understand I like women, but I had never planned to marry," he said, staring out the window. "Oh, I thought to seek amusement and connection with the rare woman I could tolerate, should she cross my path. But I generally prefer my own company to others." He turned his topaz gaze on her. "I'm too candid for social niceties and have no patience for wading through simpering women to find one I might tolerate for a time. Miss Blackwood, in fact, was a consideration only because of her convenient family ties. If it weren't for the demand that I carry on the Greenwich lineage, you wouldn't be here."

She pasted a bland smile on her face as her brain cried: *Why not me?*

"I see what you mean about those social niceties."

He rubbed his jaw and winced. "I apologize for my bluntness, but the bulk of our arrangement was spelled out from the beginning." His voice softened as he watched her. "If it makes any difference, you are by far the most interesting woman I've met in a long time. And it's been only a matter of days between us."

"My thanks for that highest compliment," she said, softening to his frankness. "But think: If you stay longer, what more might you discover?"

His lordship faced away from her, staring out the wide-open window. She noticed he highlighted interesting over womanly form or prettiness. That snared her more than any flattery to her appearance, luring her deeper into the lair of this reclusive man. Lydia wanted him, and the ways she wanted him bewildered. Her body wanted to mold to his, to test the hardness she'd glimpsed, and something deeper inside—Her heart? Her soul?—yearned for more of this fledgling bond. And if he caught a whiff of the latter wish, his lordship would shut down and shut her out as quickly as one closed a door. Best she trod carefully.

Lud, but she was turning overly sentimental.

She shut her eyes and took a deep breath.

"Very well, we still have the matter of my artwork," she said, opening her eyes to see him studying her.

"You failed to disclose those intentions at the Blue Cockerel. I cannot support the Countess of Greenwich selling artwork—"

"Then what were all those fine words about commerce?" she said, the grip of her fingers tightening. "And you, I might add, failed to disclose a few things as well, my lord."

He shrugged and crossed his arms loosely over his chest. "I hate to admit it, but my mother's right about England's rigid rules when it comes to noblewomen.

You're only good for carrying on family lines and hosting dinner parties."

That his eyes glowed with a teasing light when he said that saved him from having a biscuit hurled at his head.

"You've said yourself my sketching's quite good. And I've been painting since my days on the Somerset Estate."

"That long?" He rubbed the back of his neck and stared out the window. "Where are those paintings now?"

"I've nearly a dozen stored in Wickersham. I had to scrape paint off some of the canvasses and reuse them. Others I painted over." She adjusted her shawl. "A poor girl does what she must."

He moved to his desk and opened a drawer. He withdrew foolscap, a nub of a broken lead stick, and what looked to be the Greenwich seal. He ignored the quill and ink pushed aside on his dish-strewn desk and scribbled a rapid note. He folded the note and yanked on the servants' bell rope near the window.

"What are you doing?" Lydia asked, watching him hold a chunk of red wax over a candle flame.

"Solving at least one problem, which I consider a small victory on this disastrous day," he answered without looking at her.

He took a quick view of the melting wax, dabbed it on the folded missive, and pressed the seal into splotched wax. The door opened on the other side of the study, and Rogers entered, his gloved hands tugging his green waistcoat into place.

"My lord, you called?" He spoke from the doorway, not stepping foot into the inner sanctum.

"Come in, man." Lord Greenwich waved him into the room, and he held out the missive. "Have the coachman deliver this to Miss Montgomery's great-aunt's house in the village of Wickersham...a Miss Euphemia Carson. Tell him he's to take whatever conveyance he needs to bring back all of Miss Montgomery's paintings. Make sure he wraps them with care."

"Very good, milord." Rogers accepted the folded note, but the footman hesitated, clearing his throat.

The young man tried to keep a servant's stoic face, but his eyes spread wide, and his Adam's apple bobbled up and down. The earl glanced up from putting away his seal.

"You've something to say, Rogers?"

Rogers nodded slowly, as if he were about to impart news of the Holy Grail. "Yes, milord. There's a delivery for you. A chest. It just arrived."

"Very well." And Lord Greenwich closed the desk drawer firmly.

"The chest, milord...it's from King George himself, sir."

Fourteen

So divinely is the world organized that every one of us,
in our place and time,
is in balance with everything else.
                                    —Johann Wolfgang von Goethe

NEW CLOUDS GATHERED OVERHEAD, FAITHFUL WIT-
nesses to Greenwich Park's stormy drama that played
over three days. With those new clouds came an extraor-
dinary storm and nighttime freeze. Outside, dormant
grass and bare tree branches frosted silver and white
everywhere, so heavy that some branches broke from
the burden and tumbled to the ground. The air chilled
inside and out with news of Lord Greenwich's impend-
ing journey. The household moved in a state of shock,
whereas Lady Elizabeth vented in a way that rivaled any
storm. Lydia, like the servants, tiptoed through marble
hallways and tried to lose herself in the euphoria of work:
sketching for the earl when required and painting for
personal pleasure when not.

What was she to make of this mess?

She planted both elbows on the wood table, her place

of penance in the greenhouse for snooping about the earl's room. Lydia's fingernail etched designs on heavily frosted glass as she stared at the dreary downpour outside. The concoction that poured from the heavens vacillated between a mix of rain and sleet.

Sometimes she touched the alluring, exotic Chinese pear tree, now within easy arm's reach. Huxtable had shoved a high bench against brick and glass across from his lordship's workbench, all the nearer to the earl's watchful eye as she labored. Neat piles of well-illustrated pages testified to her skill, but the tapping of her lead stick at this moment testified to thin restraint of another nature.

What was in the chest the king sent to the earl?

The unassuming wooden chest, bound by buckled leather straps, sat on the earl's workbench for three days, begging to be opened. There was no lock. Only twine knotted through the latch, but the tamperproof knot was a tight one. Was Lord Greenwich so distracted by the ongoing drama that he *forgot* the king had sent him something? The mysterious chest was the size of an overlarge hatbox, yet she dared not investigate, not after the disaster of poking about his room.

Perhaps he needed a gentle reminder?

Lydia swiped at a vexing strand of hair that came loose, and she glanced sideways. At the moment, another mystery was unfolding: his lordship sequestered himself with a heavily cloaked Miss Mayhew. Sequester really was a thin description, since they discussed something rather heatedly in the wide-open greenhouse, but the way they bent their heads from time to time, one could only guess both sought some privacy. Yet their words often bounced and echoed off the glass ceiling, raining down like misty tidbits.

Lydia's gaze went to the manse. She counted a row of well-lit windows on the eastern side of the house that made up the countess's apartments, where that lady stewed with some malady or another. Even to Lydia's eye, unfamiliar with detailed Sanford family lore, Lady Elizabeth battled for and attempted gross manipulation of her son from, as she called it, his folly on *The Fiona*; however, for three days Lord Greenwich battled back, speaking in firm, clipped tones of his intent to sail on the fifteenth of June. Lady Elizabeth graced few with her presence, but when she did, well, damage was done, and the pall cast over the estate wore down everyone. Servants whispered as they scurried from one place of hiding to another, all wearied of the strain.

That Miss Mayhew spoke with emphatic hand thrusts further demonstrated even the calm, collected house-keeper had had enough. As the earl and Miss Mayhew moved into Lydia's vicinity, she averted her eyes to the lanceolate leaf before her. The pair passed by on a parallel path, and Lydia clutched her shawl, sketching as Lord Greenwich's words fell on her ears.

"You always have a safe haven here."

"Thank you. Greenwich Park is the only home I've ever known. This will be hard. But that's just the prob-lem, isn't it? I've hidden too long," said Miss Mayhew behind elbow-high greenery. "If we don't force ourselves beyond comfortable boundaries, we stagnate and die."

"Resurrecting old arguments?" he asked. Then his tone turned clipped and firm. "Promise me you *will* see him. Let him look after you."

Soft, feminine laughter filtered through the leaves. "That sounded rather like a command, not a request," she said. "Time I looked after myself, don't you agree?"

"At least take the jewels to him, Claire. Don't try to do that on your own." The cultured, lordly voice finished with a coaxing, "Please."

Their footsteps made a slow rhythm as dirt and gravel crunched underfoot. Miss Mayhew's calm voice dropped in volume.

"Very well. I'll visit David."

Voices muffled and blurred from a heavy onslaught of fat raindrops drilling the glass roof as they moved out of earshot. Lydia stretched tall on her stool for a view of the earl and Miss Mayhew at the greenhouse door. She indulged her blatant need to know. Why shouldn't she? In the distance, the door opened to the watery storm, and like a dark wraith, Miss Mayhew vanished in the gray.

Lord Greenwich disappeared from view, and Lydia buried herself in the papers she was copying meant for a pamphlet, a gratis service provided in sympathy for the printer who would try to decipher the earl's atrocious handwriting. But much niggled at her brain, and soon neat rows of words blurred under her nose as she lost focus.

What were they talking about?

The earl's footfalls behind her meant he was again at his bench, but he didn't deign to share. His lead stick scratched paper, and one of the tiled Swedish stoves rumbled anew in the background, spewing heat into the damp chill. Lydia flicked at a piece of lint on her woolen sleeve and stared at the misted glass, stewing over being left out in the cold.

The most deplorable truth hit her square in the face: the green monster of envy had grabbed hold of her.

Lydia huffed at this, creating a lighter round spot on the glass that quickly clouded over again. Miss Mayhew shared a deep friendship with Lord Greenwich, the rare kind that only time and traumatic events could create. She rubbed her neck, acknowledging that she was no expert on the topic of intimacy and closeness.

She'd taken a tumble or two in the past, but what did that have to do with truly knowing a man? Or deep, abiding friendship with a man?

How well she kept people at arm's length…for how long? The sad truth of that made her feel wobbly inside. She hid herself so well in painting, but true depth with people was another matter altogether.

Bothersome wisps tickled her neck, which she brushed aside, all the more reason to shift on the stool for a better look at the subject in question. There he stood, engrossed in his work. Lord Greenwich was, she had learned, as protective of his time as he was of his space.

But this latest development, a midday greenhouse visit by Miss Mayhew for a cryptic conversation, needed explaining. Wasn't he at least going to share the bare bones?

She slanted a tentative stare over her shoulder. His lordship planted one palm on the table, while the other hand scribbled notes. One shoulder blade shifted under his shirt, while shoulder and back muscles bunched under linen. Lydia's gaze wandered lower, where his firm buttocks rounded nicely under brown breeches. She smiled to herself, recalling her fear the first night that his lordship might have a terrible paunch.

How wrong she was on that score: he possessed a very fine form.

Lord Greenwich's head shot up. He dropped the lead stick on the table and turned around, glowering at her.

"You're staring holes in my back. Something amiss?" His black velvet queue hung lower on his neck, the only sign of a long day. "And what's with the mischievous smile?" His arms clamped across his chest, and he leaned his backside against the table, crossing one brown boot over the other.

"Am I smiling?" She touched her lips. "Smiles aren't unwelcome, are they? They seem to be in short supply around here."

He grunted at her cheekiness and repeated, "Is something amiss?"

"Amiss?" She scooted fully around, tugging the corners of her shawl into her lap. "I'd say everything is. Your household's in quite an uproar."

"My mother's contretemps?" he said, snorting. "She's famous for displays of temper followed by taking to her rooms with one malady or another when she doesn't get her way."

Lydia turned her face to the greenhouse door and the frosted lawn beyond.

"And Miss Mayhew?"

"Gone. For good. To London." He leveled her with a testy look. "Now that you've been informed, may I get back to work? I've much to do before I meet Jonas today."

"What?" She tipped forward on the stool. "Why'd she leave?"

"Miss Mayhew resigned her post for personal reasons."

"Her leaving didn't have anything to do with…with me?" Lydia winced, ashamed of her petty jealousy over the beautiful woman. "A woman alone in London, without family or prospects…"

His visage softened a fraction, and the corners of his mouth quirked.

"No, she didn't leave because of you. And she'll be fine. Claire's a grown woman with a mind of her own." He unlocked his arms and moved off the bench, acting as if he were the soul of patience. "*Now*, may I get back to work?"

Her eyebrows scrunched together as she surveyed the chaotic workbench. He'd added a row of several cork-topped glass vials propped up within a wooden stand, but her gaze caught on the king's parcel.

"No."

His eyebrows shot up at that.

"Everything's work, work, work with you, isn't it?" Lydia hooked a shoe heel on one of the stool's rungs. "You have a deplorable lack of communication, my lord. Don't you think I should know something about what goes on here? Have you decided who will replace Miss Mayhew?"

His lack of willingness to share details unnerved her. That business with Miss Mayhew needed unraveling, but the king's special delivery taunted her more. These were simple places to begin unwinding the coil that made Lord Greenwich.

He slanted a look at the house and grimaced.

"Her replacement's not at the forefront of my mind, with so much to do. But Claire's leaving is only one curiosity…" His voice trailed off as he caught her sight line. "Haven't been peeking, have you?"

"Certainly not," she said, tipping her chin high. "You hold too many secrets to yourself, milord. There's a fine line between secrets and deception." She clamped her arms tight across her chest. "What with not telling me about your voyage, and all."

"Never give too much information. All the better to lure you into my lair," he said with a humorous, mocking leer.

"Oh, stop," she said, unable to hold back her smile. She loved his sense of humor over the many stories that circulated about him.

The earl canted his head, scrutinizing her anew. "Why would my expedition upset you? Doesn't it work in your favor to be free of a certain self-serving nobleman for two or three years? You'd have an incredible amount of freedom…within reason, of course."

Her mouth opened to respond, but her mind stalled. From her perch on the high stool, one leg swung like a pendulum in time with her ticking brain. Why this odd urgency to have him stay? Lydia had added her voice once or twice these past three days, albeit more quietly than Lady Elizabeth. She loathed the idea of him leaving. At the moment, his tanned skin and lionesque hair against the vibrant green background made him a kind of exotic specimen. He watched her, waiting, and the scars near his mouth puckered and twisted as the damaged side of his face curved in a sardonic grin.

"Careful, Miss Montgomery, or you'll catch flies."

She touched her lips, shutting her mouth, then grinning at how silly she must look. She enjoyed the ease that moved between them. They'd worked these past days in solidarity, and the way the earl had treated her like an equal, even when she was at a complete loss as to the finer points of botany and academics, was rewarding. Her illustrations and diagrams conveyed what he wrote, what he said. Their partnership of sorts, however new, truly gratified. And then to be left alone while he explored places unknown, possibly never returning from so hazardous a journey?

"Any woman would be upset if she were left to raise a child by herself. Assuming we accomplish that," she blurted, her cheeks growing hot under his perceptive eyes. "And in a place she's not entirely comfortable calling home."

There. That must be it.

He set one hand at his waist, where the shirt was half-untucked. But he glanced toward the Greenwich manse once more and nodded with resignation.

"On that score, I'm trying to gain my mother's assistance." His broad chest expanded as he took a deep breath. "Her guidance once I leave is crucial, but this, this is no easy thing for her."

"Then don't go."

His head, full of harsh glower, snapped around to face her. "Out of the question."

"I can't claim to understand this need of yours to roam the world, exploring strange places," she said, rubbing the pinched muscles at her neck and shoulders. Leaning over the high workbench these past days had begun to take a toll. "But I would think men have been persuaded to change their plans once or twice because of a woman."

"Not their mothers, I'm sure," he said, crossing his arms once more. "I, for one, have never been moved enough to work my plans around a woman, no matter her relation to me."

He spoke with finality, and that last pronouncement, meant as fair warning for her, chafed such that she needed to look away. She stifled the argument that he'd changed plans for family demands in the past, when her gaze fell once more on the strange delivery from King George.

"What about the king?"

He pivoted toward the much-traveled chest, with his scarred profile in view. "Would I change my mind for the king? Stay or go, I don't think he cares." His disfigured cheek twitched as a warm smiled formed. "If you're angling to know what he sent me, why not simply ask?"

"I didn't think I ought to be so bold, considering what happened in your room." She hunched her shoulders and mentally brushed off his prickly dictate about not working life plans around a woman.

"Meekness doesn't become you." He tipped his head at the unassuming trunk, and like a highwayman luring a coconspirator, asked, "Want to see what's inside?"

Lydia needed no further prodding; she sprung from the stool to join him. He chuckled at her enthusiasm, and Lydia loved the way his eyes twinkled. She imagined him as the boy she'd viewed in the Greenwich art gallery, thoroughly involved in mischief. With both hands, the earl tugged the box closer, scraping it across the table. Whatever inhabited it was solid weight. He cut the knotted twine with a small knife from his tool collection, and the rusted latch sprang free.

"Go ahead," he said, tossing the knife aside. "Open it."

She unbuckled the flimsy leather straps and lifted the flat lid an inch or two. Lydia rose on tiptoe for a peek through the rectangular opening. In the dimness, squared edges and leather mixed with a dry, dusty smell.

"They're books."

She flipped the lid back and pulled out a well-worn volume. "*Systema Naturae*"—she grimaced and handed over the volume—"riveting, I'm sure."

"Linnaeus's taxonomy of the plant and animal kingdom." He slanted her smile. "Excellent reading material."

She scrunched her nose as a strong whiff of dust accompanied the next book. "I'll have to trust you on that."

"I exchange books with King George on a regular basis. He's not an intellectual, per se, but plans an extensive library and seeks my opinion. And quite frankly, he needs it," he said without a trace of humility as he retrieved the remaining books, at least a dozen, stacking them in a messy array. "A few years ago, the king purchased six thousand volumes from Joseph Banks, but it's my insight and advice he seeks to refine the collection."

A smile crept across her mouth. His patrician nose and scarred profile, trimmed with a dose of strong male pride, made for an interesting juxtaposition. To suggest modesty about his intellect would be a waste of breath, yet he wasn't overly impressed with his connection to royalty. To his lordship's mind, King George was simply another fellow seeking his opinion, as evidenced by the mound of correspondence people sent him.

Some letters requested the sale of exotic plant cuttings, while others presented complex scientific questions on various floras. Lord Greenwich, she had learned, was a well-connected recluse who responded to the scientific minds of the outside world on his timetable.

Lydia kept up her careful review of one tome after another as they passed books to each other. Their fingers touched often, quick grazings of skin to skin.

"Let me guess: when it comes to Sir Joseph, you may be smarter, but he's nicer." She opened the only volume she recognized, flipping through the pages. "You've got quite a rivalry with him, don't you?"

He dusted off another volume with a Latin title and raised it for quick inspection. "I have my reasons."

Out of her side vision, he made a show of examining each book, but Lord Greenwich also watched her from his peripheral view, the awareness was mutual. His hip and thigh touched her, lingering, as he reached to check the chest, now empty. Her stays pinched her chest. A constricting grip made her breathing become heavier. Lydia fidgeted, adjusting the stays wrapped around her torso.

"And those reasons would be?" she asked, keeping her eyes on the table.

He replaced a pair of books inside the chest, his forearm brushing hers. Gold and brown masculine arm hairs tickled her wrist. Lydia missed how she came to stand so close to Lord Greenwich, but his body heat mixed with whiffs of his clean, earthy smell coiled around her. His shirtsleeve rubbed her shoulder, and her shawl slipped lower. Their closeness, so companionable, must've struck him as well. When she turned to him, his lordship's face creased in a genuine smile, and both the scarred and unscarred planes took her breath away. The tiny white scar on his temple disappeared into the crinkled corner of his eye.

"You want nothing hidden, do you?" His voice dropped to an intimate low. "And yet, I seem ready to open up my secrets to the most singular woman of my acquaintance."

Lydia swallowed, trying to rid herself of the lump in her throat. He gave her another of his unusual, elevating compliments. Praise, she long ago surmised, did not fall easily from Lord Greenwich's lips.

"I, I'm not sure what you mean," she said, stumbling over her words. "But I'm willing to listen and keep secrets."

His gaze swept across her eyes, down to her lips. "I'm sure those lips of yours do many things, including keep secrets."

Her heart pounded at his blatant innuendo. Gone was the brave woman making bold insinuations of her own in his study. That magnetic smile of his, if he chose to use it more often, would win the meanest shrew, turning her to melted wax.

"What? No saucy return from Miss Montgomery?" he jested softly. "I've rendered you speechless. I'll have to remember that: flagrant flirtation silences Wickersham's hoyden artist."

"You're a bit free with your word choices, my lord, and short on delivery." She held the open book against her chest. "What's this secret you're talking about?"

His smile froze. Dark-eyed flirtation shifted as the glow in his topaz eyes hardened.

"I have strong reason to believe Joseph copied my findings at university and gave them to Lord Blevins, current president of the Royal Society. Some years ago, Blevins published my work under his name, taking full credit"—more gold-brown hair worked loose from his queue, falling about his face—"because the old man wouldn't know an original thought if it knocked him on his arse."

"I'm sorry," she whispered, touching his sleeve, yet the sentiment seemed woefully inadequate.

Life had dealt the Earl of Greenwich agonizing disappointments and unfair trials. If this latest bit proved to be true, then someone who was supposed to be a close, trusted friend betrayed him, all amidst very public gossip and speculation about other areas of his life. That he bore the burdens like a true nobleman made her heart swell with admiration, for she wasn't ready to credit any other emotion at this time. Something flashed behind Lord Greenwich's dark eyes, and conciliatory softness replaced stony sharpness.

"I hope you aren't offended by my boldness. I find I like our blunt speech. It's direct, refreshing."

His frank nature appealed to her, drawing her out in new, curious ways. Direct speech could be so honest and desirable even in its bluntest forms.

"I don't mind," she said, her voice a husky alto.

The air between them roiled with warmth and more awareness in a way she couldn't slow down or moderate. Even the simplest exchange with the earl seemed to twist her about. If she didn't look him in the eye, she'd be safe, safe from being drawn into this maddening attraction. Lydia turned to the table and set down the volume she held, closing it.

"Aristotle's *Poetics*. The only book in this pile I'm familiar with."

"You've read it?" he asked with mild surprise.

"Parts." Her fingertips skimmed gold foil on the spine, and she willed her heart and breathing into calmness. "He said people are higher and lower types, divided by moral decisions and social class." She returned the book to the chest, sensing that she, not he, was the one revealing a hidden place. Lydia swiped her palms free of fine dust. "A change of fortune can knock you out of the higher social class, but moral decisions keep you there no matter your fortunes."

She looked up into sparkling topaz eyes, opened wider as he regarded her.

Lydia pulled her shawl up around her shoulders and shrugged. "I'm no intellectual, but he caught my interest. A few things he said about people and art."

Lord Greenwich reached up and touched the edge of her shawl, skimming her neck. He brushed back loose strands of hair, tickling her cheek, her ear. The move, really a simple touch, was both intimate and caring, and she drank it up like a parched woman long deprived. They were supposed to be discussing books, but her eyelids fluttered low as her body quivered from his slight touch. Lydia stepped closer to his warmth.

"An interesting facet worth exploring." His fingers curved around her nape, but his thumb slowly stroked her earlobe.

Did he mean people or art?

Her languid gaze met his. *She* was the facet he wished to explore. The blackness of his wide pupils told her as much as did the full masculine mouth looking ready to plant hot kisses somewhere, anywhere on her skin. Yet her teasing nature played along with the sensual.

"What would you like to explore?"

"You're offering personal tutoring lessons?"

Their faces were a hand's breadth apart. His long, gold-tipped eyelashes dropped lower over his darkened eyes. His warm breath caressed her skin.

From somewhere within the mass of greenery, Huxtable's cheery whistle careened off the glass walls.

His black wool cap bobbed up and down on a far pathway as he approached. Lydia lowered her head and took a careful step back, but not before Lord Greenwich's warm hand covered her shoulder and slid down to her elbow. His smoldering brown eyes promised something.

Later.

"There she is," Huxtable called over a row of potted, juvenile sprouts. He chewed his ivory pipe into the corner of his mouth, talking around the stem. "Lady E.'s a callin' for ye, miss. Wants to see ye in the Blue Drawin' Room right quick like, she does."

Fifteen

*A beautiful thing never gives so much pain as does
failing to hear it and see it.*

—Michelangelo

IRRITATION NAGGED HIM WITH ALL THE PERSISTENCE OF
a buzzing fly about his head; a sure sign that all was not
right in the world. He dealt in constant logic and fact,
methodically moving from one premise to another,
proving or disproving suppositions. People, however,
never quite stayed within those neat parameters. And
when messy emotions dared intervene—and he solidly
categorized irritation as emotion—Edward turned testy.
Wasn't he made of firmer stuff than to be bothered by,
of all things, *feelings*?

That word made him cringe. He wobbled, nearly
losing his footing, but balance and nimble feet prevailed.

"Fifty-one, fifty-two, fifty-three…" Edward puffed
his steady count, jumping rope in the ballroom's massive,
cave-like confines.

This was his sixth, no seventh, attempt to reach one
hundred without faltering, and normally he'd not miss a

beat the first time through, moving onto the next exercise. But even this sanctum had been invaded. Again. By Miss Montgomery.

How could he forget her instructions days ago to deposit all her art supplies in the ballroom? Probably because that brain-muddling embrace outside the gallery scrambled clear thinking. He recalled the distraction of burying his face in the softness of her hair. Her presence seeped into him the same way her simple lemongrass scent invaded his senses. Right now, breathing heavily from exertion, he'd swear her scent surrounded him.

"Fifty-eight, fifty-nine, sixty…" He exhaled the count with each steady slap of thick hemp on parquet as the rope's staccato noise bounced off the walls.

Of all the rooms in Greenwich Park, she'd chosen this one for her art studio. Yes, the light was good, even on this cloudy afternoon, thanks to a glazier's dream of high-paned windows and doors, now ringed with frost. On sunny days the light would be ideal. Yes, he had given her free rein to choose any room that pleased her. Yes, he would be absent from Greenwich Park—from England—in seventy-five days. Thus, *her* use of this space should not matter. But it did.

Sweat dripped from his forehead, and thin rivulets sluiced his chest.

"Sixty-three, sixty-four, sixty-five…"

His goal, not to be thwarted, remained: reach one hundred consecutive jumps without error before moving on to the next training exercise. That discipline came in handy during the confines of his first voyage, however shortened that one was. This time, though, he'd planned a healthy dose of swordplay for better defense. For that he needed Jonas. Where was his friend?

"Seventy-three, seventy-four, seventy-five…" he counted aloud as he maneuvered across the ballroom floor, closer to Miss Montgomery's paintings all wrapped in burlap, lining the opposite wall.

Nearby, a table with powders in bulbous glass flasks, mortars and pestles, flagons of oil, linseed by the puttylike smell, and chunks of plain beeswax made a neat row. Four tripods, soldiers defending the perimeter of her makeshift studio, stood with their spines facing him in their section of the ballroom. Three tripods were bare, save the one supporting a painting, and that square beckoned him.

Come see.

Edward sped up his jumps, inching closer to that curious square and the unknown on the other side.

"Ninety-four, ninety-five, ninety-six…"

Suddenly, the ballroom doors cracked open wide. Light spilled a long rectangle across the dance floor, illuminating his quest to look at Miss Montgomery's art.

"Ninety-eight, ninety—" Caught in the act of almost peeking, Edward stumbled. His stocking foot snagged on the rope. He gave an exasperated roar that bounced and echoed.

This would not be his day to reach one hundred.

Miss Montgomery cast a long shadow up the middle of the rectangular light splashing the ballroom. He squinted at the brightness and, chest pumping like a blacksmith's bellows, Edward leaned his hands on his thighs, pressing a damp outline on his breeches. All of him was hot from exertion and frustration.

"What are you doing?" Miss Montgomery called into the distance, raising a candelabrum high. Her determined footsteps clicked across the ballroom.

Edward raised himself to full height, holding the rope, a limp instrument at his side. When she came closer, her mouth opened to an O. Miss Montgomery's green eyes went saucer-round as her gaze swept from his head, lingering on his bare chest, and moving down his legs to his stocking feet.

"You're nearly naked, my lord. Quite sweaty, too." Her eyebrows slammed together in two dark slashes. "And for goodness sake, what are you doing with that rope?"

He wiped excess sweat from his forehead and gave her a marginal bow. "And may I say how nice to be in your company again."

Her pretty lips frowned at his subtle chastisement before looking over at an array of swords and equipment on the far side of the room.

"Next, I suppose you'll tell me I'm invading another of your domains," she said, setting a hand at her hip.

"No, by all means, invade them all," he said, breathing heavily as he coiled the rope. "I'm preparing for my voyage. Where you paint shouldn't matter." *But it does.*

That sounded reasonable enough, yet his words rang as testy to his ears. Miss Montgomery wasn't fazed by his irritation. Her bottle-green eyes followed the slow, rhythmic motion of the rope as if he were a mesmerizing snake charmer and she his victim. Edward felt his smirk grow. She'd blatantly ogled his bare chest and arms as if she'd never seen the like before. And, well he knew she had likely seen a male chest or two. Her reaction pleased him and made up for the intrusion.

But did he detect some irritation on her part?

"And what has you in such a state?" he asked, moving to a nearby pile that was his shirt, coat, and boots. He dropped the coiled rope there.

Her frown deepened. "Your mother and her idea of countess lessons. She was very vocal to me and the servants about my inadequacy for that post. In *her* opinion, of course." Her brows slammed together as she finished, "And say what you will, to her it's a job."

She looked away in a fit, but her green jeweled gaze went right back to him. Edward picked up a drying cloth and wiped sweat from his face, chest, and arms, aware of his spellbound audience. Interesting. At least the scars across his chest didn't repulse her. He drank long from a pitcher of water, noticing the way her full lips dropped open and she scrutinized every inch of him.

With shirt and coat in hand, he walked back to the easel where Miss Montgomery stood. He tugged on his shirt not bothering to tuck it in, since the fabric clung uncomfortably in several spots. The way she viewed those spots, he could very well have been a feast she was about to devour. Edward wasn't shy, but her lack of composure in the face of his lack of decorum made the air spark anew between them. He shrugged into his brown broadcloth coat.

"Miss Montgomery," he said softly. "You're staring."

Her bottle-green stare jerked from his chest to his face. "Oh."

Her cheeks tinged pink. She set the candelabrum on the floor, removing one flickering candle. She faced the opposite wall and moved about, all business. Smiling to himself, he decided to let her collect herself. She flitted from one mirrored sconce to another, until their end of the dim ballroom flickered alive with brighter light.

"How was the meeting in the blue drawing room?" he asked, retying his queue. "That's where you've been all day, isn't it?"

"A disaster. And yes, that's where I've been *all day*. Your mother insulted me at every turn as we practiced pouring tea." Miss Montgomery jammed the candle back into the silver candelabrum, and her green eyes pierced him as she rose to full height. "It was tea, mind you, tea. But your mother acted like I ruined a state dinner."

"She takes that kind of thing seriously," he said, moving around on quiet feet to see what was on the other side of the canvas.

Flashing green eyes held him at bay on the easel's perimeter, denying him a view.

"That's all you have to say?" She glared at him then moved in a flurry of skirts to her artist's workbench. She pinched a dash of colorful powder into a stone mortar, then scooped another into the bowl, her tiny spoon clinking stone. "You as good as fed me to the lion's den. Your mother's so concerned about family lineage? Ha!" she huffed, hugging the stone bowl to her body while grinding her pestle in the mix. The more she pounded and stirred, the more her ire built. "Maybe she ought to be nice to the current candidate. And *you*, my lord, could at least tell her to curb her tongue. She shoots daggers with every syllable."

"You held your own with her the first day she arrived." He swiped his coat sleeve across his forehead. "Why wouldn't I think your meeting in the blue drawing room would be any different?"

Her dark head snapped up at that, but she was in

the act of dribbling oil into the mortar, which pulled her back into the work of mixing pigment. She paused, distracted by the process of bringing color to life. At least the tension in her face eased as she examined the particular shade created. Funny how finding the right shade diminished her temper; his Miss Montgomery was a bit of a magician, one he wanted to appease.

"About my mother, I'll see what I can do," he murmured, slipping around to face the square canvas.

She may have said something, in fact, he was sure she did. He'd become an expert over the years at tuning out the female voice, of listening but not really hearing; however, this was not a matter of escaping a verbose female. This was altogether different.

Edward lost himself in the image before him. The painting, a tree of sorts, or… No, he stepped back, then moved closer for better focus. An up-close view of his Chinese pear tree. Dense foliage with an open, inviting space in the middle of all those leaves.

Yet the golden orb, the fruit suspended in the middle of that space looked suspiciously like…

Did his eyes deceive him?

Edward blinked again, lost in the Chinese-pear image. The aroma of newly mixed oils floated from behind. The pleasant mix of scents: paint, oils, and what was distinctly Lydia, drew his attention away from the mysterious impression. He pointed at the painting.

"When did you do this?"

"These past few nights after dinner…late." Her lips curved in a secret smile. She dipped her brush into a shade of onyx and then a vibrant green, mixing the colors. Her brush moved in a tight circle on the palette.

"And you're not tired?"

"Painting makes me..." Lydia dabbed brush tip to canvas, and her voice glowed with reverence. "It makes me feel alive."

Soft candlelight flooded the room. She painted with fervor, engrossed in her work. Her lips parted with soft breaths at each dip of the brush. Lydia Montgomery was a study of something rare. He couldn't put his finger on what he saw as she moved in close to ascertain details, then stepped back for fuller effect, but he liked the way her body moved, vibrating with energy from each tiny stroke. Brush and paint swooshed and dabbed canvas. Light framed Lydia's hair, a glossy halo on her dark crown. Color smeared and dotted the old, gray smock she wore over her dress.

He looked again at the painting, his stare catching on the tempting, pale gold fruit.

"Lydia," he called to her softly, "you're painting the Chinese pear tree."

"Very good, my lord." Her short-bristled brush finished dabbing another leaf into existence, shaping the curving ovate tip.

Warmth spread over him as her skirt twitched and rubbed his knees and calves. He pointed to the golden orb hanging in the midst of foliage: pale fruit, a nude-gold shade, nicely curved with a slight cleft down the center.

"The fruit bears a strong resemblance to a woman's bare bottom."

Or am I so randy for you I can't see straight?

She flicked a side glance at him, and her brush slowed. "Does it now?"

Her question floated between them, pure invitation. Not so much sensual invitation as something else.

Well, yes, there was something sensual, no denying that.

But what else? This facet of her was all like a new and complex puzzle laid out before him. He crossed his arms, perplexed at the inability to put his finger on the exact nature of her invitation, and his utterly male inability to grasp what needed to be said. The painting, both excellent and elemental, spoke volumes, and he was on primer reading level when it came to art, woefully out of his depth.

"Is this almost finished?" He winced at his own ineptness. *University educated, and that was the best he could do?*

"Almost." She nodded and didn't bother to look his way.

That was close to a dismissal. A chill of distance spaced itself between them, even though neither had moved. Tenacity gripped him. He inched closer to her and the canvas as if proximity could capture what eluded him.

"But this is the Chinese pear tree, yet it's not an exact rendering." He pointed to fruit hanging in the background. "These pears are indistinct...they're..." His words trailed off.

When was he ever at a loss of words to explain or define? His whole life was dissection and discovery, especially flora in all its intrinsic properties. Everything had a place and a definition, a role and a purpose.

Lydia dabbed her brush on the platter. "They're what, Edward?" she prompted him with a quiet air and kept her attention on the canvas.

His patient tutor's dark eyebrows raised a notch as she gave a slight nod. The teacher would not give up on her unskilled student; instead, she'd coax him into deeper comprehension.

"This close, the piece looks unfinished." He cocked his head this way and that, pointing at one of the leaves. "Yet, stepping back, I would call the work complete."

"What do you see?" Lydia concentrated on one corner of the canvas.

"A tree, of course."

Her shoulders dropped.

"I'm disappointed. You, who daily capture the tiniest details in your work, with plants no less, have failed to notice what's right in front of you." Her head tipped sideways, and Lydia made a satisfied moue with the spot she completed. "For someone so intelligent, you're really quite dull."

Edward snorted in good humor. "Dull?"

"Yes. I recommend rereading your Aristotle. Find out what he says about art." Her lips twitched, then softened when her brush touched canvas again. "Truly enlightening."

Her mild condescension didn't bother him; he welcomed the energy that vibrated between them. Glimpses of his exemplary education, years of private tutors, discussions with some of the best minds, from physicists to philosophers, flew through his mind—a carousel of vivid scenes from youth to maturation.

And all he could come up with was that snort and to repeat the word *dull* used to describe him.

Miss Lydia Montgomery had out-nuanced him today, and that interesting facet both stimulated and pleased. His pretty tutor gave him a patient sigh and finally faced him. Her suspended brush, heavy with scarlet paint, pointed at him.

"You demonstrate a deplorable capacity to miss what's right in front of you." Her serene smile held mysteries that made the set down worthwhile.

"So that's it. I'm to receive low marks today." He grinned wide, thrilled to the core at this woman.

There was something else in her smile, a touch of knowing that he hadn't quite grasped. Something beyond art. She wasn't being smug, though she enjoyed this moment of superiority with him: Lydia exuded depth. The paintbrush twirled in the air, pointing at the artwork.

"Try this. Look again. Study the piece in a different light or a different time. In the same way you'd study your plants." Her whole visage warmed from the topic. "Of course, not with your magnification glass." Her voice softened. "I mean *really* look at it. Accept whatever you see, whatever you feel. There's a difference between looking and seeing in the same way there's a difference between studying and learning."

His gaze swung from her to the painting and back again to her. She laughed, a light sound like a soft feather to his skin.

"Oh, Edward, such consternation. You really are befuddled, aren't you?" Lydia tapped the red-tipped bristles on her palette. "To think there exists a subject the great Earl of Greenwich hasn't mastered."

What could he say to that? She was right. And she'd called him by his Christian name, a few times, in fact, the sound of it vibrating over every inch of his flesh. Did he let her name slip as well? He was tired of being "my lord" to her and hoped to breach formality with the "Miss" salutation.

Lydia lowered her lashes, pondering the hue she'd just created on the palette. "Art isn't purely academic: step one, step two, categorize, dissect, and define. There is discipline yes, but there's also an element of emotion involved, quite a lot. Creative pursuits, like life, are not an exact science."

She held her brush over the palette as she pondered the right pigment from the messy globs.

"Ah, this will do." The corners of her mouth tilted upward. "More than satisfactory." Lydia turned to the work in progress and dabbed the canvas. "The best advice I can give is ask yourself what you feel when you're considering a work of art. In time, the answer may come, or it may not." She shrugged off this last acknowledgment.

Her face transformed into a subtle, translucent quality before his eyes. Her eyes went wide then narrow, her lips opened slightly, as if she breathed life into her work. Fascinating.

Following her movements, he broached the personal. "I like that you called me Edward."

"Did I?" That jerked her out of the painting. Her dark lashes ringed wide-open eyes.

"Yes, and I called you Lydia."

He noticed a dab of red-hued paint on her cheek now that she fully faced him. He smiled at the attractive mess she made: loosely pinned hair, an old gray smock dabbled with color, and fresh-faced, even with that smear. She was more attractive than any of the Society women peacocked in all their finery. The pad of his thumb swiped away the pigment on her cheek, and his hand lingered close to her silken skin.

"I'd like very much that we address each other by our given names…forgo formality."

Her head tipped, as if drawn to the warmth of his hand.

"I'd like that very much too—"

"Edward!" The countess's shrill call into the ballroom jolted them apart. Her rapid heel-toe strides sounded like a volley of bullets fired across the room.

Edward pivoted to his mother and tipped his head in greeting. "Mother. You fare well?"

He hadn't seen her since yesterday, but the light line of artful kohl around her eyes failed to hide the swollenness. She gave him a scathing glare.

"You know I don't fare well at all. Not until you give up this nonsense of yours."

He studied her for a second, unsure if she meant his voyage or his pending marriage. Perhaps both. But he'd let the matter rest and tried for a less contentious approach.

"I see our conversations of the past few days availed nothing in the realm of understanding." He clasped his hands behind his back. "But I'm glad you're up and about."

Tourmaline-blue eyes, the whites of which were bloodshot, swept from him to Lydia and back to him, catching on his feet.

"And where are your shoes?" Her fine-arched eyebrows knit together, but she held up a soft pink-white palm and rolled her eyes. "Never mind. I came to alert you to a domestic imbroglio that demands your attention."

"Speak in plain English, if you will."

"Very well. Since you lack a butler, and with your housekeeper's sudden departure, there's a deplorable void of authority in your home." His mother clasped her hands together at waist height. "Your staff's in an uproar. That Colonial friend of yours took Miss Lumley to the village to attend a family emergency. The kitchen's in mild chaos without clear direction, thus, at the moment, dinner's not even a glimmer of a thought. To keep everyone in line, you need to announce the new housekeeper, and I'll not do it, since you've told me under no uncertain terms that Greenwich Park is your domain. How's that for plain English?"

"Excellent." Edward chuckled and looked at Lydia. "If we're to eat, I can see I'd better attend to the matter."

He tipped his head to both women and walked away.

"Edward, your shoes," his mother called to him with exasperated sharpness.

He pivoted around, walking backward in his exit. Of course, he gave a smile of pure cheek, the kind that drove his mother mad.

"I can give orders with or without my boots." He touched his head in a mischievous salute and kept up the backwards walk another nimble step or two, all for the chance to watch his coconspirator's green eyes smiling back at him over the canvas.

He turned to walk into the light, certain of one thing. Art—mysterious, beautiful, and challenging—was growing on him.

❧

"Such dishabille," the countess said, watching Edward disappear. She faced Lydia and shook her head. "My son and his Philistine ways."

Lydia dropped her attention back to the canvas filled with color. Those Philistine ways allowed her the first glimpse of Edward's bare torso and another excellent view of his muscled calves, but that pleasant picture faded under her ladyship's gimlet eye. Lydia swiped the brush on a rag, dipping it in a small cleaning jar at her feet, and touched the tip to a new blob of green. Perhaps the countess would leave her in peace.

They couldn't possibly have any more to say after today's disastrous meeting in the blue drawing room.

The countess, her fingers linked loosely together, stepped closer to the easel, angling her powdered blond head for a better look. Oh, but she wanted the woman gone. Silk skirts and underskirts rustled in the silence. Lady Elizabeth's presence hung like an unwelcome specter peering over Lydia's shoulder, but this was one area in which the noblewoman could find no fault, though she might try. The ballroom, a vacuous amphitheater, magnified every little sound, and the countess's breathing came in abrupt huffs behind Lydia.

Tension began to form a burning knot near the middle of her back. She was sure the countess was studying her as much as the painting. Lydia stretched minutely under her smock, trying to lessen the tightness building, while her fine, tufted brush swept this way and that. Lydia increased the speed of her strokes until she snapped.

"Is there something you'd like to say, my lady?" Lydia spoke over her shoulder.

"Yes. Many things," was her unbothered, cryptic response. Silk skirts rustled, and she moved closer. "You know, I did a bit of painting some years ago. Perhaps you noticed the cupids on the armoire in my old rooms?"

Lydia chewed her lower lip and squinted at the leaf she painted. "Hmmm…yes, I noticed." Positive commentary was likely expected. Empty praise, however, would not be forthcoming. Those cupids were hideous.

"But somehow I can't imagine you've stayed in here to discuss art."

A heavy sigh sounded over Lydia's shoulders, and the countess cleared her throat.

"Very well. My attempts at social niceties aside, let me speak in plain English, since that's the mode of the day." Lady Elizabeth stepped such that she was very near the painting, her elegant features in peripheral view. "We both know you're not good enough to be the next Countess of Greenwich. You're not worthy of the position."

Lydia canted her head sideways toward the countess. "I don't think it's all that bad."

After tea, when her ladyship had spewed so much poisonous criticism, any unkind words at the moment only added to the numbing effect. She doubted the countess could do more harm, but Lady Elizabeth moved, and her arm banged a corner of the canvas, causing Lydia to make the smallest smudge. The damage was minimal, quickly fixed with a dab of her pinkie finger, but righteous anger began to build.

"Now see here, milady, I stay because Edward decrees it, and we're in full agreement about our arrangement," she said, swiping her paint-smeared fingertip on her smock's sleeve. Lydia knelt to drop her paintbrush in the jar at her feet. The green just wasn't the right shade, and she was ready to explode under such stinging commentary.

Her ladyship's eyes turned into narrow, glittering blue slits when Lydia used Edward's Christian name. Lydia swirled the brush globbed with paint and guessed that was another failure on her part. Solvent within the jar darkened to a murky hue. When did men and women of nobility, who intended to wed each other, for goodness sake, break past walls of formality? Certainly they didn't "my lord" and "my lady" one another during conjugal relations, did they?

The silly coldness of that picture made her grimace as paint thinned with each swirl of her brush. If she weren't so upset, she'd laugh at that mental picture. She was so out of touch as to what made good marital relations, both in and out of bed, and knew no wise matron's advice would come from the countess. Her ladyship was concerned only about the outward appearance of things. An impatient huff above her head pulled Lydia out of that musing.

"If you're quite through fiddling with that, I have important things to discuss. You dally overlong."

"I think you came only to pile more insults on my person," she said, looking up. Lydia stirred the brush in the jar all the while, wrestling with the perverse wish to spill that dirty liquid on the lady's fine, unblemished silk shoes. Were there diamonds on her buckles? "This is my time to spend as I see fit."

Lydia took a deep, calming breath, let that shoe-ruining impulse go, and rose to full height with palette and clean brush in hand. Lady Elizabeth's slender, straight nose tipped high, as she did her level best to look down at Lydia, though they were of similar height. It was almost comical.

"Do you really think you can stand by Edward's side when he eventually returns to Society? And he will someday." Pale blue eyes blazed. "He corresponds with the king, for goodness sake. You'll *never* be his equal."

What could she say to that truth heaped on her head? That she liked being in the same room as Edward and guessed he felt the same? Lydia turned away, needing another calming second. A mild tremor shook her body as she gripped the paintbrush and palette for steadying anchorage. She wasn't so immune to the older woman's needling after all. She went to the table that housed her supplies and set the palette down; the desire to paint ebbed. Her palms flattened on the work surface, grounding her.

"I support whatever Edward wants," she said over her shoulder, and slowly removed the smock. Yet her voice sounded feeble to her own ears.

"Do you?"

Lydia folded the smock in half and curled the material once more before setting it on a chair. The countess, every hair in place, stood statue-still by the easel in all her finery, a watered silk gown, glimmering in shades of rose and champagne. Lydia could never imagine owning such a dress. Edward had mentioned at dinner the previous night that when his mother was "well enough," she would take Lydia shopping in London for all the appropriate accoutrement a future countess would need.

More like leave me there.

Lydia saw a determined woman, one who wanted her gone. At that moment, Lady E. clasped her hands behind her back, just like Edward. Did the countess know she mirrored her son right then? Lydia studied some dots of dried paint she had spilled on the fine ballroom floor. The toe of her shoe scraped the area. The floor near her workbench had become a casualty of her enthusiasm for mixing pigments and would surely cause complaints to someone. She really was an out-of-place mess in this over-fine home.

"I see you have a *tendre* for him," said Lady Elizabeth.

Her head snapped up to face the countess. "I, we enjoy each other's companionship. That's all."

"Call it what you will, but have you considered what's best for Edward? If you truly care for him, the best, in fact, is that you *not* marry him." The countess moved closer, slow measured steps, looking more like a governess taking her charge to task on a key lesson. "If you don't marry him, he won't leave in June on this absurd journey of his. One that we both know could be his demise."

Lydia's quick intake of air let the countess know she'd hit her mark, and the noblewoman nodded her head.

"That's right. Should you marry, and should you breed, he will feel he's done his best, a version of his duty, if you will. Thus, he'll have all the more excuse to leave." Lady E.'s blue eyes narrowed. "But, if *you* leave *him*, he'll have to find another to take your place. That could take months. Many, many months."

She set her hand low on her midsection and frowned over that simple but reasonable fact. Lydia had to admit she didn't want Edward to leave either. There were also the difficult circumstances with her mother, but part of her was confident Edward would help her mum no matter what. The countess had the right of it. Simply put, their arrangement enabled him to leave, but if she left him, he'd have to stay.

She nodded grudging assent. "I know what you mean, but I gave my word."

The countess made a sound akin to a growl and marched closer.

"Don't you see?" Her fists curled at her sides. "You cannot be here."

"No, I won't go." Lydia couldn't give reasons, but she crossed her arms. Tremors of upset wracked her body. "I won't abandon him."

Lady Elizabeth's mouth pinched closed, and her nostrils flared from angry breathing. This was turning into a kind of standoff, two opponents facing each other in a ring with neither willing to give quarter, though Lydia was outflanked and outmaneuvered. She looked beyond the glass doors, hugging her arms even tighter to her chest as daylight waned.

The countess scanned the row of burlap-wrapped paintings and broke the stalemate.

"Then what about your art?" she asked, her voice lilting with lethal softness.

"What about my art?" Lydia's view of her ladyship narrowed. No one had asked her about those wrapped paintings, not even Edward, and she didn't trust the lady's sly shift in tone.

"You've expressed a strong desire to have your art featured and sold in London, like any man." Her ladyship's ghastly tone and shiver of horror reinforced her opinion of that plan.

"So I have. What of it?"

The countess folded her hands together, resting them low on her skirt, and her blue eyes turned to calculating slits. "I'll pay you a hundred and fifty guineas to leave. Tomorrow. When Edward's engrossed in his work. Go live independently and sell your work under a different name. He'll never find you."

Lydia's jaw dropped with all the lack of elegance

and comportment one could expect in an unrefined commoner.

The countess nodded slowly. "That's a lot of money for a woman like you. A hundred and fifty guineas provides very well for a London artist." The countess smiled pure satisfaction as she went for the kill. "My dear Lydia, isn't *that* what you really want?"

Sixteen

My soul can find no staircase to Heaven
unless it be through Earth's loveliness.

—Michelangelo

"THAT'S WHAT YOU WANTED, RIGHT, MILORD?" Huxtable bent near the table and pointed at another row of empty, cork-topped glass vials, all shiny and brand-new. "Just came in today, they did. And there's more, but I suspect you'll want to save those for yer voyage come June. I left 'em in the crate."

"Perfect. Thank you."

Edward gave the sparkling glass the slightest check before he positioned his small blade. He prepared to splice the *Khaya senegalensis* seed pod. The rare specimen came from the juvenile khaya tree in his greenhouse, the only tree of its kind in England. He had to get this right.

If the tree grew to full maturity, which could take twenty years, the bark could be harvested to treat bleeding wounds, or so the natives on his first voyage had told him. With sly smiles they also told him the seeds, when ground up, could serve as an aphrodisiac, not that this secondary idea was at the forefront of his mind.

He had so many other needs to attend, and at present his body, thrumming too often in Lydia's presence, needed no further encouragement in that arena. He refocused his eyes, squeezing them shut and opening them wide when Huxtable shifted next to him.

"A mite tired, are ye?"

"No," he snapped, trying for patience, however thin. "I need to concentrate."

Huxtable kept hovering and bothering, like some kind of persistent pest. Getting these particular seeds into the hands of one Dr. Finley, an Edinburgh physician and scientist of like mind, with the only other greenhouse capable of growing such a tree would accelerate the development of medicines. Edward's need to increase the chances of success in his research and save the lives of others with bleeding wounds similar to Jonathan's drove him to these many late-night sessions in his greenhouse. His working late was nothing new. Time was always of the essence, careful, meticulous planning and uninterrupted time.

Everything and everyone, though, required their own slice of his time and attention.

"O' course, did I tell ye? Someone sent the crate to the kitchen where it sat a few days. That's why it's so late." Huxtable inched closer to peer at the careful botanical surgery. "Sendin' a scrap o' seeds to that gent in Edinburgh, are ye?"

Edward paused, keeping the sharp splicing tool hovering in hand over the brown seed. In his history with Huxtable, the old man hung round the table only when he had something to say. "Yes, this is for Dr. Finley," he answered, not willing to open conversational doors to Huxtable.

Edward had piled on the work, ambitiously laboring through two treatises at the same time. As he leaned over the workbench, the weight of self-imposed demands bore down on him. He was behind on his *Agathosma betulina* paper. Work on his treatise on plant placentas sat idle, since Lydia was negligent in her duties today. How quickly he'd come to count on her, but she claimed to not feel well by way of her maid last night, escaping her duties under the same guise today.

Edward leaned over the magnification glass, inhaling and repositioning the tool.

Huxtable wheezed and coughed, too close, and the thin blade slipped.

"Ahh," he griped, dropping the sharp metal. Blood welled from a thin, harmless stripe across the pad of his thumb holding the seed in place.

"Cut yerself, did ye?" Huxtable pulled a thin strip of linen from the pile of cloth used to wrap split seeds. The old man hesitated over the small cut then began to wrap the injured thumb. "Just a tap from yer blade. Done worse to yer chin, ye have. Hardly stops ye from a day's labor." Huxtable knotted the ends of the bandage. "But I'd say ye should call it a day. It's after dinner, when most of yer kind meet in drawin' rooms and such."

"Hux, my working into the evening a few nights a week is nothing new." Edward examined the bandage and the small red spot blooming on linen.

"Aye, but ye weren't a near-married man with a fair lass about the place, neither." The plain ivory pipe twitched between thin, admonishing lips.

"If you've something to say, say it."

Huxtable scratched his head. His rheumy eyes glanced at Edward then up to a lone, faint light shining from the west corner of the grand house.

"A light's on in her room. Has been all day. She can't be all that under the weather. And if she is"—Huxtable removed his pipe and jabbed it at Edward's chest—"yer the one who should be seeing to her welfare, not the likes o' Tilly or Edith. That's if she's truly in the sick-room, if ye know my meanin'."

He leaned his backside against the bench and looked up at the bank of windows that made the earl's and countess's suites. All were dark save one.

"I have wondered," he admitted aloud.

Was Lydia taking a page from his mother's book and trying her hand at manipulation? Or escape? He scratched his bewhiskered jaw. She hardly seemed the type. But did he truly know?

"The kitchens are all abuzz over the way Lady E. was a talkin' to the miss in the blue drawin' room yesterday. Real harsh like. More'n usual for her lady-ship's sharp tongue, some said." Huxtable's bushy brows wiggled like two hairy varmints not shed of their winter coats. "What yer used to is a mite hard fer others new to the place."

Edward's finger played idly with the bandage's knot, and he looked up at the lone window dimly lit. "I advised the countess to enjoy London tomorrow, which should give us all a break. Lydia held her ground so well that first day, but you're right. Perhaps she's overwhelmed."

Escape it was.

He looked over at her workbench, where three neat

stacks stood evenly positioned. Beyond that flat surface, velvet night wrapped around the greenhouse glass.

"And I think ye missed her a mite," Huxtable said with a firm nod as he replaced the pipe between his thin lips.

"I wouldn't go that far." But out of the corner of his eye, Edward caught the open book he'd retrieved from the king's chest.

Aristotle's *Poetics*. He'd taken breaks that day, seeking out what little the ancient philosopher had to say about art. Perhaps the student needed to check on the welfare of his lovely tutor. Edward looked over his shoulder at the disarray across his workbench and turned to clean up, when Huxtable waved him away.

"Shoo. Off with ye," the old man said, pushing Edward away from the table. "I can coddle plants and seeds just as well, milord. Was doin' it back when ye were knee high to me, think I can do it now."

"My thanks, Hux." He rubbed his nape where tension formed. Edward pulled his brown wool coat tightly about as cold air blasted him upon leaving the greenhouse.

His boots tramped their way out of the greenhouse, across the graveled path, and through the infamous blue drawing room's wide double doors. That room was dark, save a pair of lit candelabra. Traversing the pale blue carpet, he imagined the trial Lydia had faced the day before in that formal receiving room. The countess was about appearances first and substance second. Perhaps yesterday's meeting was the reason for Lydia's sudden female discomfort, or whatever it was Tilly called it when she gave excuses for Lydia's absence last night and this morning.

Time he took matters in hand. He'd not tolerate female histrionics in whatever form they came, the way his father had. But as he trudged upstairs with lead legs toward the red carpet delineating the earl's and countess's suites, Edward was at a loss. Was he supposed to coddle a woman when she had a case of the contretemps? Or was a man supposed to be firm, informing said female that she was made of firmer stuff, as he'd come to believe Lydia to be?

He bypassed her door, where not even a sliver of light shone underneath, and slipped quietly into his own room. Standing in his domain, he faced a singular dilemma. How would he approach her on this nocturnal visit? This wasn't an appointment to converse about work or some other purpose: *she* was the purpose. He chuckled to himself as he glanced around his quiet room, his books and maps always a comfort and interest, when suddenly he lit on an idea. Boldly provisioned, he knocked gently on their adjoining door.

"Lydia?" He cracked the door.

"Who is it?"

"The big bad wolf." He pushed open the door, grinning. "Who else would it be from this side of the door?"

He looked around the countess suite, dim with a few burning candles, and he spied Lydia. She jumped up from the writing table, shutting its drawer with abruptness at the same time. Her eyes blinked, and her gaze dropped to the pair of glasses in his hand.

"I come bearing a gift." He held out the glass containing a dram of scotch and tipped his head toward the seating area by the fire. "Shall we?" Then he hesitated. "That is if you're at least well enough for my visit?

Strong liquor may not be the best, but I thought…" He trailed off, watching her and hoping.

She graced him with a wan smile and moved to the pink-and-yellow-striped settee. "Thank you. I'd like that."

Lydia curled her legs underneath her, tucking the white velvet wrapper around her legs and feet. She reached out to accept the glass when he seated himself on the other end of the furniture. She murmured her thanks again, and they sipped the amber liquid in pleasant silence.

This was all very nice and somewhat awkward. Hadn't they both enjoyed each other's company? Even trading barbs with Lydia was refreshing. But this, this stilted and polite nothingness made his skin tight and uncomfortable. Edward set his glass on the table and settled against a cushion, linking his hands together. He contemplated his next move, but Lydia took the conversational helm.

"How was your work today?"

He gave her a half smile. "Fine."

She nodded at that and stared into the fire, listless and inattentive. Enough of this. He wanted to pull her out of the doldrums that swallowed her. The only way to retrieve a drowning person was to reach for them. He stretched out his arm and stroked his knuckles lightly over her knee.

"More's the point, how are you?"

That feathery touch drew her out of the fog. She swiped messy strands of hair, which had come loose from the single braid that curled over her shoulder. Lydia looked like she had woken from a nap and the braid had barely survived a battle with her pillow.

"Overtired." Her thumb rubbed the side of her glass.

"Have your late nights of painting worn you down? Or is it as many in the household fear? The countess's sharp tongue has wounded you so gravely that you need to hide away to lick said wounds?"

Her nose tipped high on this second option, alerting him to the threat of damaging female pride.

"I didn't sleep well last night. That's all," she said and took another sip of the scotch before setting the glass on the table to clamp her arms under her breasts. "But I'll acknowledge all here gave me fair warning about the famous Lady E. And now I've seen, or heard, rather, her in action."

"Ah, then I need to do my utmost to repair the damage so she doesn't scare off the fair damsel I've trapped in my lair."

"I don't scare that easily, but I hope you've ordered her to sheath her claws." Her thick eyebrows drew together in as firm and flat a line as her mouth.

Her voice held that low alto quality that he'd noticed came to her by the end of the day. And he had his verdict: this was a case of clear escape.

"Better still, I've banished her for a day. How's that for helping a damsel in distress?" He grinned and stretched his arm across the back of the settee toward her. "I encouraged the countess at dinner that she visit a good friend in London tomorrow, do some shopping, and give you a reprieve for a day."

Her eyebrows arched high. "You mean we can carry on tomorrow minus the countess training?"

"Yes. You don't have to see her at all if you don't want to."

Her shoulders eased a fraction, and she hugged a pillow

to her midsection, flipping the gold tassel. That's when he noticed her face looked a shade or two paler than usual, and purplish crescents darkened the fragile flesh under her eyes. Was there something else? Edward leaned closer on the settee.

"So this is a mix of difficulties, the countess combined with a sleepless night?" he prodded. "Nothing more serious than that?"

She rested her chin on the pillow. "I've been a lot of bluster about being able to stand on my own, haven't I?"

"If that's what this is, then I'm glad it's nothing serious." He smiled and moved closer, his hand within reach of her knees. "Actually, you've given me a new trial to face."

"What's that?"

"The dilemma of talking with a woman for no particular reason over no particular subject. Usually I'd find out what I needed to know, or impart necessary information and leave." He smiled at her. "I'm learning to converse for no other purpose than conversation itself."

"Dreadful, isn't it?" she gibed with a sleepy, teasing smile. "Having to converse with a woman and not necessarily having a deep topic or explicit task at hand." A sparkle relit her eyes, and she tipped her head, exposing the part of her neck he longed to explore.

She had no idea what that tilt of her head did to him. His pulse quickened, and warmth spread through him. Edward was lost in the graceful lines exposed to his view as she continued her banter, unknowing of the riot inside him.

"Or perhaps in the hope of drawing closer to the other person?" Her siren's alto stirred him, breaking through his muddle.

He searched her eyes, languid with the evening's ease. "You're throwing down the gauntlet on this nocturnal visit, aren't you?" *And more of your diverting stretch of neck will be the prize.*

"I am, my lord. Are you up to the challenge?"

Edward faced facts right then. He wanted to truly know *her*, which was a daunting task of emotions mixed with facts. For some reason, that white desk caught the corner of his eye at the same time that stunning revelation hit him. Papers stacked in neat piles across the surface. It was on the tip of his tongue to ask what she had shut away in the drawer when he entered, but fate turned him in another direction.

"I may be revealing trade secrets of every male, but the trick is knowing when to listen and when to tune a woman out. All while giving the appearance of attentive listening. I've done that all my life. Perfected the skill to an art form."

"At least you've mastered an art." She batted the pillow against his encroaching thigh and laughed, a deep, sensual sound. "And how will I be able to tell when you're truly listening and when you're playing false with me?"

"That's my secret. Something you'll have to figure out over the years to come."

As soon as he said that, her cheerful sparkle faded, and she looked away. The bottom edge of Lydia's upper teeth showed on her lower lip, and her thick brows worked with what he guessed were myriad thoughts running rampant in her head.

"That is one thing your mother and I have in common. I wish the same as her that you wouldn't go."

She swiped away the messy lighter strands of hair that framed her face. The line of her mouth wobbled. "I don't want to make you angry by saying that out loud. I cannot even explain it. I have no claim to you, but..."

She shrugged and stared off into the fire. He wouldn't fight her on that statement. He wished for the ease to continue, but he was a swimmer beyond his depth here on female emotions and wants. Silence hung between them, an awkward kind for him, though she appeared wistful and at ease. He cleared his throat and settled his hand atop his knee, all the closer to hers. The red-stained bandage on his thumb was a flair of color and, like a conversation lifeline, Edward showed her the appendage.

"See what happened tonight?"

She reached over, and her hands cradled his larger hand. "What did you do?"

He welcomed the coddling touch.

"Not a bad cut, but I was preparing seed pods for a friend of mine in Edinburgh, Dr. Finley. We share a lively correspondence on our work." He shrugged off that explanation of a man she'd likely never meet. "I was so focused on getting things done that I tried to do the cutting at night, when I had no business doing so." He inched closer. His head was very near hers. "The bark that grows on the tree from that seed cures rampantly bleeding wounds."

Her dark lashes fringed wide-open eyes.

"Do you recall the other treatise that you're copying for me? The one on the *Agathosma betulina*?"

"Yes." She nodded rapidly and glanced over at the desk. "I worked on it some today when I was feeling up to it."

"Good. I need that done and soon. That plant has curatives for the same kidney disease that claimed my father." His hands cupped hers, and his voice lowered as he focused on her appendages.

Her skin was soft, with a few small calluses, especially on the inner part of her thumb and index finger, where the wooden stem of her paintbrush rubbed the skin. He massaged her palm, making tender circles over white-pink flesh. The act rendered her speechless, but the small, dark space between her lips was closer.

"Don't you see? There are so many lives that could be saved. Families wouldn't have to endure what mine faced."

She licked her soft lips, drawing his attention to her plush, lower lip. But she surprised him with a soft-voiced revelation of her own.

"Your father, your brother...that's what drives you," she whispered. "The loss of them."

He nodded, his shoulders shifting against the back cushion. Lydia had just peeled back a layer that left him denuded, and like any man who found himself suddenly bared, the exposure was a new, uncomfortable thing. He needed grounding. He needed her. Their fingers, still moving from the desire to explore flesh, somehow became intertwined.

"What started as youthful study and curiosity turned into something else long ago. I'd hear stable masters talk of applying poultices to a horse's damaged fetlocks, and midwives discuss herbal remedies." He shook his head and looked her in the eye. "Then much-vaunted physicians slit veins, bleeding patients as was done in medieval times."

"Sounds barbaric," she agreed.

She understood, and that lifted a burden from his shoulders.

"And now you see why I must find better answers. I planned a six-month expedition along the western coast of Africa and was stunned by what I found. I brought back as many seeds, pods, and stripling plants, trees, and bushes as I could fit on the ship. By then, Jonathan and my father were dead. I admit I skulked away for that expedition while my mother still grieved." He shook his head. "I had no business going then."

Her hand reached up and touched his scarred cheek. He froze. No one ever touched him there. The burned parts gave a slight haze of sensation and pressure, but the other scars gloried under her fingertips skimming his flesh, so hungry was he for touch—anywhere. Sublime pleasure stirred him in a straight arrow line to his loins. With his bulk leaning close, and her slender white hand stroking his hairline and feathering his cheekbones, he could be a beast calmed by a forest maiden, so still was he. Her index finger traced the skin next to his left eye.

"I noticed this half-circle scar the first night at the Blue Cockerel and wondered about it." Those fingers of hers skimmed the outer edge of his eyebrow and moved down his cheek again. "Was the countess angry?"

"What?" He blinked.

Her hand slid to his jacket. "Your mother," she said, a smile playing about her lips. "She must've been beyond upset at your voyage."

"She was furious with me when I returned, the wounds notwithstanding. At the worst moments, I imagined the attack, my scars were a form of penance. I felt guilty about not doing a better job as head of the family…that promise I gave my father." He winced at the memory. "He knew me far too well. Nor did it help matters with Jane in her flights of rebellion, but we all eventually recovered and found our footing."

Lydia's hand grazed his coat at the opening, a slow trail down near his navel that teased him. Something in her dark green eyes told him she read him again.

"You all have your own ways of adjusting to pressures."

"Even before things went bad, we did." His voice went thick and slow. "Jon conformed, Jane rebelled, and I hid away in science." His dry bark of laughter was in no way humorous. "And my mother adjusted in hers."

"What do you mean?"

Edward shrugged that off and looked her in the eye. "More the point, do you understand?"

With that quiet question, a slight distance filled in the space. They'd come full circle to his need to leave, to do, to accomplish much.

"I think I do," she ventured, tucking some hair behind her ear. "At least you're not running off after treasures of gold and silver."

Her lips parted as if words wanted to spill forth, but she wasn't altogether sure to release that dam. Edward nodded at her, wanting more of this intriguing intimacy.

"Go ahead. We can, by now, be honest with each other. That's something I've come to value about you."

As soon as he said that, her features tightened and her eyes half-closed, pinched and uneasy. Lydia let words pour out in a soft plea as her fingers slipped inside his coat.

"Then why not stay and share what you've already learned with all and sundry? Support another scientist to go on the expedition, and you stay. Present your findings to the Royal Society." She tugged on his shirt, finishing on a higher note.

Her green eyes, lighter in color yet fathomless, searched him.

"Edward, I've not simply copied your research, I've read it. What you've written is astounding. You could change so much." Her head tipped in gentle amazement. "But you must present your findings in person, otherwise the words will lose their power and momentum. Isn't it discourse, face-to-face communication that makes all the difference?"

His lips tightened, as much because she spoke the truth as he didn't want to hear that truth. Nor did he want to lose the connection building between them. He liked the subtle play of her fingers inside his jacket. But this time a new pull grabbed hold of him, one he wasn't ready to name. He shook his head.

"No. That's why I need to get cuttings and seeds out to other scientists with the minds and the means of similar greenhouses. And the supply I have is few and fragile. I must find more to prove my theories." He looked her in the eye. "To do that, I have to go to other continents."

Her questing hand on his shirt froze. She removed it to the pillow's neutral ground. The absence of her searching appendage left a void. They were at an impasse, the same as when he'd entered the room. This was an altogether different kind of barrier: they'd moved into new, deeper territory of intimacy and honesty. But the wall of differences remained, if not more entrenched.

"Besides, I don't relish going out into Society." He pulled away, sitting up straighter. "Forgive me, but I thought you understood."

"Oh, Edward, I do, I do." She inched closer to him across the cushion, the velvet wrapper loosening in her progress. "You'll forgive me for wanting you to stay."

In moving toward him, her right leg unfolded from beneath her, and she stretched the limb toward him. The action wasn't meant to seduce or attract, but he stared at her knee, shrouded by very thin linen pulled taut across that spot. The hearth's fire brought to full relief the art of a woman's limb…Lydia's.

Viewing with fascination that section of barely covered flesh, he smiled. Men could be so preoccupied with breasts and bottoms as to miss the delicate beauty of a woman's pretty knee. Too many landscapes of curves and skin and not enough time to memorize them all.

A small, dark mole dotted the center of her knee. He gave in to temptation, tracing the indents that bracketed her joint with thumb and forefinger. Her soft intake of breath from the gentle, unexpected caress was music to his ears, but her skin's response snared him as much as that subtle sound. Visible waves of reaction pricked her skin, goose bumps under her threadbare night shift.

Edward bent low and kissed the tiny mole. Her skin was warm under his mouth. He lingered over that spot, breathing in her scent and wanting to open his mouth wider and taste her. He spread his hand over her leg. His palm skimmed the back of her calf, down to her slender ankles, where he stroked the delicate shape.

"You know, I also came here because I wanted to check on you. See for myself if you were well or not." His voice was rough to his ears. "But I want to stay for very selfish reasons."

"You mean tonight?" Her head tipped with languorous invitation. "Or longer?"

He chuckled, catching what she implied, and was not bothered that Lydia pushed him to stay in England.

"Both."

Her dark green eyes widened at the admission. Strange, he wasn't bothered that he wanted to stay—now or longer. Sex was a drug, and Lydia, his wife-to-be, was turning out to be a rich, enticing elixir. Isn't that what he wanted? A congenial woman in his bed?

He chuckled at that. Sitting close with his hand exploring forbidden flesh, Edward could easily give in to the lure before him.

Most of his brain gave in to the mind-numbing sensual flood, forgoing rational thought, but somewhere in the growing haze, a section of his brain marched on, stridently reminding him of the facts: he'd be the worst kind of oaf to press her in her state of lethargy. He took a slow, deep breath, ready to dive in no matter the consequence. His hand encircled her ankle then slid along the straight line of her shin, snagging and dragging her shift higher. The act bared inches of smooth, fair leg above the ankle.

If he kissed that bare skin, he would stay.

Edward battled his urge, about to give in. And then he saw again her pallid face and the shadows under her eyes.

His other hand reached up to her face, the same as that first night at the Blue Cockerel. His palm grazed her cheek, such fair, smooth skin, and his thumbs barely brushed her cheekbones. Lydia's mouth opened, revealing that secret dark space between her lips that tempted him. His thumb traced her succulent lower lip, the wanton plushness needed testing.

"I'd better leave before I do something foolish, like press myself on a woman in need of a good night's sleep." *Or stay with you and never leave.*

His body protested the change of plans. Edward rose from the settee and winced. He adjusted his breeches from the pressure building at the placket. He faced the fire, not willing that she see the effect a little tenderness and intimacy had on him. Of course she likely knew; his Lydia was no babe in the woods.

He moved closer to the hearth to collect himself, all while planning to tend the mellow fire. Edward crouched down, his legs spread wide to give more space in his breeches. He settled another log on the iron grate and stared, hypnotized by the dancing orange and yellow flames. Coming here tonight, he played with a deadlier fire.

And why this sudden need to be honorable with a woman of some experience? A woman he'd wed and bed soon enough? Edward's loins clenched with deep ache, snapping him out of his haze. He flinched and a hoarse, dry chuckle escaped him. Gingerly, he stood up and jammed his hands in his coat pockets. When he faced Lydia, she tucked the night-robe about her legs, looking long in the mouth. Never had he seen so forlorn a face.

"You will take yourself off to bed, won't you?" he asked, not trusting himself to help her with that task.

"Yes." She gave the barest nod.

"You understand...my leaving?"

"As long as you understand my desire that you stay." *Forever.*

Sad, dark-lashed eyes had some kind of power over him. The emotion in her limpid green gaze reached inside him. The wanting pummeled his gut from loss and denial.

"Good night, Lydia."

Edward retreated to his room before he caved into temptation and never left. The air shrouded him with cool emptiness. His mind moved, but not racing with its usual speed of thought. Somehow his feet led him to his study, where he sat at his desk and propped his boots on the desktop. Tonight, even his treasured books held no allure.

❦

As the clock struck midnight...

Edward grabbed a candelabrum from a hall table, and in a fog of tiredness, strode to the ballroom. His boot-steps echoed in the cavernous spaces. All were abed in the house when he pushed the ballroom's double doors wide. He honed in on the makeshift art studio and held the flickering candles at shoulder height, unwrapping one burlap painting after another. He needed to know, to understand.

Perhaps his diminished state of exhaustion opened him, a physical weakening that affected his soul. This past year, no, these past three years had been hard. Maybe the entrancing connection he'd made with the woman upstairs, the first of its kind, opened channels he'd left solidly dammed. But his body was loose-jointed and free, ready to accept, *to feel*, what came his way. A novel notion to be sure.

What was it Lydia said? Something about letting his feelings respond to what he saw. He let himself see, all right. He chuckled dryly again. No, this wasn't an exact science. This went far beyond his realm of comfort, but he'd let come what may and not try to analyze it. Some habits, though, didn't fade away from one lesson, he decided, when gaining an inkling of victory over one piece and another.

"Let's see what you wish to tell me," he said aloud, pulling burlap from paintings, "or should I say 'what you wish to tell the world'?"

Lydia had painted proper English landscapes, two of them. Not eye-catching at all. Though of reputable quality and excellent images, nothing that stirred the soul. They could be like everyday women in sturdy English morning dresses: you'd know something covered a wall, but it didn't dress it.

Then she became more interesting by going outside the lines of acceptable subjects. Her smaller painting featured a country maid, her breast half-bare as she nursed her babe in a kitchen.

The image would not grace the wall of any grand English drawing room, but the painting, excellent and appeasing to the eye, tore back the curtain of formal veneer. Intimacy, of the deep and trusting kind, struck him with awe. Lydia had captured love and tenderness, yet the mother looked facedown at her swaddled child. There was no eye contact of the subject with the viewer.

Could one even say an art piece *looks back* at the viewer? The mesmerizing image rattled him.

How did Lydia do that?

He glanced at the lone easel. That square hidden under cloth called to him.

He walked briskly to that covered easel and tore back the cloth cover, revealing the small canvas square that vexed him most. The cover bunched in his left hand and draped to the floor like a woman's skirts.

The Chinese Pear Tree. The piece played with his insides, luring him.

"Art," he said under his breath. "What am I *not* seeing?"

Lydia's words from the other day still stung. Her instruction harangued him. This was his third time coming back to view this piece since that meeting. The first time he snuck away for a perfunctory few minutes, staring at several paintings in the family art gallery, staring at family portraits, and then viewing some of the famous pieces, but ending with this one. Seeking to examine art in different lights, he found himself going back to a few that he liked. The second time, viewing the work in daylight hours, availed nothing new.

Each time he ended face-to-face with *The Chinese Pear Tree. Why?*

Edward raised the candelabrum higher, squinted at the painting, and exhaled his exasperation. After victory with the painting of the mother and babe, why couldn't he see this one? Enough.

"I'm going to bed," he said, growling the words.

Just as he turned, candlelight flickered, and shadows flitted across the tree. The action tricked the eye, as if the tree moved. He jerked from the strange perception and squinted again. The cover cloth dropped to the ground. He hoisted the candelabrum higher. There. The half-hidden fruit, waiting like a woman dancing in the shadows. He touched stiff, dried paint.

The play of light drew his attention to the hidden fruit. Words poured from his lips.

"Lines…less distinct…a specter of an object, shapes…

rather than definitive lines showing completion." He took two more steps back. "That's why I think it's unfinished. Only the forefront has thin, completed lines. The fruit appears whole, yet—"

He moved closer and inspected the background foliage. More fruit, ethereal silhouettes, hidden behind leaves. So like a woman, layers of revelation and hidden depths.

"How did she do that?" he whispered and looked over at the other uncovered paintings along the wall.

Some were quite traditional. Others brought to mind a different feel, something primal. His eyes were drawn to the tantalizing Chinese pear tree. That center fruit still looked very much to him like a woman's nude bottom. The side of his mouth quirked at the possibility that the image could be a self-portrait of sorts.

There's only one way to confirm that.

He grinned yet, something else bedeviled him. The distinct foreground, what was at the surface, was obvious.

"What we see, what *I* see is evident, yet only surface." He smiled. "Ah, Lydia, the remaining treasures need to be searched out and wooed by the patient beholder. You and I are much more than what the outside world sees."

One needed to take a longer look to find and plumb those rich depths. The dark-haired woman sleeping upstairs taught him as much. This painting was her siren call. To him.

Edward let loose a peal of laughter, whole and round, that bounced around the ballroom as euphoria filled him. He was like a blind man newly sighted. Candles wobbled and dripped wax on the floor.

What he *felt* was primal, passionate, and pure. Like Lydia. Yes, Lydia was the best kind of pure. Honest and refreshing with enticing mystery. Her art reflected her, and she reflected her art.

Truth, like an alluring woman, sat right before his eyes.

Seventeen

When we have gold, we are in fear.
When we have none, we are in danger.

—English Proverb

No MATTER THE WOMAN, FROM SCULLERY MAID TO lofty queen, sex leveled her playing field. Hadn't that always been the case from the most ancient of times? Oh, some of the fairer sex held a trove of talents, others wealth and keen minds, but the one consistent line through the fabric of time was sex and sensuality. Women wielded so much power, much more than men, in the give and take of sensual pursuits. Then, why, why, why after only one kiss to her knee was she considering tossing all and sundry to the wind?

Stay or go? That was the question.

There was no delicate way to put this as she pushed off the answer to the last possible moment. Avoidance remained a coward's path, and Lydia ran headlong down it with both eyes shut, like some kind of fool. For two days she embraced indecision, and peace of mind was the cost, with discomfort her reward. Lud, but the pressure was horrid.

But what an intoxicating kiss. *To her knee*. And there were Edward's caresses to consider. Why did his touch fan flames wherever his fingers skimmed flesh? Just thinking about where his hand had touched caused a minor shiver.

She closed her eyes and let the headiness play out in her mind. The surprise: images of laughing and talking, trading quips and barbs with his lordship came to the fore. Was this really about the lure of sex? Of gold? Art? Or something else?

When Lydia opened her eyes, the bristles of her new ox-hair paintbrush fanned the canvas, smearing blobs of paint. Canvas stretched that morning, and already the painting had turned to a messy disaster. Like her. Lines failed to form, shapes didn't mesh. Two agonizing days had crawled by with tossing and turning over her ladyship's offer, when she should have slept. Misery and melancholy claimed her when she should have been wide awake and vibrant about her future. Today, by sunset when the countess returned, she had to decide: stay or go.

Lady Elizabeth's scandalous offer tempted her in ways she couldn't fathom.

At the same time, the offer reviled her in ways she was just beginning to probe.

The primary reason to leave was her art; the singular reason to stay was a man.

Why did Edward have to come to her room last night with his honest, sensual appeal that touched her to the core? She was certain his lordship was knocked back a step or two, as well, by that nocturnal visit. Oh, he had to be as affected as her by the surprising closeness that had filled the room, encircling them on the settee. His body had responded to the novel caresses they'd exchanged.

Strange, though they were hardly sexual, her body craved him. Her hoyden's mouth quirked sidewise, recalling the way he'd tried to hide his arousal by poking at the fire; she was glad he shared some discomfort from their unique situation.

At the moment, the tempting man was sweating in one of his silliest pursuits: Edward participated in a jump-rope race against Jonas Bacon. Both grown men had spent more than an hour practicing swordsmanship, fencing mostly with short swords. They worked to best the other at one feat of athleticism after another, laughing their way through the ballroom. In the current competition, Sanford Shipping's man of business lagged far behind the fleet-footed earl, who whipped his rope in a frantic race to reach one hundred jumps before Mr. Bacon.

"…ninety-eight, ninety-nine, one hundred!" Edward crowed his victory, dropping the long hemp rope as he raised both fists high.

His chest heaved under the sweat-dampened shirt. He gave her a bold smile and a bow, playing to his attentive audience of one. Linen clung to both men's torsos, since both had claimed with her presence in the ballroom, they would honor propriety and keep their shirts on. She glanced over the top of her new, larger canvas at the boyish display. When she looked back at the canvas, her brush had smeared a new arc of muddied color: this was nothing like the exotic specimen she'd seen, the *butterfly bush* it was called, beginning to bloom in the greenhouse.

She exhaled long and rubbed her rag so hard across the canvas that the easel's legs rattled and scraped the floor.

"Why the glum face?" Edward walked toward her, wiping a towel across his nape. He breathed heavily from his unusual sprint. "I thought you'd be euphoric with my mother gone. No countess lessons today."

He managed a wide smile that showed nice even teeth. With moisture dotting his hairline, his queue near undone, and shirt untucked, Edward looked more like a laborer ending his day than any nobleman. How could she let a man throw her off this much?

"Perhaps like you, I wish to work uninterrupted." She dropped the rag to her feet and took a step back to contemplate how she'd rework this piece.

Lydia dabbed and mixed a shade of onyx and blue and red, trying to achieve the perfect purplish hue, but even her palette had become a disarray of smeared colors. She bristled at his lightheartedness. How could he smile and be so at ease? Of course, his world was ordered and known; hers was the one thrown into disorder and uncertainty. Part of her was tempted right then to spill the news of his mother's offer, just to relieve the pressure.

"Ah, we've reached an understanding then on the importance of work, my work at least," he said with a teasing wink while moving around to see the latest project. "I'll have you know I've once again become an astute pupil of Aristotle."

"And what exactly have you learned?" she asked, cranky and out of sorts.

"That I'm attracted to a distinct and brilliant woman."

Her lips parted. Why did he have to say wonderful things like that and look incredibly handsome and appealing? The soft way he said those words was as effective as his touch, though at the moment he kept his hands to himself. Edward gave her his brash smile, and the scarred skin creased handsomely, as did the unscarred cheek. What woman in her right mind could turn away from him? Her brush hung midair, thick with purple, and she cleared her throat, trying for prim control.

"Somehow, I can't think Aristotle said that." She licked her lips, all of her warm and muddled.

That fuzzy sensation in her head from mulling over the countess's proposal melted under his stimulating presence. The corners of his eyes creased with a deeper smile. Edward looked very satisfied with the effect his compliment had on her.

"No, I came to that conclusion on my own." He clasped his arms across his chest, taking a glimpse at her latest work. His head canted to the left and then the right as he examined the purplish mess. "But he did say that art consists of bringing something into existence, and that impresses me about you. I never quite thought of art that way."

"Because you never thought about art at all," she chided gently, but her heart swelled under his second compliment. "Does my painting something or someone make the subject more real to you?"

"Says the teacher to her student." He grinned and moved closer to her.

His gaze went from her current, unformed painting to the Chinese pear tree painting that sat alone near the workbench. His lordship's arms moved loosely in front of him as he wiped the rag once more over his face and neck.

"I can't figure it all out yet. But I'm getting there."
He glanced back at the sensual fruit and grinned. "Want
to know another conclusion?"

"Please." Lydia coached herself to keep calm under
the onslaught of unexpected charm.

"The month-long mandate is too long." His eyes
sparked with new light that had nothing to do with art
appreciation.

Her sharp, involuntary intake of breath was quiet and
heard only between them. Lydia studied her palette and
schooled herself to regain composure before meeting his
newly smoldering gaze.

"You're full of surprises today, my lord—"

"Edward, remember?"

"Of course. Edward. What brought about the hasten-
ing of our bargain?" she asked, trying to regain equilibrium. "Surely not Aristotle. I don't think he wrote a
single romantic word, did he?"

His topaz eyes darkened. "No, I'm swayed by simple
biology."

Her heart dropped. She kept a semblance of a smile
frozen on her face. "And here I thought you were going
to wax on about being smitten with me."

His molten gaze lowered to the practical neckline of
her smock and then a little lower, where the swells of her
breasts pressed against the coarse fabric.

"A few things have developed between us. Something
mutual." The line of his mouth flattened. "But, Lydia,
tell me you're not developing any affection for me. I'll
only disappoint."

Could he have added another stone to her pile of confusion and discontent? She gave him her best nonchalant

toss of her head and paid attention to her palette, dipping her brush into who knows what color.

"Of course, not. Our original agreement was very clear as to what was expected. And you have been more than generous with me." Both her shoulders shrugged tightly then dropped. "We have the good fortune to enjoy certain attraction. And that works in our favor."

"Good. Because I notified my solicitor that we should move matters along...late next week, I think?"

"Next week?" she yelped.

He balled the rag in his hand and called out, "Jonas, put this with the other rags, will you?"

He tossed the cloth at Jonas, who caught it handily on his way to the pile of swords. The Colonial, his massive chest working hard to grab deep breaths, picked up a pitcher and tipped it over. Empty.

"I'll see about more water." The way his clear blue eyes assessed her and Edward, Lydia needed to hide. His skills of perception were well-honed for a rough man of business.

As Jonas left the room, the countess's proposition rang in her head, but the sound of it was as flat and unappealing as the alternative—a passionate if emotionless marriage. Then Edward dropped another offering at her feet.

"I may have been too optimistic with my timeline. Beside, all the better to help your mother. You could write her today and let her know. That'll be a tremendous relief to her." His tanned face glowed with the kind offer.

Lydia glanced at the floor and grimaced at the bald fact that she'd forgotten all about her mother's welfare, so concerned with her own wants these two days. She jabbed the ox-hair brush, thick with purple, on the canvas.

"She'd like that news very much," she murmured, not able to look him in the eye.

Edward stood near her shoulder, perusing the progress of this painting and trying to keep their earlier agreeable connection. For a man who didn't like social discourse, he sought her out often enough.

"Of course, this means you cannot escape countess lessons." He said the words with an amused thread in his voice. "We've all the more reason now we're speeding things up."

His words stirred her hair, and a tantalizing shiver grazed the shell of her ear. Edward's fingers brushed back strands that had fallen loose from their pins. Her paintbrush halted under the unexpected touch. Like a cat purring from a tender stroke, her head tipped toward his caressing hand. Lydia's body shivered under the voluminous smock.

"I suppose this means you no longer doubt me," she said quietly, trying to keep some composure while her brush dabbed here and there.

His long fingers stroked and played with wisps of hair that had come loose around her collar, lulling her with gentle movement. His hand slid to her shoulder and then slipped lower, trailing warm pressure down her spine. Her brush slipped on what was supposed to be a petal, and purple flared.

"I was wrong that first night," he said, his lips grazing her ear. "I know it in my bones I can trust you."

A bolt like lightning in a dark sky shot through her. She gave up on the pretense of painting but didn't move. Sensual quivers shook her body, spreading across her buttocks, the globes of which clenched. All of her thrummed like a plucked instrument to the man teasing and stroking her so skillfully from behind. His touch, his words made her long for more, but that gift he gave—his trust. What was more potent to her?

"And then there is this attraction between us," he said, tracing one side of her face. "But there is one other serious proposition I have for you. About your art."

Somber reason intruded. Her neck stiff, Lydia tilted her head forward a fraction, away from the earl's drugging presence. She needed a clear head.

"What about it?"

"When I wrote my solicitor about our wedding next week, I mentioned your wish to sell your art and—"

She yelped from a surge of excitement, and swung around to face him. She had read him all wrong. He would support and promote selling her art. With palette in one hand and paintbrush in the other, Lydia flung her arms around him and set her cheek to his chest.

"Thank you, Edward. You've *no* idea what this means to me," she cried.

His calloused hands gripped her forearms and carefully peeled her from him. "I welcome overtures of appreciation, but wait until you hear all that I have to say."

The cultured, factual tone of his voice didn't bode well, reminding her of stodgy requirements that always got in the way of what she wanted. Her arms hung at her sides. She waited for the latest ruling that would affect her life. Edward's face bore that serious barrister's expression, the same one he'd worn after he caught her snooping in his room.

"I get the feeling this doesn't go well for me." Lydia glanced down at her palette and brush, and the desire to paint diminished. "I'd better put these away."

Edward followed her to the worktable. "It's not all that bad. I asked him to look into the inner workings of the art world." Edward set both hands on his hips. "I want to support you, but the Countess of Greenwich is a position of some esteem and expectation. Miss Lydia Montgomery may turn Britain's art world on its ear, but the Countess of Greenwich? That's a different matter."

She rubbed a cloth vigorously over her hands. "So that's it? My art's on the shelf if I marry you."

"If?" His eyebrows slammed together, and that sharp line between his eyebrows appeared. "We already have that one resolved, don't we?" he asked sharply.

She slapped the rag on the bench. "Of course we do."

"Good. I only beg your patience while my solicitor sorts this out. You've waited this long, a few more months won't matter, will it?"

She wanted to toss his words back at him, but something worse began to happen. She refused to look him in the eye.

"I guess not."

This wasn't supposed to happen to her anymore. Hot, horrible tears formed; how long since she'd last cried? The prickling pain pinched the insides of her eyes, pushing, pushing until the first determined tears spilled.

When would this ever happen for her?

Lydia dipped her head and rubbed her forehead, hiding the wetness filling her eyes. This was not a resolved matter. And as scalding tears came one after another, she remembered the last time she wept: right after she saw Nate, her erstwhile farmer of four years ago.

She'd been politely asked by her mother to leave Somerset right after the Duchess caught her with Nate, but brimming with joy, she ran to the village public house where her handsome farmer waited. She was onto a better, different path. When Lydia, full of smiles, pushed open the door, his gorgeous eyes sparkled at her over the shoulder of a tawdry doxy giggling in his lap. He shrugged and mouthed: *sorry, luv.*

And that was that.

Her dark-haired farmer would never know the painful destruction he'd meted out in her life. She ran out the door before he witnessed scalding tears of humiliation. Lydia packed herself off to Wickersham, swearing never to cry in front of a man again, which was easy when keeping them at a distance. But Edward was not satisfied with being shut out; he was determined to witness her shame. His hand tipped up her chin.

"Lydia, what's this all about?" His palm grazed her cheek, brushing the damp streaks. "I know you want this badly, but wait. Please wait, and all will be resolved."

Edward was a watery blur, his features distorted. His fingers slipped into her hair, and something about her must have touched a caring nerve, because he groaned and drew her into his arms. Once he kissed her forehead, all fragile threads of control broke.

And how good it felt to have a man hold her with the simple gift of his tender care.

His hands cradled her head, his fingers kneading her scalp in gentle touches. Strong, sculpted lips pressed her forehead, her temple, her high cheekbone, sliding along inches of skin until meeting her lips, open and ready for him. Her tears salted their kisses. The surprise of that contact exploded the air around them. Edward pressed her, or she pressed Edward, so tight, limb to limb, fitting curves and planes together. The buttons of his placket ground into her abdomen as both tried for as much contact with the other.

She was letting herself drown in a man. Again.

But this was Edward.

Her hands, searching, moving, gripped his untucked linen shirt and found access to the smooth skin of his waist.

Someone groaned, perhaps both of them, when her fingers connected with his torso, spanning to consume every inch of flesh: smooth flesh, hard and taut, narrow, slippery burn scars, thicker ridges, and gooseflesh as her touch feathered this way and that. His skin, hot from his exertions, was a wonder to feel.

Hot need shot through her, flaring between her legs. The shock made her stiffen. Her fingers slid along Edward's ribs, and she held on for dear life. Lydia wrapped her hands around his back when her lower lip slipped between his roving lips. The gentle way he sucked on her plump lip, and his tongue exploring that wet space, her knees buckled.

Lydia swayed into him, her back arching, but his hands caught her. His warm hand splayed wide against her upper back. The other ventured lower, massaging circles, lower, lower. Edwards's hands, like his kisses, belonged to an explorer, not a ruthless conqueror. Testing and checking, his firm but gentle caresses enticed her into his web of curiosity and question. His kisses, his touch were not the rehearsed moves of a long-practiced rake, but genuine affection and sensuality braided into an explosive mix that promised to incinerate them on the spot if they didn't stop.

Her head tilted back, exposing her neck, and Edward groaned anew as his lips rubbed the smooth column. The tip of his tongue touched the pulsing beat at the base of her neck, sending another shudder through her. Lydia's head rolled to his shoulder. Her eyes opened a tiny bit, enough to see a red-faced, round-eyed footman frozen in the doorway. She gave Edward a gentle push.

"Edward," she whispered, drugged by him and not willing to let go. "Edward, there's a footman...in the doorway."

"Tell him to go away," he whispered against her collarbone, his warm lips concentrating on her flesh there.

The footman raised a balled fist to his mouth and coughed loudly, taking tentative steps into the ballroom. He waited a moment. His eyes inspected the ceiling's plaster work, and he coughed again with more volume. Something couldn't wait. She pushed harder, and cool space separated them, setting the back of her hand to her swollen lips.

"This must be important," she said, looking into Edward's near-black eyes.

He bore the presence of a man roused from a warm bed who'd hastily dressed, not bothering to tuck in his shirt. Heavy breathing from their shared passion controlled them; their chests pumped in unison seeking air, but Edward followed the cant of her gaze and slowly went about tucking in his shirt in the back of his breeches. He gave her that brigand's half smile and turned around to face the door.

"What is it, man?" he called across the ballroom.

"The countess, milord, she's returned and wishes to

see Miss Montgomery." The older, red-faced footman, shifted from one foot to the other. "I'm sorry to bother you, milord, but she was most insistent."

Lydia's shoulders dropped. All of her was a mess... her heart, her hair, the paint on her fingers. But the time of reckoning had come, and earlier than expected. She glanced outside: there was too much daylight left. Something had brought Lady Elizabeth back early.

"Very well," she said, tugging the smock over her head. "In the blue drawing room, is she?"

The footman stood ramrod straight. "No, miss, she waits for you in your room."

Eighteen

Small opportunities are often the beginning of great enterprises.
—Demosthenes

"Is your corset on too tight? Because no sane woman in your circumstances would dare tell me '*no*.'" Lady Elizabeth's eyes glittered with elegant mayhem and threat. "Thus, I'm led to believe you're light-headed due to an inability to breathe."

"You heard me, Countess. I'm staying."

Audacious words that failed to match Lydia's insides.

The pink coliseum was their battleground, with the countess claiming ample space. This time, the noble-woman came with an ally. Her lady's maid, Simpson, stood near the pink-and-white canopied bed with stacks of long, plain boxes, dresses to be sure, but strange arma-ments in this clash of wills.

Was Lady E. worried enough to bring reinforcement?

Lydia linked paint-spattered fingers in her lap and waited. The countess, bathed in afternoon light, had looked in her element, ready to square off when Lydia walked through the door. Now, her stomach aquiver from their skirmish of words, she sat at the edge of her chair, back straight. Her ladyship's plump white hands fanned her yellow silk skirts across the settee where she sat enthroned. Her fingers plucked the stylish pearled trim on her puffy panniers, which took all her focus. When she looked up, her face was tight and drawn.

"Very well, two hundred guineas."

"You must not have heard me. I'm. Not. Leaving."

Rouged lips thinned to a sharp line but opened wide enough to say, "Two hundred fifty guineas, and that's my final offer."

Lydia's head tipped back as she chuckled, a shaky, humorless sound that covered her unease. "My lady, you could offer a thousand guineas and it wouldn't matter. I'm not going anywhere. Edward and I will marry, and there's nothing you can do about it."

One imperious blond brow rose at those audacious words, but Lydia's frayed nerves improved under that bold proclamation. Her exposed skin was cold despite the nearness of the fire. This was untested ground, when she didn't want them to be adversaries. How to tread carefully and turn this around? The bald fact remained: she *needed* the countess badly, but she wouldn't let the noblewoman see anything less than full bravado.

Lady Elizabeth's chin tipped high. "Why stay? People toss over others for money all the time."

Meaning you've done that before? Lydia silenced that coy question that badly wanted out, and cleared her throat. It was time to drop the lure.

"Have you considered that perhaps we can both get what we want?"

Lady Elizabeth's pale lids dropped, half covering her

eyes, as if she were measuring this unexpected turn and didn't find this new premise wholly lacking. The notion of mutual victory probably hadn't crossed the woman's mind. She likely worked only in wins and losses, placing herself squarely in the winning category, of course. But that singular question changed the atmosphere. Late afternoon air shifted and stirred between them. The first sprout of transformation from being adversarial, to a partnership of sorts grew.

"Go on," the countess said. "I'm listening."

"I should have known all along to ask: What do you want more? To have Edward stay in England? Or that he *not* marry me?"

That defining trio of questions must've stunned Lady Elizabeth. Her chin tipped to normal level as she glanced away, though she was still very stiff of spine. Her pink-white hands curled into fists, pressing down on her silk lap. The air of brittleness about the lady cracked. When she looked at Lydia again, her mask of high decorum slipped from her fine-boned features.

"I'd marry him to a swine herder's daughter if I thought that'd keep him here."

Lydia's hands clamped together. Despite her air of composure, dampness covered her palms. "What if I promised that he'll stay? Would you help me? I mean truly help me to become the kind of wife he needs in Society?"

"How can you make such a promise?" she sputtered as more fractures in her composure spread. She gave Lydia a good once-over. "What could you possibly do to keep him in England?"

Lydia opened her mouth to answer, but the frustrated countess charged ahead.

"So you and he share some attraction. Edward's never been one to be led about by a skirt." Her earbobs swayed emphatically from the lady's twitching head. "You'll have to do better than *that*."

Lydia smiled at what was the closest thing to crudeness from the countess. "Yes, I know, but you'll have to trust me."

"What? You harbor some kind of secret?" her ladyship said, her head tilting forward.

"In a manner of speaking, yes."

"And you wish me to give you the full force of my support to transform you"—the countess scooted to the edge of the seat, her voice rising an octave—"without so much as a hint as to your plan?"

"Yes, *and* with a minimum of barbs and insults." She took a deep breath. There. She'd stood her ground, seated, of course, on a pink-and-yellow chair.

Lady Elizabeth's lips tightened. "You mean the courtesy as deserving one in *my* station. Is that it?"

"Yes."

"And you'll somehow magically"—the countess circled a hand in the air as her voice rose another octave in disbelief—"keep my son in England."

"That's what we both want, isn't it?"

Lady Elizabeth shifted, and her body tipped backward onto the cushions and pillows as if the simple force of that question felled her. She exhaled loudly and stretched her arm along the backrest. Perhaps the weight of having to hold up appearances had overcome her right then? No matter, a thrill of victory shot through Lydia, and she fought the urge to jump up and yell, "Yes!"

This peace agreement wasn't sealed yet, but Lydia

was sure it was coming. Then Lady Elizabeth did a curious thing.

She glanced at Lydia and turned away, her manicured fingers tapping the settee's back cushion. The countess stared at the white writing desk, covered with papers, an ink pot, a quill, and lead writing sticks. Ink splotched the side lip of the delicate, white expanse, but the lady viewed that furniture as if she could read it. The countess nodded, appearing lost in thought, and finally turned to face Lydia.

"Very well. Though it pains me not to know this secret of yours, I am in desperate straits," she said, her voice sounding tired and worn. Still in repose, Lady Elizabeth raised her hand from the settee and snapped it twice in rapid clicks. "Simpson."

The servant left her position as stalwart guardian of the boxes. She moved toward the settee, where the countess pushed off the furniture, keeping her eye on Lydia.

"Yes, your ladyship."

Simpson, an attractive woman of middle years, was dressed and coiffed with above-average style for a lady's maid. There was nothing mousy or timid about her. The servant exuded confidence in her simple but pretty lavender dress, complete with modest panniers.

"We have a great task ahead of us. We must transform Miss Lydia Montgomery into the future Lady Lydia Sanford, Countess of Greenwich. You will instruct her maid on all the tricks of the trade, appropriate styles of clothes, hair befitting a lady of quality, and so forth." The countess's pale blue eyes narrowed as her stare went head to hem over Lydia. "And, Simpson, summon her maid, now."

"Yes, your ladyship." Simpson moved in graceful steps across the room to yank the pink bellpull.

"We'll begin with the most crucial elements: dress and comportment. I'll compose a list of what we need to do in the short term, and what can wait for later." Nodding, she studied Lydia's face as one might review a vase for purchase. "Thank goodness your skin is of excellent quality. But those eyebrows, hideous." She shivered over that pronouncement, and her blue gaze met Lydia's. "You *will* surrender to Simpson for plucking."

On reflex, Lydia's fingers touched her eyebrows. "I'm not a chicken to be trussed for dinner," she sputtered. "They work fine, in my opinion. Plucking sounds awful…" But her words lost momentum under the identical moues of disdain facing her.

"Your opinion doesn't matter," Lady E. said with authority. "Your brows are like a pair of caterpillars marching over your eyes. That won't do. Shaping them will enhance your appearance and add to your elegance. And you need great doses of the latter, my dear."

Her brows were thick but not all that bad. Lady Elizabeth's insults weren't really insults anymore, more like marching orders on this road to transformation. There was no sharp-edged meanness, and that's when the inkling struck her: becoming a countess, the Countess of Greenwich, at least, was about much more than putting on a new fancy dress.

Lydia's hand dropped to her lap. "Whatever you say, my lady."

"That's better. If I'm to trust you, then you need to return the favor." The countess didn't wait for an answer. She gestured to the stacked boxes. "I purchased some dresses while in London."

Right then, Tilly poked her head through the doorway,

holding the doorknob and leaning forward. "You called for me, miss?"

"I did," Lady Elizabeth announced. "And don't dawdle half-in, half-out. Bespeaks poor training."

Like a foot soldier trying to please a general, Tilly pulled herself upright and stepped into the room, head held high as she shut the door. She folded her hands demurely in front of her and waited.

"That's better." The countess nodded, her own spine ramrod straight with her hands clasped at her waist. Her elbows jutted from her side in perfect angles, dripping with pearled lace. "Tilly, we have a great deal of work ahead of us. To begin, I need you to bring two spoons and a basketful of eggs to the blue drawing room. Lots and lots of eggs."

Tilly's hazel eyes opened wider, but she curtsied. "Yes, my lady."

The young maid hesitated as her blinking eyes went from the countess to Lydia, but the countess clapped her hands twice and snapped her order, "Now."

Tilly sped from the room. The countess and Simpson bent their heads in quiet conversation. Lydia's composure started slipping. What did she need to know about more? The boxes? Or the eggs? Was the countess planning to toss them at her when she flubbed at tea service? Spoons and eggs, however odd, weren't right in front of her. Those dresses were.

"Countess." Lydia cocked her head at the secretive pair and pointed at the boxes. "How did you know?"

"How did I know your measurements?" A smile of pure feline satisfaction curved Lady E.'s lips. "My dear, divining that information was the easiest task on my list of how to get rid of you. However, finding *finished* gowns of quality with which to tempt you was another matter." The countess raised a hand toward the stacked boxes. "They were meant for a woman who fell out of favor with her protector and can no longer afford them."

Lydia's jaw dropped. "Protector? Just what kind of gowns are they?" She shook her head. "Nor can I believe that you would have given me the guineas *and* some dresses to get me to leave."

"Any woman in her right mind knows the importance of looking her best. I was prepared to tempt you with pretty gowns. But here we are." The countess linked her hands at her waist. "The quality is quite up to standards, excellent creations all of them. They're from one of London's better mantua-makers. Day dresses and two evening gowns with panniers, hooped petticoats, and shoes, though nothing fit for a ball, mind you. You'd be surprised how many courtesans move about in Society." Her nostrils flared as she took a deep breath, and as she rose, she gave Lydia a quick once-over. "But we digress. There's much to do. Meet me in the blue drawing room in half an hour. We begin work today."

The countess quit the room, and Simpson herded her to the dressing table to begin the rapid disassembling of one Lydia Montgomery. Her old dress and patched underskirts fell slack on the floor into a faded fabric puddle. Simpson picked up the old garments, and pinching them between two fingers, dropped them out of sight on the other side of the bed.

A long box opened, and from tufts of fragile tissue, a gorgeous swathe of burgundy with gold embroidery emerged. Lydia's heart beat faster, and she laid a calming hand over that place. Her reflection in the mirror was a comfortable one, but today was the last she'd see of her. Lydia accepted that she'd never see that woman again. Ever.

So bemused was she, that questions about eggs awaiting her downstairs were a mere footnote in this, her metamorphosis.

Nineteen

When you're finished changing, you're finished.
　　　　　　　　　　　　　　　　　—Benjamin Franklin

"MY DEAR, IT'S NOT WHAT'S IN YOUR HEAD THAT MAT-
ters, but how you look, your comportment. Those two
priorities are vital to your success."

Silk-clad and iron-willed, Lady Elizabeth sipped from
a fragile rose-petal dish, issuing pearls of wisdom as Lydia
concentrated on a most difficult and trying task: walk the
length of the spacious blue drawing room, holding two
spoons aloft that cradled fresh eggs—without dropping
said eggs, of course.

She wanted to be a perfect countess, but the skill of
walking and talking at the same time was apparently new
to her.

The silliness of that revelation should have been
enough to make her laugh, if she hadn't wanted to groan
her agony at the evidence of her lack in that simple
pursuit. Splats of eggs, casualties of her shortcomings,
dotted the pale blue carpet over which she trod. She
lost count at how many. Rogers and Tilly were down

on all fours, rapidly whisking cleaning cloths over lots of sticky explosions. Miss Lumley stood nearby in her new housekeeper gray, directing the two as she held a bowl to collect broken shells and yolk in one hand, and a bowl of cleaning solution in the other. She gave Lydia a wink on this latest pass.

"Doin' grand, miss. You're doin' grand," she said under her breath.

The worst of it so far wasn't the embarrassing lack of skill; rather, the loss of her newest beautiful gown, streaked with viscous yellow, hurt more than any damaged pride. Yet the countess seemed to take that loss as a matter of course. A surplus of lovely dresses made for a novel notion to Lydia. She tried a surreptitious peek at her hem, but was caught by the ever-watchful eye of her vigilant teacher.

"Ah, ah, ah. Head up at all times. It is the most gracious of comportments."

Lydia's head snapped up as she rounded a pair of chairs and delicate table. "This makes it seven, right?"

"Six." The powdered blond head of the countess shook an emphatic "no." "You won't succeed by short-changing yourself on this exercise." She set her teacup back on its saucer with a definitive clink and put the dishes down. "You will complete ten perfect rotations. That is my mandate if you are to have a successful walk. We will practice this every day until you get this right."

"And here I thought I'd walked well enough all these years." Lydia couldn't resist the temptation to smirk.

But her smirk at the countess was costly. Her knee bumped an ottoman, and down went an egg.

"Lud, another one down," she groaned when the

spoon's load lightened, followed by the inevitable crunch and splat.

Lady Elizabeth snapped her fingers for a fresh egg, which Tilly supplied and then dropped on fours to commence cleaning the new mess. The countess sighed and repeated her same instructions.

"Let's try again, shall we? Head up, shoulders back, arms to your sides, bent at the elbows, of course, to accommodate the spoons and eggs, level and forward. Think: always look forward."

"One," Lydia said aloud to denote the first of a new round of ten rotations.

"Know the landscape of the room, my dear, because that will enable you to *know* the landscape of a room." Her ladyship's rouged lips pursed on that mysterious advice.

Lydia moved past the large pale blue settee where the countess sat, and kept her face straight ahead. "I don't suppose you'll enlighten me on what you mean by knowing the landscape of a room? Something tells me there's more to it."

"Very good." Lady Elizabeth's head canted at a gentle angle, following Lydia's progress.

Then the lady was behind her, and she dared not turn around to look her in the eye lest another egg drop.

"Apprise yourself of who will be in the room as soon as you arrive, if not before. We'll start you off with small engagements, simple dinner parties to win over a few of the top matrons of Society. Always greet them immediately after your host. You may discuss the weather, your painting, simple estate matters, but *never* let on about your intentions with your art," she said, finishing with brusque tones. "And to those you've determined are hostile, give a gracious greeting and move on." Lady Elizabeth's silk skirts rustled under what must have been her preening hands. "Many will be jealous of your sudden position, but I'll be sure to catalog a list of those to avoid."

Lydia snorted at that. The egg wobbled, she slowed, held her breath as her body tensed for the worst, but the minute back-and-forth rolling stopped, and she relaxed. "I didn't realize people would be so unwilling to accept me. A list of people to avoid sounds very like a list of creditors to avoid until my debt is paid."

"Society can be like that…full of jealous cats who resent your sudden social credit, if you will." Lady Elizabeth made a small, thoughtful, humming sound. "There will be some social tremors from Edward's marital decision. Nonetheless, you will charm them with your astounding elegance. I'll make sure of it. You'll be a trendsetter."

"That may be a tall order."

Nor did the lady ask Lydia what she wanted, but that was not at the forefront of matters in the blue drawing room.

Her rotation turned her to the wide double doors opening to the balustrade at the far end of the room. Beyond, she glimpsed the greenhouse, its chimneys swirling smoke into frigid air. Edward and Mr. Bacon strode across the curving graveled path, deep in discussion as they headed toward the house. A small groan escaped her. Now she'd have more witnesses to this indignity. Yet part of her thrilled to the knowledge of more contact with Edward. Her footsteps slowed, which the countess must not have noticed.

"Keep Edward in England, give me a grandson, and I'll make sure you have my full, unwavering attention."

At this end of the drawing room, Miss Lumley was in sight, and her bright blue eyes widened over red cheeks. Lydia and the older woman grinned like two connivers. All and sundry couldn't wait to be free of Lady E.'s unwavering attentions, but Lydia, for now, was stuck.

She had made so many rotations about the room in her new heeled shoes but was still unused to the slight juxtaposition of her body from flat heels to high. Even stepping from the blue carpet onto wood floors in the drawing room threw her off kilter. Down went another egg. Her chin dropped to her chest and she eyed the latest casualty, when her other arm drooped, and that egg crashed near the toes of her brand-new shoes.

"Blast it! Will I ever get this?"

Rogers and Miss Lumley came to the rescue, smiling encouragement and cleaning up the mess.

Lady Elizabeth sighed. "Come. Take a break."

When Lydia looked up, Edward and Mr. Bacon pushed open the glass door, their breath still huffing small clouds of frosty air until they crossed the threshold. Edward froze, his dark eyes roving over her, catching on her messy skirt but rising to her face. His eyes spread wide, as did Mr. Bacon's. Lydia, clutching empty silver spoons at her sides, laughed. What else could she do?

"I'm a fright with my egg-smeared skirts."

"You sound like Lydia," Edward began, and then his narrowing eyes lit with a low smolder. "But you're a different version of the woman I stole from the Blue Cockerel. Who is this vision?"

Even Mr. Bacon's bright blue eyes glowed with male appreciation. "Good afternoon, miss. You're looking lovely." He dipped his head in greeting, but his stare remained on her.

Lydia took a fraction of a second to register their responses to her, the subtle differences that went beyond the beautiful dress. Her hair was swept high off her face with only a few hot-iron curls falling artfully in the right places, since time was of the essence with Simpson. A thin line of kohl had been applied to her lower eyelid, and a touch of rouge to her lips. Simpson had plucked her brows into elegant arches, and earbobs dangled from her ears, teardrop in shape and identical in color to the burgundy dress, cheap paste to be sure, but pretty. Of course, there was more of her to see: two plump, cream-white curves rose from her square neckline. Could those few changes make that much difference in male reaction?

"May I escort you to your seat?" Edward offered his arm to her in what also looked like a subtle crowding out of Mr. Bacon. His gaze lingered on her cleavage then strayed to the spoons. "That is, if you promise not to slay me with your spoons."

His lips twitched with humor, and Lydia slipped her arm into his. She turned her face into his sleeve, hiding a snicker at his jest. The day, odd and exhilarating, just got better, because Edward was here and close to her. Then he leaned his head near to hers, adding to the intimacy.

"I see my mother's subjecting you to the same torture she exacted on my sister, lessons in graceful walking with eggs," he said low enough for her ears only.

"My apologies to the Greenwich floors, my lord."

"You and the eggs improve the place. Never liked it in here. Everything's icicle blue, like being on a Nordic expedition."

She giggled and leaned into his body warmth as they strolled to the seating area.

"Perfect. Lydia can practice her tea-service skills," the countess crowed her pleasure across the room. Then she dismissed the servants with a quick clap. "That'll be all for now, Miss Lumley."

Edward delivered Lydia to a delicate white chair, bending deep with her as she took her seat. He dipped low and close, such that his warm breath fanned the top of her bosom. Some of her hard-earned decorum slipped. A rash brigand's smile crossed his face, visible to her alone, and the spoons dropped in her lap with a rattle.

No matter, the voices of the countess and Mr. Bacon floated in the background, engaging in social chatter. Edward set a hand on the back of her chair, a move that was possessive and claiming, and she wanted to sink into him. His lordship's sculpted lips twitched, and he looked pointedly at the sliver of dark space between her breasts as if he would like very much to explore what he could and couldn't see.

"I find that I'd like to continue our discussions tonight, if that meets with your approval," he said for her ears alone.

His voice vibrated over her skin, and her body turned puttylike by his presence. When she responded, her voice kept their quiet, intimate thread. "You mean such as we had last night? Your talking with a woman for no particular reason over no particular subject?"

One corner of his mouth hitched up at that.

"Exactly the kind of discourse I had in mind," he whispered and rose to full height.

Lydia licked her lips, purely feline in nature. She

followed him as he circled behind her and took his seat on the settee between her and the countess. He looked the same as all the other days since she'd arrived at Greenwich Park: plain woolen coat, brown today, with black breeches, unadorned linen shirt, and the same scuffed and worn brown boots, clean at least, and his queue tied but loose. But something about him looked delectable. She wanted to put her mouth to him and test him, and yes, nibble certain parts of him. Perhaps he read her mind, because a predatory smile curved his mouth, welcoming such exploration from her. But they were in one of England's once-finest drawing rooms, and other matters beckoned.

"If you're ready to practice with tea service," the countess announced in a loud voice.

Her ladyship had likely tried for her attention, but that flirtatious interchange with Edward singed her ability to hear. Lydia's fingers, scrubbed free of paint, linked together, a mutinous move, since they were needed to pour tea.

"Countess, do you really…" Her plea wilted under her ladyship's starch stare. Lydia licked her lips and positioned her hands as gracefully as she could and proceeded to move through tea.

She passed a fresh cup to Lady Elizabeth.

"Mmmm, well done," the countess said, setting down the cup she didn't need, since she already had some. "Now offer to serve me with a motion of your hand like this—" She gently waved her open hand over the biscuits and petit fours. "And I'll say, 'No thank you.' Then make the offer to our guests."

Lydia mimicked the lesson, a little embarrassed that

Edward and Mr. Bacon witnessed this, but they went along nicely with the lesson, accepting their refreshments. For Mr. Bacon's plate, she heaped high the small dish with delectables, especially the tasty biscuits they both liked. When everyone was settled, her stomach growled for a biscuit, and she nearly reached for the golden delight with her hand.

Lady Elizabeth raised a single finger. "Ah, ah. Think again."

Lydia's hand floated gracefully to a plate and small silver tongs, which she had just used for the others. She wanted to heap it high for herself, but another of her ladyship's pearls rang in her mind: at tea, never take more than one item. This isn't luncheon, *and* your mantua-maker will appreciate not having to take out any seams.

She set a solitary biscuit on her plate and took a tiny bite. Between the tiny waists of her new gowns and the stiff whalebone stays squeezing her into place, she'd have to maintain correct posture just to breathe. As she chewed, Lydia dabbed the corner of a neatly folded napkin to her lips, hiding the rotation of her mouth behind the cloth. Then the countess offered up her latest lesson.

"Now, about your language. We never say blighter, blasted, or lud," she instructed. "You must strike those words from your vocabulary."

"Don't worry, Countess. I've a lot of other salty words I can replace them with," she said, grinning, and took a healthier bite of biscuit.

Mr. Bacon chortled, wiping crumbs from his beard. "Like a regular sailor, you are."

For the first time, her ladyship cracked a smile. Her head dipped as if she couldn't let her charge see the teacher taken in by that bit of cheek. How nice to see this side of the grand dame. The countess coughed a polite sound of redirection, but her lips pressed into a smile-suppressing line.

"Be that as it may, you must strike all such language from your vocabulary. You're surprisingly well-spoken, but my best advice is find someone who speaks well and mimic her."

A compliment from the countess.

Edward, who sat closest to her, raised his cup in salute to Lydia at the hard-won positive comment.

Lydia swallowed the morsel in her mouth and ran the tip of her tongue over her lips to capture crumbs. "You mean someone like you, minus the verbal daggers, if you'll beg pardon for my directness."

Jeweled blue eyes stared back at Lydia with the first reflections of honesty and openness. "My dear, noble-women since the time of the Conqueror wore their daggers about their waists. Today we are more civilized and refined." She looked blankly across the tea table into open space. Her lips turned in a bitter line as Lydia guessed she was surely recalling a past incident. "We still keep daggers of our own, our tongues, which are no less lethal in bloodletting."

"Your lessons are well and good, but I like Lydia exactly as she is," Edward said as he returned his cup and saucer to the table. "I wouldn't change a thing."

Edward's blunt statements were as good as bringing in the sun on the still-dreary days. Lydia sat up taller, and her smile spread wider, brighter she was sure, and all for him.

"Thank you," she said, her heart beating a little faster

after she'd calmed from his blatant sensuality while seating her. Lydia rubbed her finger over a gold-embroidered swirl on her skirt and schooled her breathing. "But I promise not to traipse about with egg-covered skirts."

"Good." Then his gaze rose to her hair. "And no powder on your hair."

"Of course that must be part of her toilette, Edward," Lady Elizabeth said, her voice firm and decided. "To attend a ball unpowdered would be gauche."

"No powder." He said that as if it were a king's edict. "I'll not have her stuffed and trussed like so many woman, peacocked and ridiculous. Powder would dull the color of her beautiful hair."

"And what do you know of fashion?" the countess sniped. "She must have powder. We go to London tomorrow to begin selection of ball gowns *and* powder for her hair."

That Edward had such strong opinions on her hair surprised her. She didn't even think he noticed what shade sprouted from her head. Yet he and the countess shifted on the settee, two combatants about to square off in this latest challenge, and Lydia witnessed a fragment of the infamous tension between the two.

"If I have to work it in the wedding vows, I will."

Lydia laughed at his last proclamation. Of course she planned to honor her vows, but what he'd said teetered on the ridiculous.

"I've never heard of anything so silly in my life," Lydia said, her gaze bouncing between Edward and the countess.

He turned to her, and his strained visage softened. "I *request* that you never powder your hair." And then he added, "For me."

She knew right then she loved him, at least her imperfect

understanding of something so perfect as love. Her heart belonged to Edward, and there was no going back on that. His quiet words, a request over something as un-life changing as hair powder, tilted the world upside down for her. Benumbed and exhilarated at the same time, she set her plate in her lap, lest she drop the thing as the skirmish of wills continued. Both combatants, however, were blithely unaware of her earth-shattering revelation.

This was not a matter of mind-muddling attraction, though all of her was drawn to him and longed for his hot friction. His fine form folded on the furniture, a feast for her eyes. He planted one tanned hand on his knee closest to her, and the same question that probed her at the Blue Cockerel came to the fore: What would it be like to have those tanned hands all over her?

The discussion between Edward and the countess escalated: powder or no powder, go to London for ball-gown fittings or stay at Greenwich Park to continue the neglected scientific illustrations. These became the hotly discussed topics around her and about her. Then Edward turned and tried to draw her into the fray.

"What do you want to do?" Edward held up a hand to halt his mother's verbal onslaught. "Lydia?" he called again and dipped his head for eye contact with her. "What do you want?"

She looked at him and the countess, drawn back from her stunning revelation. "I...I..."

Want to paint. Be naked with Edward. Tell him how I feel.

Another honest admission from her heart and mind, but she'd stifle those words and choose a diplomatic route. "Why don't I go to London tomorrow for the fittings, and the next day I'll catch up on the illustrations? I'm behind only a few days." She gave Edward a triumphant grin. "One would think you've always had me around to labor for you. I'd say you've grown accustomed to me in your greenhouse."

"If you must," the countess said in a huff, though oddly sounding not too put out to have lost this battle. She smoothed her skirts and addressed Lydia. "I shall return later in the week to find a dance instructor, and you must have your own stationery. Don't worry, I can decide that for you." She tapped her fingers against her skirts. "Very well, I'll take care of the other items that don't require your immediate presence."

"Going to London tomorrow, are you?" Mr. Bacon asked. "Then would you mind dropping off a small chest at Buckingham House? Saves me a trip."

"Are we talking about the books you exchange with the king?" The countess turned to Edward, her eyes rounding at the mention of Buckingham House.

"Yes." Edward nodded. "The chest's manageable for your carriage."

"Of course we can deliver them."

Lydia guessed she'd find a way to drop that royal connection into conversations at tea with friends for weeks to come. But the recipient of that chest opened a new door on an idea that had been brewing. Timing and opportunity rarely fell so fortuitously in her lap. This was as near an invitation as she'd ever have.

She chewed her bottom lip, contemplating what would be her boldest move yet.

∞

As the clock struck midnight…

Sitting comfortably at her white desk, Lydia chewed

her thumbnail. The plan, bolder than brass, scared her. A few deep breaths for courage, and she opened the drawer of her writing desk. But easing the drawer open gave her a surprise.

Someone else had gone through this drawer.

She hadn't noticed earlier in her haste to be done with the letters, but her three sketches of Edward were not in the correct order. Someone had looked at her simple lead-stick sketches. That had to be what had happened, since the sketches were tucked in the back of the drawer.

"The countess," she said, hissing that woman's name.

How invading, leaving her bare in a most personal way. But she paused, glancing at the adjoining door, and admitted the lady's methods weren't so far off from her own. Instead, Lydia was drawn into what she held in her hands.

She loved these sketches. Tenderness filled her from this late-night viewing. Her favorite, a close view of Edward's face, embodied the way he looked the day she untied his queue outside the art gallery. He had shown her Jonathan's portrait, and revealed that Miss Mayhew was not a woman of any romantic consequence.

No. He revealed much more than that.

Her fingers skimmed the lead pencil sketch, showing equally the planes of his face. The fierce fire in his eyes leapt off the page, the same as when he had proclaimed staunch loyalty to his friends. She grinned at how those sculpted lips had frowned this evening when she chased him away after so short a time of *discussion*. She had covert work to finish.

With that, the sketches went back into the drawer. Lydia retrieved two letters hidden away inside, written a few hours ago. So nervous was she then that she'd failed to notice the sketches out of order. She set one letter atop a pile of papers, and the other on an identical stack of sheaves and illustrations. A third stack, sketches and diagrams, made a neat pile already atop her desk.

Heart thumping as loud as a drum, she walked to the fireplace, and tossed that third pile into the flames.

Hot yellow and orange flames curled the white sheaves, turning them to gray dust. The shock of what she'd done washed over her. So final. A stall tactic to be sure, and wouldn't do near the damage of those letters atop the desk. But what was burned was gone forever. Emboldened, Lydia grabbed the remaining papers, cracked open her door, and sped along the vermillion path, down the stairs to Edward's study.

Reaching his study, she shut the door behind her with a click. She leaned back, grateful to have the heavy walnut hold her up until her breath calmed. She'd come this far...

She went to the drawer where he kept his seal and blotting wax, and moved methodically through her steps, disembodied from what she was doing. Across the mahogany surface, her hands folded letters inside the packets. Those same hands melted wax to the right spot. But when Lydia held Edward's seal over the formless red wax, she paused, loosening her grip on that ancient token of good faith. Her stomach quivered and roiled.

Words of Wickersham's vicar echoed in her head, when he recounted an Old Testament story last fall: Jezebel had used Ahab's seal.

Twenty

Whatever deceives men seems to produce a magical enchantment.
—Plato

"CHANGE BRINGS DISCOMFORT, EVEN IF IT'S FOR THE better." Edward tapped his lead stick on the Sanford Shipping's account book.

He halfheartedly listened to his mother's commentary and responded, though his head was filled with numbers: numbers to calculate in their accounts, numbers of days 'til he left England, and number of days until his self-imposed one-month edict was done. All three numbers pressed down on him, demanding their due.

Beside the account book rested the special license. That document's arrival had initiated this latest flow of conversation with the countess, whose presence in his study was for no particular reason that he could tell. One trait he shared in common with his mother: neither did anything without a purpose. For the countess, conversation, whether social chatter or deep dialogue, always served an end. As he tallied this final column, she was blessedly silent.

He scratched a number in the book and looked up across his desk. "And speaking of change, you've sung a different tune about Lydia this past week."

Straightening her sleeve, the countess smoothed the lace and silk, banishing creases and wrinkles. "She's adapted rather quickly to her lessons, but she's not fit to be a countess."

"I don't care."

The countess tilted forward in her chair and touched the edge of his desk. "Bear in mind, I do like her."

He snorted rudely at that shocking admission and tossed the lead stick onto the open book.

Her mouth pursed, and she pressed on with her agenda, something at which the countess was very skilled. "But it's not too late. Why not let me assist you in finding more suitable young ladies? I could—"

"Stop." He raised both hands, disliking the direction this interview was going. "We have been over this too many times. I refuse to dance attendance on empty-headed chits."

"But, Edward," she pleaded, "I'll carefully preselect ladies of the highest quality, those amenable to marriage to one of your stature."

His short bark of laughter was barely suppressed ire. His mother never knew when to quit. He rose from the chair, restless and wary, sauntered to the widow. A long-suffering sigh came from behind him when he leaned a shoulder on the window frame. He folded his arms across his chest and crossed one boot toe to the floor in front of the other as he drank in the scene before him.

Outside was warmth and bluster, pleasant and pastoral. Pure Lydia. She wore one of her old dresses, something dark brown and practical, with a high neckline. She was flying a kite with John, the stable master's son, and the tail of the kite swirled and trailed through the grass. Its diamond shape twirled low, and woman and boy ran, laughing as they tried to capture the wind. Lydia tugged on the line just before the kite dropped to the ground, saving its flight.

Both enthusiasts cheered their success. The lad slowly unwound the string, letting the kite dance and soar higher and higher. Lydia was like that with him: she unwound him in places he didn't even expect were coiled and tight. So lost was he in his reverie, Edward failed to hear his mother's approach. Her silk skirts rustled as she inched closer to him.

"She still has a rather bracing walk." The words came as judgment, but one corner of her mouth tilted up as she delivered what was close to a tender proclamation.

Edward faced his mother—his beautiful mother—who reflected on the same scene as he. Emotional nuance was new to him, a gift from Lydia, but the truth of his situation—no, his life—blew across him as surely as the wind blew winter clouds away outside.

"What bothers you more?" he asked. "That I'm marrying Lydia? Or that you think I'm *forced* to marry Lydia because no one else will have me? Scarred beast that I am?"

Her eyes spread wide, but she flinched as if someone had hit her.

"Edward, that's not true. There are many women who'd have you. You simply have to put yourself in the position to meet them, take the time to court them." The skin around her blue eyes strained, creating tiny wrinkles.

"You didn't answer me, but that alone gives me your answer," he said, shrugging that off. "No matter."

The countess tipped her head against the chilled pane and said nothing.

"You mean for me to go back into Society. The very same Society I despised even when I wasn't scarred," he groused as mocking bitterness tinged his voice. "The assemblage of garrulous bloviates. Couldn't stand them when my face was intact. Like them even less now that it's not."

"Oh, Edward." She reached for his forearm, but her hand hovered, not making contact. "It's not good to hide away from people, however flawed we all are." Then she raised her hand, and the backs of her fingers stroked his smooth, unscarred cheek. "You were so handsome. Your brother was dashing, but you were always so, so much more…" Her lips pinched into a painful line. "My beautiful boy."

A teardrop sparkled from her lower lashes, a well-cut crystal that liquefied and slid over her cheek. That the countess still harbored pain over his injuries, injuries earned from a younger man's rash decisions, caused an ache within him. Wasn't it a boyish need to always have the praise and adoration of one's mother? No matter, he was a man now. The responsibilities of these past three years had molded him into who he had become. Yet another dawning crept in, truth that failed to bother him. Edward gripped her fingers in a gentle vise but kept her hand aloft between them.

"That's what bothers you," he said, viewing his mother in a clearer light. "You hate the fact that I'm scarred, probably more than I do."

Her sharp intake of breath must've been like a knife to her, so pained and broken was her visage. She stepped back and dabbed her knuckles to new tears forming.

"How can you say such a thing?"

"Because it's true." He nodded, allowing her to collect herself a moment. Then he pressed on as gently as he could. "All my life you've thrived on the appearance of things. I pity you your world of empty vanity, but I love you all the same, Mother. I made my peace with what happened to me. Now you must make yours."

The countess wrapped her arms about herself, and her shoulders drooped. She touched her mouth where the beginnings of a small, bitter smile was forming.

"You must think me so very awful."

Edward glanced out the window in time to catch John passing the kite's handle over to Lydia. Her hair, most of it fallen loose from its pins, whipped about her head, but she accepted the proffered honor of kite-flier, and both followed the diamond shape high above.

"Embracing truth is a kind of freedom. Don't you think?" He glanced back at his mother, who sniffed and dabbed a handkerchief to her face. "I understand the framework from which you've established your world, your environment."

"Heavens." She sniffed. "You sound like you've made me into one of your scientific studies." She stared out the window, but not at the scene beyond, rather, he noticed she was checking her own reflection in the glass before facing him again. "You sounded just like your father right then, you know."

Edward's arms went lax, and he clasped his hands behind his back. "What do you mean?"

The countess dabbed her eyes and tipped her head in a doting way. "At first he was all science. Work at night. Sleep all day, since astronomy was his field. Dinner was transition time. The only time to see him. But yes, I soon changed that." Her head raised a proud notch. "Someone had to make him aware of his responsibilities elsewhere, duties to the estate, and yes, to attend me. I make no apology for demanding such. No marriage would survive otherwise."

Was his mother about to give him advice? Spread marital wisdom his way? He stiffened at the idea, but her eyes, older and sadder-looking, kept him quiet. Handkerchief clutched in one hand, the countess spread her arms wide.

"Take a look around you. Someone had to look to all this. You may denigrate my concerns, but you have an excellent place in this world. Growing up, those tutors of yours didn't visit based solely on your brilliance, you know. Nothing here happened by accident. I helped build the Greenwich name in Society. Yes"—she arched her dark gold eyebrows, and her hands dropped to her sides—"the same Society you castigate so freely."

The strange push and pull of truth tugged at him, weighing down like a gentle burden on his frame. His mother showed more depth in this single meeting than he could remember seeing in her in a long time, perhaps because he made his judgments and was never willing to look again. But time and circumstances changed people, wearing them down the same way water worked over stone.

With all sincerity, Edward tipped his head in a small salute. "Your talents have never been fully appreciated."

Her lips wobbled as if another flood of tearful emotions was about to erupt. Both turned to the window, taking in the boy and Lydia enjoying the sunny, windy day. At that moment, Lydia turned and caught sight of them in the window. Fingers splayed wide, she smiled and waved her arm emphatically at them. Then she pointed at Edward, and beckoned him outside to join her. She exuded cheer, so full of life.

His mother sighed, a sound of relief and tiredness mingled together. "Life is a series of choices, great and small. Choose wisely."

Edward waved back to Lydia. "I already have."

Lydia waited awhile for Edward to show. When he didn't, she handed the kite's wooden handle back to John and walked briskly around to the back of the great house, expecting to find him somewhere inside. She trotted up the back steps, more than ready to get back to her long-neglected painting, when she heard her name on the wind.

"Miss, Miss Montgomery. This away," Huxtable yelled to her, both hands cupped around his mouth. The gardener waved her over to the greenhouse. He cupped his hands and called out once more, followed by a frantic gesturing of his hands. "Come quick, miss!"

She sprinted full speed through the grass, down the hill to the greenhouse, imagining every sort of trouble. Her shoes pounded the ground. Chill wind snapped her cheeks. Lydia stopped short of the door, her heart thumping hard.

"What's wrong? Is it Edward?" She rubbed her side where a cramp pinched from her sprint.

Huxtable gave himself a good-natured slap to the head. "Sorry I gave ye such a fright. Hisself is fine as usual." He set his pipe between his thin lips and finished, "We didn't want ye to miss this. Come quick."

His gnarled hands held the door open for her, and once inside the balmy warmth, Lydia unclasped her cloak. Her wind-chapped hands went back to rubbing the nagging ache at her side. Huxtable moved down a central path through the middle of the greenhouse. His fast footsteps crunched on gravel, and she followed that noise into thicker greenery. Midway through the path, Huxtable turned and grinned around his twitching pipe. He jabbed his thumb at an open space off the path.

"Here." He wheezed a quick chuckle and touched his cap before disappearing.

Edward stood amidst juvenile butterflies floating about, and some spread brand-new wings, damp and sluggish, as they clung to stick-thin branches. Their pastel colors fluttered against vibrant green leaves. One landed on his shoulder, and another flitted closer to his forearm, where it settled on his wrist. With care, he raised his wrist for her closer inspection of the pale green butterfly.

"May I introduce *Callophrys rubi*, or green hairstreak, if you prefer the King's English," he said, and right then a pale blue butterfly with a smattering of black dots found sanctuary on his arm. "And here is *Celastrina argiolus*, sweetly known as holly blue."

"They're so pretty."

"Stand still, and they'll come to you. Dozens of them newly emerged from their chrysalides," he whispered in his cultured voice as he rattled off the strange word.

She chuckled low at his scientific talk. She stretched

out her arms, and one green hairstreak flitted in front of her nose to flutter, drop, and settle on her arm. "When you say chrysalee…or whatever, you mean their cocoon?" she asked, matching his whisper. "They've just hatched?"

Another type, bold orange, with eye spots on its wings, landed on her arm. Edward's warm breath touched her forehead.

"That orange one is the peacock, *Inachis Io*. And yes, hatched, emerged, whichever you prefer."

The closeness of their confined space and the lovely insects drifting into flight above their heads made a dreamlike haze. A bird chirped a song and flew overhead, its wings flapping the loudest sound in their peaceful paradise. A single green hairstreak lingered on Edward's arm. The body was fuzzy and white. The wings changed from a subtle pale green to a richer light blue-green shade closer to the body.

"I should like to paint this one, if I can remember all the subtle colors and textures. So lovely."

"This one reminds me of your eyes on certain days," he murmured close to her ear. "And I would like that butterfly painting to remind me of your eyes."

When you're gone.

She pulled away, couldn't help it really from the unspoken words that hung between them. That vertical line pronounced itself between Edward's eyes.

"I shouldn't have said that." He spoke in normal tones. The butterflies abandoned him.

"Why not?" She concentrated on the one butterfly, a beautiful jewel, on her arm. "You're not one to avoid facts."

The tender butterfly left its perch on her forearm. She

followed the halo of young butterflies over their heads. Sun shot through greenery. Everywhere new flowers flared in a profusion of pinks and yellows, exotic oranges, scarlets and reds. Birds chirped their songs so busy at building nests. Outside, English weather gave its last winter shout with bone-chilling gusts. Inside? Paradise, and Edward was its architect. He set his hand on her elbow, guiding her to another path.

"Amazing. I'm mesmerized by color and sound," she said, whisper-soft, still taken by the brilliant kaleidoscope before her. Your greenhouse looks more alive than ever."

"Spring. It has that effect on species of all stripes. But if you want to paint the butterflies, better hurry. Those three you just saw will not stay. They like to venture to other places."

"Sounds like you," she said.

Their footsteps crunched a slow cadence on gravel. Edward's hand slipped lower to her waist.

"I know, but I'm not gone yet."

Gone was the intractable scientist, determined to explore the outer world's scientific treasures. Edward sounded...different. She looked askance at him and found a randy grin on his face. It might have been the effect of their small slice of Eden, or it could've been the age-old rhythm of man and woman, but Lydia's body hummed to his tune.

"I haven't checked the calendar, Edward, but we're nearly at the end of your month-long edict, aren't we?"

"Next week is the end of the waiting period."

He led her past the Chinese pear tree to her work-bench. All was in order, if a little bare from her recent neglect. The undercurrent hummed between them, a silent reminder of what would pass between them. Edward's eyes smoldered darker than usual. She'd become used to the sparks that flew between them. Comfortable in his domain, Edward leaned his backside on the workbench and braced his hands on the wood.

"Do you feel ready?"

"It's what we agreed from the beginning. Nothing's changed, has it?" Lydia planted her bottom on the high stool, facing him. "I suppose I need lots more lessons in comportment."

She gave him a cheeky grin, but couldn't shake jittery nervousness. She rubbed her fingers, chilled at the tips from gloveless kite flying. Edward's eyes, his face, everything was too intense. Did he know somehow what she'd done? The letters?

"I was going to take you worming today, but that's not the most romantic outing a man can offer a woman, is it?" He studied her with keen eyes.

"You are if anything, a surprising man. Worming…" She laughed. "I was hoping to paint, really. I haven't had the chance at all this week. The countess has been relentless, demanding all my time."

His gaze flitted to her workbench. "Yes, I see your pile of illustrations hasn't increased. What about your promise to help me? Your recompense for snooping in my room?" His eyes turned fierce for a playful second of mock judgment.

That incident seemed like it happened years ago. She fidgeted, making a study of her hands on her knees. She squeezed her eyes shut, about to blurt out the full truth of what she did, when Edward tossed what must have been his own theory to her hesitancy.

"Lydia, what's wrong? Is this about what I said over by the butterflies?"

She breathed a sigh of relief. He didn't know.

She shook her head. She had to give him something. "The fact is I burned the illustrations—"

"What?" He sprang off the bench.

"It was an accident. I was cleaning my desk and tossed good pages in the fire with my mistakes. But don't worry, the originals are here." She turned and picked up a pile of his first-draft diagrams and illustrations, a pile about an inch thick.

He grabbed them from her and shuffled through them, clearly needing reassurance that the originals were sound. He set the stack down and rubbed the back of his neck.

"These are for my treatise on the *Agathosma betulina*. How far along are you on the pamphlet?"

"Up in my room and almost done." She touched his arm. "You know I'm fast. I can get them all done quickly enough."

"Good, because I wanted to publish the pamphlet before I left, rather than leave the work hanging." He tapped two fingers to the bench. "I need you here every day without interruption."

With him standing so close and irked, she wasn't put off by his bristling irritation. She found him quite appealing this way. A smile flirted across her lips.

"I could say the same about you, my lord." She let her voice drop, a lure for him to flirt back with her.

"Ah, Lydia." But there was no bite to him.

She leaned closer, liking the smell of his soap.

His knuckles grazed her cheek, her lips, and she

captured his warm hand and kissed his knuckles. She'd burned those copies in a thin hope to slow him down, but that was a weak gamble on her part. He knew how quickly she worked.

The other, bolder effort was what truly scared her. The letters. His seal. Her stomach fluttered unpleasantly when that deception came to mind. Instead, she shoved it away, ignoring it. Part of her wanted to explode and tell him, and part of her was scared what would happen. She held his hand to her cheek and shut her eyes, not able to bear the honesty that always shone from his.

He brushed back strands of hair that fell about her face. The way he touched her, she could be a fragile treasure that he adored and would keep forever.

"And so the red-hooded hoyden of Wickersham tames the Greenwich beast." He dropped a kiss on her forehead, her hairline, and skimmed her temple. "Or the phantom...not sure which name I like most today."

"Jest if you must," she said, letting her lips brush his cheek. "But people hold misconceptions about you because you fail to show your face in public. No one will ever know the truth."

He pulled away, but not with anger. He stood too close for that, and for the first time, something like consideration for that argument reflected in his eyes. What was it about intimacy that tore down barriers? The good people of Greenwich Park had laid out their arguments in the same vein to him these past three years, since he was first scarred. She knew as much, since all and sundry told her, as did Edward. He looked at her with a satisfied smile.

"You know the truth about me." And he kissed her

lips, a feathered touch. "That's good enough for me." He pulled away again, and his gold-tipped lashes hovered over his topaz-brown eyes. "You really don't see my scars when you look at me, do you?"

That startled her. She reached up and stroked the cheek, knotted and shiny. Her fingers skimmed lower to his shirt's neckline, where dark-edged scars showed. Lydia's hand slipped just inside the linen fabric to explore enticing flesh.

"I see a great deal, but not scars." Her voice was low and throaty.

The scandalous idea of sketching him without his shirt on made her blush, but he didn't notice. She held that secret idea to herself as Huxtable came up the path, two buckets swinging at his sides. The gardener plunked the buckets on Edward's workbench.

"Are ye goin' to sit there playin' patty fingers all day? Or are ye goin' wormin', like ye said?"

"We're not going worming today, Hux."

The old man removed his pipe and twirled it at Edward. "Good, 'cause I wondered if I needed to teach ye a thing er two about courtin' a lady. Draggin' 'em through mud doesn't work." His bushy brows twitched over his rheumy eyes. "If yer not goin' wormin', what are ye doin'?"

"Getting married. Today."

Twenty-one

Whatever you can do or dream,
begin it.

—Johann Wolfgang von Goethe

SITTING AT EDWARD'S DESK, LYDIA TWIRLED THE quill between her fingers as she peeled back time to that summer of "firsts." Every girl remembers her first kiss, her first love. Twelve summers ago, Rosalba Carriera, an old Venetian artist visiting the Duke of Somerset, was the first to take her talent seriously and teach her about art. That was the "first" she savored most until today.

Today she would marry the man she loved, but the torture was whether or not to admit those feelings to a man who didn't want them. Oh, he wanted *her*, all right, but not all the parts she wanted to give, and therein rested her dilemma. Bits of old wisdom played in her head: Mrs. Carriera's thick Italian accent, textured by time, tutoring her in the discipline and beauty of drawing and painting.

Art, like love, grows as much from what you put in as from what you keep out.

Should she add love, the most nettling emotion to her evening with Edward?

Now at his desk, she composed a quick missive to her mother, or tried to. The half-formed letter wouldn't end. Instead, Lydia kept connecting art and love with sex and marriage, but without a completely willing partner in all aspects of wedded bliss, she was destined to be incomplete... a painting not quite finished. She needed him to stay.

Late-day sun reflected the time ticking closer to the magical hour. Lydia dipped the quill in ink to finish what was meant to be a quick note.

"Hello, miss. Surprised to see you here." Mr. Bacon strode into the study with a packet stashed under his arm. "The kitchen's all abuzz. You're to wed. Tonight."

"Mr. Bacon." She glanced up, distracted, as she added her signature to the letter. "Yes, tonight."

He must've entered through the kitchen, since no footman had taken his coat or hat. Sanford Shipping's man of business was as comfortable moving abovestairs as below, moving with stealth and collecting information from both areas.

"What're you doing in here?" He set the leather packet on the desk and removed his black frock coat, tossing it on the back of the chair.

"Writing a letter to my mum...ran out of paper at my desk upstairs," she said, waiting for the ink to dry. "If a woman's to enter the state of matrimony, her mother ought to know the day. I owe her that."

"One could argue much is owed you." He settled himself in the chair and crossed one leg, setting his ankle over his knee. He balanced his cap on his thigh in a most informal fashion.

"We all take care of our mums in one way or another." She folded the missive, but when she looked up, he stared at her with his bright blue eyes, a penetrating observer. "I'm assuming you have a mum somewhere in the world?"

A leading question, since Mr. Bacon was a mystery to her. The man always looked more pirate than businessman to her, but he had genteel moments.

"We all come from somewhere." He twirled one of his pitch-colored beard braids. "You seem calm for a woman about to attend her own wedding."

"I've got Lady E. and two maids upstairs to worry for me." She smiled and held the sealing wax over a candle, not focusing on Mr. Bacon. "They're all aflutter over what I'm to wear. I had to escape the feminine excess."

Believing the conversation done, she concentrated on the task of closing the letter and stamping Edward's seal to the back. But Sanford Shipping's man of business rumbled from across the desk once more.

"Don't let them change you. Edward needs you just as you are."

Lydia took a good look at the man across the desk, the man by all accounts Edward would surely call one of his dearest friends. Jet-black hair had begun to sprout from his pate, less than an inch, but clearly he was not naturally bald. His bright blue eyes stayed guarded but alert in every social transaction she'd ever witnessed him partake of.

Why had she never probed into the mystery of Mr. Jonas Bacon?

"That sounds like a version of a compliment. I think," she said, smoothing her dark brown skirts as she rose from the chair.

He stood up as well, a rough-and-tumble version of a gentleman, but a gentleman nonetheless. A thickly muscled man, he set cap in hand and stood tall. She gave a polite nod, about to retreat into mental preparations for the biggest promise of her life, but Sanford Shipping's man of business wasn't finished.

"He told you about the scars." Both his meaty hands clutched the cap as if he would wring it dry. "But I don't think he told you everything."

"Barbary pirates attacked the ship in search of treasure, right?" Lydia stayed on her side of the desk. "Is there more?"

"We were not prepared for the attack, outgunned and outnumbered three to one," he said, taking a breath to recount the facts. "They herded us below deck, but we could see from the hold."

"Edward?" Her hand went to her mouth, despite what she already knew.

"No, the captain…" He braced his curled fist on the desktop and leaned closer. "You know how Edward dresses. They didn't even take him for a third mate, that and his age. He was below, like all the rest of us."

"They took the captain, thinking he'd hidden something from them. The man was old. That was to be his last voyage, and then he'd settle down in some Cornwall cottage." He shifted his stance. "Do you see what happened? Edward sacrificed himself for the captain…yelled he was the one they wanted…that he had a treasure map."

"Oh." She breathed the word. "I can't believe it."

"Believe it, miss." He glanced away from her, but a sneer twisted his lips within his heavy beard. "I'd been running like a rat from my past, and here was this stripling nobleman almost a decade younger than me, willing to take on the world to save an old man."

Her hand slipped from her mouth to her chest. "That's how you met? On that ship?"

"Yes, I saved Edward's life, and we've been friends since the day."

"How did you save him? I thought you were locked away and outnumbered?"

Mr. Bacon settled his hip on the desk. "Getting in and out of places is a skill of mine." His oak-solid voice finished the story, at least what he would tell. "The pirates were half in their cups by then, easy pickings, but damage had been done to Edward."

"I see." She took a deep breath, but a hollow ache for Edward settled in her chest. "Thank you for telling me."

From the doorway, Rogers coughed into his white-gloved hand. "Miss, her ladyship's asking about you. She wishes you'd finish your letter and quit dawdling." He winced and turned a shade of scarlet. "Pardon me, but she bade me say those exact words. Said I couldn't leave you until I escorted you to the red hallway."

Lydia and Mr. Bacon exchanged smiles.

"I'm on my way."

Jonas gave her a curt nod. "Many ways he's given me my life back."

His blue stare was strained and tense, but his message was solid.

Give my friend his life back.

༺❀༻

"Of all the days to wander off."

The countess held court on the settee, fussing over

her own skirts and venting opinions. Her ladyship's work was complete. But Tilly and Simpson labored on with the countess directing the bride's assembly.

Lydia had been poked and prodded, cinched and pinched. She was dangerously close to being *peacocked* as Edward would say. Her sable-colored tresses had been swept high off her forehead.

Tilly completed the picture by pinning jeweled stars at strategic points within the dark curls. The countess did everything in her power to visually transform Lydia into a noblewoman, everything short of powdered hair. Not that her ladyship didn't try.

When Simpson held the talc-covered puff, Lydia raised a staying hand. "No powder."

"Really, Lydia. You can wear powder if you want," the countess fussed from the settee. "Even if he puts *that* in the vows, it's not like it matters today. You're not honor bound to obey him until after the wedding. And believe me, most women give those words a liberal interpretation."

Lydia rose from the dressing table. "I think this is quite acceptable."

"Oh no, miss," Tilly gushed, breaking one of her ladyship's cardinal rules of silence until spoken to. "You're a vision."

"Thanks, Tilly." Her blue-silk court dress not only showed a good deal of bosom, but shoulders as well. "His lordship's bound to see lots of me up here."

She wanted to wrap a shawl around her shoulders, but the countess banished that practical item. The dress was severely plain, except for tiers of extravagant white and silver lace draping from her elbows. A twine of silver and white embroidery threaded a simple design up the center of the bodice. She took a tentative step, and the countess echoed in her head: *head up, shoulders back, face forward… always face forward.*

"There's lots more underskirts," she said, looking down in alarm.

The countess rose from the settee. "You'll get used to that." She stepped into the hallway, where she checked her own appearance and waited for Lydia. "Aren't you coming? The vicar awaits us in the Dutch Salon."

The volume of fabric and a sudden sense of power made her hesitate. The idea playing in her head, delicious and powerful like champagne, was pure imp's mischief. Lydia stroked her skirts.

"In a minute. You go ahead." Then she looked at Tilly. "I need your help."

Give a man his life back? She'd certainly try.

"I can't be sure if you're happy to have wed me or to get a child on me." Breathing heavily, she pulled away from Edward's voracious kisses.

"Both." He pressed her back against the wall. His lips worked their way along her hairline down to her earlobes bare of jewelry.

He worshipped those plump bits of flesh, spreading goose bumps all over her with soft bites and attention. That was the first part of her he undressed when they were alone in the vermillion hallway. Earbobs glittered somewhere in the sea of red. Bubbling over with euphoria, her head tipped back. She laughed when his mouth skimmed her neck, tickling her. Lydia needed him to lose control, craved it as much as she craved feeling him inside her.

But others mingled belowstairs within earshot. The visual image of Edward finishing his hardly touched dinner played in her mind. Her new husband had barely got them away from the others when he began feasting on her. He had growled away poor Tilly when the maid offered to undress the bride. Instead, he wrapped Lydia's arm possessively through his and took her from the dining room's civilization. The beast would take the damsel to his lair and do the undressing.

Faint celebratory voices floated from belowstairs, champagne poured for servants and guests alike. Now, inches from his door, she wanted to explode. Under Edward's potent attention, the evening's joy morphed into a slow opiate, seeping into her limbs. Kisses and roving hands stirred the brew that thrummed her veins. But, the precipice of being caught in this passionate state excited her.

Lydia's arm stretched out, as much to hold her up as to find the doorknob. All the better to get them to the right place to reveal her surprise. Sculpted lips pressed hers, insistent, teasing…demanding. His hands framed her face, and long fingers slipped into her hair, kneading and pressing. A jeweled hairpiece fell to the floor.

"Your mouth," he growled. "Open for me."

She opened her eyes. Edward's eyes burned hot and black. Annoyed even. Her brain registered satisfaction to have upset his sense of order. Obedient to his command, she tilted her head back, needing the solid wood. Her lips parted, giving him that sliver of control over her. He groaned, eyes shuttering, and lost himself in her mouth.

Yielding was its own kind of power. The beast, barely tamed a split second ago, ravaged her, wanting more.

Her knees buckled. Fingertips dug into smooth walnut paneling, bracing her from falling into a puddle. Her mouth barely moved, receiving Edward's unbanked fiery passion. His kisses, deep and passionate, sought and explored. His hands slid over her silk dress, circling her hips. Volumes of silk sang whispered music when he caressed her there.

Breathing heavy, Edward stepped back. His predacious eyes, pitch black with sensual fire, narrowed. "I want you more than I've wanted anything or anyone in my life."

Anger and desire twined together in those words. She smiled. His lordship didn't like intense wanting.

Lydia leaned on the wall, arms spread out like some maiden in Greek stories left as a sacrifice for men and monsters. At the bottom of her vision, twin white curves, plump and high, pressed her low neckline, straining the fabric with every breath. Everything was too tight. Edward's smoldering gaze dropped to those soft, round parts. His nostrils flared over the offered sacrifice.

"But I know well enough"—breath surged from his chest in heavy doses—"not to take you in the hallway."

He grabbed Lydia's hand. They sped into his room, locking the door firmly behind. Then for good measure, he locked the adjoining door. There'd be no escaping this night.

Lydia leaned against his bedpost, thrusting her bosom and rocking back and forth like some kind of tart. Her brazen motion wasn't lost on him. Edward's head snapped to attention where she waited, but control, for the moment, was his. He stood in the middle of the well-lit room and removed his brown velvet jacket, letting it drop to the floor.

"This is a first," he said, loosening the cloth at his neck. "I'm more talkative than you."

"I want to watch."

His fingers froze on the knot. All of him tensed, showing muscle and sinew under his breeches in relief. A moment passed. Edward fought for restraint, and she loved witnessing the battle. One corner of his mouth kicked up, and he finished working the tie.

"Aren't you full of surprises."

Her fingers stroked high on her embroidered bodice. "More than you know, my lord."

"Lucky for me, one evening of sex doesn't necessarily make a child." His neckwear dropped to the floor.

"Neither does getting a woman with child make a father." Her gentle rocking slowed against the bedpost. "Is that all you want?"

"A child? No." His dark stare swept her from head to hem. "I want all of you."

Pewter buttons slid from buttonholes on his waistcoat, donned for the formal occasion. She swallowed hard. By the wicked smile playing on his face, Edward enjoyed giving her the display. His fingers slowed, moving over one tedious button after another. The controlled Lord Edward was back, relishing this power over his new countess.

Lydia's lashes lowered, half over her eyes. "Please hurry." Her body's gentle undulation increased. "I liked the beast who almost devoured me in the hall."

His chuckle was deep and full of sensual promise. But

those tanned fingers took their time until the last button slipped free. Down went the waistcoat.

"Patience, Lady Greenwich," he said softly. "You wanted to watch, remember?"

Her head lolled back, rubbing the wide bedpost. More of her meticulous hairstyle came undone, slipping to her shoulders. A star pin dangled from a curl, skimming her right breast. He sounded triumphant and in control, yet Lydia smiled…a secret, feline kind. Patience was hers. The reward was coming.

He approached, untucking his shirt from his breeches. The carved shape of his chest, the view of his flat, muscled stomach, enticed her from his open shirt. She reached for him. A solitary finger grazed firm flesh from sternum to navel, making a slow, meandering trail to the brown hair low on his navel. Edward's warm skin quivered with waves of gooseflesh from her touch.

"Edward?"

"Mmmm?" He inched closer, kissing her mouth tenderly, as if he'd put away the beast and would take his proper time with her.

"Untie me?" She rotated, presenting her back.

His hands moved across the silk, loosening the tie that trussed her. His fingers worked the myriad rows of back-and-forth lacing with even, methodic attention. She didn't want that.

When the gown slackened, Lydia whirled around and licked her lips. Her clothes couldn't come off yet, but she wanted him out of control and senseless with wanting.

She rubbed her bottom against the bedpost, and her upper teeth nibbled her lower lip. Edward's head canted to the side as if she were an unknown creature.

"Lydia..." His voice trailed off.

"Please, my shoe." She almost bubbled over with laughter from the long evening of waiting, but Lydia covered her mouth. Anticipation had tortured her all night. The time had come.

Edward obliged, dropping to one knee. He made a fine sight, kneeling before her with his shirt open, glancing up at her in all his dark-eyed glory. Her new husband was beautiful with his blade-straight nose and sculpted lips. He gave her a tolerant smile and brushed back her hem. Both his hands bracketed her shod foot. The bow untied, and his thumb skimmed her upper foot.

Bare flesh, pale and delicate.

He pushed her skirt higher, checking her ankle. His hand explored the slender, convex curve of her nude calf. She gloried in his light, investigative touch. Her eyes shuttered with pleasure when he made soft circles behind her knee.

"Lydia," he said, thick-voiced, "you have no stockings on."

He leaned closer and kissed her knee, shrouded behind ample silk skirts.

"Please...please..." she said, her words coming in huffs. "Go higher."

His gold-brown head touched her skirt, her legs, an inviting place to rest as his fact-finding fingers caressed her. His queue for once stayed neatly tied. The only civilized part of him. Edward's eyes sparkled when he looked up at her. His hands stayed hidden under her dress. The beast's dangerous light glowed dark again in his eyes.

Her new husband did as she bade and went higher,

his hands discovering her bare thighs for the first time. She moaned. Anticipation melted her in the right places.

When would he get *there*?

He gripped her hips, and standing up, slowly pushed volumes of silk with him. Blue fabric puffed and pillowed between them. His hand traced a slow caress the length of her from knee to hip. Edward's nostrils flared, as did his eyes, when his roving hand slipped behind her, grappling bare skin. She quivered from tantalizing male touch exploring forbidden flesh.

Lydia read Edward's face, the flush of tanned skin and mouth unable to close, as knowledge seeped into his brain: she'd said her vows, eaten dinner with the utmost decorum, and chattered politely with all and sundry in this secret state of undress.

Edward groaned and jammed her body hard against his.

"You're naked under your skirt."

Twenty-two

Some identify Happiness with virtue, some with practical wisdom, others with a kind of philosophical wisdom, others add or exclude pleasure…

—Aristotle

IN THAT SECOND, LYDIA BECAME HIS BELLADONNA. Few ever tasted the small, sweet berry of the dangerous plant and lived.

Memories of a reckless university prank haunted him right then. Edward's heart banged fast and hard in his chest tonight, same as it did after savoring the lethal fruit then. A single foolish lick proved enough to fulfill the dare. Any more, and he would've died, yet living to see another day, provoking fate, made a dangerous snare. Temptation lured the best of men that way. Made a man think he could walk to the edge of a cliff in darkness and not fall.

Now, he tested Lydia, tasting her neck, not getting enough. She became sought-after piquant fruit and he the hapless adventurer in an unknown land. Her smell invaded his senses. He wanted to take her right there against his bedpost.

"I want you, Edward," she said, as though she'd read his mind. Her hand slipped lower to his breeches, stroking his erection with her artist's hands.

His hoyden wife knew exactly what she was doing. Dark green eyes glittered back at him with triumph when her fingers scratched his bollocks and trailed slowly up his rock-hard erection. His body convulsed, Edward had to brace one hand on the bed for support.

"Lydia…" he whispered. "The lights…the bed."

Two feminine fingers gave careful ministrations, scratching low between his legs, dawdling over his placket, rubbing his pulsing flesh. Her husky laugh was pure sex.

"I don't require darkness or a bed." She leaned forward and kissed his neck, hot and openmouthed. "Don't you want to see?"

His body shook at her intoxicating question. He throbbed against the restraining placket. Everything spiraled into a cloud of heady sensuality. This was supposed to be about her comfort, her pleasure, about…

He lost all sense of thought.

Lydia's fingertips swirled high on his placket and loosened a pewter button. Edward's forehead dropped to her sweet-smelling shoulder. His lips found the moonlike roundness of her left breast and sucked. He'd mark her as his. Yet that intent felt feeble when her capable hands slipped two more buttons free. He shivered like an untried lad.

Who marked whom?

Edward opened his eyes, and knowledge of being well dosed by a woman's touch danced at the edges of his sex-dulled brain.

"Lydia…" His left hand clenched the coverlet. "This was supposed to be done right."

Her head lolled against the bedpost, and the bodice slipped lower. Tender nipples poked over elaborate embroidery. He had to suck. She breathed deeper, freeing more flesh.

"This *is* right," she whispered.

His mouth clamped down on that pinkish point, pulling soft and hard. She arched against him, and her cry of pleasure sated him. 'Bout time she was as uncomfortable and bothered as he was. But Lydia started more undulating against him. A faster rhythm.

He looked down, and lots of blue silk bunched intrusively about her waist. Roundish white breasts stared at him over her bodice, and the softest, bare white legs, with one shoe untied, stretched to the floor. He couldn't imagine a more erotic sight.

"Take me," she demanded. "Now."

Those three words. Potent. He bent to kiss her other breast, lingering there. An offering like that couldn't be ignored.

"Lydia…I…" His voice muffled against her chest as his lips grazed and nibbled her breasts.

She said something, but the opiate's haze of sex pulsed stronger, rushing through his ears. His belladonna spoke. Or was gentle laughter shifting her breasts under his mouth when he slavishly kissed their softness? Her fingers slipped inside his shirt, and somewhere in the fog, words…

"The stool, Edward. Get the stool."

He did as she requested and brought the stool, unsure what she had in mind, but all parts of him were game.

Lydia shimmied out of her bodice and then her skirt. She tossed yards of shimmering fabric aside and stood there naked, save for one tied and one untied shoe. He placed the stool at the base of the bedpost, and her shod feet stepped onto the square cushion. Her seductive, impish smile touched him. He reached out and plucked the gleaming star that dangled from a lock of hair onto her breast. He tossed the jeweled piece atop the skirt. She needed no adornment.

With hair a tumble and naked splendor in candlelight, Lydia hooked two fingers inside his breech's placket, pulling him closer, loosening another button. And with that button, his erection sprang free.

Lydia's hands tugged on his breeches, and the placket opened in a wide V. Her artist's hands moved up his abdomen, pushing open his shirt and exploring his flesh like a practiced sculptor. Lydia's fingernails skimmed his flat nipples. She took control, and he was the recipient of her attentions—a novel sensation to simply feel.

Her lips parted, tasting his upper lip, his lower lip, moving to his scarred cheek. She kissed the marred flesh, small kisses soft and sweet, and the flame that had stirred his earlier fogged haze came roaring back. And when he looked down, her fingers slipped inside the glistening sable curls at the apex of her thighs. Feminine flesh, slick pearled pink, opened to him. With her other hand, Lydia angled his stiff flesh, poking the head into those dark curls.

This was her plan.

Shocks of pulsing intensity, ripped through him, powerful as any ocean wave knocking down a lone swimmer. Edward grabbed the bedpost behind her, breathing hard and holding on for dear life. Lydia guided him to her opening, a safe, wet place.

Whatever threads of logic and control he wanted to maintain evaporated the instant Lydia opened herself to him in life's most intimate of ways. Edward pushed up, and in one freeing moment, slid inside her. They moaned. Together. A symbiosis of pleasure and fulfillment, rocking slowly against each other until they found their bodies' cadence.

He gripped the bedpost with one hand and her ass cheek with the other. He squeezed her hard. There'd be tiny marks. Mouth to mouth they rocked, crying their satisfaction as wonders built from one frantic stroke after another. There'd be no languorous sex tonight. Edward couldn't feel the floor beneath him. All faded in the sensual shroud that wrapped them both. When their peak of pleasure came, and it did come fast, Lydia clutched him as tightly as he held her. Her sex pulsed around him, the aftermath as sweet as the orgasm.

And he was lost.

She was virtually naked, and he was half-clothed. He ought to see to her comfort, her warmth. He started to pull away.

"Lydia, a blanket—"

She held him tight. "No," she whispered against his neck. "I want you inside me. Please. Please stay…just as you are."

Lydia rested her head on his shoulder, an act of trust that undid him. Tenderness surged through Edward. Candles blazed around the room, turning into melted wax columns. Like him.

Nothing went as expected tonight.

He held Lydia, stroking her tangled hair. He tasted her on his tongue and reveled in the wonderful newness that she was his. Yet an altogether different tremor shook him as their connected bodies recovered. His belladonna did something hazardous: she freed him from his mind, his plans. All that remained was potent sex and emotion.

Very alarming indeed.

Twenty-three

*I hope that I may always desire more than
I can accomplish.*

—Michelangelo

IS IT POSSIBLE THAT A MAN YOU'VE SHARED MIND-muddling kisses with is the same one you'd want to throttle? A fortnight of marriage, and Lydia bounced between heights of pleasure and vexing irritation. That mad pendulum of emotions came from the man shuffling papers across his desk in that distracted man's way of his. But she wanted all of his attention, thus her leaning forward to plant her palms on the mahogany.

"I'm sorry, did I misunderstand?" she said, trying for calm. "Because I distinctly heard you request that I hold off on selling my paintings until you return from your voyage."

Never mind that I'm still working on you staying.

He held two papers up and glanced at her over the edge. "Misunderstand? Yes, that wasn't a request; that was a command." His topaz gaze flicked back to the items before him.

Lydia jammed her arms across her chest. "And once again, a man impedes my progress."

He frowned at her outburst and stacked the papers, tapping them on his desk. "Convenient for you to blame men for your lack of progress in life."

Her mouth moved, rather like a fish just caught out of water, when he said that. His words, delivered with matter-of-fact directness, were as good as a slap on the face, but she was speechless at his blunt pronouncement. Edward set the papers in a folio and stood up, dispensing more of his problem-solving insight.

"You had three years before you became the Countess of Greenwich to make things happen. What stopped you?"

He set his hands loosely at his hips, and she was quite certain he had no idea the damage he inflicted with his pearls of wisdom.

"Lydia, if you want something, think it through, balance both sides of an argument, then act." He raised his hand and tapped unseen points in the air. "Make your progress from step one, step two, step three with clear logic until you reach your destination."

"You mean such as spending the past two weeks working madly on *your* diagrams and illustrations, so that *your* pamphlets are completed in *your* timeline." Her voice rose in volume, but she kept control. "At the exclusion of my own plans to paint."

He sighed and linked his arms across his chest. "I see where this is going, and I adore you Lydia—"

"You adore me?" That shocked her.

The horizontal line between his brows showed up. He was cross at the interruption. "Yes, I have some fond affection for you, but while you have a lot of passion, you lack a certain discipline. Whereas I've developed both."

She snorted at that as much from his arrogance as his decided edict about her. He'd given her some thought, and she'd come up lacking. "You wouldn't know passion if it hit you in the head."

His eyebrows raised a challenging notch. And when he was arrogant, he didn't even see it as arrogance. That was the exasperating thing about him.

"I don't refer to passion in the marital bed," she sputtered.

But even as she was ready to continue their battle, part of what he'd said rang true in a painful way. A twinge of discomfort made her shift in her seat like a scolded child. She smarted from the fact that hit a truth: she went into great bursts of enthusiasm for her art, and then could be distracted by aiding others with whatever were their pursuits and their needs. There was no discipline and order about her process. Sitting there, she wanted to pour out excuses that he had so many advantages, while she did not. But that didn't stop some of the female artists she admired greatly. Rosalba Carriera was a lace-maker's daughter, and that good lady was single-minded in focus.

Edward walked around the desk and planted a kiss on top of her head. He couldn't be too awfully upset with her. But then why should he? He was getting everything he wanted and more. Right then, the countess breezed through the doorway.

"Greetings, I haven't missed anything, have I?"

The countess had graciously made herself scarce the first week after they wed, then returned with reminders of ball-gown fittings and such. Lydia was certain the countess had come to check on their progress, and in particular, *her* progress at keeping Edward in England. Lady Elizabeth would be disappointed.

Benumbed, she moved to the study's seating area with Edward and the countess. They chattered on about something, but Lydia couldn't say what. Her mind turned over and over again Edward's stinging pronouncement. The arrival of Miss Lumley and Rogers with a tea tray gave her mind some reprieve. Lydia looked at Lady Elizabeth and motioned to the tray in a halfhearted fashion.

"Would you mind doing the honors? I'm a bit peaked." She set another pillow behind her to help prop up her flagging body.

"My...so soon? To be *enceinte*?" Lady Elizabeth's face perked up, and she glanced back and forth between Lydia and Edward. "Of course, how silly of me, but one can only hope."

She picked up the teapot and began to pour, in her element with them both. Lydia declined tea but listened to Edward praise her work on the illustrations and diagrams. His topaz eyes glinted at her from his great chair.

He tipped his head toward the desk. "Because of Lydia's excellent work, I was able to focus entirely on the research and improve my first draft. And all the work was done in less than half the time." He raised his cup in salute to her. "We make quite a team."

The countess sipped from her cup with watchful eyes. "Then you will work together in the future?"

"Yes."

"No."

They spoke over each other, with Edward giving the surprising affirmation.

Lydia folded her hands in her lap and explained, "That is, I need to concentrate on my painting." Her chin tilted at a stubborn angle. "Become more disciplined and the like. And, of course, Edward still plans to leave on his expedition in June."

"What?" Lady Elizabeth's cup rattled on the saucer, and she set the dish on the table. "Your wife could be breeding at this very moment. I had hoped you came to your senses and changed your mind over that."

Edward set his cup down and dug his elbows into the plush leather arms of his chair. His steepled fingers tapped as he appeared to consider how to respond. The way he looked at Lydia and his mother, she was sure he was trying to add up the changes between Lydia and the countess, the sudden shift a few weeks ago. Had he guessed they'd become allies? Lydia brushed an imaginary speck from her lap, finding her red-and-white-striped skirt of great interest.

"The two of you haven't cooked up something, have you?" he asked.

"Cooked up something?" the countess sputtered. "You make it sound as if there's a conspiracy behind every shadow."

At the same moment, Rogers knocked on the door, and when he entered, he bore a silver salver held out perfectly level. The countess had busied herself getting everyone and everything in excellent working order at Greenwich Park. Rogers bent near Edward, from the waist, and held the position until Edward removed not one, but two missives from the platter.

"The king." Edward proclaimed the sender of the first letter, but when he picked up the other, his eyes opened wider. "And Blevins."

He set them in his lap, but the countess tapped her chair's arm. "Come, come. You must open them. Don't keep us in suspense."

He broke the seal, and Lydia cringed. Today was the day of reckoning. She couldn't take back what was already done, so she folded her hands and watched and waited. Edward's face was a study in concentration as he read the letter, unaffected by the fact that he corresponded with his sovereign. The way his eyes flared over one part of the page, this letter was not about books, but was the expected and hoped for response…a consequence of her gamble.

Edward let the letter drop to his lap, and he flicked a glance her way. Her cheeks grew hotter under that quick attention. What would he do in anger? Would he yell? Drop to his knees and kiss her hand with thanks? The latter was a silly hope.

Then, he opened the second missive from Lord Blevins. The damaged plane of his face faced her, and as he perused the letter, his muscles ticked under the scars. Edward's mouth went into a flat line, and his eyes locked on her.

"Do tell. Don't keep us in suspense," said the countess, scooting to the edge of her seat. "What did the king say?"

Edward kept his dark stare on Lydia, not facing his mother. "The king says he's delighted to attend my lecture on the healing properties of the *Agathosma betulina*. A lecture that I'm apparently giving at the end of June to the Royal Society." Edward's voice went soft. "Which is an impossibility, since I'll be a fortnight into my expedition by then."

Lydia set a calming hand to her waist and took a deep breath. "I can explain."

"Yes, please do, because I find it astonishing how the king and Lord Blevins have already read my pamphlet, when the finished product sits on my desk. Completed today." His voice stayed quiet, but there was a threatening hardness growing.

"What are you talking about?" the countess demanded.

Lydia took a deep breath, keeping her focus on Edward. "The illustrations…I burned some and sent copies to the king and Lord Blevins with the treatise I'd already copied. I wanted to slow down your progress." She paused and took a gulp of air. "And I sent a letter and signed your name."

"So we can add forgery to your list of crimes," he snapped.

She winced, rubbing damp palms across her lap. "I made sure to send a copy to the king and to Lord Blevins…to ensure that his lordship doesn't steal your work. And as to the lecture, I left the date open." She chewed her lip and flinched. "Apparently the king or Lord Blevins decided on the date."

"How very thoughtful of you to make plans for me," he said, his sarcasm growing. "But Blevins stealing my latest work is not a concern of mine, since he's never been to West Africa, nor does he possess the Agathosma tree, a detail your overworked, deceitful mind failed to consider." He stood up, and a menacing scowl crossed his features. "But neither did you consider that I want nothing to do with Blevins."

"Edward..." Lady Elizabeth fretted from her seat. "Let's all take a calming moment—"

"No." He went to the fireplace and paced the area like a caged animal, but the way he glared at Lydia, he wasn't done with her.

Something in her snapped. She flung her hands in the air and tilted forward on the settee, perilously close to falling off. "What are you afraid of? Don't you think it's time to forgive Blevins his error?"

"*Afraid?*" His face screwed up in distaste. "This has nothing to do with fear and everything to do with you meddling in my affairs." He clamped his arms across his chest. "Forgive Blevins?" He snorted. "I'd rather kiss a pig's arse."

"Edward, please," the countess interjected into the fray.

Edward tipped his chin at the countess. "Are you in on this?"

Flustered, Lady Elizabeth went saucer-eyed, but despite her ruffled feathers, she maintained composure. "No."

His presence was overpowering. Lydia had to get equilibrium and diminish the anger that washed out from him, at least explain her intentions. "I thought I was doing the right thing, helping you to get back into Society, your science..." she finished lamely, her words wilting under the heat of his glare.

"You warm my bed, and now you think you know me?"

Lydia jumped up, scalded by his words. "Do *not* demean our time together. And I *do* know you."

It was on the tip of her tongue to add *I love you*, but she held back. He would likely think she was showing emotional histrionics, and this tense situation wasn't how she wanted those beautiful words to come.

He groaned a sound of frustration as he looked up at the ceiling. "Of all the women in England…I find the meddling, quarrelsome one."

His chest moved under his shirt with labored breathing. He was angry, a controlled kind that frightened her, because he'd do or say something that would be utterly final. And he did. Edward stretched his arm and pointed to the door.

"Get out."

Of the room? The house? England?

His harsh face went blank, not giving her anger or hope. The biggest, blackest pit swallowed her up right then, even though she was still standing. Lydia's body jerked from sharp pain, a tearing sensation in the pit of her stomach. She wanted to curl up on the floor like a small child and cry her eyes out.

This time the countess, however, intervened and kindly guided her toward the door. What was done was done, a risk she'd taken and lost. At the door, Lydia turned around, as surprised that no tears flowed as at the revelation that came to her with startling clarity.

"You asked me once why I never married." With her hands at her sides, she stood tall, but her voice wavered and cracked. "I feared I'd turn out like my mother. Freedom to paint meant everything to me. I swore I'd never let my art run second-best to any man." A bitter laugh bubbled up from her. "It appears that's what I've done."

The countess tugged Lydia along with gentle hands and shut the door. From within the sanctum, a loud roar resounded as dishes smashed and crashed.

Twenty-four

Waste no more time arguing about what a good man should be. Be one.

—Marcus Aurelius

"YOU DON'T HAVE TO GO." JONAS'S VOICE PULLED HIM out of a mental fog. "You're not the type…the kind with a bad itch for adventure."

Edward balanced his empty glass on his knee, making a game of how long he could keep the glass level. The odd midnight game epitomized the kind of empty pursuits that had filled the last month. The crystal wobbled, but he saved it from a crash, letting the glass fall into his palm.

"Adventure?" He poured more scotch into his glass and repeated the word, as if that were a profound question. "That's not the issue." Edward sipped from his glass and let the peat-smoked liquid pour into him before looking through bleary eyes at his friend. "No, the problem here is that I can't be in two places at the same time, on a ship exploring exotic flora, or in England exploring my wife…my lovely, *errant* wife."

"She made a mistake."

"Damn right, she did." He glared, but the effect was useless. He was as weak as a kitten, too worn out and worked over.

"And it's time to forgive and move on." Jonas linked his hands together across his midsection as he had so many other nights, sitting in that chair and giving the occasional comment, but listening, yes, mostly listening.

Tonight, however, was to be different. Jonas looked different. Could be the black hair growing from his head. That had to mean something, but Edward, neck deep in his own muddle, was too overwhelmed to ask. Jonas was not content to be a giant ear tonight. He observed Edward like one might read numbers on an instrument.

"Going out to sea won't bring them back," Jonas's deep voice rumbled.

His father and brother.

Edward's fingers pinched the glass. That bitter truth bit through his haze. A bubble of emotion, of all things, wanted to gurgle up his chest and erupt. He tamped it down, kept it barely in check.

"I know," he said with another kind of sadness. "I miss them. Life would've been so different if…"

He couldn't finish. He was tired of emotions, exhausted of them. He'd had a month of the worst kind of feelings. Lydia had been a glimmer of the best kind, new and different when she was here. She excited him in ways no woman had ever been able to do—in mind and body. That she'd hardly read any books in her life didn't matter. She reached inside him and touched places he had hidden away—the good and bad parts. His friend was not content to let things be either.

"I can only think your father and brother would've liked her." Jonas tipped his head at Edward. "Would want you to stay and tend her."

Edward scratched his whiskered jaw and frowned. "You make it sound like Lydia's a plant I should take care of."

"It's what you do," Jonas said and one corner of his mouth quirked. "You can take care of her and do your science here."

Edward set down his glass and pressed the heels of both his hands to his temple, rubbing. His head ached. "I'm so tired of thinking."

"Never thought I'd hear you say that."

"It's true." His fingers massaged their way across his forehead. "I'd like nothing more than a quiet evening with Lydia."

Finished by wrapping ourselves naked in bedsheets or against the bedpost...if she'd have me.

"Well?" Jonas prompted.

"It's no use. She won't answer any of my correspondence." He examined the dying fire, all the orange pieces of wood were disintegrating into pieces of charcoal.

"You've got to do better than that." Jonas shifted in his chair. "Remember, you sent her away."

"I know," he groaned, recalling the shock followed by agony on her face when he made that grand pronouncement. "But the die is cast. The expedition leaves in less than a fortnight."

Jonas sighed, a long-suffering sound as he leaned to the side of his chair. "I didn't want to do this, but..."

Edward's dreary stare snapped away from the fireplace to Jonas, who opened his plain leather folio. Jonas raised the flap and pulled out folded broadsheets, three of them, and tossed them on the table before Edward.

Each paper was folded with odd geometry, such that the eye was drawn to a particular caption and piece. Edward picked them up and read the painful print out loud.

"*Stunning Countess of Greenwich Wins the Hearts of London's Art World.*"

That, however, wasn't so bad as what was inferred underneath. The writer fairly drooled over the new countess, describing throngs of male admirers flocking to her Grosvenor Square town house. He scowled at the paper, but the next broadsheet went right to the heart of the matter.

"*Famed Architect Sir William Garth Courts Newly Married Lady Greenwich*—What?" He glared at Jonas over the broadsheet, and then read on. "*Sir William has attended Lady Greenwich's art salons and hopes she'll lend her support to establish a Royal Academy of Art*"—the paper dropped as heavy as a hammer—"a Royal Academy for art?"

"Keep reading."

"*One site under consideration for the Royal Academy of Art is Piccadilly, where the two have been seen of late. Of course, this writer speculates Sir William escorts her with more than art in mind*—" Edward crumpled the paper and flung it in the fire. He balled up the other two papers and fed them to the flames.

The fledgling embers took a moment before devouring the paper with shoots of yellow and orange. Edward rubbed his unscarred cheek, where longer, more troublesome whiskers needed scratching.

"It's only vile gossip."

Jonas lifted one massive shoulder in a shrug. "Maybe. Maybe not. Only one way to find out."

Edward's head tipped back against his chair, and he stared at midnight shadows flickering over the plaster ceiling. Something between a groan and a roar erupted from him.

"Time for hiding's over," Edward said, scrubbing both hands across his face.

"Funny that you chose those words." Jonas looked at him with a crooked, uncomfortable smile of his own.

Edward's gaze narrowed on his friend. They usually didn't miss much about the other, needing few words, yet communicating much over these three years. Sudden recognition made Edward cock his head. Another novel piece of news was about to sink its teeth into him.

"You're returning to the Colonies."

Jonas gave the barest smile of acknowledgment at that profound decision. "The Colonies by way of Plumtree first. But, I'll find my replacement for Sanford Shipping, and go to Plumtree in August, if all goes as planned."

"Some kind of friend I've been." Edward braced a hand on his thigh. "When did you decide?"

"Been a long time coming." Jonas's curt nod was as good as a solid promise.

"You're certain?"

"Yes." Jonas rumbled with a chuckle. "What a pair we make, Ed. You hiding from your life, me running away from mine."

They sat in silence, watching the last of the gossipy broadsheets burn into gray dust before Jonas stood up and stretched, likely as tired and wearied as Edward. Jonas picked up his leather folio and snapped it shut as puzzlement formed on his stoic features.

"You said 'time for hiding's over.' Does that mean you'll stay or go?"

Twenty-five

Pure gold does not fear the furnace.

—Chinese Proverb

PERFECTION, A PAINFUL PROCESS, WAS NOT IMPOSSIBLE. Strains of fragile violin music played, and the diamond brilliance of three chandeliers glowed over the heads of London's best—all scions of Society having delayed their summer sojourns to the country simply to attend her art salon. All moved in clusters, garbed in the finest, colorful attire. This evening would be a success. She willed it to be.

Thronged in the crowd was Mr. Cyrus Ryland, his broad-shouldered frame moving methodically from one painting to another. Well-dressed hangers-on followed behind him, vying for his attention. Tonight, the Marquis of Northampton, "Lord Perfection" many called him, had won the prized spot on Mr. Ryland's right. Rumor named the marquis first choice for Lucinda Ryland's hand in marriage. Rumor also claimed Northampton sought a coveted piece of the business empire. Likely both avenues provided the same end.

Lydia had always been on the outside of this strange glittering life, wanting only to sell her art. Now she was part of the parade.

She achieved everything she wanted, hadn't she? Yet the cost was brittle hollowness. When she left Greenwich Park and its scarred master, she invited emptiness that not even beautiful, perfect art could fill.

How could a woman gain so much, yet be so lacking?

She was surrounded by elegance. The newly redecorated conservatory reflected neutral shades, an ideal foil for the vivid paintings dotting the room. Footmen liveried in champagne-colored attire dispensed trays of fine, pale gold champagne for this elegant victory. On walls and easels, a few of her paintings were secretly on display, under another name, along with those of several other prominent artists. Rumors abounded that the king would establish a Royal Academy of Arts this year. She should be happy, ridiculously happy.

But she wavered between angry and miserable and empty, with very little time to sort out those emotions. She was marvelously "peacocked," as Edward would say: her gown of deep blue and green brought to mind that exotic bird similar in vibrant hues and richness. Clothing, however, was part and parcel of her battle armament. The evening required self-control, restraint, yes…even discipline. She breathed in air, as much as her sharp stays allowed, girding herself for the first hurdle, a man of great importance who graced her gathering.

She smiled and sank into a deep curtsy. "I'm honored with your attendance, Your Grace."

Voices hummed all around, and when she rose, Lydia placed her fingers in the duke's proffered hand.

"My dear, I think the patrons will find you the greatest work of art in the room." The Duke of Somerset bent over her hand, his head not quite touching her.

A sphere of awe surrounded the duke, a man of average height and thinning hair. She kept a respectful arm's length from him, but he would have none of that, pulling her into the rarified space next to him, tucking her arm over his.

"Let's take a turn around your salon and admire the outstanding art, shall we, Countess?"

The broadsheets would have much to say about his simple gesture, an elevation in status no doubt for her. Clusters of people parted for the duke, giving an unspoken radius of distance. Conversations lulled as people nodded and greeted him with polite refrains of "Your Grace."

They were rewarded with his tight smile and coolness. In the midst of one frozen smile, he spoke to Lydia.

"You've come a long way from the wayward miss of Somerset." The duke's nose was in the air, the erect pose everything his position required; the surprising twinkle in his eyes when he glanced her way was not.

Lydia pasted a pleasant smile on her face and nodded greetings to a pair of ladies. She hesitated on how to answer that, but the duke was the one to save the day. He slowed their progress and steered her toward an easel, pointing at the modest landscape.

"I admire that piece." The duke pinched his monocle in place and leaned in for closer examination. "The whimsy of the clouds in the distance. Brings to mind the work of one Rosalba Carriera." He withdrew his monocle and used the glass as a pointer. "But this one done by a certain L. Wright, I see. Fascinating."

Nervous pinpricks spread over Lydia, moving a flush of uncomfortable heat. Would the duke connect the initial of her first name and her true maiden name? She'd gone by Montgomery for many years, but of course His Grace wouldn't forget her father. Her hands fretted, but she pinched them together near her waist, prodding herself to calm.

"There are many other artists of greater consequence that I can show you, Your Grace."

"Oh no, this one captures my fancy." He waved his monocle at the painting. "Lady Greenwich, I must have it, a gift for my daughter's birthday. She delights in Carriera's work, and this is so similar." He tucked his monocle into his waistcoat pocket and went on with some bluster. "Though a woman artist…the very idea."

The friendly sparkle in his eye was the only acknowledgment—he knew. She smiled graciously, and her hands relaxed at her waist.

"The world is changing, isn't it? Sometimes for the worse, sometimes for the better." Lydia paused, and they both took a glass of champagne from a passing footman's tray.

A good hostess was not supposed to partake, instead looking to her guests' need for refreshment. Lydia needed the bubbly liquid and let the chilled gold beverage tickle her throat a bolstering few seconds.

"Hmm." The duke's thin gray brows raised as he sipped from his glass. "True. But women artists?" He shook his head and took another sip. "Then again, what else can you expect from the Italians? All that sun makes them hot-blooded, I'm sure." He tipped his head at the modest painting beside them. "But this L. Wright, an English painter of some quality. I hope to see more."

Lydia set her champagne glass on another passing tray and let elevating victory lift her. She smiled at the Duke of Somerset, thankful for his support. A Russian diplomat and a marquis of someplace or another approached His Grace, and she benignly stood there, nodding from time to time as if fully engaged.

Her art filled a place sublime and wonderful, but she'd tasted heaven at Greenwich Park. Funny how she had no time to paint in London, yet painting in that empty ballroom, having Edward hover as he tried to understand art, had thrilled her. She was more alive those weeks with him. But like a coward, she never said those magical three words: *I love you*.

But what would he have done if she gifted him with that deepest emotion, love?

Edward should be here. Tomorrow he'd be gone.

The whole room grew too hot, and the voices, so loud. Lydia set her hand to her waist. She'd have to warn Tilly not to pull her corset so tight; she could barely breathe.

"Edward…" She breathed his name, and her head bobbled as she pulled herself out of the haze.

The duke touched her elbow, his face writ with concern. "Yes, Edward." He gently pivoted her to the other end of the room, advising her under his breath, "Steady, Countess. People are watching."

The footman could just as well have announced the *Greenwich Phantom*, but to her, he was a knight in shining armor. Impeccably attired in black velvet, Edward stood tall, surveying the room with his hands clasped behind his back. His waistcoat shined a deep red silk, with the barest flounce at his neck, the minimum formality required, but worn nonetheless. The whole room hushed. Even the violins thinned to quiet.

Then one brave soul greeted him. "Glad to see you back, Greenwich."

That broke the dam of silence as greetings trickled and then flooded around him. "Looking well, man... Greenwich, hale and hearty you are...Good evening, my lord..." And so poured forth the goodwill as Edward stepped into the conservatory.

Music resumed. Edward greeted people, nodding his way through the room, even smiling now and then, but his dark eyes were on her. Lydia, for all her newfound courage to set the art world on fire, was timid as a lamb. Her feet would not move. The duke put subtle pressure on her elbow.

"Go to your husband as befitting a wife."

Lady's E.'s voice chided her: *Never let them see your discomfort. And for goodness' sake, glide!*

And glide she did to the man who claimed her body and soul. To all the world, this was part and parcel of the evening, a social morsel that would be rehashed at summer house parties.

Lydia extended her hand to Edward, and with all the cheer she could muster, said, "How nice to see you, my lord."

Edward bent low over her hand, but his stare locked on her low neckline. "How nice to see so *much* of you."

He kissed her knuckles, and his thumb stroked her fingers. He held her hand longer than was decent, standing upright and letting his fingers linger on hers before finally letting go. Nearby, a trio of ladies fluttered their fans, having witnessed up close the sensual interplay. It would be known that the Phantom Earl of Greenwich found his countess appealing.

Her breath hitched. "You're looking well." Her gaze dropped to his waistcoat. "A red waistcoat, a bold choice in fashion, but it suits you. You may win a few ardent female admirers this evening."

"I seek to win only one." He flashed his brigand's smile, and something eased in his stance. "You like it then? It's claret, not red, or so my valet informed me." He leaned closer and his warm breath teased her skin, "I'd expect an artist to discern the difference."

Just having him step closer to her made her body rejoice at the powerful draw he had on her. She worked to maintain composure, but Edward was more practiced in high decorum.

He saved her by nodding at the room. "We must take a turn around the room and welcome our guests." He slanted a glance at her hair. "Thank you for not powdering your hair."

She dipped her head, certain she was blushing like a schoolgirl, but glad he'd noticed. Tilly followed her strict instructions to pile the glossy dark curls high and never powder them.

Lydia linked her arm through his. "Of course, and when you have a moment, you'll have to tell me about this valet you hired, my lord."

Did that mean he was staying?

His right hand covered hers as they began their stroll. "The valet? A gift for my ambitious art-salon wife."

An elderly gentleman and his wife approached. She'd greeted them in the receiving line but had forgotten their names. Edward recognized them.

"Lord Ellerby, Lady Ellerby," he called, stopping to chat.

"Good to see you're out and about, man," Lord Ellerby said, giving Edward the gimlet eye. "Your father would never have approved of your hermitry. Not even for the sake of science. Turn over in his grave he would."

Lady Ellerby, a stout matron with a prim smile, tapped her fan on her husband's shoulder, admonishing him. "Now, Hugh, that's hardly the ideal greeting for a peer and fellow scientist." She turned her smile on Lydia. "We should instead congratulate Lord Greenwich on finding so lovely a wife, and one so ready to enliven Society's artistic circles." The lady's turquoise ostrich feather bobbled atop her hair as she spoke to Edward. "Your mother must be so proud."

"My mother was beside herself when she found out I was to wed Lydia. It was all very quick, and done at our estate. I was quite smitten," Edward said, smooth as silk.

"How lovely," Lady Ellerby gushed, her chubby cheeks making her eyes small spots of color. "And romantic."

They made their excuses and continued through the room.

"Quite the charmer, my lord," Lydia said under her breath.

"I learned from the best, remember?" He scanned the room. "Speaking of that grand dame of social instruction, where is my mother?"

"She said Jane needed her…something about 'if my children insist on marrying beneath their station, they will need my help for a leg up in this world' or some-thing of that nature."

Intimate words ebbed in the sea of banal conversation. More people approached, among them Mr. Ryland and the Marquis of Northampton, with a throng of well-wishers. The Marquis of Northampton smiled and tipped his head.

"Edward, it's been a long, long time."

"Gabriel, good to see you." Edward tipped his head at Mr. Ryland. "And you, Ryland."

"Greenwich." His gaze traveled from Edward to Lydia. Tonight he sported a yellowing bruise on his right cheek, but no one dared ask how he got it.

Mr. Ryland's fathomless pewter stare missed nothing. At every social event, he gave the minimum niceties required, but nothing passed his notice. The man was like solid stone with the thinnest veneer of Society painted over him. Lydia guessed he was aware that much more hummed under the surface of this husband-and-wife meeting. But he stayed silent.

The well-dressed Lord Gabriel, however, took in Edward's attire. "I don't recall your wardrobe veering from anything other than brown or black. This suits you." He flashed a brilliant, practiced smile at Lydia. "Something tells me you're the cause of this transformation."

She touched Edward's sleeve, as much for needful contact as the desire to shield him from anything unpleasant. But that was silly. Edward didn't need her to take care of him.

"I'm glad to see him, whatever color the wardrobe." Her tone bristled with irritation.

Lord Gabriel's brows shot up, but Edward jumped in quickly.

"Gabriel has a long history of summer days at Greenwich Park with Jonathan." He gave Lydia's hand a gentle squeeze. "He's well acquainted with my past antics."

They made polite excuses and moved on, finishing their agonizing rotation around the room. So many questions swirled in her head. Was he planning to leave? Surely not if he hired a valet. Or did he do that to help her, a small token before he left? Edward didn't wear a wig this evening, but his queue was as impeccable as his clothes, and he went out of his way to engage in social chatter.

What made him come tonight? Was it her? Or because he was leaving tomorrow? She agonized over the crowds of people still in the house and wanted a private moment. The chamber music was cloying, the guests too loud, and even the elegant chandeliers burned excessively bright. When sending out the invitations, she had wanted so many to come. Now she wanted them all to leave.

Lydia spied a potted palm and tugged Edward's arm to follow. On the way, another footman passed with a tray of champagne, and she grabbed another glass, but this one she would finish.

Behind the safety of the palm, Lydia gulped down champagne.

"Easy, Countess," he chided.

Lydia stopped gulping, but the glass rim touched her lower lip, and she blurted, "Did you do this for me?"

"Of course," he said, his smile full of mischief. "Unless I have another ambitious wife waiting in the wings."

She lowered the glass, clutching it with both hands in something resembling a prayer. "Edward, please…I need to know."

Under normal circumstances, his humor would make things perfect, but in this strained, fragile state, she needed certainty. The past month had been a series of steps, one and two and three, with very specific goals in mind, yet she was empty. Oh, her art took front and center, but everything was out of balance. She needed him, but when his dark stare dropped to her slender waist, Edward turned into the earl.

"Are you pregnant?" There was a small light of hope in his eyes. "I was sure you'd write to me if that were so."

The abrupt shift in conversation startled her. Their arrangement was fundamentally the same from that first night at the Blue Cockerel. When they'd exchanged wedding vows, she'd had her hopes, and he'd had his. Something died right then, growing small and hard within her. Lydia poured her remaining champagne into the planter and set the glass in the dirt. A scale of armor surrounded her, the same as the day she'd walked out of the public house when her first lover had callously mistreated her. Lydia smoothed both hands over her peacock-blue bodice.

"No, I'm not. As a man of science, you know the chances increase with more *activity* between husband and wife." Her shoulders squared as she took a step away from him. "Not that there will be any of that in the future."

He grabbed her wrist. "What's this? Am I being dismissed?" He scowled. "I came with good intentions to help you."

She faltered for a second, the part of her that turned to jelly at his closeness, his clean smell. Edward's sculpted lips that she loved to kiss hovered close, though they curled now in anger. She guessed as well what steps he'd taken to be here tonight, and that was in no way easy.

She loved him, but he didn't love her back. Lydia took a deep breath.

"Thank you for coming tonight."

"I'm not a guest to be brushed off. This is my home."

"And mine," she said staunchly and pulled away. He let her wrist drop from his grip. "I really must get back to our guests."

Lydia took a few steps back toward the conservatory, where the crowd had thinned but still thrived. He would leave. *Tomorrow*. She stood in the doorway, a voice near shouting in her head to dismantle her safe harbor of pride and tell him how she felt, but when she turned around, Edward was gone.

Lydia's sleep-grained eyes opened, and she was out of sorts. *What time is it?* She was in her nightclothes, but... Edward. She'd never had the chance to finish talking with him last night, or tell him...

She sprang off the settee where she must have dozed, waiting for him, and ran to the windows, yanking back the curtains.

The sky was predawn gray. *His ship*.

"What time is it?" she yelled, scrambling out of her nightclothes, so fast and hard that fabric tore.

Running to the bellpull in only her chemise, she yanked hard and yanked again. Lydia flung open her bedroom door and bellowed like a fishwife.

"Carriage! I need a carriage!"

She ducked back in, leaving the door wide open. She'd barely pulled a simple gray dress over her head before Tilly and a footman appeared, both blinking from sleep-lined faces. Her dress gaped in the back, and her hair was in wild disarray.

"His lordship? Have you seen Lord Greenwich?"

The footman, an older man she didn't know, adjusted his wig. "He, he left this morning for the docks—"

"No!" She bellowed her agony, both hands gripping her head. "I must see him before he leaves. Get a carriage. Quick!"

The footman disappeared, but Tilly stood saucer-eyed at Lydia. "Don't gawk, Tilly. Button me up."

Lydia planted herself on the ground and slipped on her stockings, while Tilly kneeled behind her, hastily buttoning up the back of the dress.

"There's no time for this," she snapped and scrambled off the floor. Cool air slipped into her back where the fabric gapped from what must be missed buttons. She started for the door.

"Wait, my lady. Your cloak." Tilly flung a brown cloak at Lydia, who tore down the hall to the mews in her stocking feet.

She had to tell him she loved him.

Even if he never loved her, she had to say those words to him. The carriage awaited her in the back, and the footman must've conveyed her upset, for they moved with great speed. Lydia pulled the curtains back, clenching the fabric in her hands.

How could she have been so foolish? Did it matter if someone loved you back?

To love someone like this was a gift, not something to be hidden away. Share that love, give it, say it, and hold nothing back. Sitting in the rocking carriage was pure agony. They moved through near-empty streets. Palatial homes turned into practical midtown businesses, a blur of buildings which gave way to older, crowded structures of taverns and warehouses.

Had *The Fiona* left?

Then, the carriage lurched to a halt. Voices yelled outside. She pressed her hand on the carriage window.

Why weren't they moving?

She cracked open the door. A sleepy-eyed footman poked his head inside the carriage.

"There's an overturned dray, my lady."

Lydia looked past the footman, half out of the carriage. Barrels scattered in the road, and two flustered men argued over them.

She smelled briny air. Gulls swooped low onto bits of scraps in the road. People milled about, gawking at the mess despite the early hour. She gripped the carriage door and leaned far. They sat in the middle of St. Catherine's road. Ahead was Sanford Shipping.

"No, I can't wait." She sprang from the carriage with agile feet and picked her skirts up to knee level. Lydia broke into a full run with the green and black Sanford Shipping sign her target.

She had to find him. Find Edward.

Behind her, one of the livery men called out, "My lady, wait. You can't go there alone."

She sped past a crossing carter, almost upending him and his goods. The man swore vilely at her back. Her stocking feet beat the ground. Lydia threaded through half-drunk men emerging from a tavern. Air, cool and damp, swished her calves, so rucked up were her skirts. The ground squished under her feet.

Her side knitted with a horrid pinch. But she kept

going. A trio of schooners listed in the quiet water. On the dockside, men hoisting heavy sacks stopped to watch her. Lydia's lungs burst, but she kept her eyes on the green and black. A clerk stood at the base of Sanford Shipping's warped wood stairs, writing notes on a tally sheet. She slammed into a barrel when she tried to stop short.

Lydia grabbed the barrel with both hands for support. "*The Fiona?* Where is it?" She panted, her body rocking from the extended sprint. "Lord Greenwich, I must speak to Lord Greenwich."

The clerk pushed his spectacles higher up his nose and pointed at a mast far out on the Thames. "There be *The Fiona*, ma'am—"

"No," she cried, turning to see where he was pointing. She clutched her roiling midsection.

"Left just under an hour ago…"

All of her went numb. Hot tears spilled from her eyes. Lydia walked across the narrow street, the stink of fish offal everywhere. She stood on the planked walk, staring at the ship floating down the Thames. Hope ebbed from her, leaving with that vessel.

A pair of frizzy-haired harbor doxies sidestepped her, whispering behind their grimy, fingerless gloves. Sobs gushed freely from Lydia. Her body doubled over from the ache pummeling her.

"I'm such a fool."

"Female histrionics. I never understood the need for all that drama and blather," an amused male voice said behind her.

She spun around.

"Edward?" He was a watery blur. She swiped her eyes

with the heels of her hand, and another gulping wail shook her body.

There he stood, blond-brown queue a mess, the same scuffed boots he wore in his greenhouse every day, and his black tricorn hat pulled low.

"I myself make it a rule to avoid such women." His lips twitched, then broke into a broad smile. "But with you, I could make an exception."

"You're not on the ship."

"Very astute observation, Lady Greenwich."

He closed the distance between them, and she launched herself into his arms. The buttons of his great-coat smashed her chest. One hand brushed the hair from her face, caressing her jaw. His thumb stroked her cheek, wiping away rivulets of tears, but she couldn't stop the flow. She held him since the world melted into watery shapes again.

"You're a mess," he said softly, keeping up his gentle ministrations.

Lydia gulped. "I thought you'd left me…that I wouldn't see you again for years…if ever." Her voice dropped to a hoarse whisper. "I couldn't bear the thought."

"You're not getting rid of me so easily."

She dropped her head to his chest and listened to Edward's steady beating heart. The assurance that he was real, that this was Edward standing with his arms around her, calmed her. Lydia loathed to separate even an inch from him, but she tilted her head back and touched his face, loving the smooth and scarred flesh with her fingers.

"What happened?"

"I came to bid one Dr. Ian Finley farewell and give him a parting gift—my jump rope." He grinned. "My

colleague from Scotland. I asked him to go in my place."
He took a deep breath. "It would seem I've become
one of those men who changes his mind for a woman
after all."

Her eyes flickered back and forth intensely over his face.
He looked thinner. Why hadn't she seen that last night?

"This isn't some kind of joke? You aren't leaving on
another ship, are you? If you are, I'm going with you."
She said it boldly, her whole body leaning into him, her
hands gripping his wool coat. "Do you hear me? I won't
keep you from what you love so much. I'll, I'll just go
with you."

"I don't have another expedition in mind. This one
took plenty of gold to finance, as it is." He looked
softly at her and kissed her full on the mouth, lingering for a moment. Edward pulled away, keeping his
arms around her. "But I thank you for the offer. Some
captains, however, have strict policies about no women
on their ships."

"Can't you find one and persuade him with your
gold?" She leaned archly into his chest. "Or persuade a
captain with your arrogance?"

"Wench." He smirked.

They stared at each other, drinking in the visual
promise of each other. A trio of seagulls squawked over
a morsel on the ground, and Lydia pulled away, needing
a fraction of air between them to think straight. Edward
offered his sleeve for tear drying. She dabbed the scratchy
wool to her cheeks. Lydia tasted the salt of her own tears,
felt the marks of them drying in slender streaks across her
face. Every inch of her felt taxed.

"Edward, why didn't you go?"

"I faced facts. You've seared me, left your mark deeper than any drunken pirate could've done." His gaze lifted to the top of her head and traveled down her face. "This may be the only time you'll hear me wax maudlin, Lady Greenwich, so listen well. I love you and couldn't bear the thought of not seeing your impertinent face. I need you needling me to present my papers to the Royal Society, to keep me going out in public…in small doses and"—he stopped to drop a kiss on her forehead and spoke softly in that voice of his that sent shivers down her spine—"I want us to have a family, which is difficult to negotiate if we're on opposite ends of the earth."

"Oh, Edward," she sighed, and moisture threatened to spill from her eyes yet again. "I was supposed to say I love you first." She buried her nose against his wool-covered chest. "I was such a coward not to say it weeks ago."

Above her head, his warm lips touched her, kissing her head. "Doesn't matter."

Edward took a step back, but kept both hands solidly on her arms. "And I think you may have need of my guiding hand when it comes to your wardrobe, Countess. You've not availed yourself to a maid to fix your hair." His eyebrows shot up when his mocking gaze dropped down to her untrussed bosom, visible from her open cloak. "Shocking. And you're without a corset. What will London's Society have to say about this?"

"Your lordship?" A footman beckoned from the street. "We have the carriage here for you and her ladyship."

"Excellent," he called over his shoulder.

Edward offered his arm, but noticed her lack of shoes and shook his head. He swept her into his arms. Lydia buried her head against his neck and sighed. He laughed, a low sound reminiscent of the first night they met. Edward said something under his breath.

She could've sworn he said *hoyden*.

Epilogue

That is the true season of love,
when we believe that we alone can love,
that no one could ever have loved so before us,
and that no one will
love in the same way after us.

—Johann Wolfgang von Goethe

1770
On board The Glory

"LAND'S AHEAD." EDWARD TIPPED HIS HEAD AT THE razor-thin brown line.

Lydia visored her hand across her forehead for a better look through the distance. "Yes, I see. Is that Scotland? St. Andrews?"

Beside her, a young boy in leading strings strained against the side of the ship to no avail. Edward picked up his son and settled him at his side. He pointed to the far-away spot and repeated, "Land."

The glossy-eyed, curly haired boy could only squeal in delight and chew on his hand. Drool covered his scandalously tanned skin for a British heir, but he was the picture of health, with chubby cheeks and a few white spots for teeth in front of his grand smile. Edward kissed the top of the tawny curls.

"He's going to be England's next greatest scientific mind."

"Or artist," Lydia chimed in beside him.

Edward snorted and raised an eyebrow at that, but wisely chose restraint. "And speaking of art, how go those sketches, Countess?"

She braced both hands on the ship's rail and leaned into the breeze. "Well, I'm no Maria van Oosterwyck, but I think I captured the essence of the azalea's stamen."

Her hair hung free, and the sea air brushed her tresses gently past her shoulders. She closed her eyes and faced the sunshine. At present, the Countess of Greenwich was an unfashionable, though glowing, shade of creamy tan. His heir, Jonathan, clapped his hands in glee at nothing in particular. Edward was blessed with a joyful son—and a wife who understood and respected him to his very core. He grinned at the bountiful blessings right in front of him, and kissed the babe on the cheek. The lad rested his curly head on Edward's shoulder.

Lydia opened her eyes, pointing at their son, whispering, "He's half-awake, Edward. You might take him to Nurse so she can watch him for his nap."

Edward pulled back to see little Jon rouse and fight the invading sleep. He whined and mumbled sleepy childish noises.

Lydia stroked his tousled head, cooing at him. "Oh, love, I think he wants you to tell him a story. Please tell him a story and walk about the deck. Your voice will soothe him." She winked at Edward. "Not unlike the effect you have on me."

Lydia slipped her hand over his arm and they began a slow circle around the deck. The woman at his side gave him lots of inspiration.

"Your mother, the Countess of Greenwich, has many talents," he said, rubbing the youthful halo of curls under his chin. "She's a very good worm hunter. But she's known throughout the land as the woman who tamed a horrible beast."

"Oh, Edward," Lydia chided him, but her tender laugh erased any starch reprimand.

Wind gusted across the ship, but they were a tight, cozy bundle, the three of them. Lydia moved closer to Edward, and Jonathan burrowed into his warmth. Profound satisfaction poured its rare kind of balm on Edward's soul right then. He knew exactly the tale to tell.

"Once upon a time, there was a midnight meeting…"

Acknowledgments

My husband Brian said, "It's your turn." That kind of support can't be measured, yet makes all the difference. My agent, Sarah Younger of Nancy Yost Literary, works tirelessly on the behalf of me and the other writers she represents. She's cheerleader, adviser, and all-around sage. Without her enthusiasm, this would've been a half-finished "someday" story on my laptop. To the Sourcebooks team, thank you for looking beyond the first "title-challenged" manuscript. I appreciate your enthusiasm and warm welcome to Sourcebooks.

About the Author

Growing up, Gina wanted to be an author. Fast-forward past college, into the working world, marriage with two boys, and that's when she discovered that sleep's a luxury. With shelves of history books and a fertile imagination, it didn't take long for her to put the movies playing in her head onto paper. Ever the introvert, she was thrilled to partner with her excellent agent, Sarah E. Younger of NY Literary, because that's when the fun really began.

When not exploring adventure and romance on the page, she enjoys life in southern California with her husband and two sons.